# THE BLACK ANGEL OF THE LORD

# THE BLACK ANGEL OF THE LORD

A NOVEL BY
**NORMAN** AND
**LYNN REED**

PRINCIPIA
MEDIA

Principia Media, LLC
678 Front Avenue NW
Suite 256
Grand Rapids MI 49504
(www.principiamedia.com)

Scripture quotations marked (NIV) are taken from the Holy Bible, New
International Version®, NIV®. Copyright © 1973, 1978, 1984, 2011
by Biblica, Inc.™ Used by permission of Zondervan. All rights reserved
worldwide. www.zondervan.com The "NIV" and "New International Version"
are trademarks registered in the United States Patent and Trademark Office
by Biblica, Inc.™

Scripture quotations marked "KJV" are taken from the Holy Bible, King James
Version, Cambridge, 1769.

ISBN 978-1-61485-317-6

**Disclaimer**
All characters appearing in this work are fictitious. Any resemblance to real
persons, living or dead, is purely coincidental.

19 18 17 16 15 14          7 6 5 4 3 2 1

Printed in the United States of America

Cover design and interior layout: Frank Gutbrod
Cover photos: Shutterstock
Author photo and digital imaging: Sherry Baribeau

*Dedicated
to our children*

# ACKNOWLEDGEMENTS

Our special thanks go to Dan Vant Kirkhoff and Kathy Boeve for their early encouragement, to Dirk Wierenga for his guidance and advice in the publication process, and to our wonderfully steady editor, Sally J. Smith.

# TABLE OF CONTENTS

1. The Early Years of Ramtouses  *1*
2. The Lion Hunt  *9*
3. Meditation of Holofernes  *19*
4. Sennacherib: The King of Assyria  *39*
5. Judith  *52*
6. Assyria's March on Babylonia  *74*
7. Destiny Dream  *86*
8. Kinky Mane  *96*
9. Ramtouses and Carnabrara  *110*
10. Hezekiah Reforms the Kingdom  *144*
11. Confrontation with the Vassal Districts  *153*
12. The Siege of Jerusalem  *167*
13. The Agony of Ramtouses  *184*
14. Building An Army  *209*
15. Damned Environment  *222*
16. Tales and Deeds of Ahikar  *238*
17. The Eclipse  *259*
18. Holofernes Meets Judith  *286*
19. Eternal Night  *301*
20. Day Light  *331*

# CHARACTERS

**Abi** *(a-bi)* Mother of Hezekiah, King of Judea

**Adzua** *(ahd-zoo-ah)* Niece of King Tasmeria of Tungul

**Ahaz** *(a-haz)* King of Judah and father of Hezekiah

**Ahikar** *(uh-hy-kahr)* Hebrew servant, cupbearer and scribe for Sennacherib

**Arki-kudam** *(ar-kee-ku-dam)* Oldest son of Sargon II, half brother of Sennacherib

**Ashur-nadin-shumi** *(ash-er-ney-din-shoo-mee)* Older half brother of Sennacherib

**Astarte** *(a-stahr-tee)* Daughter of King Sargon II and sister of Sennacherib

**Baal** *(bahl)* King of Assyrian deities

**Baako** *(bah-kol)* Oldest second brother (nephew) to Ramtouses

**Baduga** *(buh-doo-guh)* Egyptian officer and advisor/scout for Ramtouses

**Carnabrara** *(kar-naa-brah-rah)* Daughter of Tasmeria and betrothed to Ramtouses

**Ell** *(ee-l)* Superstitious evil spirits who take on human form

**Esarhaddon** *(ee-sahr-had-n)* Younger son of Sennacherib and successor to the throne of Assyria

**Eventha** *(ee-ven-thah)* Holofernes's second wife

**Flulano** *(floo-lahn-oh)* Holofernes's first wife

**Grandfather**, Nutombi's grandfather

**Hephzibah** *(hef-zeh-bah)* Queen of Hezekiah, King of Judea

**Hezekiah** *(hez-un-kahy-uh)* King of Judea

**Holofernes** *(hol-uh-fur-neez)* Assyrian Commander-in-Chief

**Isaiah** *(ahy-zey-uh)* Prophet of Yahweh

**Judith** *(joo-dith)* Hebrew woman with red hair

**Lizoka** *(leh-zoh-kuh)* A village girl from Juba

**Lozato** *(loh-zah-to)* Oldest son of Nutombi

**Manasses** *(meh-neh-sehs)* Judith's husband

**Merari** *(meh-rah-ree)* Judith's father

**Merodach-baladan** *(mair-oh-daak-bal-ah-dahn)* King of Babylonia

**Nutombi** *(nu-toom-bee)* Ramtouses's mother

**Padi** *(pah-dee)* Assyrian governor of Ekron

**Peninnah** *(peh-nee-nah)* Judith's mother

**Rabsaris** *(rahb-sahr-eez)* First Assyrian General under Holofernes

**Ramtouses** *(ram-tu-seez)* Youngest son of Nutombi and betrothed to Carnabrara

**Sargon II** *(sahr-gon)* King of Assyria and father of Sennacherib

**Sennacherib** *(suh-nak-er-ib)* King of Assyria and son of Sargon II

**Shabaka** *(shah-buh-kuh)* A Kushite descendant and Pharaoh of Upper and Lower Egypt

**Shalmaneser** *(shal-muh-nee-zer)* Army general and mentor of Holofernes,

**Shebitku** *(sheh-beht-koo)* A Kushite descendant, brother of Shabaka, and a Pharaoh of Upper and Lower Egypt

**Taharga** *(tah-harg-uh)* Ethiopian officer and advisor/scout for Ramtouses

**Talia** *(tuh-lee-ah)* Youngest wife of King Sargon II

**Tasmeria** *(taz-mair-ee-uh)* A Kushite descendant and King of African nation, Tungul

**Urentu** *(u-ren-tu)* Oldest son of King Tasmeria

**Yahweh** *(yah-we)* God of Judah and Israel

# PLACES

**Assyria** *(uh-seer-ee-uh)* Dominant kingdom of the
Mesopotamian world
**Babylon** *(beh-buh-lon)* Capital of Babylonia
**Egypt** Region along the Nile River delta on the coast of the
Mediterranean Sea
**Ekron** *(eh-krah-n)* City allied with Jerusalem and trade center
of region
**Ell** *(ee-l)* The underworld realm of the Ell people, an
African tribal superstition in which evil spirits wreck the
environment and bring death upon all humans
**Eltekeh** *(el-tek-a)* City in Philistia
**Israel** *(iz-rey-uhl)* home to ten northern Hebrew tribes
**Jerusalem** *(ji-roo-suhluhm)* Capital city of Judah
**Juba** *(joo-bah)* Ramtouses's home village in what is now South
Sudan, Africa
**Judah** *(joo-duh)* home to two southern Hebrew tribes
**Lachish** *(ley-kish)* Judean city
**Meroe** *(mer-oh-ee)* A Nubian city and pyramid location
**Nineveh** *(nin-uh-vuh)* Capital of Assyria
**Nubia** *(noo-bee-uh)* Country south of Egypt, formerly part
of Goshen
**Philistia** *(fil-lis-ti-a)* Country bordering Judah
**Samaria** *(suh-mair-ee-uh)* Capital of Northern Israel
**Thebes** *(theebz)* Capital of Upper Egypt, Kushite domain
**Tungal** *(tuhn-gal)* Capital of African nation, Tungul (tuhn-gul)
in Northeast Africa

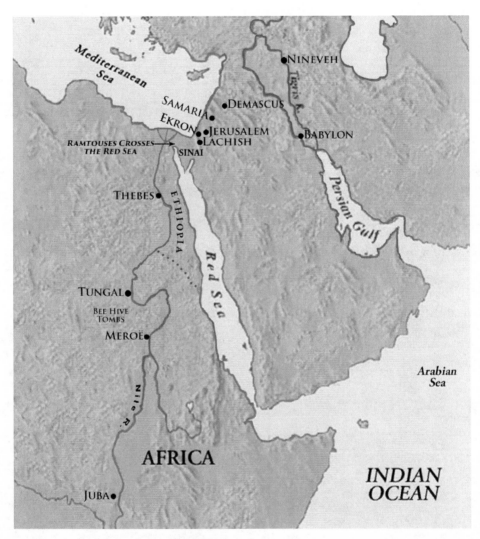

Middle East circa 701 B.C.E.

# INTRODUCTION

A mysterious arrowhead was unearthed along with pottery pieces and a partial spear during a modern day Jerusalem expansion. The whole group lay buried within the same archeological timeline.

According to carbon dating, all the items found dated back to around 700 B.C.E. Further examination revealed the arrowhead was made of copper and primitive in design. It could not be identified as Assyrian or Jordanian. In fact, its origin could only be East or North East Africa. Why was this arrowhead in the fields outside Jerusalem of old?

Take it. Hold the arrowhead tight. Press it into your palm. Do you feel its strength? It is a weapon designed to kill. Even an arrowhead has a story.

# THE EARLY YEARS OF RAMTOUSES

## 728 B.C.E.

The day was stifling hot.
In the small village of Juba in Africa, a woman lay inside a hut surrounded by three women.

⁘

Nutombi shook and sweated, fearing the worst with each contraction. The pains came closer together and grew more intense. With a final push a baby boy slipped out into the arms of another village woman and started to yell lustily. Nutombi found great comfort in the sound of his cry and rejoiced he came into the world without the problems she expected.

The birth of her last child eight years earlier was extremely painful, and she had feared the Ell would pull her down. Her dread of Ell and its minions held a strong grip on her. The beliefs went back as far as the ancestors. The Ell dried the skies and prevented rain from falling, killing crops and animals. It was said when the Ell emerge from their domain, they will kill and swallow the villagers then carry their spirits down to the kingdom of Ell. There, they will regurgitate the spirits to writhe in torment forever.

She believed childbearing was no longer part of her life when her husband took a second wife. Then he sought comfort in her bed one night and this boy child, her surprise child, was born. He brought renewed purpose to Nutombi. She resolved

1

to enjoy every moment with him. When he was eight days old, she presented him to the village elders to suffer the traditional circumcision. On that same day the villagers first heard his name declared, Ramtouses.

No child learned as fast as Nutombi's Ramtouses. He accompanied his mother wherever she went—working in the fields, hunting, fishing, cooking and toting water. At night, they slept together.

Nutombi was wise in the ways of nature and knew many things about the forest, animals and plants. She had traveled many years with her grandfather and he taught her everything she knew about their world. During those years she also gained keen insights into the behavior and nature of men and women. Nightly she told Ramtouses stories of her grandfather's travels across the land, teaching him all that she had learned from Grandfather. Nutombi valued honesty and compassion, and recognized the damaging influence of forces like greed and envy. She spoke of these things to her young son.

"Listen closely, my son, and learn," she said. "One day something I have taught you might be one of life's crucial lessons.

Ramtouses did listen. He reviewed all that his mother taught him while standing watch over the fat bean pods in their fields, guarding against marauding monkeys and occasional poachers from neighboring tribes. By the time he was eight years old, he could climb the tallest trees and drop a raiding monkey with his slingshot.

The march of life and its demands left their mark on Nutombi. She grew ill. Each day delivered more pain to her body. There was no relief, and she could no longer hide her exhaustion from young Ramtouses. At the end of the small cotton harvest, Nutombi sought out her eldest son, Lozato.

"Mother," Lozato's voice was full of concern. "You are not well? You look so tired."

"Each week it worsens." She leaned against a straight-backed stool and looked him in the eye. "I will die soon, son, and I have one request of you."

"What is it, Mother? I will do anything for you."

Nutombi smiled at him. Her heart filled with love for her oldest son. "I want you to promise me you will watch over little Ramtouses."

"Of course, Mother. You know I will."

Yes, he would. She had needed to hear his pledge. "One of the village elder women will care for him, but a brother's guidance will help him become a strong man."

"I promise I will watch over him, but, Mother, I do not want you to die. Can I do nothing to help you? You have always been so strong. I cannot bear to see you weakened in this way. Have you seen the healer? Surely there must be something we can do."

Worry stretched tightly across Lozato's face, and Nutombi's heart skipped a beat with sadness. She loved all her children. She did not want this coming death, but Lozato was right. She had little strength left to fight it.

"Lozato, do not press me more. There is nothing to do but wait and then care for Ramtouses and yourself when I leave."

⁜

A few days later as Nutombi and Ramtouses walked home after a hot day in the field, they took a detour to a certain tree her grandfather showed her years before. Ramtouses filled his sack with the plump fruit he picked from the tree.

"If you embark on a long journey, Ramtouses, a sack of this dried fruit will sustain you, give you life. Every hunter should carry dried figs and dates. This is only one of many lessons Grandfather learned from his travels. He was a wise man."

Nutombi's breathing was labored as they walked back to the village. She asked Ramtouses to fetch the water by himself. *She is tired.* They prepared the meal, exchanging few words.

Ramtouses awoke the next morning aware of a strange stillness. The usual sounds his mother made as she prepared for the new day were absent. He went to check on her. She lay still. Her body felt cool. She did not awaken with his soft nudge.

When the village women came later that morning, he was curled beside his mother. Ramtouses did not speak when they questioned him. He saw them and heard them as if in a dream.

⁛

The village elders prepared a stately funeral for Nutombi. A drum signal was relayed a great distance informing all of her death. The drums were a common language understood by all the tribes in Northern Africa even if their spoken tongues differed.

The people of Juba and hundreds of others from the bush gathered for the ceremony. Ramtouses gazed in astonishment at the seemingly endless trail of people who came to show respect for his mother. His second brothers and sisters, children of his brothers and sisters, stood beside him. They, too, seemed astounded.

Lozato called together Ramtouses and all the children of his brothers and sisters.

"Many years ago, your ancestors lived in a land far to the north of Juba. Your great-great-grandfather told my mother stories of the days he traveled to those faraway lands. Would you like to hear those stories?"

The children clustered close while Lozato told of a man he called Grandfather. This man was Lozato's great-grandfather who traveled to many places where he experienced different cultures and made friends with special people.

"While traveling to the north in a country he called Egypt, Grandfather came upon a caravan. He waved his arms to gain the attention of the man he presumed was in charge. The man signaled his guards to stop the procession and let Grandfather come forward. His name was Ramtouses." Lozato glanced at young Ramtouses and caught a big smile.

Ramtouses already knew the story of his namesake and was happy all his second brothers and sisters would hear it also.

"Grandfather respectfully declared his desire to trade some shiny yellow stones for food, water and a sorely needed bath, or he would work for them.

"Ramtouses took a liking to Grandfather and invited him to stay with his servants for a few days. Eventually, he employed Grandfather to observe the country's farming systems. Grandfather earned many privileges through this powerful Egyptian nobleman. He gave our great-grandfather a signet ring. Grandfather eventually grew wealthy and employed many people to journey and study with him."

Lozato pointed to his youngest brother. "Our mother gave her last child this man's beautiful name to honor his memory."

The children all looked at Ramtouses.

Lozato continued. "Grandfather learned all he could about agriculture. He understood how vital that information could be for the many who faced drought. When he returned to his homeland, he traveled from village to village, tribe to tribe and taught farmers about the care of our land—what grew well in this climate, how to irrigate the fields and maximize the use of water, how to strengthen the soil and store the seed. He also designed farming tools that made the work easier and faster, and he showed the village craftsmen how to make these tools."

Lozato's voice enraptured the children, and they listened intently. He told stories of Grandfather's travels and promised further tales of the many things Grandfather saw and learned. He told the story of Nutombi's life with her grandfather after the death of her family.

"Grandfather took her from the elder woman who housed her. He said, 'You are mine.' And from that time to her marriage age she stayed with him.

"Our people have long memories," Lozato said, "and they remembered the old man who traveled to their villages with his young granddaughter boasting about her wherever he went. People respected and loved him but never had the chance to say farewell. No one really knows what happened to him. He went into the forest one day and never returned."

From Lozato's story, it was apparent those who attended Nutombi's funeral to remember and honor her, also honored her grandfather.

⋅⊹⋅

It rained on the day of the burial, a heavy rain that continued for hours, wetting and soaking Ramtouses like all the other mourners as they lowered his mother's body into the muddy earth. Tears flooded his eyes and ran down his face, but the rain concealed them on that very sad day. He vowed to never forget how the people helped him and his family when his mother died. The respect and honor they showed touched him deeply.

⋅⊹⋅

The tribe had a basic social structure that attempted to meet every individual's needs. When a village child was orphaned, an elder woman who lived alone accepted the role of caretaker and became a foster parent to the child in need.

As a village orphan, young Ramtouses stood at the mercy of that system, and when an elder village woman requested the honor to adopt Ramtouses, Lozato agreed. He thought staying with her might be the best for his young brother at this time in his life. She offered him a place to sleep in her hut and welcomed him to share the food she cooked.

He could have taken Ramtouses in, but Lozato felt his brother would receive more of the needed attention from a solitary woman than from a family with many other children to care for. Lozato accepted the role of male guardian over his young brother and became seriously devoted to him as their mother wished.

⋅⊹⋅

Growing up in the tribal social system required active membership in an age-set or age group. Nutombi had selfishly kept Ramtouses apart from this aspect of tribal life. After his mother died, Ramtouses's life changed from one of near solitude to a life filled with training necessary for his age-set.

Village elders took the lead role in teaching the beliefs and ways of tribal life. Ramtouses and his age-set companions learned the principles that bound the village together, creating a strong entity. They honored the ancestors, and upon death, their spirits would rise and join the ancestors for all eternity. Behaviors and attitudes contrary to harmonious village life were disallowed. Those tribesmen who had wicked hearts were vulnerable to the Ell.

Ramtouses never tired of learning. His training enabled him to continually search for more understanding of everything around him.

When Ramtouses reached the age of twelve his guardian mother allowed him more liberty at night in the woods. Ramtouses liked the way his eyes adjusted to night vision, away from all light except the moon and stars. Early one evening, just after sunset, he noticed a very bright star.

"Aah," he whispered into the night. "That must be a special star. It shines so brightly."

Just above the horizon, this star moved in line with the setting sun. Ramtouses sat and watched to see how much time it took to set.

The next night he noticed the same star had moved to a new location. *I thought stars stayed in one place. Why has this one moved?*

He tested his theory about the stationary nature of stars by picking another bright star, comparing its position with others around it. He also measured how far the star near the horizon had moved. Ramtouses could not wait to see if other movement occurred.

The following night, the star above him had not moved. Its location remained the same in relationship to the stars around it. However, the star near the horizon did move again. Ramtouses laughed, happy to see that one star, among all the stars of the night, shine so brightly and wander the sky freely.

He announced aloud to the night sky and all life around him, "I will make this my favorite star and look upon it for good luck and peace of mind."

Ramtouses soon found a very, very bright star in the dark sky preceding the sunrise. It did not take him long to figure out that the same star whose movement he had followed at night now appeared in the morning sky. He tried to tell others about this amazing star, but no one took interest in his observations.

The years went by, and Ramtouses gained enough knowledge from watching his star to predict where it would be when he looked for it. Whenever he had a bad day, he meditated beneath the star to restore encouraging thoughts.

Ramtouses named the stars he observed. He watched the phases of the moon as it traveled across the sky. He also discovered stars that appeared to streak through the sky. He called this phenomenon *raining of the stars*. After some time he would see the raining of the stars return to the same area of the sky. When this occurred, he calculated one rotation cycle of the heavens over time. He knew when and where he would see it again by successfully calculating its arrival.

# 2

# THE LION HUNT

## 712 B.C.E.

A male child was born into an age-set and went through the various stages of physical and mental growth with that group. The boys' ages fell within a four to five year span. Tight discipline and extensive training given each age group proved exceptionally effective in preparing the future shamans, master hunters, toolmakers and leaders for tomorrow. The skills needed to hunt, farm and protect the village were also exercised daily in the age-set training.

⁙

The final test for a young warrior was participation in stalking and slaying a lion, and a primary ambition of these young men centered on becoming a member of the twelve-man team selected for the semi-annual lion hunts. Participation in a lion hunt was a sign of bravery and personal achievement, and would catapult each young hunter into manhood, into the class of warriors.

They studied the habits and environment of lions and learned how, when and where they hunted their prey. Everything they learned had the potential to play a vitally important role in the game of life or death between man and beast. Such experience testified to the bushman's bravery and courage, and without this prestige, his courage could be challenged.

Unlike the others in his age-set, Ramtouses did not devote all his time training to become an exceptional warrior.

9

Ramtouses enjoyed the forest environment. It fed his thirst to understand his world.

When they missed him in the ranks of his peers, the call went out. "Look to the trees and animals for our lost brother."

But though he might lose track of time, he never lost his sense of location. He knew the forest and open plains as well as he knew his village layout.

Through the years he gained an extraordinary amount of knowledge concerning life in the forest. Ants became one of the many creatures that captured his interest. He came upon a large, industrious colony of red ants and settled in close by to watch them. The activity never ceased and sometimes hours passed before he coaxed himself back to the village.

As he observed ant behavior, he realized the ants constructed their colony mounds close to existing food sources and modified the surrounding habitat to ant life. They built entrance and exit pathways and drainage systems that would prevent flooding on rainy days. They also erected barriers against invaders. If an ant did not belong to the colony, even if it looked like them in color and size, it was immediately attacked.

Ramtouses described what he saw to others in his age-set. He called the ant colony a super life-form.

"The ants appear to function as a unit, working collectively toward one goal, the survival of the colony."

His friends listened then ran off to train with spears or wrestle and swim together.

÷

Ramtouses arrived at the red ant colony early one morning. To his surprise, a massive body of large black ants advanced toward the red ant mound. Fighting began. The size and color of the ants defined the armies. When the red ants launched a counter-attack against the intruders, the black ants created a wall-of-ants around their attack force. This enabled them to withstand anything the red ants mustered against them.

Eventually the red ants began to withdraw and the intensity of their attack diminished.

The black ants expanded their wall creating gaps and weak spots along it. They moved forward in pursuit of the retreating red ants.

*Do they believe they are winning the battle? Do they smell victory?*

Many of the red ants were injured, but not dead. The bigger black ants trampled over the thousands of bodies of dead or injured red ants. Those red ants that were able began pulling on the legs of their enemy, greatly impeding their movement and causing further disruption to the organized wall. The retreating red ants turned around and were suddenly joined by thousands of their own who appeared from the far side of the mound.

The black ants were unable to break free and realign their broken wall. The red ants charged through and fighting escalated. Ramtouses believed the ants knew their opponents only by their scent. The aggressive black ants were defeated. The red ants marched victorious.

Ramtouses watched, fascinated. *It is almost as if the red ants executed a superbly well-formed battle plan.*

The conflict lasted for hours, well into the evening. It tested the determination, cunning, strength and resolve of the red ants. No black ants survived.

All through the evening he replayed the amazing conflict in his mind. *That is one of the most remarkable events I have ever witnessed.*

⁙

The day approached when the elders would select the young hunters for the lion hunt. It was a ritual of passions rather than amusement and played an important role in village culture.

Among Ramtouses's peers, conversation centered on who might be chosen for the twelve-man team.

Ramtouses's agility and speed were superior to others his age but those attributes were not certain to rank him over the bigger, older boys in his age group. The likelihood he would be chosen for the lion hunt this time seemed meager.

*However, in case I am chosen, I need a plan for bringing down the lion.*

For many days, early in the morning and again in the evening, he contemplated the nature of lions, their habitat and behavior. He committed what he learned to memory. This was important information to have when one planned to hunt and kill any prey, but particularly a lion. His life could depend on what he learned.

After weeks of consideration, he thought of a way he could defeat the lion without even throwing the spear. *If I face the lion in tall grass where he can move without being seen, I must have an offense capable of taking him down.*

Most warriors, even the best, would not pursue a lion in tall grasses, but Ramtouses devised a plan he thought just might work. It required a bigger and heavier shield, one more protective than those commonly used. It had to cover him from his neck to his knees.

He envisioned his spear to be two-thirds as long, yet heavier than the customary spear.

*If I have to throw such a spear at him in the open plane, I will have to wait a little longer for reliable accuracy. That would be my only disadvantage, but otherwise, this design should be effective.*

⁘

Lozato joined Ramtouses sitting near his caretaker's hut. "What are you doing, Giraffe Legs?"

Ramtouses smiled at the affectionate nickname. "I am making a new weapon to bring down a lion."

"How does it work?"

Ramtouses showed his brother the shield. It was much like shields used by village warriors but twice the size and weight and constructed with thicker rawhide. A hole at the center was reinforced with leather-laced edging. Ramtouses's spear was also twice as thick around as the typical spear. A knob at the base afforded a tight hold, and grooves carved at the end would keep it from slipping through the hand.

Ramtouses eagerly explained the maneuver in full to Lozato.

Lozato waited until his brother finished then, "I think the best and safest way to bring down a lion is with eleven other well-skilled warriors around you, each with his own spear. Eleven others greatly put the odds in your favor. If a lion menaces human life or cattle, you will need to chase after him even in the high bush. I can see that your weapon may be superior in a situation where the lion has the advantage and can hide from you."

"I can only imagine how the hunt might play out," Ramtouses said. "I am happy you understand the need for such weapons in case of certain conditions."

⁘

Ramtouses usually found solitude in the woods after an intense training session, but on this day tension and excitement ruled the air. The word went out calling together all the young men of his age-set. The day everyone waited for had arrived— the day the elders announced the names of those young warriors selected for the coming lion hunt. Ramtouses had just passed his sixteenth birthday. He took a position between his two second-brothers. The elders stood in the center as the young warriors circled around them. They seemed to debate the final decision among themselves.

An elder suddenly called out the first name. "Baako," he shouted. Ramtouses's oldest second-brother jumped up, gave a triumphant shout and ran to join the elders. At nineteen years, he ranked among the oldest of their age-set. Ramtouses and another second-brother held hands as more names were called. Ten more thrilled young men yelled and jumped up to join the inner circle of elders and the future lion hunters.

Just one more name remained to be called, the twelfth member of the new lion-hunting team. Ramtouses's heartbeat accelerated, his muscles tightened and his breath quickened. He looked around at all the other wide-eyed boys, each hoping to hear his name called.

He turned to his second-brother. "If I do not get the honor, I wish it to be yours."

The words had barely escaped his lips when one of the elders yelled, "Ramtouses."

He stood and walked to the circle of junior warriors. The new twelve-man hunting team embraced each other and celebrated.

⁖

Hunting lions was a perilous task. If a young warrior is mauled in a lion attack, the hunt is stopped and his replacement is selected from those remaining in the age-set. The young warriors not selected for this lion hunt would have another opportunity in six months, or in a year or more.

After the ceremony, the newly formed team left to prepare for the hunt. During those few days of seclusion prior to the hunt, the group selected a leader. It would fall to him to make all final decisions.

The day before the hunt, passions ran high. There was feasting and celebration throughout the village. The twelve young warriors dressed in red, and the people of the village cheered them on to a successful hunt as the young men danced the traditional dance of victory.

⁖

Lozato came to Ramtouses.

His face showed high approval and great happiness. "Such an honor does not often come at age sixteen. You have done exceptionally well in your training, Ramtouses. Our mother would be so proud, and I am very happy for you."

Ramtouses basked in his older brother's praise. "Thank you, Lozato."

"Heed my word of advice for you and your fellow hunters. When you are stalking the lion, if the beast threatens another

14

member of your hunting party, you must warn him by yelling
'*Olamayio!*' That one shouted word sends an immediate alarm
to the warrior in danger. Pass this along to your fellow warriors
so everyone knows the call. It takes only one word to save a life."

⸭

The hunting journey started at dawn. The twelve young
men armed themselves with one spear and one shield apiece.
They were clothed in the same red dress worn during the
dance the day before.

They tracked their prey by following footprints, animal
droppings or by the circling of vultures over recent kills. Tribal
law prevented them from hunting a lion weakened by illness
or injury. Lions were not hunted for food. Nor, for the sake of
their cubs, were lionesses targeted in the hunt. Juba people
believed females to be the givers of life in every species.

Noise agitated lions. Once a lion was found in a wooded
or bushy area where it could swiftly and effortlessly conceal
itself, the warriors beat their shields to anger him and lure him
to an open plain where they could encircle him.

In his own territory, a lion was as smart as a man. It could
maneuver through the bush faster than a human, and facing
a lion in the open savannah could become the memory of a
lifetime, should the person survive.

⸭

Ramtouses and his fellow lion hunters walked most of the
morning before spotting a big and healthy older male lion. The
large cat struggled to devour a wildebeest while fighting off a
small pack of spotted hyenas.

The leader divided the hunting party into two groups that
moved slowly toward the lion from different angles. Within a
safe distance of the combative animals, the team began to beat
their shields. The hyenas ran off, but the lion stood his ground,
his mouth red with blood. The warriors moved in, still beating
their shields.

The lion roared, hissed and broke away from the kill, charging the nearest group. The young hunters turned and ran to open fields. The second group of warriors moved in behind the lion. Once in the open, the lion slowed to a walk, snarling and hissing.

The hunters surrounded the lion closing him within a large circle. They shrank the circle, beating a soft, steady rhythm on their shields. The lion charged in one direction, stopped then started another charge only to stop again. The powerful animal seemed agitated and angry, but the young hunters continued to shrink the circle.

The leader yelled, "Get closer!"

Just when they were close to accurate range, the lion gave a deep, long roar that tailed off into a series of short ones. He took off with blinding speed toward one of the junior warriors and just as the young hunter threw his spear at the big cat, the lion leapt up and over him. The spear missed its mark. Other tribesmen did not chance a throw and saved their spears.

"After him!" cried the leader. "Do not let him get to the high grass."

Ramtouses's advantageous position gave him the best chance of intercepting the monster. He dashed across the plains with long strides like a panic-stricken giraffe. Man and beast in a race that could determine the outcome of the hunt. The other hunters also rushed after the lion, coming from different angles. The lion veered away from Ramtouses and disappeared into the high grass.

When the lion entered the thick bush, Ramtouses boldly went after him, reluctant to relinquish his pursuit. He focused solely on pursuing this powerful and quick-footed beast. He frantically dashed here and there as he glimpsed the lion moving up and down through the tall grass.

He stopped suddenly. He could no longer see the lion. Many trees and bushes disrupted the straight line of the horizon in the distance. He was alone in waist-high grass separated from his hunting companions. His situation was serious.

Sweating profusely, his heart racing, Ramtouses garnered his courage and willed his nervous shaking to stop. He swiftly inserted his spear into his shield. The air was still. Even the grass and trees quieted. He clutched the spear firmly and held the shield up to eye level. He moved his head in quick jerks from one spot to another, scanning the grass all around him. Each second was like an eternity.

The lion could be stalking him, creeping closer and closer. The animal could crawl so low and so silent, the tall grass would hardly move. Ramtouses knew an attack was inevitable.

Abruptly, the huge cat was flying through the air toward him. Its snarls broke the silence. A wave of terror coursed through the young hunter who barely had time to brace himself before the lion crashed into his shield. He fell backward and slammed to the ground, flattened by the weight of the animal.

Somehow, he kept his shield over his body and the butt of his spear rammed firmly against the ground. Ramtouses lay unmoving and slightly dazed. The lion made no further effort to attack. Ramtouses sprang to his feet, looking around for the lion. His spear was broken off halfway. Where was the other half?

Blood spotted the grass and ground. Ramtouses followed the bloody trail for a good distance before hearing the low groans that came from further off. He walked cautiously toward the sounds and there, before him, lay the lion, panting. Ramtouses's thick spear protruded from its chest. Ramtouses did not hesitate. He ran his knife through the lion's heart. A beast so noble should not suffer. The big cat made a loud and final meow and died.

The other hunters were halted by the leader before entering the thick bush. When they heard the sounds, they rushed in and found Ramtouses standing over the prize. Their faces reflected astonishment at what they saw—a tall lanky youth, standing beside an enormous lion. For a few moments no one said anything, then, their cries of jubilance rang out. Sounds of laughter and cheering dominated the jungle. The young warriors jumped and danced, hooted and howled shouts of triumph around the lion's corpse in celebration of their victory.

Baako ran and hugged him. He wore the biggest smile. The leader of the hunting group knelt down beside Ramtouses, urging him to climb upon his shoulders. Baako assisted him, hoisting the young lion killer up onto the shoulders of the group leader. This gesture meant: *You are the highest.*

Their leader sent two hunters ahead to spread the news of their success.

⁜

Many villagers came to greet and congratulate them, looking with astonishment at the surprisingly big cat. All the junior warriors received credit for the kill, but Ramtouses received the greatest recognition. The successful lion hunt brought excitement to the entire community, and Juba prepared for seven days of celebration.

Village women came together to shear the lion's mane and pull its claws and teeth for trophies. They made ornaments of these trophies. They braided the lion's mane beautifully and hung it around the neck of the warrior who speared the lion, Ramtouses. He touched it with pride. The other young hunters wore their ornaments made from the trophy teeth and claws around their necks on leather thongs or as skin piercings.

⁜

The drums beat a low rhythm during the celebration and spread the news throughout the region. They beat the story of the victorious lion hunt with Nutombi's son, Ramtouses, one of the youngest ever to slay a fully grown male lion. People who heard the drums' story retold it again and again.

# 3

# MEDITATION
# OF HOLOFERNES

## 719-711 B.C.E.

Holofernes was camped an hour's march away from the city of Nineveh, the capital of Assyria. The young Assyrian general had waited all his life to be in this position. Tomorrow morning when his men arose and readied themselves as best they could after months of battle, Holofernes would lead them home to Nineveh and glory.

Holofernes sat in deep thought, his hands folded behind his head as he reviewed his life. The memories flowed freely, all the way back to his childhood when his widowed mother took on the serious task of raising him alone. She spent much of her wealth to obtain the finest training and education for her young son.

She came to him one evening in his sixteenth year, 719 B.C.E.

"I want you to be a champion among Assyrian leaders, feared and loved by everyone in our country all the way to the throne. Your father is no longer with us and there is no male relative to take up his responsibility. As is our custom, it falls to me to teach you to be a lover of women so they too will know your grandeur."

She removed his garments and continued speaking. "Always examine what your woman looks like unclothed."

She shed her own clothing and turned completely around, showing him her body. She moved to the bed and climbed over him.

"Now I will begin teaching you how to entertain a woman."
These instructional sessions occurred randomly.

"Never underestimate the influence of a woman," she said.

Holofernes was an adept student, both physically and mentally. His mother made it clear her intent was solely to provide him with the knowledge of women and prepare him for future relationships. She warned him of trickery some women played and cautioned attentiveness to avoid being fooled by girls who might seek to deceive him for personal gain.

⁘

After two years these lessons ended. One day when he returned home from a session with Prince Sennacherib and their military tutor, General Shalmaneser, his mother and all her belongings were gone from the estate.

A servant delivered a note to him. *My son, Holofernes, I have provided and arranged for your training. It is you who must now forge forward. Farewell.*

Why his mother would simply leave was a mystery without clues. He hurt deep inside but did not weep.

Holofernes held no memory of his father who died in battle. Now the son sat alone, a nestling whose mother bird left after teaching him how to fly and find his own way. Grown into a young man, he was dependent upon no one to make whatever decisions life would require of him. She had done her work well.

*Surely, I have a strong body and a fine intellect. I have my father's estate and my mother's dreams for me. I can forge forward.*

⁘

During the months following his mother's departure his existence was secluded and solitary. The march of days and nights never seemed to end. He lived alone in the fabulous villa with marble floors and statues lining the long corridors. The house was a labyrinth stretching on in four directions. Holofernes was haunted by loneliness.

He slept poorly, and the long nights crept slowly toward morning while he walked aimlessly through the villa. Some nights the wind through the many windows howled along the hallways at every turn. Moonlight created grotesquely shaped shadows of the familiar statues and household items as they morphed into strange and darkened figures over the course of the night.

He came to relish the discipline his life demanded and threw himself into the daily regimen of hard physical and mental training. General Shalmaneser declared him to be the most talented student he ever taught when it came to war strategy and the sword. Holofernes and Prince Sennacherib trained together most of the time and became close friends. Ahikar, the prince's tag-along servant, often shared their company.

⁘

One day, as Shalmaneser illustrated how a wall of shields could control the line of contact with an enemy, a large chariot carrying Prince Sennacherib's lover, two sisters and their driver arrived at the training site.

One of the women called out, "Prince Sennacherib, when will you be finished?"

Shalmaneser recognized the futility of continuing instruction and soon dismissed the class. He said, "That will be all for the day, men. I am a poor match for such lovely distraction."

Prince Sennacherib ran to the chariot. Holofernes followed but stopped halfway there. He was a large youth, already a beautiful specimen of man at age eighteen. Sennacherib's woman greeted the prince with a big kiss, seeming oblivious to their audience.

Holofernes noticed the Prince's sisters were watching him. His face grew warm when one said to the other, "How right you are! This Holofernes has turned out to be quite a beast."

Sennacherib's lover said, "We are planning an *akhatuti* outing two nights from now on my family's estate. Normally no men are allowed at such overnight gatherings of women, but you, my prince, are welcome in my tent."

The older of the two sisters looked straight into Holofernes's eyes. "Will you come with Prince Sennacherib?"

A smile lit her eyes, and Holofernes had no trouble guessing her thoughts. "Of course," he said. "It will be my pleasure."

⁜

On the evening of the *akhatuti*, Holofernes and Sennacherib slipped onto the estate in an inconspicuous area, as planned, and found the girls' tents. The prince stayed with his woman, while his sisters led Holofernes to another tent. The girls disrobed then quickly covered themselves with a blanket.

He remembered his mother's words. "Examine the wares before you buy."

Holofernes went to the tent entrance where two candle poles were set in the ground. He brought one near to the young noble women and held it up. "I must see each of you fully from all sides before I can join you. Arise and let me see your stunning bodies."

Their eyes wide, the two slowly began to smile behind the hands covering their mouths. They seemed shy and surprised at Holofernes's request. However, with unspoken agreement, the two giggled, jumped up and spun around, arms up and hands swaying over their heads.

Holofernes stared at their beautiful, unclothed bodies before they leapt back beneath the soft sheepskin, still giggling. He blew out the candle and joined them.

Holofernes had no doubt he would always remember this night as his triumphant night.

⁜

Three nights after the *akhatuti,* the young Princess Astarte's chariot arrived at Holofernes's villa.

Summoned by his servant, Holofernes greeted her from the main doors. She stood tall in her chariot, covered head to feet with a long, hooded, black cloak. He started down the steps to her. Her beautiful, unblemished face was golden in the light of the setting sun, but her eyes were like cold daggers. He touched her hand.

She looked down at him with indifference. "I am not sure what I think of you, Holofernes. I require a man who can entertain me. I do not know whether you can fill the role. I need to make certain before I decide. Alone, with no one else involved."

Holofernes rubbed the palm of her hand with his thumb as he looked up at her. "Will you come inside?"

"No, I will not." Astarte's attitude was condescending, but Holofernes would not let her think for a moment he was shaken by her behavior.

He climbed aboard her chariot. "Then I will go with you."

Astarte nodded to the driver and they pulled away. She released her grip on the handrails and moved behind Holofernes, putting her arms around him. Each time he looked back, she was staring at him with a haughty expression. Her cloak and gown were of a silken fabric so thin he felt her softness pressed against him.

"Where are we going?" he asked.

"Off into the wild," she told him, "in the dark of night where no one will find us."

A distance from his villa, she stopped the driver, picked up a blanket from the floor of the chariot, leapt down and ran into the bush. Holofernes chased after.

He caught her around the waist. "Astarte, you have no fear of animals or anything that may be hidden out here?"

"No!" she called out.

He gently pried the blanket from her and spread it on the ground. He laid down on it. She jumped on top of him.

"You should be boisterous and show a bit of roughness with me if you want to win the job." She laughed.

Holofernes and young Princess Astarte had an exciting time in the field.

Walking back to the chariot later that same night, Astarte surprised him with her question. She asked, "How is it you show so much experience in the art of entertaining a woman at such a young age?"

"You command my best," he answered.

She held him around the waist again as they returned to the villa. When he stepped down from the chariot, she said, "I will see you again. You passed the examination."

✧

Because Shalmaneser believed Prince Sennacherib would someday become king over the empire, he advised him to build a network to collect information. "You should not wait on this matter, my prince. Never underestimate the importance of being aware of everything and everyone around you. A king with knowledge becomes a living god. He must know everything that goes on in his world.

"To accomplish this he must spy on all his subjects, no matter who they may be. Your spies must be very well trained and totally reliable. A king's strength equals the measure of his knowledge. An uninformed king is weak and easily outwitted. His reign will not be long."

✧

When Shalmaneser came to Holofernes's villa to train him and the prince, he often brought the same young girl, Flulano, with him. She sat a short distance away, giving no notice to the prince and attempting to hide her interest in Holofernes.

Holofernes tried to take the same nonchalant approach toward her. There was no profit in pursuing her as she was always with Shalmaneser, for whom he held great respect.

Before too long, King Sargon II sent General Shalmaneser off to war in Israel. King Ahaz, of Judah, had pleaded with Assyria for help when Northern Israel and Syria threatened to attack.

Holofernes waited a few months then went to the house of his tutor's companion, the beautiful Flulano, and asked her to walk with him in her family's large gardens. She seemed happy to walk with him.

In the following weeks he frequently arrived at her villa and together they strolled through the gardens talking and laughing freely. Finally, one afternoon Holofernes gathered the courage to kiss Flulano.

She resisted his advances. "Why do you come to me with your hunger for a woman?"

"I think I may love you."

"Stop trying to kiss me," she said firmly. "Have you no respect for Shalmaneser? He thinks highly of you."

Holofernes turned the questioning to her.

"If you do not want me as I want you, why do you continue to see me?"

Flulano hesitated. "I don't know. I think I wanted companionship while Shalmaneser fights the war in Israel."

Holofernes pressed. "And why did you accompany Shalmaneser when he came to my villa and look directly at me with your lovely eyes?"

"I came with Shalmaneser because I asked him to bring me." Flulano glanced shyly at him.

His heart beat fast. It was the answer he wished to hear, and it implied she wanted him also. He took her in his arms and kissed her. Flulano resisted only a moment before she kissed him back. They kissed passionately, as if a mountain of suppressed desire had finally been released. Holofernes picked her up and carried her to a secluded thicket where he watched her disrobe in the warmth of the late afternoon then turn full circle before him. He reached for her, and the entertainment began.

It was evening before they walked back to her parents' villa. They held each other's hand tightly.

Before going inside, Flulano asked, "Will you come tomorrow?"

Holofernes nodded. "Come ride with me tomorrow. We can go to my home."

She threw him a goodbye kiss and turned to hurry up the high stairway. The breeze whipped her long dress against her legs then around and in the air and against her body again. Holofernes thought she looked incredibly beautiful moving in the wind.

⁂

When he came to pick up Flulano the next day, she stood at the top of the steps with her two younger sisters. *I see how it is. Perhaps this day we will just share a meal.*

His chariot carried the three girls to his villa for games and a midday meal in the gardens.

After he returned them to their parents' home, Flulano waited until her sisters were out of sight then said, "I will come to you later. My parents leave the house every night. So after my sisters are asleep, I am free to do whatever pleases me."

⁂

The two of them met in that way for months until the day Holofernes heard news the war had ended, and General Shalmaneser would be returning to Nineveh.

That evening when Flulano arrived at Holofernes's villa, she ran and threw her arms around him. "What can we do? I do not want to return to Shalmaneser. I do not love him. My father attempted to arrange this marriage against my desire."

Holofernes held her close. He moved his hands gently up and down her back, trying to comfort her. "We will think of something," he whispered. "We both knew this day would soon be upon us. I love you, Flulano, I truly do."

Flulano returned to her parents' home, leaving Holofernes to wrestle with his problem. His mind and heart filled with conflict. Shalmaneser knew the young men he trained as well as they knew themselves. He would discern something amiss once the lessons resumed and then what? *Will we fight for the love of Flulano?*

*I respect Shalmaneser, admire his knowledge and skills and am forever grateful to him for tutoring and mentoring me, a fatherless boy. How can I go to him and tell of my love for Flulano, the woman he now courts? Certainly she and I cannot continue as we have for the past eight months.*

Shalmaneser was a commanding general whose powerful family ranked second to none in wealth, and only the king held more authority. *How will he respond to our relationship?* The questions soared through Holofernes's mind.

*If he loves Flulano as dearly as I do, why has he not taken her as a wife? She is so young and beautiful.* Holofernes could not answer the questions.

All the next day he walked the halls of his villa, trying to solve the dilemma. At one point he found himself before the large fireplace in his great meeting hall. His father's collection of fine weapons hung over it. He reached up and removed one of the bronze daggers.

*If I kill Shalmaneser, my troubles will be over.*

He suddenly realized that thought was in his mind all along, waiting for him to acknowledge it. His grip tightened on the hilt of the dagger. "I will not give up Flulano, no matter what!"

⁜

General Shalmaneser returned a hero after carrying off twenty-seven thousand Hebrews to captivity. The elite of Nineveh gathered at King Sargon's palace to celebrate.

Shalmaneser would sleep in the palace quarters rather than travel the distance to his own villa after the late night of revelry. Holofernes discreetly determined the location of the general's sleeping quarters. The rooms were heavily guarded by Shalmaneser's own men. It would be impossible to get to him through them, so Holofernes went outside the palace walls where he came upon a sturdy vine that climbed beside the balcony of Shalmaneser's quarters.

He made his way back inside. The celebration had progressed to music and dancing. Flulano came near him and whispered, "Are you going to tell him tonight or wait until morning?"

"I will talk with him tonight if I get the opportunity," Holofernes lied.

Flulano drifted back to her family while Holofernes mingled with the crowd.

It was late when the aristocrats and noble families began to take their leave. Flulano smiled and eyed Holofernes as she and her family departed.

He left soon after, taking his chariot outside the palace walls then circling back to conceal it in the bushes. He returned on foot, careful not to be seen. He climbed the vines to the balcony of the general's still-empty chamber and hid, waiting.

*I am insane! I love Shalmaneser as a son loves his father.*

The longer he waited, the more jittery and upset he became.

Shalmaneser finally returned to his quarters. Holofernes blotted out all thoughts except the love he had for Flulano. He listened to the muted voices of the guards and the sounds Shalmaneser made as he readied for sleep. The general muttered and stumbled around clumsily, obviously tired and very drunk. It wasn't long before the general's heavy snoring was the only sound coming from inside.

Holofernes crept from his hiding place, moved swiftly into the room and stabbed the sleeping general's intoxicated body twice before making his escape.

⁘

The next morning Flulano came to Holofernes's door. She was excited and anxious. "Did you talk to Shalmaneser?"

"The man was too drunk to talk. I will speak with him this morning, when he is recuperated." Holofernes couldn't look her in the eye. "Wait here, Flulano, until I return."

Flulano noticed how agitated Holofernes appeared. He seemed distracted. She took his hand and brought it to her lips. "I will wait."

⁘

When he arrived, the palace was in an uproar. Holofernes walked the palace, eavesdropping, hoping to hear news of the attack on Shalmaneser. When the news came, it wasn't what he expected.

"Shalmaneser lives! He will recover from the wounds."

Holofernes stumbled away shocked yet filled with relief. Shalmaneser had survived the attack. When it came to killing, Holofernes's inexperience had prevailed. Because of his admiration and respect for the general, he had hesitated and the two wounds he inflicted upon Shalmaneser were too shallow to kill.

*Should I be thrilled with my failure or chilled with the dread of facing Shalmaneser's vengeance?* Whatever happened, Holofernes needed to carefully consider his every word and action for the coming weeks while the attack was investigated.

He returned to his villa where Flulano waited. He took her in his arms. "Shalmaneser was attacked last night as he slept. He will recover from the assault, but I was unable to speak to him. We must wait to see what happens."

The question in Flulano's eyes told him she believed there was more to the tale, but she spoke not a word of doubt or suspicion.

⁙

The Shalmaneser family and their supporters wanted to point the finger at the Sargons. The two families had vied for power for generations. The Sargon family insisted the inept attack on the general could not be the work of a person trained to assassinate. If they had done this it would have been professionally executed and Shalmaneser would be dead. No one could counter that claim for they knew it to be fact. Thus, the investigation into the attempted assassination continued.

When Shalmaneser's wounds began to heal, he sent for Holofernes and Prince Sennacherib. "The time has come for me to leave this business of war to those younger and stronger. Of those I have trained, you two are the best. Prince

Sennacherib, your skills will carry you far as a leader and a king, the best our land has known. And you, Holofernes, will be a military leader and master. I have seen no one better than you with the sword."

He paused briefly. "My intent is to marry and live out my life in peace. I chose Flulano, the young woman who frequently accompanied me to our training sessions at your villa, Holofernes. After this attack on my life, I changed my mind. Earlier today I spoke with Flulano's father. He has graciously relieved me of my obligation to marry his daughter. This freed me to choose a woman from my own clan for the honor, one who will always be at my side."

He raised his hand and a woman entered.

Holofernes and Prince Sennacherib watched as an elegant and stunning mature woman strode across the room to Shalmaneser's bedside, sat and took his hand. Her demeanor was of love and respect. The two younger men stared, speechless.

⁘

For a moment, Holofernes could not move. Confusion ruled his mind. Then fear sliced through him as he considered the truth was known. But as he watched Shalmaneser and this beautiful woman, he realized Flulano was free to become his woman.

⁘

Shalmaneser spoke to them again. "Go now, out into the empire, and never forget treachery is a constant threat. Be on guard always. Let what has happened to me serve as a lesson."

⁘

Holofernes walked out of the villa aching inside. He shook all over, and it was hard to breathe. Ahikar offered him a drink of fresh water.

"What is wrong?" asked Prince Sennacherib.

Holofernes only said, "I hate to lose him."

But later, when he had calmed down, he confessed his crime to Prince Sennacherib, his lifelong friend, relating the entire story including how he came to love Flulano.

"I feel so guilty. I thought for certain he would take Flulano from me."

Sennacherib listened to it all then said, "No one will ever hear this secret from my lips. Do not look back with regret. Only sorrow can come from that, my friend. Yet do not forget the past either, learn from it."

"I will," Holofernes said. "But should I confess to our teacher?"

"No, neither for your own sake nor the general's. Shalmaneser is shrewd. He may already suspect it was you and your admission would humiliate him. Stand strong. You did what you felt in your heart to be the right thing."

Holofernes decided his friend's advice might well be the best course. For the next two years he concentrated on his studies and training with Prince Sennacherib under new instructors.

✢

Prince Arki-kudam, the oldest son of King Sargon II, returned from a trip to Babylonia. He came upon a group of Hebrew servants and field workers gathered in the countryside near the road. He ordered his driver to stop and watched the Hebrews for a few moments while one of them spoke and the others all listened attentively.

Arki-kudam was curious about the gathering, as well as suspicious. He alighted from his chariot and walked over to the group.

The speaker turned at his approach and bowed. "Please forgive me, dear prince, I did not see you until now."

"You are the servant of Prince Sennacherib," the prince said.

"Yes, I am Ahikar."

"What are you doing here?"

"I am teaching them the Assyrian language so they can be better servants for their masters. These people know nothing."

The prince asked, "Did you get the overseer's permission?"

"No, I did not. I thought it would be helpful for both them and their Assyrian lords."

The prince said, "If you should decide to do anything like this in the future, make sure you ask if it is their lord's bidding first. Now, return to your duties and your master Prince Sennacherib."

He watched as Ahikar bowed again and left right away in a single horse chariot.

The prince turned to the Hebrews. "Return to your assigned work and see to it you make up for the time you loitered around that man."

Arki-kudam began to observe Ahikar regularly. The Hebrew moved about freely to do whatever he wanted. Also, he never attended the temple to pay homage to Baal, as did the other Israelites whose lordships granted special liberties because they worshiped Baal.

One day he approached Ahikar and said, "The hour for all Hebrews to pray to Baal in his temple has come. Why have you not joined them? Baal has blessed you with many freedoms."

Ahikar bowed down before the prince. "I am sorry, my prince, I will go at once."

*Does he think so loosely about his responsibility to Baal that he must be reminded of worship? If one servant behaves like this, others will follow. His insolence must be addressed.*

⁘

Soon after, one of Prince Sennacherib's many spies informed the prince of a plot to assassinate Ahikar involving four Hittites.

"My lord," said the spy. "I grieve to inform you it was your brother, Prince Arki-kudam, who organized this evil scheme." He trembled as he spoke.

Prince Sennacherib asked his servant, "How did you come to know all of this?"

"Four strangers came to the prince's villa outside the city. Your brother offered them living quarters. I suspected something out of the ordinary and decided to investigate further. So I exchanged duties with the servant assigned to them. I served the strangers wine and kept a close ear. I am only somewhat conversant in their language, but I overheard and understood enough to learn of the plot, as I have told it to you."

Sennacherib stood. "Good work, my fine servant, you will be handsomely rewarded."

Holofernes stood and put his arm over the spy's shoulder. He said, "The prince and I will go forward from here. You must hurry back before your absence is noticed."

⁜

The very next day Ahikar went to Prince Sennacherib and asked leave to travel. "I have received word my cousin lies seriously ill, perhaps on his deathbed."

The prince nodded his permission. As Ahikar hurried away, the Prince exchanged a conspiratorial glance with Holofernes who followed him. Ahikar knew nothing of the plot against him nor of the counter-attack Prince Sennacherib conceived.

⁜

Ahikar arrived in the countryside late the same afternoon and went straight to the landowner for consent to visit the Hebrews' field quarters. Just before he entered his cousin's abode, four men ran up to ambush him. At that very instant Holofernes and his keen-eyed bowmen slew the attackers. Ahikar stood trembling, seeming stunned and confused, unable to recognize the reality of the situation. Then to his relief, he saw Holofernes coming toward him.

"Go inside, Ahikar. Tell them not to worry."

Ahikar entered his cousin's abode. He said, "Everything outside is fine, but no one should go out right now."

The Assyrian property owner heard the commotion and just before he came out, Holofernes's young officer hurried to the door. "Sir, a few unruly slaves from neighboring properties attempted to escape and had to be subdued on your land. Prince Sennacherib's guards have control, but you should stay inside for your own well-being."

As Holofernes's men removed the Hittites' bodies and cleared the area, two other men approached them. They behaved suspiciously, and Holofernes suspected their mission was to pay the Hittites. His men apprehended them and discovered large sums of gold and silver. Holofernes had the men tortured until they admitted Prince Arki-kudam had supplied the coins to pay for the assassination thereby corroborating the story told by Sennacherib's spy. Holofernes showed them no mercy and ordered them executed on the spot then he divided the gold and silver among his own men.

⁙

Arki-kudam paced his chambers, waiting for the return of his servants. *Did the Hittite men accomplish their deed? Why have my servants not returned? Did they make the assassination payment?*

It was then a guard came to him. "My prince, it is said the two servants you sent to the countryside have absconded with the gold and silver you delegated them to deliver. It is also said a man lies dead on the road nearby."

*That may be Ahikar.* As there was no confirmation from the thieving servants, the prince took several of his guards and went out to view the scene himself. Upon reaching the location where the body lay, he halted the company of guards and went forward alone.

"Get out of my way, you inept fools." He threw aside the blanket covering the body. It was not Ahikar, but his own servant. He dropped to his knees.

"What went wrong?" he yelled out in frustration. "What went wrong?" Suddenly, he knew. He leapt to his feet. "Get me back to the palace. Hurry."

But he was too late. Arrows soared in from opposite directions. After a short fight, all his men lay wounded or dead, and Arki-kudam stood alone.

⁘

Holofernes walked up to the prince who quaked before him like a rabbit caught in a snare. "What frightens you, Prince Arki-kudam? What have you been up to?"

The prince cried out. "Holofernes, spare me. I can give you a fortune."

Holofernes only said, "You underestimate a man's loyalty. Now, draw your sword and fight like a man."

"My father, King Sargon, will put you to death for this. You must be mad to think you can get away with murdering me."

Holofernes's smile seemed more like a sneer. "It is said you are skilled at handling a sword. Let me see how much talent you have."

The prince responded. "How can I have a fair chance with all your men around me?"

Holofernes looked around at his men with pride. He said, "Swear to me no harm will come to the son of Sargon II if he prevails over me. All of you declare it now before Baal. Your loyalty will be to this man, and you, Prince of Assyria, must also swear before Baal that when you reach safe company no harm will come to these men for following my orders. Swear it on Baal."

After all the oaths, Arki-kudam checked his armor then drew his sword. The prince was known to have killed several men, and Holofernes had never even faced a man in real, single combat, much less killed one. These facts did not diminish his confidence. "The oaths will come to nothing, Prince. For you shall not prevail over me."

The clashing of the swords rang out, over and over, as the blades swung. The two men fought furiously, but in the end Holofernes slew the prince, the oldest brother of his friend Sennacherib. He suffered only a minor leg wound himself.

⁘

35

Holofernes sent word to Sennacherib of the deed. He made his way back to Sennacherib's quarters in the palace and found him sitting at a large, marble table. Holofernes sat down at the opposite end of the long table.

"Holofernes," his friend said, "you do understand why I had to do that. He was my biggest adversary. If he had succeeded at killing Ahikar, his ambition would have targeted me in the future. My other older brother, Ashur-nadin-shumi, is not a dangerous rival. He has no ambitions to the throne. I can force him out of the picture anytime."

Holofernes nodded. "I do understand."

Sennacherib stood. "Tomorrow my brother will be a hero. He fought courageously against the Hittite spies after he and his guards uncovered their hiding place. Now, my loyal friend, I noticed you are walking with a limp, go visit a healer for the wound."

⁕

True to Sennacherib's prediction the city of Nineveh learned of this tragedy the next morning. For six days Assyria mourned. The high priests prayed to the gods. Then the fires of cremation consumed the body of Prince Arki-kudam.

At the end of the ceremony King Sargon II announced before the people, "My son resides now among the gods. Let all the citizens of Assyria remember he gave his life for his kindred."

⁕

Nearly a year passed since the death of the first prince. Holofernes and Prince Sennacherib completed all the tutoring and training required to become leaders in the Assyrian nation. Prince Sennacherib became involved in governing the empire. Holofernes received word that his induction into the Assyrian military as a high ranking officer received approval. All noble young men who complete their physical training and required study do not necessarily qualify for acceptance into the higher corps of officers. King Sargon II determined that he would conduct the induction service himself at Holofernes's villa.

On the day of the ceremony over a hundred guests waited in the villa's main hall. Holofernes had not heard from the one person he wanted there more than anyone—his mother. He repeatedly sent someone to see if his mother had arrived. Each time the answer was "No."

In the center of the large room was a statue of a human-faced winged bull, representative of their god Baal. A hot fire burned inside a bowl directly in front of the statue. King Sargon II walked to the left side of the statue, Holofernes to the right. He knelt down, placing both hands upon the side of Baal's statue. The king gave him permission to speak. He spoke in a clear, loud voice, his eyes fixed on the statue of Baal.

"Hear me, my god, Baal. I, Holofernes, swear before you and your living son, King Sargon II, that I dedicate my life in service to you, to enforce your will upon those who defy you. I will eliminate all enemies who war against you. My loyalty will forever be unblemished. Before my god, Baal, my king and the people of the Assyrian nation I declare it with my life." Holofernes bowed his head and remained kneeling in silence.

King Sargon II removed the red-hot branding iron from the pit. He took Holofernes by his right arm, holding it high, and said, "O Baal, with this seal I emphatically appoint Holofernes as your loving servant. May this seal express to everyone that he has your authority to act in your name."

The King brought the seal down hard on the arm, searing into the flesh a print of Baal. Holofernes made no sound and no movement. He had accomplished one of his mother's wishes for him and could only hope the news would reach her wherever she might be. Then he gave recognition to his mentor and tutor, General Shalmaneser, and to Prince Sennacherib, his life-long friend.

⁘

Holofernes remembered those early years while sitting in his tent on the eve of returning victoriously to Nineveh. It had not always been a happy childhood but certainly wonderful people and moments filled most of his years.

# SENNACHERIB

711-704 B.C.E.

After the Assyrians overthrew Merodach-baladan's kingdom of Babylonia in 711 B.C.E., the two nations united as one. However, within a few years, Merodach-baladan reappeared and incited another revolt against Assyria.

King Sargon II called a council with his son, Prince Sennacherib, and included Holofernes. He spoke first to his favorite son.

"The hostilities between our nation and Babylonia have erupted into a confrontation between Merodach-baladan and our governing authority. I am assigning you the task of restoring order in Babylonia. You will become a fearless leader on the battlefields."

He turned to Holofernes. "You, Holofernes, will stand beside my son as a high-ranking officer in this conflict. Experienced generals will supervise the strategy of the military operation, but you two will be the focal point of the campaign. War is eminent."

÷

King Merodach-baladan originally expected the full support of Babylonia when the Assyrian troops crossed their borders, but he soon realized the situation had drastically changed. Forty percent of the Babylonian provinces went neutral putting the Babylonian king at a huge disadvantage. However, he knew a strong cavalry could dictate the outcome of a battle so he negotiated with the neutral Babylonian cavalry, securing their service for a large payment.

King Merodach-baladan brought his army out to meet the Assyrians in battle, led by his cavalry. He gave the command to attack. The forward rush of men and horses across the field made a daunting scene.

Prince Sennacherib gave the order to meet the oncoming horsemen and the two opposing cavalry forces clashed between the two opposing armies. The Babylonians defeated the Assyrian cavalry but paid a heavy price in casualties for the victory. The remaining Babylonian cavalry raced on.

The Assyrians interlocked their wall-of-shields and braced for the impact. The Babylonian infantry chanted the call of war as they came across the open fields behind the horsemen.

Holofernes watched the enemy's fast approach and waited to give the order for the archers to release their arrows. At firing range he shouted the order and the Assyrian arrows came down like rain upon the Babylonian cavalry.

The cavalry was decimated but successfully breached the pavis wall. Their infantry forged into the Assyrian interior. The Babylonian archers, coming in behind the infantry, reached their position and exchanged arrows with the Assyrians. The Assyrian infantry crowded into the huge breach to defend against the thousands of Babylonian soldiers now fighting their way in.

As they battled to stop the penetration, Holofernes spotted a powerful officer at the center of the front line of the Babylonian fighting machine. He fought skillfully and with great strength, killing many Assyrian soldiers who ran up against him. Clearly this man dressed in silver and gold led the battle. His helmet displayed an especially long crest of horsehair that ran from the front to back and ended in a long horsetail that danced with his every movement. He was frightful to gaze upon and stood prominently over all the other fighting men. Holofernes knew immediately this man's identity—the Babylonian supreme commander and ruler, Merodach-baladan.

Both Holofernes and Prince Sennacherib rode upon their chariots. Holofernes signaled the prince he would fight his way through the battle and confront the Babylonian champion in war. Prince Sennacherib followed. They encountered heavy resistance but ultimately faced the Babylonian leader.

⁖

King Merodach-baladan recognized the opponents before him as high-ranking Assyrian officers. This fight could determine the outcome of the war. The one to his left in black armor decorated with highly polished iron had to be the military leader, Holofernes. Already a giant among the Assyrians, he stood even taller with all white horse hair mounted high on his helmet and a long white horsetail in the back.

Holofernes stepped off his chariot. Merodach-baladan followed suit. They would fight hand to hand on foot.

The two men circled, shields held high. Their soldiers battled around them and held off interference. Holofernes and the king charged each other. Swords clashed and clanged. It was certain victory for one, the end for the other. Two skilled heroes landed and received blow after blow. It was a dance of death for two mad warriors, neither of whom gave either ground or quarter.

Bodies of fallen Assyrian and Babylonian soldiers piled around them as they continued their skilled swordplay, whacking at one another whenever the opportunity arose. Sennacherib fought back-to-back with Holofernes, cutting down any Babylonians who threatened his friend.

Neither man showed weakness or weariness to the other. It was Holofernes whose sword first struck flesh through Merodach-baladan's plate armor. The Babylonian king fought on as if no strike had landed. The tip of Holofernes's sword was red, and like a shark with the scent of blood, he intensified his attack.

He struck another blow on the shoulder. It slowed Merodach-baladan's rush and he withdrew. When Holofernes pursued him for the kill, he sustained an ear-ringing blow to the helmet from behind by a Babylonian soldier who eluded the Assyrians. Prince Sennacherib saw the attack and felled the Babylonian with one powerful stroke. Merodach-baladan escaped into the ranks of his infantry.

As the day progressed, the battle slowly swayed in favor of the Assyrian forces. Prince Sennacherib and Holofernes continued to fight alongside their men until early evening when the last of the Babylonian men of war ran for their lives. King Merodach-baladan and a number of his officers fled into a wooded area.

⁕

The Assyrians wanted to restore order to the province, not destroy it. They took no civilian prisoners but all had to commit and swear allegiance to King Sargon II of Assyria, or die. King Sargon II's oldest living son, Ashur-nadin-shumi, received an appointment as King of the entire country of Babylonia.

Prince Sennacherib and Holofernes returned as heroes. Word of the bravery with which Holofernes fought King Merodach-baladan had preceded their arrival. King Sargon II orchestrated a welcoming parade and the entire city turned out to join the celebration.

Princess Astarte sat near her father. She waved and threw Holofernes kisses. Flulano sat with the nobles and aristocrats, waving excitedly at Holofernes.

Later, at the feast, the princess came to Holofernes. "You will entertain me tonight, my he-man. Flulano can have you for the rest of the year, for all I care, but tonight you will be with me."

Holofernes was puzzled. "How on earth is that going to happen?"

She saw someone else approaching and moved away, whispering, "You will see. You will see."

Before the feast ended, Flulano came to him, "I am ill. My family insists upon taking me home. I will come to you in the morning, my love."

⁕

When Holofernes finally exited the celebratory party and went to his assigned quarters, Princess Astarte lay in his bed with her arms held open to him. He said as he disrobed, "You are a powerfully bad, bad goddess." She was insatiable, staying with him until the early morning hours.

⁕

Flulano came to his quarters early. She would be suspicious if he did not show interest in her body, so Holofernes created a diversion that was sure to work.

"Flulano, will you be my wife? Will you marry me right away?"

Flulano danced around the room. "Yes! Yes!"

Her excitement told Holofernes his secret night with the princess would remain a secret. He loved Flulano and believed she would be a wonderful wife.

She suddenly stopped dancing. "I have to make plans. Everything must be perfect. You have been at war, and they say you fought like a lion. You deserve a reward, but please forgive me for not laying with you. There is so much to do, and I must hurry home to tell my family. I promise to return to you later."

⁕

The wedding ceremony was flawless, and following the final words of the high priests, Flulano stood before her new husband. Together they thanked everyone for attending and invited the guests to take pleasure in the lavish celebration in honor of their marriage.

The wedding chariot rolled up and the two mounted it and rode away, waving to everyone. The firelight of the wedding party grew dimmer and dimmer. They found happiness and peace for a few weeks before Holofernes received a message from the king commanding his presence.

⁕

King Sargon II had held his anger until his military officers recuperated then he called a debriefing wherein he expressed his outrage at the devastating defeat of his horsemen. He demanded a new, elite cavalry be assembled, one greater than any the world had ever seen.

·:·

While his father was off on a new campaign testing the excellence of the improved Assyrian cavalry, Sennacherib revealed himself to be a man of the people. He spent his time with influential and wealthy subjects, statesmen and military officers. All the while, Sennacherib continued to strengthen his personal network of spies.

For the first time Holofernes controlled the whole of the army that remained in the capital. He had never been quartered in the palace at Nineveh, but once Prince Sennacherib appointed him Commander in Chief, he was given rooms on the upper floors.

·:·

He spent long hours seeing to his many military obligations and often spent nights in the palace rather than traveling home to Flulano. As he returned to his rooms after one such day, Holofernes discovered Queen Talia in his quarters.

"What are you doing here? Hiding under a drapery?" He smiled, curious yet pleased.

"What do you think I am doing here? I have a husband who is away most of his days fighting wars leaving me, a young woman in the prime of her life, to wilt. What is it with you men? Do you not understand women also have feelings and desires?" She paused briefly then smiled. "I have heard of your reputation with women, and I also know you fear no one."

Holofernes shook his head. He doubted the wisdom of a relationship with the queen. "I don't know," he said. "What happened to loyalty and respect?"

Queen Talia made a move to pass him and leave, but he took her by the waist and held her tight. The two of them stood close, not saying a word. He felt each breath she took and bent to kiss her face and neck, enjoying the faint taste of freshly washed and scented skin.

Wisdom did not prevail. "Remove your clothing."

Queen Talia slowly lowered her gown.

"You, my queen, are exquisite. There is no component of beauty you lack."

Grinning, she said, "I made your approval."

The young Queen lay with Holofernes but could not stay with him for long. "I must leave. I have enemies with spies everywhere."

Holofernes said, "Does the king know what a wild young thing you are? I want to see you as often as possible."

"I do not know if I can. His older wives hate me." She thought for a moment. "I found you very satisfying also, and I would like to see you again. Even if they found out I do not feel they would dishonor me. I have enough dirt on them to sink the palace." She kissed him lightly. "What they want is to dispose of me altogether, but without drawing suspicion to themselves."

Holofernes sat up. Her courage impressed him as well as her determination to fight back against her enemies. As he controlled all the palace guards now, he was well aware of the potential danger she faced, and he truly wanted to protect her.

"I will first get rid of all your personal guards. There may be spies among them. I will assign some of my most loyal men. What about your servants? Do you trust them?"

"Yes," Queen Talia said. "They are all hand-picked by me."

"Well, how did you get in here in the first place?"

With a slight smile, she responded. "One of my maidens removed some of her clothing and distracted your guards. I crept in from the opposite direction behind them."

Holofernes shook his head. "Naughty girl, but clever."

When the time came he lured the guards away from the door himself and she left unnoticed.

⁘

That evening, in her own rooms, Queen Talia thought about what she had done. She remembered the day she sat looking out of her window, watching the activities of the city when her close friend, Prince Sennacherib's older sister, came to her.

She said, "Oh, Queen, why do you look so sad?"

"I am young, in the early years of womanhood, and I rarely see my husband. He spends most of his time off on the business of the government or the likes of war. I am lonely."

Her friend massaged her neck and shoulders. "Why don't you bring some adventure into your life?"

"Such as...?" the queen asked.

The now happily married princess who once trysted with Holofernes and her sister in a friend's beautiful garden replied without hesitation. "Find yourself a secret lover."

Queen Talia shouted "What?"

The princess remained nonplussed. "I know just the man to fill your desires."

She told the queen about Holofernes, the ideal candidate.

Talia's curiosity was aroused. "Why would Holofernes want me?'

"You are young and beautiful, and he has the heart of a lion."

Queen Talia had grown warm at that remark and rolled her eyes. "He is newly married to the lovely Flulano. How much can one man handle?"

"The gods are in his blood. Trust me," her friend had answered. "He is always lusting for new young beauties."

Talia sighed. *She proved to be right, and I do believe neither of us has any regrets.*

⁘

Only a few days later, he sent one of his most trusted guards to deliver a message to Queen Talia requesting she visit him that night.

He dismissed the guards outside his quarters, so no one stood beside his door when she arrived. He kissed her passionately and discovered her face wet with tears. "Talia, what can be so troubling?"

Talia shook as she answered his question. "The senior queen came and tried to convince me to imbibe a poisoned drink. She told me I brought shame upon their house by sleeping with you."

Holofernes's stared at her. "How did she learn of our tryst?" His voice was whispered.

"I do not know. Maybe I was followed."

"I thought you said our affair would be of little value to your enemies."

"Yes, but now I have doubt," she said. "I flung her many affairs in her face, but she only laughed and said she had told Sargon about her affairs. He had neither care nor interest since he has not slept with her for many years.

"Then she said to me, 'However, to hear such things of you, his little charm, would make him very angry.' I threw the poison away and sought protection behind the new guards you posted for me." Talia buried her face in her hands. "She followed me and said 'I am not finished with you yet.' And then she pointed her finger at me and walked away."

Holofernes took Talia in his arms. "I feared something like this would happen. Don't worry. I will protect you. I have a plan."

He led her to the bed and tried to make her forget the ugly threat. "When the time comes for you to return, I will arrange safe passage back to your rooms. Your cupbearer needs to test everything you eat or drink. I will also add more guards."

"What do you plan on doing?" she asked.

He smiled. "Relax, my love, all is well and under my control."

The very next day Prince Sennacherib and Holofernes met for their usual consultation during which time the affairs of the empire were the number one topic addressed.

Holofernes asked casually, "What do you think of the first Queen? Is she as sweet as she would lead one to believe?"

Sennacherib sneered. "I view her as a miserable woman who is jealous of everyone. She loves to exercise her power over the other queens, including my mother who should be second to no one!"

Holofernes began, "What if something were to. . ."

Sennacherib cut him off. "Don't say another word." He stared Holofernes in the eye. "I do not want to know."

With that, the conversation ended.

They discussed a few other matters and Holofernes left, anxious to move forward with his plan.

Before he could take further action, word reached the nation that King Sargon II had died in battle. Holofernes's duty was to Prince Sennacherib who was mired in mourning. However, Holofernes's thoughts focused on his own problems, and he formulated a plan. By midday he had readied it for implementation.

---

News of Sargon's death reached the senior queen and her entourage at the king's villa. She immediately made plans to return to Nineveh.

Holofernes knew this would likely be her course of action once she learned of her husband's death. His mind raced. *This is the ideal time to act upon my plan.* He quietly gave the order to replace the senior queen's guards around her palace chambers with his own men.

---

Late that afternoon an assassin entered the queen's chambers before she and her servants arrived. He found a weapon in Sargon's collection of trophy daggers and concealed it in his robes, then hid behind the draperies near her open balcony and waited. When the queen arrived and retired for the night, he awakened her ever so briefly as he plunged the dagger into her abdomen.

All accepted the tale of the queen's tragic suicide due to her depression over the death of her king.

After hearing the news, Holofernes spoke quietly with his head guard. "Well done," he said.

Queen Talia came to him that very night. "We are free to love each other as we wish."

Holofernes only smiled and kissed her passionately.

⁘

Sadness and mourning wrapped the city of Nineveh for the people loved King Sargon and his Queen. Prince Sennacherib promised a large ransom for his father's body but no one came forward. The body of King Sargon II could not be found.

The royal funeral pyre burned a wooden likeness of King Sargon II with the body of his senior queen.

Before the royal family departed the funeral site, Prince Sennacherib spoke to his mother. "Now you are the most powerful woman in the world. Does that suit you?"

She clearly saw her reflection in his eyes and said, "I did love your father. He once told me my son, above all his sons, would one day be king. I could never be certain of anything he said, but that."

Sennacherib enclosed her in his arms. As Holofernes looked on, standing a short distance away, Princess Astarte, daughter of the now powerful queen, stood behind Holofernes and whispered, "I am so happy for my mother and brother. I do not know what role you played in this, but I sense you had a hand in it. I want to reward you and will meet you in your quarters in two hours."

Holofernes turned, surprised to see her standing there.

"Yes. Yes, and I will have a surprise there for you as well."
She backed up and disappeared into the crowd of mourners
and bystanders.

⁘

Prince Sennacherib demanded an explanation regarding
the failure of the army to protect his father, and he called for a
debriefing of the battle in which he died.

The cavalry general spoke, "Our scouts missed the
approach of a second attachment of Cimmerian soldiers who
overwhelmed the King's position. Emperor Sargon II died
along with his finest guards, away from the major battle."

⁘

Because King Sargon II did not name an heir to the
throne, a minor confrontation developed between Prince
Sennacherib and his older brother, Ashur-nadin-shumi, who
their father sent to govern Babylonia. However, Sennacherib's
brother had actually become quite comfortable in his role as
King of Babylonia. Sennacherib quickly rose to the Assyrian
kingship for he already held the overseer role of the empire
and easily won the approval of the majority of the noblemen
and statesmen.

⁘

Less than a year following his father's death in 704 B.C.E.,
the high priest of Baal anointed Sennacherib the living god
of the entire Assyrian world. Upon his anointing, the newly
crowned king said, "Baal has entrusted to me an unrivaled
kingship from the upper sea of the setting sun to the lower sea
of the rising sun. He has brought all mankind in submission
at my feet."

As king, Sennacherib immediately began to design and
build new public centers, temples, and monuments. However,
as soon as the news of his father's death became known, King
Sennacherib faced extremely serious problems. Rebellions

broke out in the Mediterranean districts and in Babylonia, Phoenicia and Philistia.

Holofernes held a monthly conference with the officers to discuss the security and operations in Assyria at large. For two years Sennacherib had immersed himself deeply in his many building projects, and the generals were concerned about the political health of the empire. The Assyrian kingdom might collapse around them. They warned Holofernes he must convince Emperor Sennacherib to redirect his focus to the many developing rebellions.

Holofernes shared their opinion. Assyria did not require the provinces to make tribute, but the provinces still responded rebelliously and attempted to gain independence. Though Holofernes expressed his concerns related to the provocation of the rebellious colonies, King Sennacherib continually ignored the increasingly serious issues and tended only to the beautification of Nineveh.

"My king, you are doing wonders for our beloved city, but you are neglecting your obligations to the well-being of our realm. There are revolts in all corners of the empire. Only a handful of the conquered still pay tribute. Not one of the Babylonian provinces remains completely in alliance with us.

"Your brother serves as the king over Babylonia, but he is Assyrian and more Babylonian people turn from us each day that goes by. Merodach-baladan is once more raising his evil head, trying to lead a revolt. We must address the real danger these uprisings present."

Sennacherib finally seemed to hear the words of his advisor. "So badly did I want to finish this work in the city, but now I must act."

However, before the battle cry sounded, Ashur-nadin-shumi, Assyrian King of Babylon, became a victim of treachery. He lay dead by the hand of rebels, while the Assyrians old enemy, Merodach-baladan, renamed himself Emperor of Babylonia. It signaled yet another war.

# JUDITH

727-705 B.C.E.

When Peninnah gave birth to their daughter, Judith, she and her husband, Merari, praised God for the blessed joy and thrill of a newborn in their lives. Until this gift, children had eluded them. Women throughout the city came to see the new baby with the surprising red hair. In the collective memory of all, no one remembered any other child with red hair. In her early childhood, the servants gave Judith the nickname of Rufus, meaning redhead. The name stayed with her through to adulthood.

During her early years, Judith lived in a wing of the palace designated for high ranking government officials and their families. Her father's days were filled with work on his large farm and the responsibilities that accompanied membership on the elders' government council. Her mother tutored other Hebrew women on the history and laws of their people, as written in the Torah by the Prophet Moses.

Young Judith had a large playroom and many servants, but only a few children her age came to play with her. Without sisters or brothers and sheltered from children outside the palace, Judith lived a lonely life. She watched other children from her balcony as they played in the streets below. She yearned to play as they did.

Judith snuck out of the palace one day and was caught playing in the street with the children. After the incident her father realized she needed better supervision. He decided she would accompany him to the council meetings of the governing elders.

"I can keep watch over you there and it will give you something to do. The governing council comes together at the king's directive when an issue arises in need of discussion by the governing elders, as often as four days a week."

Judith was nine years old.

⁛

Judith sat back with the rest of the audience and onlookers. She developed a curiosity in the proceedings and with each passing council session her interest to learn more increased. Her understanding of Judah's business and political activities grew also, and accompanying her father to the meetings quickly became a priority for her.

⁛

"It gladdens me to see your satisfaction in the business of your people," her father told her.

Judith became his full-time companion. At the time, most of the meetings ran smoothly with little disruption or disagreement. Rather routine issues dominated the agenda with few conflicts.

However, over the upcoming months, neighboring countries threatened war. The council meetings changed dramatically and debate became quite volatile with various members exhibiting strong responses to the issues discussed. Judith began to learn of a world where turmoil, wars and religious rivalries frequently occurred.

The entire court often fell into anarchy where hostile, intense bickering and angry discussions became the norm for the day. Embroiled in the controversy of each day, Merari seemed to be oblivious to how volatile the debates had become or how it affected Judith through the years.

She did not ask her father questions about the meetings, especially when he grew irritated from the gatherings. She feared he would stop taking her and she was terribly interested in what happened and needed to understand the troubles of her people.

Peninnah educated her daughter in the evenings when the family nestled at home.

⁝

Through the years, Judith witnessed one dismal episode unfold after the other. The subjects discussed at the council meetings revealed the political and military struggle that King Ahaz faced. His dilemma was whether Judah should join Syria and Israel in the fight to secure independence from the dominating Assyrians. King Ahaz rejected the idea, and this left many of the council questioning the wisdom of their king.

Merari was one of many who wanted the merger with Syria and Israel. He constantly voiced his opinion. At the time, the vassal state of Judah paid tribute to Assyria. Merari and other council members who shared his position were concerned with Assyria's strong drive to push their pagan beliefs on the vassal states. They feared the heathen gods of Canaan would become the new gods of Judah.

King Ahaz and his disciples defied any alignment with Syria or Israel, fearing if Judah joined the vassal states and aligned against Assyria, war would come to the entire region. Not only did the king not trust their Israelite brethren, he worshiped the pagan gods of Assyria.

Listening to all the disagreement overwhelmed Judith's young mind. She struggled to understand what it meant for her city and its people.

King Ahaz's rejection of Syria and Israel created no small amount of strife. Syria and Israel joined forces in a threat against Judah to control them by force. Judah had only months to choose either to align or prepare for battle. Ahaz chose to fight and met them in a military confrontation. The armies of Syria and Israel slew one hundred twenty thousand in a single day and marched on all the towns before them.

In Jerusalem the council members raged in fury. They begged the king to somehow make peace before Jerusalem faced destruction. King Ahaz refused, even in the light of two hundred thousand women and children, the sons and daughters of Judah, carried to the Israeli capital city of Samaria in captivity with copious spoils of war. Each day the cries grew louder. The ongoing situation captured Merari's full attention daily as he held Judith's hand, rushing back and forth between council meetings and home.

Judith pretended to be oblivious to the whole matter, never letting her father know how she felt about the violent affairs before their country. She sat on her hands in the audience, nervously watching every move the elders made during the discussions.

When Judith accompanied Peninnah to the Temple, she beseeched God to save Jerusalem. "Oh, my God, I ask you to save the women and children of Judah."

She prayed and cried for the women and children taken into captivity as slaves. In a low murmuring voice, she prayed, "My God, women and children do not wage war. They only suffer the consequences of it."

One day, shortly after returning home from a trip to the Temple with her mother, Merari called to Judith. "Come on, sweet daughter. Hurry!"

He rushed down the stairs into the street, leading Judith by her hand. "A messenger has come with favorable news of our people taken into slavery."

Judith wanted to hear the news as much as he. *Did God answer my prayers? Almighty God, I know you heard my prayers! I know you love your people!* She could barely keep up with her father as they rushed to the meeting hall. With each step she softly chanted her prayer.

Every council member was present and all seemed anxious to hear the latest report.

The messenger wasted no time. "The prophet of Israel went out before the returning armies of Israel and confronted them in the name of our God. He told them the children of Judah and Jerusalem had brought to rage the anger of our LORD so the LORD delivered them into their hands. He continued to speak to the returning armies of Israel, saying, 'But are you not also guilty of sin before our God, the God of Israel? Do not add to your sins with further crimes before our heavenly father. Now, hear me therefore, and return the captives whom you have taken captive from your brethren for the fierce wrath of the LORD is upon you.' Upon hearing the prophet speak, the army of Israel set free all the captured people of Judah and moved them to Jericho."

The room exploded with shouts of joy and jubilation. Everyone knew someone who had been killed in the battle with Israel and Syria or ripped away into captivity. The joyous news gave great cause for celebration.

Judith looked up with gratitude. A small smile spread across her face, and she beamed with happiness. She mouthed a prayer of thanksgiving. *Oh holy God, you have answered my prayers. Thank you, my God, thank you.*

King Ahaz stood. The room grew quiet. The king informed the elders he had sent messengers to Assyria requesting their assistance to defeat the Syrians and Israelites. He took silver and gold from the Temple and treasures of the palace and sent it all as a gift to the Assyrian king. As in the past, the council elders were divided in their opinions. Many elders supported the king's action. However, many others held strongly to their position that the king should reconsider negotiating with the Assyrians.

A short time after the Judah's offerings, the council received word that King Sargon II of Assyria accepted Ahaz's request. The Assyrian army, led by General Shalmaneser, came up against Syria at Damascus, defeated them and killed their king.

King Ahaz traveled to Damascus where he met with General Shalmaneser to celebrate their victory. While there

Ahaz saw an Assyrian altar that greatly impressed him. He commissioned a copy of the altar and sent the design and details of its construction to the high priest in Jerusalem. King Ahaz ordered the removal of the original bronze altar from its rightful place in front of the Lord's Temple and relocated it to make way for his new altar. He made pagan sacrifices on the new altar daily.

When Judith realized what the king had done, she began to shake all over and was still trembling when her father took her hand to leave the council.

Immediately upon arriving at their palace quarters, Judith asked her mother to take her to the Holy Temple. Peninnah turned to question Merari. He told her about the new altar in front of the Temple of the Lord, and straightaway, Peninnah took Judith to see.

The big altar stood boldly beside the entrance. Peninnah covered her eyes in horror. "What evil is this placed before the house of the one God?"

Judith's eyes grew large and she covered her mouth to keep from crying out. "Mother, what does this mean? Will we not love our God as before?"

Peninnah answered, "We will never stop loving Almighty God. He is the one true God."

*Why do people from other countries believe in other gods? Who is right? Is there more than one god? Can there be more than one heaven? If other gods exist, do they have other heavens?*

Questions flew through Judith's mind. She could not stop thinking about it. *How do people come to know other gods? Isn't the God of Abraham and Isaac the Father of all mankind?* Tears ran down her face as they walked back home. *When I die, I want to be with the God of Abraham, not the other gods.*

Soon after when Judith fell ill, her father left her at home in the care of her mother. She recovered, but he did not resume taking her to the council gatherings.

She ran to him asking, "Please, dear father, why do you not take me with you? I am so accustomed to accompanying you that now I feel withdrawn with nothing to do. I want to go with you again. Please."

Merari recognized his daughter, a child of twelve years, possessed a keen desire to learn and understand her world and resumed taking her to the council meetings. Soon after her return to the spectator pews, yet another episode of conflicting discourse reared its ugly countenance.

King Ahaz stood before the elders, yelling intensely. His anger was directed at the Philistines who had invaded, annexed and occupied several towns in the southern lowlands at a time when Judah already suffered from the onslaught inflicted by their adversaries, Syria and Israel.

In this time of crisis, the council met daily while King Ahaz grew more and more frustrated with the ordeal. He requested help again from Assyria and once more withdrew large sums from the Temple and palace treasuries as payment. This time the Assyrians did not reply. The manner in which Ahaz governed appalled Merari and his contemporaries, and resulted in many angry and aggressive sessions of debate at the council gatherings. Still, no solutions could be found concerning the invaders.

⁙

Once again Judith lived with sadness for her people. She prayed for God to forgive King Ahaz. Each time she and her mother went to the Temple they had to walk past the large, bold altar of a pagan god at the entrance. Each time Judith trembled in fear.

*If I am afraid of the altar, then how strong is my faith and trust in my God? If I truly love Almighty God then nothing should stand between him and me.*

Her belief in Almighty God, the God of Abraham, strengthened and reinforced her determination to always place her trust in Him. After this day she walked fearlessly past the heathen image at the Temple.

⁙

King Ahaz called the elders together. "The Philistines do not withdraw from our towns, and the Assyrians show no further interest in my gifts, but there remains one more thing that will garner the support we need from Assyria. We will show that we are with them, that we accept their god, Baal, fully as our god. We shall build altars and make sacrifice to Baal."

⁙

For many fortnights, King Ahaz spoke of more conversion to the worship of idol gods. He built altars to the heathen gods in every corner of Jerusalem. He robbed the holy place of gold, silver, ivory and decorations. He tore down the canopy of the holy Temple, originally constructed for use on the Sabbath day, and ultimately closed the doors to the house of the LORD.

Some elders protested. "Is this necessary? Is there no other way? Please, we beg you." They pleaded to no avail. Ahaz would not move from his determination to win Assyrian approval and, therefore, potential protection.

Judith felt she lived in a nightmare.

As they returned home from a harsh session, her father said, "We will find a way, my child. We will never abandon the God of Abraham."

"You promise, Father?" Her heart was broken, her eyes full of tears. "I am so sad for the king. He will not let God love him."

⁙

Word reached the council that the prophet Isaiah warned of fierce wrath against Ahaz from the LORD God of Abraham, Isaac and Jacob. Queen Abi, wife of King Ahaz, sent a message to Isaiah telling him the faithful would never abandon their love for God. Isaiah instructed her and the faithful believers to enter the Temple from a side door and go to the walls enclosing the Holy Sanctuary. They should pray there, against that wall.

So the queen organized a secret congregation by word of mouth. She divided the people into small groups and dictated when a particular group would have access to the Temple. Judith and her mother became members of the queen's party. They continued to worship at the marble sanctuary walls as Isaiah instructed. King Ahaz feigned ignorance of the worshipers to avoid a confrontation with the believers and his wife.

The Assyrians would not be coming to drive out the Philistines from within their lands. After all the additional tribute sent by Ahaz, and even after switching their worship to the Assyrian gods, the king's pleas were ignored and his ambassadors turned away at Nineveh.

Judith listened to King Ahaz's tirade from where she sat in the upper viewing area of the council room. *Has our God tested our faith?* Thousands flocked to worship the heathen gods only to find their efforts accomplished nothing. What would the king do now? *Will he be encouraged to come back to the God of our fathers Abraham and Isaac, and will he allow the people to freely do so also?* King Ahaz did neither.

⁙

Judith's daily routine changed little. She still regularly observed the council gatherings. She entered her teenage years with less strife in her young life. The previous years of war and uncertainty seemed mostly concluded, replaced with a relatively peaceful time with much less talk of war. It had been a perilous era for the young girl in which she feared continually for her people. She had believed either King Ahaz's actions would bring down the wrath of Almighty God upon them, the powerful Assyrian army would attack and destroy Jerusalem, or the men on the council would erupt into violence right there in the meeting hall.

⁙

King Ahaz sickened and seemed to tire more quickly with each meeting. Often, his son, Hezekiah, was present and assumed control. The king died that year of natural causes. His reign had been consumed by turmoil, yet through it all he sustained independence for Jerusalem, a truly remarkable feat.

At the auspicious funeral, all of Judah mourned his death. Because Ahaz believed in idol worship, he received the customary ritual burial for worshippers of the pagan faith. The heathen priests burned incense. His body was cremated. Ahaz's remains were not brought into the sepulchers of the kings of Israel, but were placed in a heathen tomb. The majority of the Hebrew population behaved inconspicuously when it came to their ancient beliefs so the Assyrian overseers would be appeased. Other than the faithful few who continued to worship at the Temple, the Hebrews seemed to be under the influence of a powerful sedative that blocked them from their natural worship of the one true God.

Ahaz's son, Hezekiah, was his mother's true son and never believed in the pagan gods. Because of his belief in the one God of their ancestors, he wanted his father to receive the proper burial prayers of Hebrew worship.

In the year 711 B.C.E., Hezekiah, was anointed and crowned the new King of Judah. He was twenty-five years old. King Hezekiah sent word to Isaiah who had been banned from the city during the reign of Ahaz and asked him to come and pray at the tomb of his father. Isaiah came before the new king and granted his request.

Judith went out with her father to see this man of God, named Isaiah. His hair was white. He wore a long robe and carried a long staff. Judith's curiosity prompted her to stay in his company and observe his every move, but she did not speak with him.

When the prophet concluded his prayers, King Hezekiah invited Isaiah to return to Jerusalem.

Isaiah declined. "The city is full of evil and Canaanite idols. The Temple of Solomon has been desecrated."

⁙

Nearly four years passed and Judith grew into a beautiful woman. No one called her Rufus anymore.

Her father said, "It is time for you to become acquainted with the young men of Jerusalem, so I will escort you to some of the town gatherings and events."

"That sounds enjoyable. I will be happy to go," Judith said.

He cautioned her. "Take care, my daughter. Many men will say they love you." He placed his hands on her shoulders. "You are a rare prize. The man you choose will be fortunate, but there are men for whom your wealth may be their primary focus. I will die someday and you will inherit everything. My hope for you is a happy and wonderful life."

Her father did as he had promised. He went with her to many places, introducing her to young men. Suitors began to seek her company to one event after another.

⁙

A year later Merari collapsed while working in the fields on a blistering hot day. He could not be revived. Judith was on an outing with a young man and returned to the dreadful news of her father's death. She fell to her knees in grief. Regret clung to her like a cold, wet drapery.

*I should have been there with him in his last hours. He was alone.*

During the funeral Judith stood in silence, uttering not a whimper. Her mother wept continuously for weeks afterward. The two walked about the palace—Peninnah, in black clothing with her head down and sobbing. Judith also wore black clothing with haircloth upon her loins and back. She held her head up but felt stripped of all emotion, as if all joy in life died with her father. Judith retreated into a shell.

Judith and her mother moved from the palace to their estate on the farm. Judith had a large room built on the roof of the farmhouse. During the day she cared for her mother, but at night she went to the quarters on the rooftop to meditate and pray. Prayer became her only solace and the one avenue to sleep each night. Almost two years passed before she and her mother returned to live in the palace.

Slowly, Judith renewed her interest in the city and finally began attending the governing elders' council meetings again, always sitting in the observation area where she had so often sat as a child. She continued to dress in robes of mourning with her head covered and haircloth over her loins.

Hezekiah spoke to her. "How forlorn you seem, Judith, even after these two long years. Our heart bears a heavy sorrow for you."

⁘

Many weeks later the king and his queen, Hephzibah, spoke to each other of Judith's grief.

The queen said, "Hezekiah, why do you not persuade the elders to offer her the seat of her father?"

He was quite astonished by the queen's suggestion. "What?"

Hezekiah thought for a moment, scratching his head while remembering that no one had filled Merari's empty seat. Slowly, the idea began to sit well with him.

"That is an excellent proposal. Her insight is keen. She knows the duties and the process. It should stimulate some life back into her sad soul and perhaps even profit the council."

Such a move had never been done before and he anticipated resistance from the elders. He made a plan to be forceful and persuasive with them. They needed new blood and another perspective. Why not from a woman who would bring fresh ideas and a new light to the meeting? He did not want Judith in the audience when he presented the idea to the elders, so he asked the queen to lure Judith from the spectator area when the time came to introduce his idea.

On that day Queen Hephzibah took Judith outside the building on the pretext of wanting to talk with her regarding her mother's health. King Hezekiah knew his voice would carry weight, but gaining approval to give the empty seat to a young woman would be difficult.

He had not been wrong in his assessment. After hearing their king speak, the elders all stood and began talking loudly against the idea of a woman member of the governing elders.

"Surely, you jest."

"This is outrageous!"

"There has never been a female member of this group, especially one so young."

One elder shouted. "Is it your purpose to insult us?"

Hezekiah held his arms high. "Peace, sirs. Peace. This is not the end of the world. This young woman was present at every one of our meetings for years. I believe she knows as well as anyone here the laws and policies."

For a moment he said not a word. No one spoke.

He concluded his thought. "I am fully behind her, and she does not know I have made this proposal. So, please, go home quietly, and think about what I have said. We will cast votes when next we meet after the Sabbath."

The meeting adjourned.

✜

Judith and the queen stood at the bottom of the council steps when the elders filed out. Each gave Judith a long stare. She did not understand why but ignored their behavior and went home.

✜

Hezekiah made plans to open the great Temple of Solomon. Only the usual small groups of worshippers entered for prayer on their scheduled days. Judith visited the Temple very early every morning without her group of believers.

A few days after her talk with Queen Hephzibah, she went to her favorite spot on the sanctuary wall and knelt.

After a long meditation, she lifted her head and opened her eyes. There was something new in the Temple—a huge bust of a man in a space that had been veiled for weeks. Now the veil was down. She rose and walked closer to get a better look. Why would such a statue be set in front of the sanctuary? Judith could not take her eyes from it.

It was carved from beautiful highly polished marble. The form was that of a man with eyes of fine jewels that seemed to follow her every motion. With its arms stretched and palms open to the heavens, the statue exuded power and even menace. It was awesome to behold.

The statue was not yet solid upon its base and leaned to one side. Several ropes held the massive statue in place. An inscription near the bottom read, *YHWH,* and in smaller letters beneath, *Who made man in His image.*

Bewildered and confused, Judith stood still, slow to comprehend the meaning of what it all meant.

"This is an idol of our God?" She uttered the words quietly at first, as a question, and then repeated them, again and again, as the truth of what stood before her took hold in her mind. Her body grew rigid, and she drifted off into a spiritual daze.

A servant at the Temple heard Judith muttering. He witnessed her strange behavior and immediately hurried away to inform King Hezekiah. He found the king making his usual early morning stroll through the city.

Judith walked very slowly toward the sculptors' workbench as though in a trance. Nervously fumbling her fingers over the tools, she picked up a knife and moved to the ropes that held the bust in place. She raised the knife and began hacking at the ropes in fury. Her efforts caused her to make grunting sounds in a high-pitched voice.

The first line took several strokes to cut through it. The statue began to wobble. The second rope cut easier, as did the third. The statue crashed to the stone floor and burst into a thousand pieces. The impact seemed to shake the whole building. A thick cloud of marble dust rose, cloaking Judith in it. She began to cry.

Priests charged in and ran toward her, screaming. They looked at the destruction in horror.

One priest wrung his hands. "What have you done? You, daughter of evil, look what you have done!"

Another shouted, "This was our gift to the king upon the reopening of the Temple. You have destroyed the image of the king's God."

Another priest ordered, "Take her! We will use the stones from the statue to stone her to death."

She shouted back to them in a loud voice as they ran to take her. "Let no man lay their hands on me, for our God is not an idol. My God is not an idol. Did you read the scripture? We shall not worship idols in the name of the LORD our God!"

Still, the priests took her by force as she screamed and yelled and tried to break their hold. As they exited the Temple door, King Hezekiah walked up the steps.

"Stop!" He demanded. "Let the woman go."

The priests released her at once, and Judith ran to the king and dropped at his feet. The priests were frenzied, all shouting and yelling at the same time.

"This woman destroyed our statue. It was for you, oh King"

King Hezekiah said, "Priests, priests, stop. This madness will not serve anything."

A crowd had gathered in the Temple courtyard.

"To be fair," Hezekiah said, "we will hold judgment on this matter according to the laws written in the Torah."

A priest yelled, "She has a demon in her. We must stone her."

The king was firm. "As long as I am king, there will be no such punishment. Now, go clean up the Temple." He went on to say, "The judgment will be made in my court the day after Sabbath. Now, go home, everyone. There is nothing else to see."

Judith still knelt at the king's feet, shuddering with revulsion at the memory of the graven image. King Hezekiah lifted her by her arm.

"Get up, my child. You have been filled with sadness too long. I, too, loved your father. We shared our faith in the LORD our God, the God of Israel, and also our hopes for Judah. Go to your quarters. I will have additional guards posted outside your door to be certain you are safe."

"Thank you, my king," she said, "You are kind."

Judith went to her quarters. Two guards walked behind her.

⁙

On the day of the judgment, Judith again wore haircloth upon her loins. An off-white garment covered her from head to foot. The priests gathered to one side of King Hezekiah and Judith on the opposite.

The king said, "We will abide by the laws of the Torah. The high priest will speak first."

The priest said, "The bust of your God was to be a gift for you, my king, to honor the reopening of King Solomon's Temple. The statue serves only as a representation of the god it symbolizes but not purposed to be worshipped as God. Secondly, the statue serves to make the people feel closer to their God."

The priest pointed his finger at Judith. "This woman is possessed by evil spirits and should be burned or stoned to death for the crime she committed."

King Hezekiah looked to Judith.

She spoke slowly. "I do not know what came over me. It was as if I had no control of my movements. I moved, unable to stop myself. I do know this statue was an idol, representing the God of Israel. They contend that it served only as a symbol of our LORD. The Torah does not support man making graven images of our LORD or idols, to worship in His name."

She turned to the priests. "My understanding comes from the writings of the law. We are told we are not allowed to look upon His face. When Moses stood atop Mount Sinai He gave him the law that no graven image may be cast and worshipped as our God. I believe our LORD God desires us to know Him in spirit. An idol can never be a true portrayal of Almighty God."

"I have heard enough." King Hezekiah said. "I do not need more time to think about this case. I stand with Judith. There will be no images of God whatsoever. However, I rule Judith will pay for the cost of the marble used to build the bust, for the work of the sculptors, as well as the restoration of order to the Temple. That is my judgment, in accord with the Torah. This matter is closed."

King Hezekiah retired to his chambers and in conversation with Queen Hephzibah, he said, "After this, how do I persuade the elders to vote for Judith? It is an unfortunate time for this to have happened."

The queen replied, "You could give her the seat outright."

"Yes, but I need the members to want her."

⁕

The following morning, the elders entered the hall and took their seats. Hezekiah studied their faces. He saw nothing to indicate their position and had no thought as to what to expect from them. Judith entered the observation area after everyone was seated. The members stood and a loud cheer went out.

They chanted. "Judith! Judith!"

Shouts came from all directions.

"You bested them!"

"What courage."

"Judith, we need fighters such as you."

King Hezekiah could not believe what he was witnessing. He was quite overwhelmed.

Judith, too, seemed bewildered. She stood still with her mouth open while the council continued to cheer and applaud her.

Queen Hephzibah went to her and held her hand. "They love you, Judith."

Judith was so stunned by this sudden attention that she could not move. When the queen took her hand, she followed without resistance as Hephzibah escorted her to her father's old seat.

"What is this all about?" she whispered. *How should I interpret this situation?*

Queen Hephzibah spoke in a low voice only Judith could hear. "Quiet. You are to become the newest member of the governing council."

As she sat down in her father's old seat, Judith's mind reeled. She could not focus and tears rolled down her cheeks. "Oh God, what is happening? Why have the elders considered me for such an honor?"

She looked around the assembly hall at her father's peers, the men who had just selected her for the highest honor possible. Tears long locked inside her since her father's death broke through, and she openly wept.

Approval was unanimous. Her father's seat in the governing elder's council became her seat. The senior council members swore in Judith. A small ceremony honored her as the customary goblet of blessed unfermented wine was passed, and each member acknowledged Judith's presence on the council.

When the cup had moved to every member, the king stood.

"Before the meeting begins," he said, "we will give our newest member time to compose herself then say a few words."

Judith calmed herself after a few minutes then stood and began to speak nervously. "God is great. Thank you from my heart. This is an honor beyond belief. As a member of this group and in my father's memory, I will give all of my very soul to serve my king and my people. Thank you all, again." Unable to say more, she covered her mouth with her hands to control her emotions and quickly sat.

⁙

Times had changed since the days her father sat on the council. King Sargon II died in battle, and his son, Prince Sennacherib, became the new king of Assyria. Closer to home, Judah occupied Philistia, not to enslave the people but to make them a provident state under Judah. King Hezekiah wanted to put down any resistance to that end. A great number of smokehouses existed in Philistia, and thousands of iron weapons could be forged for times of war in their fires. To reunite the people with their brethren, Hezekiah also sought to recover the border territory and towns that initially belonged to Judah.

At one meeting King Hezekiah made it known he wished to alter Judah's position in relation to Assyria. "During my father's reign, Judah became a dependent vassal-state to Assyria with an annual payment of tribute. This tribute has become an insufferable burden."

He walked from the head of the long table with his hands folded behind his back. "I intend to stop payment of the tribute and negotiate a new commitment with King Sennacherib. The agreement we have was put in place by my father and his many years ago."

A few elders voiced their opinion such an action could be looked upon as an act of war.

"I do not think so," said Hezekiah. "This King Sennacherib appears more interested in his beloved city than his conquest territories."

Judith stood. "How long before the tribute is due?"

"Within thirty days the tribute must have been gathered and be on its way to Nineveh. We will send a message asking for the two of us, Sennacherib and myself, to come up with our own settlement of tribute."

Again, the elders expressed concern. The nature and manner of the new Assyrian king were unknown. Such a move might be a risk. However, at the end of discussion, they concurred that the tribute amount needed to be renegotiated because the treasury neared depletion.

⁂

Before the next meeting, King Hezekiah became suddenly ill. He lay in bed, thinking he would soon die and sent for the prophet Isaiah to come.

Everyone prayed daily for a miracle recovery of the much-loved king.

Queen Hephzibah sat beside the king when the prophet came to him.

Isaiah walked to the bed, bent and looked into the eyes of the king. Without a word, he took Hezekiah's hand in his, placing his other hand on the king's forehead. The prophet closed his eyes and began to pray. Hephzibah held her husband's other hand until Isaiah finished. The prophet left but promised to return the following day.

The royal physicians could not agree as to what ailed the king and knew of no treatment. When the prophet Isaiah returned the next day, he joyfully announced that the king would live. Queen Hephzibah looked at him with doubt in her mind.

"Last night, as I meditated, our LORD God spoke to me, saying, 'King Hezekiah shall not die at this time. I shall add a number of years to his life.'"

Isaiah knelt at the foot of the king's bed and laid his staff on the floor. With his head bowed and his hands stretched out, he began to pray:

"Almighty God of Israel has forgiven you for turning your back on Him for the sake of these idol gods of Assyria your father placed all over the city and in God's house." He went on, the very voice of authority and knowledge. "David became king over all Israel and Judah. Many generations past, David is a long time great-grandfather to Hezekiah. He conquered the Philistines, the walled city of Jerusalem and in doing so he set up his capital. David, the king, begot Solomon of she who had been the wife of another. Under his son, King Solomon, the tribes of Israel were united. It was he who built the magnificent stone palace and the Temple. Solomon's ambitions put a strain on the people and when his son came to power he said, 'My father punished you with whips, but I will whip you with scorpions.' At that the ten tribes of the north broke away, set up their own kingdom and made Samaria their capital. For over two hundred years, the two kingdoms have antagonized and occasionally attacked each other.

"We are now threatened by other nations from the north, believers of idolatry who worship heathen gods. They strive to destroy us, the children of the one true God."

The prophet Isaiah continued to speak of the future. He told how the line of Hezekiah would bring a child who would be the light of the world.

"Almighty God has foretold the coming of the Savior of the world, a child from the seed of David, from whom Hezekiah is descended. Many generations from now his granddaughter will give birth to that child. And that child shall serenade the land with the gospel of the good news to come to every corner of the earth, knocking down all idol worship forever."

The prophet Isaiah began to weep loudly and said, "King Hezekiah, the LORD God loves you dearly." Isaiah picked up his staff and stood slowly, his head lowered. As he backed from the king's chamber, he said, "Blessed be this family. Blessed be this family." He could be heard saying it after he left the chamber.

⁘

A few days later, King Hezekiah arose from his bed and walked about. Judith visited his chambers daily. Each time she rejoiced seeing his continual improvement and recovery.

On one of her visits she heard him say, "I will soon make an appearance from the balcony. I am eating and feeling well—getting stronger every day. The time has come that I speak of the words from the prophet Isaiah to me, and of the promise our LORD God has given his people."

Judith bowed her head. "The hand of Almighty God must truly be upon you, my king. I am exceedingly thankful God has granted me the privilege to witness His miracle come forth in you."

# 6

# ASSYRIA'S MARCH ON BABYLONIA

## 704-703 B.C.E.

The body of King Sennacherib's brother, Ashur-nadin-shumi, was returned to Nineveh and funeral arrangements were hastened. Other than the day long prayers conducted by the high priests, the ceremony progressed quickly.

The Assyrian people did not hide their outrage and bitterness at the failure of the military to secure and protect the prince in his position as the appointed head of the Babylonian kingdom.

King Sennacherib stood alone with Holofernes on his palace balcony. The king's anger engulfed his face.

"I should have finished off Merodach-baladan when I had the chance." Holofernes spoke first and though the words seemed rather frail, they were true.

"Maybe you will have another chance." Sennacherib turned to face Holofernes. "You are promoted to Field Marshall Commanding General of the Assyrian forces. This will be your expedition. You will oversee the entire operation. You will earn the total glory of bringing the Babylonians responsible for my brother's death to their knees. I will remain here in Nineveh to continue building my new government."

Holofernes did not expect to hear this news. "Thank you, my lord. You will not be disappointed."

An emergency war council convened. The discussion focused on revenge and retaliation. At one point Sennacherib stood and raised his fist. "In the war seven years ago, we gave them liberty. We spared them from slavery, left them to determine their own destiny."

He paced. "And how do they, a conquered people, repay our generosity? How do they respect our gift of the right to be free citizens? With a slap in the face!"

King Sennacherib stood silent for a long moment. He looked at his army officers and the men who served in his government. Each man stood, focusing on him.

"They repaid our kindness with the murder of my brother! It is time to go to war."

He made it clear the expedition would start in Babylonia. Suppressing the revolts in the Mediterranean would have to wait until the provinces were once again united with Assyria.

During the war council, King Sennacherib pointed out that some of the Babylonian provinces might want to stand neutral as before. "We will let them go neutral if they wish. It will work in our favor. Weeding out the guilty will be easier. But," he told his officers, "keep in mind, no one in Babylonia will be exempt from all punishment for this crime. We will grind and pound our enemies to particles beneath our feet. We will show them the power and glory of Assyria."

Sennacherib announced the promotion of Holofernes along with the news his personal servant and scribe, Ahikar, would accompany the troops to make a record of the war effort for the archives.

Holofernes looked around the room. He knew his promotion wouldn't be received well by all. He received word long ago that there were those within the ranks who believed both King Sennacherib and Holofernes were reckless on the battlefield. That faction held to the strategy the commander should stand apart to oversee the flow of battle and direction of attack. They spoke of their military leader as being too valuable to be put in the path of danger, both for the sake of the battle and the sake of the troops' morale. The army that suffered such a loss would be dealt a terrible blow, indeed.

This campaign gave Holofernes an opportunity to demonstrate his military and leadership skills to Assyria and the entire world. His successful military campaign would reflect favorably on Sennacherib as Emperor of Assyria to all the nations.

Planning was critical. The most obvious question was how to implement an attack on Babylonia and annihilate the self-proclaimed King Merodach-baladan, his followers and his propaganda forever. Holofernes burdened himself with an additional challenge, to find victory with minimal casualties.

·⁚·

The commanding officers spent many days preparing their army to march. When General Holofernes gave the order to assemble the troops and advance south to the border of Babylon, all preparations had been completed and the army was on the move within hours.

Holofernes planned to position his massive army at the border to intimidate the Babylonian provinces. The ultimatum before the provinces would give them two choices—stand neutral or be utterly destroyed.

·⁚·

Holofernes retired to his villa to spend time with Flulano and his two young sons before joining his men.

"I am called again to war," he said. "You understand the requirements of my position, and you knew this day would come."

Flulano nodded. "I love you greatly, and though I know what you say is true, my heart still has a strong aversion to it."

Holofernes said nothing. He sat by the fire and called his sons to him.

"I love you two more than anything, along with your mother. Forgive me for not being here with you in the days to come, and please think of me often. I will return soon with gifts from far away."

On the morning of the eighth day he climbed upon his chariot, waved and called out to his family. "Remember, my sacrifice to Assyria is so that you can grow up as free citizens in a nation of wealth."

Holofernes reached the encampment the next evening. At dawn the following morning, he led his army across the border into Babylonia in the name of Emperor Sennacherib.

⁘

The Assyrian army met little resistance early on. Babylonian communities had remained semi-independent states over the years. When the mighty Assyrian war-machine moved across Babylonian territory, most of the lesser provinces withdrew from the rebellion and claimed neutrality as they had done in the past.

Babylon, the capital city, joined other provinces in neutrality. They had thrown out those associated with the rebellion and held prisoner any suspected of playing a part in the Prince's assassination.

The larger provinces combined their armies, under the leadership of King Merodach-baladan at Kish about a half-day march from Babylon for the coming battle.

Merodach-baladan's infantry transformed the city into a well-fortified position of defense, using the structures within the city as barricades. Thousands more encamped around Kish. He assigned the cavalry to the high grounds at the mouth of the Euphrates River where the irrigation dams and locks could be controlled. Any attempt to destroy the dams meant facing his cavalry, the great *men of iron* who defeated the Assyrian cavalry seven years earlier.

⁘

Field Commander Holofernes studied the terrain and placement of the Babylonian forces. With all the preparations and fortifications, it seemed as if Merodach-baladan presented the Assyrians with an ultimatum—go home now or come in and try to eradicate our city. Meeting the Babylonian forces within the city would cost many Assyrian lives. Holofernes continued to analyze the situation closely while approaching the territory.

After a thorough evaluation, he and his generals concluded the Assyrian cavalry had to go up against the Babylonian *men of iron* to gain control of the high ground and the canal locks above the city.

Holofernes stood before his cavalry as they waited, poised to attack. "Remember your brothers who lie dead at the hands of these Babylonians, our enemies. Remember them each time your lance finds another adversary."

The Assyrian horsemen presented a vision of might and beauty astride their strong mounts on a crusade to return the glory of victory to the Assyrians. The Babylonian cavalry came out to engage them and the powerful forces met in a furious clash near the Euphrates River. Hundreds went down at first contact.

The arrogant Babylonians taunted their Assyrian opponents, lax to maintain a tight formation as the Assyrian horsemen did. A long and bloody battle ensued, which saw the Babylonians overwhelmed by the new and improved Assyrian horsemen of war.

Holofernes watched as thousands of the *men of iron* fell at the hands of his magnificent forces. When the Assyrians rode down the last of the Babylonian cavalry and put them to death, his extreme pride came in a rush of emotion.

*What an unbelievable victory for Assyria, and what a devastating loss for Merodach-baladan! O King Sargon, I believe you are watching from the kingdom of Baal. How pleased you must be to see your newly-built cavalry come to such grandeur!*

As the two armies positioned for the coming fight, Holofernes's strategy began to unfold. Just as the flooding played an important role in the battle of seven years earlier, it would be critical in the battle today. The advantage lay with Assyria now that the Babylonian cavalry could no longer protect the vital canal locks, and he ordered the locks to be opened.

The wall of water burst onto Merodach-baladan's forces. They scrambled for higher ground, plunged into total disruption. Hundreds drowned and thousands more were brutally slain as they attempted to fight their way to higher ground. The Babylonian army suffered extreme losses. The surviving remnants sought safety in flight, including Merodach-baladan himself. Again.

Holofernes turned his forces toward the capital city of Babylon, but found no resistance. The city had not prepared for a siege. The Assyrians entered without difficulty and plundered King Merodach-baladan's palace of everything valuable. Following the orders of King Sennacherib, Holofernes and his army did not loot the possessions of the city's citizens.

Holofernes was grateful to the city's people who had held the assassination conspirators until the Assyrian army arrived. They cooperated fully with his order to impale all the prisoners, including those charged as instigators of the revolution and sympathizers of Merodach-baladan.

After departing the city of Babylon, Holofernes led his army on a march through all of the provinces that had supplied Merodach-baladan and ransacked them all. Thousands were killed or taken into slavery.

⁜

When Emperor Sennacherib received the report that all the provinces had been re-established under his supreme control, he handpicked a Babylonian man raised in Assyria and named him the new ruler of Babylonia.

General Holofernes brought the king immeasurable glory in this campaign which covered more territory than any other single war operation in Assyrian history. Assyrian troops fought in over a hundred cities and villages and captured tremendous spoils of war along with thousands of slaves. The Assyrian casualties had been, as Holofernes desired, minimal. The campaign with the revolting provinces had reached its end, and now they traveled the long trip home.

⁙

Holofernes ended his reminiscing and climbed into his chariot. He led the way down the main road into Nineveh with his mighty army behind him and all the captured treasures, gold and slaves in full view. He wanted the entire city and country to see the extent of their booty with thousands of captured slaves. His men stood tall and proud as they marched into the city.

Thousands came to cheer the army's triumphant return. They flocked into the city from all over the empire. What a glorious day for Holofernes and the Assyrian nation. Holofernes stopped the march in front of the palace and knelt before King Sennacherib. He declared in a loud voice, "All these spoils from the Babylonian conflict your loyal servants present to you, living god, King Sennacherib."

A seemingly endless cheer erupted.

One of the highest-ranking noblemen in Assyria held a banquet that very evening on his estate in honor of General Holofernes. All the people of nobility attended the banquet. Field Marshall General Holofernes arrived with Flulano. The guest of honor was greeted with cheers and loud applause.

After a sumptuous dinner, Holofernes stood. "I am proud to be here this night. We, the people of Assyria, the sons of Baal, the superior people of the entire world, will exert our might when we are angered. Today we have a united empire, accomplished with an iron fist. Tomorrow we will utterly destroy all those who oppose our authority. Our swords will wave across the lands as lightening across the sky, leaving only cinders of those who stand in rebellion before us.

80

"Thank you, my fellow Assyrians, for your devotion and for joining here this evening with me. We thank our host for this banquet. And to Sennacherib, my king and my friend, I thank you for appointing me commander of the forces to restore order in the empire."

He turned to his wife. "Thank you, Flulano, for being such a loving wife." At that, more applause was raised.

A beautiful young woman hovered near him the entire evening and directed the servants to fetch him food and drink, as he needed it.

He turned to her, "Who are you?" She lowered her face ever so slightly and averted her eyes, but her smile was lovely and sweet.

"I am Eventha, the daughter of your host. My father asked me to see that you receive everything you may want this night."

Holofernes took in her beauty then turned back to the table and said to Flulano, "I am going out to the terrace for some air." He stood and looked at the young woman, then strolled out to the open deck.

She followed anxiously. "Do you want anything, dear sir, General Holofernes? What can I get for you?"

He walked down the steps to the courtyard. *What was her father thinking sending this beautiful girl to be at my side? She was quite charming.* He turned and placed his hands around her small waist. She gasped as he raised her high in the air and examined her body.

"Delightful and alluring," he said, as he walked her back inside.

As it grew later, Holofernes spent time with the nobleman who hosted the celebration, hoping to become more acquainted with the gracious man who had made him his guest of honor.

It had been a night to remember.

He and Flulano departed. She turned to him. "Holofernes, my husband, thank you so much for showing me and your children loyalty. In your absence, we dedicated all our energy to praying to Baal for your safety and well-being. We are grateful and joyous you have chosen to spend the first night of your return home with your family."

He stayed silent for a long while. When they finally approached their home, he spoke. "You are the first woman in my life. There is nothing in the entire world I would not do for my children and you." He pulled her close to him. "Whether or not you believe me, it is the truth."

They slept well in each other's arms that night, and for the next seven days he enjoyed being at home and playing with his children. However, on the eighth day, he jumped upon his chariot and bade them farewell until nightfall.

⋄⋅⋄

Holofernes arrived at the home of Eventha's father. He greeted the old man with a handshake. Before he could even ask if he could see Eventha, the young girl ran past them and jumped upon his chariot.

Holofernes called to her. "Where are you going?"

"I am waiting for you to take me for a ride."

Holofernes barely had time to give his former host a nod before he turned and ran down the stairs. He leapt onto the chariot and stood beside her, his heart thumping in his chest. He snapped the reigns and his horses pranced away from the villa.

Holofernes found a secluded location in a far corner of the property and stopped the chariot. He turned, put his arms around her and gently kissed her. His kiss became more intense. She responded equally.

He carried her off behind some bushes and lay her down in the soft grass.

Holofernes slowly removed her many-layered garments. Seeing her naked body he said. "How could anyone be more luxurious, if such a word can describe a woman's body?"

Eventha smiled at his compliment. They enjoyed the day until the dinner hour approached. Reluctantly, he returned

Eventha to her father's mansion and made his way back to his own estate.

Holofernes and Eventha continued to see each other frequently, some weeks as many as three and four times. He strolled with her publicly through Nineveh's finest bazaars and market places while shopping for gifts for her.

His involvement with Eventha reached the point where marriage became a glaring factor. If he continued to see her like this it would be a total embarrassment to her and her family. He asked her to be his second wife. Eventha wanted a large wedding but Holofernes persuaded her a closed ceremony was more appropriate. A second wedding was almost always a smaller affair than the first. Thus, Holofernes and Eventha became man and wife before family members only and Eventha shared his villa.

⚜

He returned home following a day of leisure spent with Eventha to discover a company of his men led by his highest ranking officer waiting.

"Why are you here? I have not sent for you."

He wasn't so much surprised at their appearance as irritated. He did not want such a lovely day to be spoiled.

The officer stepped up. "Commander Holofernes, King Sennacherib has ordered us to accompany you to the palace immediately. The king has been trying to reach you for weeks. He will tolerate your absence no longer. You must understand the importance of King Sennacherib's demand for your audience."

Holofernes had, indeed, been avoiding the soldiers as well as his king's summons. *There are no excuses, and I have little choice in the matter now.*

He went with them to the palace and straight to Sennacherib's chambers.

It was easy to see the king was furious. "What in the name of Baal has gotten into you? I have prepared and organized the entire campaign against the rebellious vassal states without you. I have left word over and over for you to join me. Your cooperation and input are vital to the war plans. This expedition to the Mediterranean coast requires your expert involvement. Don't you know that? Assyria depends upon our critical evaluation of the preparation for such a lingering and difficult undertaking, and where are you? Off showing imprudent behavior contrary to your prominent status, wooing an aristocrat's young daughter. You ignore my every bidding."

Holofernes silently suffered Sennacherib's ranting. "I understand you have taken a second wife in a whirlwind relationship. I don't have a problem with that, but you of all people certainly understand the value of priorities. What could you possibly have to say for yourself?"

Holofernes stood before his king with his head down. In a low voice he said, "I am not going."

Before he could say more, the king cut him off with a yell louder than a crack of lightening. "What did you say? You are not going?"

For a few brief moments, silence ruled. Not even the wind blowing through the windows dared to be heard.

Then Sennacherib screamed, "What is happening? Is my whole kingdom collapsing before my very eyes? Holofernes, utter some words other than the ones I think you just said."

Sennacherib stood close to Holofernes, their faces nearly touched.

Holofernes said, "I cannot leave her. I must be mad to even think such a thing, but I love her more than anything."

Sennacherib's face filled with anger. He grabbed his friend's uniform and screamed in his face. "Stop it! Stop it! Stop! There is nothing before your king and country. Nothing!"

He quieted suddenly and his stillness shouted in the room. He shook his longtime friend, now the commander of all his forces, and in a voice so very low it could not even be called a whisper, he said, "Pull yourself together, man. This is war." The king looked sad yet there could be no doubting of the unmovable force behind his words.

Sennacherib turned his back to Holofernes and walked to the terrace.

In a more conversational tone, he said, "There is nothing you enjoy more than a good fight. I know you, Holofernes.

Holofernes moved up behind his king, reaching for his knife. His face distorted with anger. He raised the knife to stab his friend, but when the laughter of children reached his ears, he backed away and sheathed the knife.

A servant and several guards entered the king's chambers. The servant said, "Sire, I could not control them. They would not wait until you sent for them."

Sennacherib turned as three of his young sons ran into the room, jumping around his chambers in great excitement.

He looked at Holofernes. "Go to your quarters, here in the palace. I think you will be rejuvenated. The fire in your blood will be rekindled, and your hunger for the battle cry will prevail."

Holofernes turned to leave.

*Am I mad? What was I thinking? Am I enslaved to my beautiful Eventha whom I love so dearly I nearly committed a hideous crime? Have I pitted my whims against you, O Baal, and my king?*

Holofernes spent the night in prayer to Baal, lamenting his actions. When morning came, he was assured of Baal's favor as he walked into his army camp.

⁙

King Sennacherib made it known Holofernes would oversee the expedition, in the name of Baal. "I will see the faces of those who spat upon our gods. I will be the eyes of Baal as he executes his revenge, skinning the offenders while still alive and cutting them into pieces."

War was coming again to the lands of Abraham, Isaac and Jacob.

# 7

# THE DESTINY DREAM

## 712-706 B.C.E.

T he village of Juba was alive with excitement. The junior warriors had returned jubilant after the successful lion hunt, and every person in the village worked to prepare for the celebration of this special occasion. Large amounts of food hung over low fires, readied for the feast. Drums carried messages to distant tribes of the successful hunt and the coming festivities; the village anticipated many visitors. Everyone, particularly the newly transformed young warriors, was eager to eat and dance for a week of celebration.

The lion's tail was displayed by the elders while the rest of the remains, other than the trophy items, were taken away for burial in a place reserved for lions killed in a hunt, a place that signified the courage of both man and beast. If a man-eating or menacing lion was killed, it was not buried but fed to wild birds instead.

Ramtouses stood with his fellow warriors on the first day of the celebration. One of the village women placed the braided lion mane around his neck. The other ornaments and trophies were distributed amongst the other hunters.

Throughout the week, people from smaller surrounding communities came each evening. The smaller villages joined the celebration of larger, nearby villages. Often, their young warriors joined in the lion hunts to earn warrior status.

Each day Ramtouses walked around boastfully with his lion mane draped around his neck. His brother, Lozato, took him aside. "I have seen how the young girls watch after you, and while there is a new moon wedding dance soon, I do not feel it is good for you to choose to marry at this age of sixteen. Others have done well handling the responsibility of a wife and children. But, Ramtouses, you are not yet seasoned enough to take on such a duty. You should heed my words."

⁙

Lizoka, one of the many young girls eying Ramtouses, sat on the bank of the river where many of the young women went to bathe. She waited until she saw Ramtouses coming her way then disrobed and languidly waded into the water to her waist. From the corner of her eye, she saw him stop and watch her. Feigning surprise and embarrassment, she looked up and gasped.

"Ramtouses, please go. I am bathing."

He turned and walked quickly away.

Later, she saw him in the village. "Did you like what you saw?"

"No doubt!" He smiled. "You are beautiful, Lizoka, and I have been thinking of you ever since."

Now, she smiled. "Are you going to pick me at the wedding dance coming with the new moon?"

A small frown creased Ramtouses's brow. "I would love to, but I am not certain whether I should marry at this time. Also, I thought Baako would be your first choice."

"Oh, no, Ramtouses, you are the prize," Lizoka said. "Have you not noticed the girls are always looking at you?"

⁙

Each new moon the village held a feast followed by a celebration. They sacrificed a burnt offering and a spiritual renewal welcomed the first day of the new moon cycle. Traditional singing and dancing also played a large part in new moon celebrations, whether for a good harvest, honoring the ancestors or newborns, or another reason.

87

Twice in a year the new moon celebration observed a wedding dance. All the virgins and unmarried women in the village participated. Men seeking a wife were seated around the dance area in a circle.

The young lion hunters were given first choice of dancing partners. The woman could choose to spend the evening with him only. If she moved on to others, he continued to dance with other women until one stayed with him. By the end of the evening each man had a partner. In the morning, all the couples were declared man and wife.

⁘

One day when they were finished working in the fields, Lozato asked Ramtouses to join him in his hut. He once again spoke to Ramtouses of the inadvisability of marrying at such an early age.

Ramtouses nodded. "I have the same misgivings, my brother and would not dance at this new moon, save for Lizoka. She has taken my heart and I do not want to see her joined to another."

"If she loves you in return," Lozato said, "perhaps she will withdraw from the wedding dance until you are ready to participate. If you wish I will talk to her and try to learn her desires."

Ramtouses agreed.

⁘

Lozato sought out the young woman and on finding her quickly came to his purpose.

"My brother Ramtouses will not dance with you this new moon," he said.

Lizoka appeared visibly shaken upon hearing the news.

Lozato was quick to put her mind at ease. "He loves you and wants you. I have come to tell you he does care for you. You are his choice. If you are willing to wait, he will, without a doubt, pick you when he does attend a new moon wedding dance, when the time is right."

Lizoka's voice quivered. "I love Ramtouses and wish to be with him, but my family may force me to attend the dance. They do not wish to provide for me indefinitely."

"Your father is in my age-set. I will talk with him."

Lozato left her, went straight to speak with her father and committed a stipend to cover Lizoka's food and lodging until Ramtouses took her in marriage.

⁘

A few days before the new moon celebration, Ramtouses entered the hut of his caretaker.

"I will not take part in the next wedding dance and wish to remain in your hut for the present time. Will that be all right with you?"

She seemed happy. She took both his hands and held them up and kissed the back of each one, over and over. "Ramtouses, you will be a hero among our people. You have a shining light about you."

He felt shy at the exuberance of her praise. "I will pass the coming time in the fields of my farm, or the woods surrounding the village, and, too, I will share company with my age group. At night I will come here with you. You are my second mother."

She laid her head on his shoulder. He put his arms around her and rubbed her back.

⁘

Sometime later, Ramtouses went to Lizoka's family farm where she worked in the field.

"Will you work all day without resting or perhaps you can spare a moment to enjoy a drink of cool water with your friend?"

Lizoka stopped and ran over to meet him. She drank the cool water greedily.

Ramtouses laughed. "Go slowly, and save some for me." Seeing her made him happy. He asked her. "Are you sixteen yet?"

"Yes, I grew to be sixteen a few weeks ago."

"Would you walk with me?"

She didn't hesitate. "Yes, but not for too long. I must finish the field work today."

As they walked, they came to a nearby wooded area where berries grew in the wild. They picked some of the ripe ones.

"Thank you for waiting until I can dance with you." Ramtouses said. "I love you, Lizoka, and until we are joined I wish to talk with you and be with you whenever you can see me."

Finding the words to express the love in his heart proved to be more difficult than he expected, but she seemed to understand. They walked back to the farm, making small talk on the way.

⁘

Ramtouses worked every day for over four years, increasing the size of his farm. He employed several boys from a younger age-set to work in his fields. Each week he took his produce to the central market and traded for items needed on the farm.

One day, he saw Lizoka there.

*She grows more lovely daily. I can wait no longer.*

He took her by the hand and led her away from the crowded market.

"What do you think is going to happen on the coming new moon wedding celebration?"

Lizoka's eyes lit up. "You are going to sit among the warriors looking for a wife." Her voice trembled with excitement.

"Yes, and I hope you will be amongst the dancers."

Lizoka jumped into his arms and kissed him passionately. "I must return to my home quickly and tell my family."

Ramtouses watched her race across the village. He smiled.

⁘

And then it was time for the new moon wedding ceremony. The day before, drums announced to the area villages that

90

Ramtouses, the lion slayer, would sit among the many warriors looking for a wife. Young girls from far and near welcomed the chance to dance for Ramtouses and perhaps be selected as his wife.

The celebration began and the women made their way into the dance circle, each presenting her individual moves. Lizoka moved in front of Ramtouses, spun and swayed, undulated her belly and kicked her long legs high. The firelight behind her silhouetted her graceful figure. He couldn't look away. She took his breath.

The women danced most of the evening until the shaman, leader of the elders, gave the signal for the men to choose. As Ramtouses got to his feet, Lizoka ran to him and shook her shoulders, then her hips. She jumped against him and shimmied all over. He took her by the waist and danced with her, and she with him.

They danced as one, leaving no opportunity for the other girls to dance with Ramtouses. When the dancing was done, they sat together hand in hand, as all the new couples did, and fed each other the specially prepared food. Everyone with eyes could behold their intent to marry the following day.

··

Lizoka went home, gathered her belongings, and slept, dreaming of the elders declaring Ramtouses and her united in marriage in the way of their tribal custom.

Ramtouses slept in the open beneath the stars.

··

In the early morning hours Ramtouses slipped into in a deeper sleep than he'd ever known. In his dream the whole of heaven and earth were cloaked in obsidian night and he stood alone in nothingness unable to see anything.

*Yet, my eyes are open!*

He blinked a few times to verify they could open.

*Where is the earth? Where are the stars? What am I standing on? Am I standing?*

*Do I exist in this void, this emptiness?* A chill seeped into his body dominating him. Was there a future? A past? Was there even a now? A heavy sorrow and sadness filled him. It crept into his heart, and he felt hopeless.

He looked around. *Does anything exist in this empty place?* Upon looking down, he could finally discern he stood on what appeared to be a road that extended as far as he could see.

Relieved he could finally move, he began to walk slowly down the lonely road. He laughed. Who would build a road so narrow only one person could walk upon it?

After a long while, he saw someone or something coming from the other direction, moving very slowly. He knew instinctively that it meant no harm. He was not frightened. Whatever it was coming toward him, it was extraordinary. He was unable to determine its size or height. It had substance, and it was shimmering and luminous. Its gait was easy and steady. Two dark spots on its strange visage appeared to be eyes that never shifted its glare from him.

The figure came closer and Ramtouses tried to step aside or turn around, but his body kept moving forward. Walking the narrow road no longer amused him.

Just as Ramtouses opened his mouth to scream, the being spoke in a firm, soft voice. "You will rise tomorrow and go to the town of Tungal. There you shall know your mate, the most beautiful, nimble, and fruitful woman in all the land."

With those words, the figure disappeared, and so did the road.

⁕

Ramtouses awoke in a cold sweat, shaking all over. He looked for the sun in the eastern sky, but it had not yet risen above the horizon. In the western sky, a light of intense brilliance hurtled straight at him.

The being from his dream had come toward him in the same inexorable manner. He could not look away as the light drew ever nearer, ever brighter until it passed over him, high in the sky, careening toward the eastern horizon. This was not a dream, not a vision. It was real.

⁙

He calmed when the strange light did not fall upon him, just as he had when he did not collide with the strange being in his sleep. The furious light disappeared near the horizon. He viewed it as an augur, confirming the legitimacy of his vision. Yet, there was something so vital about the dream.

*Was someone here talking to me as I slept?*

Fear and cold fell upon him. He stood hoping to calm his fluttering heart. It did not quiet, until he began to think of the dream again.

*Where is Tungal? To the north. How would I get there? Why Tungal? I know nothing of the people in such a faraway place.*

For some reason he did not comprehend, he could not bring himself to think of his upcoming marriage. It was as if some uninvited outside force controlled his mind, banishing thoughts of his marriage.

It was the dream that remained fresh and clear in his mind, as if it had really happened. The wedding. He thought of it then. Perhaps he would postpone the wedding until after he came to know what this all meant, until he travelled to Tungal. He had been told he would find his mate there. He shook his head. This matter had to be settled once and for all. The urge to be on his way to Tungal overtook him. And so he found himself packing for that reality.

Lozato came to his living space as he readied to leave.

"Are you ready for your big day?"

Ramtouses did not reply, but continued packing.

"What are you doing? Are you leaving with Lizoka?"

93

Ramtouses looked up at his brother. "No. I travel to Tungal. Alone. You know the land. What is the best route to go there?"

Lozato laughed nervously. "What is going on, giraffe legs? Is this a jest?"

"It is no jest. I must know the way to Tungal."

⁙

The response mystified Lozato, in fact, he could think of no explanation revealing his young brother's actions, and the seriousness in Ramtouses's behavior left him totally baffled. He had to sit down and think about this one.

"Tungal?" Lozato sat and stared at his brother. "Please, Ramtouses, are you crazy? What about your wedding plans with Lizoka? You told me of your love and respect for her. You are obligated to her for the years she waited."

Ramtouses spun to face his brother. "I know all this. It hurts me, but I am driven to do what I must. The fire that burns in me will bar me from being a loving, caring husband until I learn what awaits me in Tungal!" Ramtouses could hear the hysteria in his own voice—hysteria and anger. "I do not want to hurt Lizoka, and this will surely hurt her."

Tears burned his eyes. He shook his head. "Lozato, I had a dream or maybe a premonition last night and I cannot dislodge myself from it. I cannot escape. I am compelled to comply with the vision. If I do not follow the road to Tungal, I fear my life will be destroyed. Leaving Lizoka now is the hardest thing I will ever have to do, but leave I must!"

Lozato looked at him long and hard. He laid his hand on Ramtouses's shoulder. "Meet me at night fall by the bend of the river. We will talk about the best route to Tungal."

⁙

As the sun sank low in the sky, Ramtouses paced in circles at the appointed meeting spot. Guilt and sadness weighed heavily on him. He looked up as someone approached. Here finally was Lozato, just as he had promised.

Lozato stopped before his brother and immediately answered the question not yet spoken. "Lizoka and her family know you are in turmoil, but they do not understand. There were tears, anger and recriminations."

Ramtouses hung his head.

Lozato continued. "She was devastated! I do not think I have ever seen someone that distraught. I offered the gift of our mother's farm in Lizoka's name as you wished. While it did not quell her sadness, it was enough to soothe the embarrassment and uphold the standing of her family."

Ramtouses breathed a sigh of relief, even though his heart was still burdened with remorse. He clutched his brother to him. "I am grateful for your help." He looked at the ground beside Lozato where a large bag lay. "What is this?" Ramtouses asked.

"I travel with you, Ramtouses, the entire distance to Tungal."

Ramtouses searched his brother's face. The determination and loyalty shining there touched him deeply. "Such a pledge, but it is many days' travel," he said simply.

Lozato nodded. "As much as thirty days."

"And who will care for your family for such a time?"

Lozato shrugged. "I have the word of those in my age-set. My family will be cared for. They will join us in Tungal after we have prepared a place for them."

Ramtouses was astounded. "You will do this for me?"

"I will. I made a pledge to our mother. I will be with you in Tungal."

Ramtouses was overcome. He did not deserve a gift so generous as this. "I love you, Lozato. Never has there been a brother such as you."

They slept where they were, under the stars, the sounds of the night their lullaby. In the morning, Ramtouses and Lozato set out for Tungal.

# KINKY MANE

## 705 B.C.E.

On the morning of the twenty-sixth day of travel, Ramtouses and Lozato came upon a beautiful landscape. Crops grew lush and plentiful. The bounty of this land lay in sharp contrast to the sparse and brittle vegetation they had often seen along the way where thousands of acres of land suffered from drought.

They encountered herdsmen and farmers who assumed Ramtouses the slayer of lions traveled to Tungal to kill a man-eating lion called Kinky Mane. The drum system relayed news of their coming. One man even offered to guide the two to Tungal. Ramtouses was surprised to hear their language differed only slightly from that spoken in Juba.

Lozato shook his head in disbelief. "I cannot believe the destiny that came to you in your dream is to travel this great distance to kill a lion. It confounds me. I am like a log in the river, caught up in the rushing current with little control over the direction of my travel.

⋆

The day after they came across the lush fields, they sighted Tungal. The town consisted of a cluster of villages strung across high hills and low valleys. A network of creeks and roads wove throughout. Midday, senior warriors who guarded the town joined the brothers and walked beside them.

The lead warrior spoke to Ramtouses. "Do you require an audience with the king?"

"Yes." The king would likely answer his questions about the killer lion.

The Tungal warriors led Ramtouses and Lozato to a lodging area reserved for visitors. They began to settle in but were interrupted by a young tribesman.

"King Tasmeria wants to meet with you, Ramtouses. He will see you tomorrow. I am to be your servant and escort for the time you wait."

After a satisfying meal, the young tribesman offered to accompany them to a tournament. Ramtouses and Lozato were eager to experience the competition.

Ramtouses knew everyone, including the king, believed he had come for the lion. He expected the king to broach the subject when they met. It seemed an excellent idea to learn as much about the problem as he could.

On the way to the competition, he asked their young escort, "What about this lion problem?"

The servant did not hesitate. "The hungry lion does not eat his normal prey. He stalks and kills people for food. Some lucky man who saw him and lived said the lion's mane was very kinky. That name became attached to him." The young man grew agitated, waving his arms and hands as he spoke, punctuating his words. "Day and night our best warriors search to find and destroy him, but this man-eating lion terrifies all the villages. The king's men are baffled. They do not know where or when the beast will strike next. We only know he will strike again."

His voice quivered slightly and Ramtouses barely heard the next words. "The cries of the people become louder and louder."

They walked in silence for a few minutes before their escort spoke again. "Other proud and mighty warriors like you have come to kill the cat, but no one has succeeded. Some lions have been slain. None were Kinky Mane. The people are still hunted and eaten by this predator."

Lozato and Ramtouses listened without comment.

Their escort spoke further. "King Tasmeria encourages champion warriors and known lion slayers to come and help. He announced a reward, a king's treasure, to one who kills the lion. The reward includes the promise of any of his unwed daughters as wife, except the Princess Carnabrara."

As he mentioned the princess's name, they arrived at the event, and the young man's attention shifted to the sporting competition.

They watched several contests. The winners have bragging rights for six months, until the next contest. Suddenly, a cheer went up around the crowd.

"What is happening now?" Lozato asked.

The servant laughed. "It is the highlight of the tournament, the women's long-distance race. It is a great race."

Ramtouses stepped forward to see the race from start to finish. More than thirty women lined up at the starting point. Someone blew a sharp blast of a bilah horn and the women burst forward. The race had begun.

Everyone yelled and cheered for their favored contestant to forge ahead. At the beginning a large pack of racers clustered together. By the halfway mark, five or six racers had broken away. When they reached the three-quarter mark, three girls ran close together ahead of the others. One girl slowly pulled away. At the finish, she ran well ahead of everyone else. She slowed only a bit as she passed the winner's line and crashed into Ramtouses, knocking them both down.

He climbed to his feet smiling and laughing then he lifted her up, his hands on her waist. When both were upright, their eyes made contact.

She was a beautiful woman with no markings or piercings on her smooth skin. Her bushy hair was long and thick. His laughter choked to a stop. His heart caught in his throat. He removed his hands from her waist.

Both stood quite still, looking into each other's eyes. She spoke. "Thank you for helping me to my feet."

A slight frown creased her brow as she turned and moved away quickly. It was promptly replaced by a grin of jubilance and victory.

Her hips swayed enticingly as her long legs carried her into a sea of fans. Colorful strips of cloth held her long hair together, and it danced behind her with the rhythm of her prance. He could not believe how beautiful she was or how taken he was with her. He finally turned away, muttering.

"What was that? Does such a female actually exist?" He looked again but did not see her in the crowd. Ramtouses turned to the young servant and asked, "What woman in this entire world looks like that?"

He replied with excitement, "That was Princess Carnabrara!"

⁘

All that night her image haunted him.

*Can this be the answer to my dream? She is beautiful and quick. Like the gazelle. And her eyes saw only me for an instant.*

Her eyes were large and shaped like almonds. The centers shone like deep onyx stone—so beautiful they captured his heart with a glance. He closed his eyes and relived the race as this fantastic creature flew past the finish line and crashed into him.

A sudden thought of Lizoka pierced his revelry. *What about Lizoka? How can I return to her as if nothing happened? Will she even want me after I abandoned her?* It was clear sleep would escape him that night. These questions had to be answered as soon as possible.

⁘

Their servant left them early in the morning and returned near noon. "The king honors the victors of the competitions. When he is done, he wishes to see you. The award ceremony has already begun."

Ramtouses turned to his brother. "Let's get there in time to see the trophies awarded."

Lozato nodded. "But I do not believe you have interest in the trophies," he teased.

⁙

When the three men arrived only a few trophies remained to be given. The woman's foot race trophy was the last. Princess Carnabrara accepted her reward—a red waistband. The king proudly made it known Carnabrara finished first in the three previous tournaments, a rare happening. She held her band high and circled the court displaying her prize. Ramtouses stood close to where she passed.

He spoke in a whisper, shaking his head in awe at the splendor of this woman. "I wondered if I saw an illusion last night, but I see now it was no illusion." *She is more beautiful than I could have imagined!*

⁙

As the ceremony ended, four senior warriors escorted Ramtouses and Lozato to the king.

King Tasmeria considered the two men before him. "You are a handsome man, big and strong, more than a meal for the lion." The king smiled, but the smile faded quickly. "I should not jest. It is not a subject for laughter. Many people have lost loved ones to this ferocious animal. Have you come to kill this menace and save the lives of many of my people?"

"Yes." Ramtouses's voice was quiet, the tone serious. "I have come to kill the lion."

"I offer a treasure of gold, silver, jewels, livestock and land, also the hand of one of my unwed daughters. The choice is yours, save Carnabrara."

100

"Your people deserve to be safe at home, here in their villages. No gifts can equal their lives. I ask for no treasure. But I will petition one wish and one wish only when I present proof the man-eater lion is dead. I will bring his corpse to you, and we will wait to see if the killing has stopped. Then I will ask for my one wish."

The king listened. "Ramtouses, you speak with compassion and humility, and yet your bearing is confident. The lion has fed on a half-dozen good warriors sent to hunt him. I pray you, young man, are the answer to our nightmare." King Tasmeria made a decision. "I will grant you your one wish upon the killing of this lion we call Kinky Mane."

Princess Carnabrara came close as the king spoke to Ramtouses. "It was you I ran into yesterday?" she asked.

"Yes, it was."

"I wish you good fortune in finding and killing the lion."

"Thank you. With fortune on my side, I will slay that lion and return to the king the honor, love and respect of his people."

King Tasmeria smiled. "Join me at my table tonight, Ramtouses, you and your brother."

Ramtouses arrived with Lozato for the evening meal. He hoped to see the beautiful Princess Carnabrara, but she and the other daughters ate their meal at a different location.

⁕

Servants came the next day to collect their few belongings from the guest lodgings and brought them to a selected hut on the royal grounds.

Ramtouses wasted little time surveying the surrounding villages. He talked to as many villagers as possible. He listened to anyone with information about the lion attacks. He drew a map on the ground of the many villages making up Tungal and marked the location and date of each attack.

He began to see a pattern. Attacks on high hills were never consecutive, nor were the valley attacks. The order went either from high ground to low ground, or vice versa. Lions hunted in the dark of night, the darker the better. Ramtouses smiled to himself. He had a theory.

By charting the cycle of the moon on the nights of the attacks he discovered when the moon was full, the attacks occurred in the valleys. On nights of the new moon the danger lay in the hills. This pattern proved to be very consistent.

The two nights coming would be a full moon. Ramtouses predicted the lion would be looking for prey in the lower valleys. There had not been an attack the past four nights. The beast should be hungry.

He requested the village leaders evacuate the valley villages to higher ground. The elders cooperated with Ramtouses and moved their people. Only a few senior warriors remained in the low valley villages. Ramtouses worked on his specially made spear and shield for the remainder of the day.

⁙

Ramtouses slept a few hours early in the evening so he would be fresh through the long night. Even a moment of inattention, of not being aware and alert, could cost him his life. He strapped the shield tightly to his arm then set out along the perimeter of the lowlands. He focused totally on the lion.

The first night was uneventful. The following afternoon he again slept. Come nightfall, he returned to patrolling the low-lying village perimeters.

Small groups of Tungal's senior warriors patrolled the lower villages. Lozato accompanied them on these patrols. They knew the lion might appear there for on more than one occasion the beast had stalked through a village, entered a hut and dragged the victim out by the throat.

⁙

The second night the full moon hung low in the sky. The tall hills cast shadows over the villages below. Stealthy lions preferred shadowy hunting grounds where they could prowl unseen. Ramtouses stayed within the darkest areas he could find.

In the wee hours before dawn the jungle rested in perfect silence. Ramtouses moved as one with the stillness. He felt a presence, eyes watching him.

He kept moving, turning quickly to his right then to his left as he had in the lion hunt back in Juba. Two orange spheres appeared just above the grass about the distance of a well-thrown rock. They disappeared quickly. A charge was imminent.

Where had it gone? His weapon only worked with a frontal attack. Vigilance with every breath was key to survival. He held the spear tight with his shield just below his eyes. There was no sound save the whisper of his breath.

Suddenly, a colossal cat sprang out of the grass and soared through the air directly at him.

The force of the impact flattened Ramtouses. The butt of his spear slammed against the ground. His shield covered his body. The air blasted from his lungs and for a moment he could not move or breathe. As his breath caught and his sense came back to him, Ramtouses heard a loud meow.

He slowly moved his shield back and sat up. He did not see the monster cat, but his spear had broken off nearly to the hole in his shield. Stunned from the violent impact, he climbed painfully to his feet, threw aside the remains of his spear and drew his long dagger. Another loud meow rumbled through the morning air followed by two more at a lower pitch. Hundreds of villagers heard the loud cries in the early morning hour and most of them chose to remain in their sleeping places, huddled close with loved ones.

Ramtouses let the animal's sounds guide him as they moved away from the site of the attack. Eventually the cries stopped and so did Ramtouses. He needed the rest. There was no way to determine which direction to go in the dark. He would wait for sunrise when he could pick up the lion's trail.

❖

Lozato and the senior warriors heard the cat's loud cries as well and judged from the sounds that the cat might be wounded. They knew nothing of Ramtouses welfare but followed the sounds until they ceased. Like Ramtouses, they stopped and rested until sunrise.

⁘

The sun soon lit the horizon and though the light created some visibility as it chased away the darkness, Ramtouses could barely identify the cat's bloody trail. The early morning silence ended suddenly when broken with another loud meow.

Heading in the direction the cat's cry led him, he spotted the lion's blood trail again in a rocky area with many large boulders. The large rocks provided crevices and outcroppings where the lion could conceal himself. Ramtouses kept a cautious watch for any sign of the wounded animal. Spotting a lone, barren tree with long dark branches, he headed in that direction. He could climb it to look over the area. The closer he drew to it, the more he realized the blood trail also led toward the tree.

He heard it before he saw it. Low hissing and heavy panting betrayed the lion, Kinky Mane. The cat lay on its side, unmoving. Was it near death? It looked to be. Ramtouses stepped closer. With a burst of strength, the huge animal bounded upright and fanned his mighty claw.

Ramtouses lurched backwards and nearly lost his footing. The cat swayed then fell back to the ground. The spear had dislodged itself from the animal's upper belly. Blood oozed from the wound.

Ramtouses rushed over to cut its throat. It took many thrusts of his dagger to complete the task. This lion was the largest he had ever seen. The cat struggled briefly before it fell limp, its suffering ended.

Ramtouses climbed onto a giant rock near the tree and leaned with one arm against the trunk, resting.

⁘

Lozato and the senior warriors had picked up the bloody trail that morning and followed it to the rocky area. Scanning the area, Lozato yelled. "Look! There he is. There is my brother!" He and the warriors hurried over the rocks to Ramtouses and the brothers embraced.

Lozato said, "My heart floods with joy to see you."

The monster cat was like none ever seen before. The men looked upon it with amazement.

Ramtouses stood on the big rock with a grin that seemed to grow each time Lozato looked at him. "This is the biggest lion I have ever seen!"

The tribesmen gave him no argument. They all agreed this had to be Kinky Mane because of the animal's huge size and large, thick mane.

Ramtouses jumped down from the rock. He took a deep breath and said to his older brother, "I will never, ever, fight a lion again."

With that declaration, the senior warriors and Lozato began to dance and celebrate. Ramtouses moved over to the lion and placed his foot upon the lion's side as the warriors and his brother danced around them.

A messenger was sent to carry word of the slain lion to the king and villagers. After a long while tribesmen came to the kill site just to see the spectacle.

Several strong men came to carry the lion's body back to Tungal.

When the party got back to the village, two warriors raised Ramtouses to their shoulders and carried him before the lion. The drums reverberated loudly and the people of Tungal chanted Ramtouses's name.

Lozato laughed and beamed as crowds of villagers escorted his brother to the king's royal grounds. The entire royal family and the village elders had already assembled. The warriors lowered Ramtouses from their shoulders, and he bowed before the king.

"Here is your lion, King Tasmeria."

The king looked at the dead lion in astonishment. "I cannot believe my eyes. Look at the mane. This must be Kinky Mane." He stared at the huge cat, and then reached down to one of its front paws and spread open the claws.

*This man came to us. He hunted and killed this lion, a huge beast, but is it the killer cat? Can we say, "Kinky Mane is dead!" without a doubt?*

King Tasmeria looked directly at Ramtouses. He said, "A few days ago we negotiated the terms of bringing down this monster. Are you certain this is the man-eating cat that has terrorized my people?"

Ramtouses nodded. "I speak with great confidence. This is that cat. However, we will wait a full seven days. Hopefully, we do not lose another one of your people."

"There is wisdom in your words. I, too, believe this is Kinky Mane and I will make you and your brother citizens of Tungal. We need men like you in our communities. You will feast with my family tonight. This is a happy day throughout the land of Tungul. One we will always remember."

Princess Carnabrara stood beside him. "You must be elated. How did you hunt and slay the killer lion?"

"It was the good fortune you brought me."

She smiled. "I am happy to know that."

There were no further attacks over the next few days, and the villagers dared to believe their sorrows had come to an end. Someone suggested that the three-day celebration should start early. The idea spread.

King Tasmeria shared their joy and granted permission to begin the celebration.

Warriors who helped in the search for the lion, including Lozato, received trophy ornaments of the lion's teeth and claws. Princess Carnabrara wove a beautiful neckpiece using the lion's mane and placed it around Ramtouses's neck.

Each night the villagers and visitors enjoyed the singing and dancing. Finally, Ramtouses was asked to speak before the large gathering of people.

"Greetings to you all." He paused as they all cheered. "I am a stranger in this land yet you treat me and my brother with warmth and friendliness. Every day I see kindness in the faces of the people I meet, evidence of good hearts. And I ask myself, 'Are we not all worthy of a good life? Do we not all deserve to escape a horrible fate? To not endure the strain of never knowing who will be next, fearing each day a monster may steal away someone precious to us?"

He looked out over the crowd. "I put myself in your position and ask, 'What if my sister, or son or daughter was suddenly stolen from me? Would it be the only time I would know the pain? Would it have to come to that?'

"When I first slew a lion it was for pride and honor. Today the reward was to save lives. We all deserve to have family, a place to live and the right to work our own fields and graze our cattle, to live and be happy. And, if any beast or tyrant tries to take that from those who cannot defend themselves, I will stand up for them. I will fight their battle.

"My reward is the great pleasure I receive from hearing the happiness in your voices exclaiming how much my efforts are appreciated. Thank you for making me your hero."

Loud cheers followed Ramtouses as he departed.

⁘

The king summoned Ramtouses to receive his promised gift for killing the man-eating lion. The king approved of Ramtouses now even more than he had initially. He saw a humble young man, generous and honest—a man he could trust with his life.

⁘

Ramtouses and Lozato walked together to the royal reception. "What will you seek from the king?" Lozato asked.

Ramtouses smiled at his brother. "You know what I am going to ask of him."

"I want to see the king's face when you ask him for Princess Carnabrara's hand." Lozato laughed and laughed.

"This is not a laughing matter. I will have to win her heart."

But Lozato continued to laugh all the way to the king's presence before speaking again. "May destiny be with you."

⁑

The audience consisted of many elders and the king's family. Ramtouses approached the king and bowed down. When he arose the king put his hands on Ramtouses's shoulders. "Speak to me, young man. Tell me what you desire."

"Dear king, I desire only one gift, as you promised. I want the hand of Princess Carnabrara in marriage.

King Tasmeria withdrew his hands. His eyes grew tight.

"You knew as well as everyone that Carnabrara was not included in the transaction."

"I rejected your offer of payment and made an offer of my own. In your payment Princess Carnabrara was excluded, but when I asked for my single gift, you did not exclude her. You said, 'I will grant you your one wish upon the killing of this lion.'"

"Is this some manner of ruse?" The king cut his words short. His face gave no evidence of the day's earlier celebration.

"King Tasmeria, I do not want you to give Princess Carnabrara to me as if she were prize livestock. I only want your approval. I have to win her heart before I will marry her. You must give your word that no one else may marry her unless I fail to win her love."

King Tasmeria looked over to Carnabrara. He could tell she stewed with anger.

Her feelings on the matter were painfully obvious to Ramtouses. With her arms akimbo, her eyes like burning coals and her mouth turned in, she had a look about her that said, "Beware!"

The king nodded. "Yes. That is an acceptable condition. As a matter of fact, I will grant you one full year. If you have not won her heart at the end of that time, I will withdraw permission to marry Princess Carnabrara."

The entire compound was in an uproar. Some seemed happy about King Tasmeria's decision whereas others acted as if they hated it.

Carnabrara walked up to Ramtouses, looked him in the eye, turned and swiftly left without saying a word.

"From all appearances, your task will not come easily, Ramtouses." King Tasmeria laughed. "Won't I enjoy watching this play out."

Lozato put his arm around Ramtouses's shoulder. "I never would have believed you could pull this off."

The king and Lozato may have been the only ones laughing.

# RAMTOUSES AND CARNABRARA

## 705-703 B.C.E.

Over two new moons had passed since arriving in Tungal. Ramtouses and Lozato were accepted into their respective age-groups as if they had lived in Tungal their entire lives.

Lozato made the long trip back to Juba and returned to Tungal with his family. Both men were also appointed tutors for the older youth age groups from several different villages. They hunted and fished and became familiar with the land surrounding Tungal.

Ramtouses noted where flowers bloomed and the best berries grew. *Doing little things is always appreciated. I will place fresh flowers and ripe fruit outside Carnabrara's hut each morning.*

The first time Carnabrara's serving attendants saw the flowers and fruit and brought them inside, she said to them, "Don't tell me. Ramtouses?" They only smiled, and nodded.

⁕

On his way to the royal grounds, Ramtouses reminisced about his every encounter with the princess since his arrival in Tungal. He fondled the lion's mane around his neck, remembering how her scent intoxicated him when she placed it there. Even now, the memory of it captivated him.

Immediately after he named her as his reward, the princess sought him out to confront him.

At the time he stood alone, looking over the space allotted him to build a hut. She was taller than most of the village women, and walked toward him quickly. Her hair moved like a bush in the wind. She had tied it back with dyed leather strips. Her long, shapely legs and wide hips caused her body to sway from side to side below her small waist as she strode to meet him. The movements were in complete harmony, making her attractive approach most pleasant to watch.

She stopped very near him and looked him in the eyes. She said nothing at first, then very slowly and with a puzzled look on her face, she asked, "Who are you?"

He did not answer and again, silence separated them until she repeated, much louder and more intensely, "Who are you?"

He remained silent, just gazing into her eyes. Eventually she spoke to him in a more conversational manner.

"I was happy to present you the gift of the lion's mane necklace because you became a hero among my people for what you did, but that does not mean I love you or want to marry you. Many men from my father's domain and other places say, 'I love you, Princess Carnabrara. I want to marry you. Pick me. I will be a good husband for you.' But never do they ask what is in my heart or what I am feeling. They do not stop to find out who I am."

The more Carnabrara spoke, the more emotional she became. "How are you different? You come here and kill the lion, Kinky Mane. Now you want to marry me. You're the same as the others wanting to boast of sleeping with the beautiful Carnabrara and having the king's wealth laid at your feet."

*She's both fiery and beautiful at once.*

Ramtouses enjoyed just looking at her, but when he did respond to her, it was with a lesson on the nature of living creatures.

111

"Life exists in a *nyumba,* surroundings of endless extremes. It is a hit or miss journey through time. Nature has developed a mechanism for improving itself to survive this challenge. The gazelle, for example, is a very timid animal that runs in fear from any movement, yet it will lock horns and fight a furious battle to insure the survival of the fittest of his species through mating. You and I have a natural compatibility, a dominant blood line that would ensure strong offspring."

Princess Carnabrara looked perplexed after hearing this.

*Is he for real?* She questioned silently. She had never heard anyone speak like that before.

Aloud, she said: "If what you say is true, I should seek out the biggest and strongest man among my people to marry and have many children to make certain strength and fitness will prevail for generations to come." She moved her head from side to side as she talked, showing a little of her snobbish attitude.

Even to his ears his response sounded somewhat presumptuous. "Life works its miracle of mating among animals in yet another way. Here is another illustration of life's unrelenting effort to overcome obstacles. Scent plays a major role in who will be attracted to whom in the passion of reproduction. Consider the way of elephants. They live in a herd, but the males stay away from the females, except at mating time. Because of their poor eyesight, the male would have great difficulty finding his lifelong mate during mating season if not for the odor she releases at this time, which is different from any other female elephant."

He clearly recalled that moment and the look his words brought to Carnabrara's face. He heard his words as if he had just now spoken them. "I was first stimulated by your scent when you ran into me at the race and again when you placed the necklace around my neck."

His words brought a slightly awkward moment of silence before she quickly moved away from him. "My scent?" Princess Carnabrara seemed quite taken aback. "I will never love you." She thrust the sharp words at him over her shoulder.

Undaunted, he watched her walk away. After all, she had stood still and listened to him. That was the important thing to remember.

⁙

As Ramtouses reached the royal grounds, he went before King Tasmeria and bowed down.

"My King," he said. "I wish Princess Carnabrara to accompany me on a hunt. Will she agree?"

The king lifted his shoulders and waved his hand. "She will respond to anything you want to know. It is best for you to ask her yourself."

Ramtouses nodded, thanked the king and left.

⁙

On the morning he planned the hunt, one of Carnabrara's serving attendants stepped outside to pick up the usual basket of fruit and flowers.

Ramtouses stood by the hut, waiting, holding the fruit. "Will you please ask Carnabrara to come out?"

The young woman turned and ran back into the hut.

When Princess Carnabrara came, she went straight up to him. "Thank you for the flowers and fruit you bring each morning. I am certain it requires much of your time to find such pretty, fresh blooms and fruit at the peak of ripeness."

Ramtouses smiled. "It does, but you are worth it."

"Do you require something from me today?"

"Will you go hunting with me?" he asked.

At first she hesitated as if undecided then she asked, "When do you want to go?"

He tried to hide his excitement behind a calm and steady voice. "Today, if your schedule allows."

"I am free today," she said.

He felt a huge smile spread across his face and thought, *You, Ramtouses, are as a child, unable to conceal your pleasure and excitement.*

113

"I shall prepare the hunting tools then meet you at my hut when you've readied yourself. Is that acceptable?"

"Yes," she said. "Of course."

⁘

All was ready and packed when Carnabrara walked up the pathway to his hut. He handed her two small backpacks. "Here, these are for you to carry."

They set out across an open plain leaving the village behind. By noon they crested a hill and saw the river below. Ramtouses spread wide his arms. "Isn't this a beautiful sight!"

Sunlight reflected off the serene blue-green water. Walking closer to the river, they spotted many types of marine life, all visible as the creatures moved about in the clear water.

"It is remarkable." Princess Carnabrara wondered why the beauty of this view escaped her eye until this moment. They stood silent, side by side, absorbing the river scene.

⁘

"Time to fish," he said.

He picked up a slender wooden lance with a slim line of rope knotted around it at one end and started toward the water's edge. Carnabrara waded into the water with him. Ramtouses concentrated, his eyes scanning the clear water. Then he launched the spear. When he pulled in the line, a large fish flopped about futilely impaled on the spear.

Fishing was not Carnabrara's favorite activity, and she tried and missed on multiple attempts, quickly realizing her fishing skills needed improvement. He described the fish's position relative to the reflected angle and line of sight. He told her she must adjust her aim accordingly. She listened, not directly admitting her limited skill. Instead she shrugged. "With practice, I'll do better."

Ramtouses built a small fire, wrapped their catch in thick green leaves and laid it on the embers to cook. They sat together and ate while discussing hunting strategies to be certain both followed the same line of attack. They hoped to come upon gazelles or impalas grazing and drinking along the river's edge. Devising the plan together came easily. Both contributed and agreed it was an excellent plan.

No game was in sight as they proceeded to follow the shoreline upstream. Tall grasses grew densely along the river's edge. In some places it towered over their heads, easily concealing them. Both were armed with long, thin spears.

A good distance up the river, Princess Carnabrara waved her hand back at Ramtouses. He stopped. She peered through the grasses and whispered, "Impalas—a small herd."

He silently crept up beside her and whispered back, "You know the plan."

Ramtouses circled around to the other side of the herd.

The animals moved slowly in and out amongst themselves, stopping to drink along the shoreline in an open area with little growth around them. They lifted their heads, turning this way, looking that way, alert but seemingly unaware of the hunters.

Carnabrara crouched and waited until she could see Ramtouses raise his spear. She raised her spear to acknowledge his signal. She moved in stealthily, her eyes focused on the target she had selected. At her point of effectiveness, she gathered herself for the throw. Suddenly, one of the impalas on the far side of the herd went down and the entire herd turned and raced in her direction.

She never relinquished her concentration on the target, a large buck that came dashing toward her. He took a giant leap and her spear met him in midair. He fell dead instantly and the rest of the herd disappeared quickly.

Princess Carnabrara took pleasure in pointing out her kill was the larger of the two. As Ramtouses cleaned both animals and prepared a sled to carry them home, he agreed she was quite the skilled hunter.

They were still several hours from home when storm clouds gathered, rolling in quickly. They knew the thunder and downpour would soon be upon them.

"Hurry," Ramtouses said, "we will take shelter on that hillside up ahead."

Once they reached high ground, he looked for an opening in the rocks. They hurried into a shallow cave just as the rain began to fall hard. He left the impalas outside the entrance where they could see them.

The temperature dropped, and their wet bodies chilled. He had used a mat and one blanket to cradle the catch, thus there was only one blanket for them to share. Ramtouses removed it from his backpack and spread it on the cave floor. He lay down and patted the empty spot beside him. "Come, Carnabrara, lie down. Warm yourself."

She didn't hesitate, but lay down beside him and wrapped part of the blanket around herself.

"Was this part of your plan? I think you knew bad weather was coming so you planned the hunting trip to get me here with you."

He burst out with a loud laugh, catching Carnabrara completely by surprise. She had not heard him laugh so heartily before. "What do you think? That I am a miracle man—even able to predict the weather in order to win your love? You give me too much credit."

When he was warmer, Ramtouses rose to investigate their shelter. Laughter bubbled up and over a few times when he thought of her words.

He said, "Your miracle man must find openings for smoke to escape so he can build a fire and keep you warm."

When he found crevices that would draw out the smoke, Ramtouses gathered enough dry wood from inside the cave to build a small fire. Carnabrara unpacked the food she brought. They sat near the fire enjoying the fresh fruit and talking about their hunt, the weather outside, and life in the village.

The rain outside was heavy, but the cave was warm and dry.

Dusk fell, then darkness, and their only light was the glow of the fire. Ramtouses moved the blanket nearer the fire. Carnabrara lay down first this time. He lay beside her.

"You can sleep beside me, but do not touch me," she warned.

He turned toward the fire with his back to the darkness and soon they both slept.

⁙

When they awoke the rain had subsided. A mist covered the ground below the cave and masked the bottom of the hill. The sun peeking above the horizon would soon burn away the moist air. Ramtouses and Carnabrara packed their few things and started down the hill, pulling the prize impalas behind them.

They walked in silence for some time.

*I like this fellow, Ramtouses. He is handsome and he certainly has some interesting things to say, but words and ideas will not win my love. The man I marry will be an Egyptian nobleman.*

*Maybe I should find out Ramtouses's real reason for coming here and killing the beast.*

*Did he concoct the entire plan to marry me long before we met? What really brought him to the land of Tungul and why? If he came for me, then how did he come to know about me and how can I discourage him?* Numerous questions flooded her mind as they walked.

"When you left Juba, did you come here to kill Kinky Mane and to marry me? And how did you know of me?"

Ramtouses said, "I knew nothing of the lion or you, the tenacious princess of Tungul."

"I don't understand," she said. "What was your real reason for coming here?"

"I had a dream. It left a compelling force that dictates what I must do. It is stronger than a natural instinct."

Princess Carnabrara stopped short of laughing. "You are a strange man. Is it this force that convinces you that you shall win my love? I do not succumb to love every time a bushman comes to me and says, 'You are the one. I love you.'"

For a short time neither one said anything, then Carnabrara spoke. "What about my visions, my force? What if it tells me not to fall in love with you. Do my dreams count?"

*A fair question*, Ramtouses thought and he answered accordingly. "Your wishes are most important. That is why I asked your father to allow time for us to know each other and see if our hearts can come together. If you do not grow fond of me and want to be with me for the rest of our lives, you will be under no obligation to marry me. I desire your heart, Carnabrara, as well as your hand."

*That's reasonable. Still, why did his force pick me?*

✣

When they neared the village, warriors met them. Princess Carnabrara pointed proudly to her kill and danced a small victory dance.

King Tasmeria came with his household to see Carnabrara dancing and proudly admiring her trophy kill before all the onlookers. His eyes grew large when he saw it.

"Save the horns," he said. "I shall add them to my collection."

Then he said to Ramtouses, "I grew worried when you did not return last night before the storm, but I know you are both very capable young people and would find safety."

✣

A band of travelers arrived in Tungal with wagons drawn by mules. Lozato and Ramtouses wondered who they were and from where had they traveled. King Tasmeria came out to greet the visitors and beckoned Lozato and Ramtouses to come to him.

"These men come from Egypt. They bear merchandise to trade." He flipped back a heavy cloth covering one of the wagons. It was full of weapons, mostly swords, bows and metal-tipped arrows. The metal had a bronze color.

"I have brethren in Egypt, governors. I trade with them. We have materials they need, and they have items we need. Princess Carnabrara and I had planned to journey to Egypt with them on their return. However, because of my promise to you, I have delayed this trip to a later time. When I told the princess, I was surprised she did not appear to be disappointed. She understands the slaying of the lion benefited our people, and she respects that I am keeping my word. But it will serve you well to know she has spoken with anticipation of this trip for a long while."

Ramtouses was grateful for the good news that the king would not take Carnabrara from Tungal. He was also glad to know she could bear the frustration of having to cancel the journey.

⁙

Through his years of gazing at the night skies, Ramtouses knew of an annual shooting star event in the heavens. During the time the stars would rain down through the skies, as Ramtouses liked to call it, he asked Princess Carnabrara to go out with him to view the village and night sky. She accepted his invitation thinking it might be interesting.

Together they walked to the apex of a high hill overlooking the villages. A cropping of large rocks capping the hill still radiated warmth from the sun. They leaned back against them. The cloudless sky glistened with bright stars. Gazing into the sparkling night sky, Ramtouses directed her gaze to a certain area.

Soon she saw a few flashes of light streaking toward the earth and then a huge display of shooting stars followed. Carnabrara gasped in surprised. "So beautiful. I have never seen the like of this." She turned to him. "Ramtouses, you planned this, but how did you know such an event would happen tonight? You never cease to amaze me."

His quiet voice framed the raining of the stars as he explained the event took place annually, the same time to the day every year. The picture wooed her.

He said, "I also have a special star that I love very much." He pointed it out to her and told her he had been watching this star in the heavens for many years. He told her it wandered across the sky.

"When it is close to the sun, for a while it shows up in the morning sky just before sunrise. May we call it our star? I can show you the trail it makes across the sky so you can find it at any time."

"No, Ramtouses. I like you and enjoy being with you, but do not think there is more to our relationship."

Ramtouses quickly responded. "I see, but perhaps you will still think of me when you see it in the early morning or evening sky."

They watched the skies and the shooting stars all evening until Carnabrara said, "I used to come here often to watch the village fire lights. I forgot how beautiful the flickering lights of Tungal look from up here."

She sighed so softly he barely heard it. "I want to leave now," she said. They stood and he pulled her to him and tried to kiss her. She pulled away at first, hesitated then gave him a light kiss on the lips.

"That is not a love kiss. It is a thank you kiss for a marvelous, enlightening evening."

They walked back to the village. She talked easily about her life, sharing the time when, as an eight-year-old, she traveled with her father north to Egypt. She spoke of streets paved with stones, buildings made of stone, marble statues, people with fine clothing and jewelry, no markings on their bodies or faces. The women wore long hair. Men rode astride horses. Large boats sailed on open water. As a child she had been enthralled with it all, and it became the impetus of her lifelong dream to live there, to marry an Egyptian prince or nobleman.

There was an ache in her voice. "I know it's hard for you to visualize having never been to see these beautiful places. However, these images are engraved on my mind. This has been my desire all these years since that trip. Please, Ramtouses, do not rob me of my dreams."

Ramtouses tried to disguise his unhappiness, but he had been unprepared for it and felt certain it showed on his face as if it were painted on.

Princess Carnabrara suddenly turned to him, excitement in her voice. "I have something to show you. Can you be ready for several days of adventure? Starting tomorrow?"

He smiled. "I can."

It was plain she did not love him, but he would not leave off his efforts to win her until the last minute of the last hour of the last day of the year he was granted.

⁘

The following morning he left with Carnabrara and traveled with her for a day and a half on what seemed to be a vigorous adventure leading nowhere. They traveled southeast and by the second day Ramtouses saw only barren, rocky hills, and wondered when it would all end.

At one point she said, "We are going to a place a short distance ahead, just beyond this next ridge." And she turned to continue the trek.

When they emerged from the desolate hills onto an open plain, Ramtouses almost stumbled from the surprise. Off in the distance several monstrous structures stood as guardians over the empty land, giving the impression this space held huge importance. Ramtouses gazed with awe, aware his mouth gaped as he tried to comprehend what he saw. His life experience provided nothing to help identify the strange erections.

Princess Carnabrara pointed to the objects with great enthusiasm. She yelled, "You see them? You see them?"

Ramtouses regained his composure and made his way quickly toward them. His astonishment only increased as he drew nearer. "How big are these giants?"

Carnabrara laughed aloud, a full rich laugh. The two of them came around to the entrance of the first structure. Up close it was even taller than he first thought, well over five or six times his height, and made of stone. It was a truly imposing sight. Ramtouses simply did not know what stood before him.

The odd shape brought to mind the beehives in the forest. But why would anyone build such a gigantic beehive? *Are the people who built these trying to imitate bees?*

She watched his confusion. "I have come to this place twice, once with my family, once with my father," she said. "These are tombs built by our ancestors. The elders from throughout Tungul come here on holy days to worship."

Ramtouses examined the tomb from top to bottom. A stone path led to a giant entry with double doors between two half-columns of marble. It was absolutely amazing.

"Carnabrara, this gift is as surprisingly marvelous to me as the gift of the raining stars was to you."

The brass fittings on the double doors bore damaged seals. It appeared the tomb had been broken into. He forced open the doors and went inside. It was hollow. As his eyes grew accustomed to the dark, he looked all around. "I find it hard to believe such a place could be built. I am so thankful you brought me to these tombs."

The masonry was smoother on the inside walls than the outside. The lower portion of the wall was decorated with a beautiful band of artwork that circled the entire structure with carvings of animals and people, embellished with jewels and gold. Only half of the decorations remained. The rest had been chiseled out, stolen by thieves.

"My father told me a mighty king from ancient time sleeps now underneath this floor, in a deep shaft. People who do not care about our ancestors come in and steal the sacred things belonging to him."

Princess Carnabrara knelt and placed her hands on the stone plaque. Ramtouses did as she did. They stayed there for several minutes as she prayed to her ancestors.

**Ancient beehive tombs in Old Dongola, Sudan**

It was evening before Ramtouses was done inspecting the tombs. They shared a meal and made ready to sleep outside along the wall near the doors. He built a small fire to keep them warm as the night temperature dropped.

In the morning, he said, "I would like to stay here and explore this site."

"A short while, yes. But our final destination remains another full day's journey or more."

Later, as they moved away, Ramtouses kept looking back as the monuments grew smaller until they disappeared behind them. The day came to an end. The night sky was a cloudless field of brilliant stars. It had been a nearly perfect day.

Sunrise found them packing for another day of adventure. As they walked they noticed an increase of trees and other vegetation. The nearly barren, rocky hills were left behind. By early evening they approached a large city still under construction. Ramtouses was eager to see it and began to walk faster.

"Wait for me," Carnabrara said. "We will get there."

A multitude of people labored on a project so huge it stopped him in his tracks. "What is this marvel?" he shouted. "More tombs?"

Carnabrara caught up to him. "Yes, but you can see these are different. They are called pyramids."

A colony of buildings stood a short distance from the construction site, some made of stone, others of wood. Roads connected the buildings.

Carnabrara said, "Let me do the talking."

He nodded.

Three tribesmen met them. They were dressed differently than the people of Tungul. They wore robes and pieces of leather strapped to their feet. The tribesmen spoke a language similar to Ramtouses's own space "Who are you?" they asked.

Ramtouses understood what they said.

Carnabrara answered, "I am Princess Carnabrara, King Tasmeria's daughter." She showed them her father's seal. They clapped their hands and seemed happy to greet her. They welcomed her with a bow, showing respect for her father.

The tribesmen led Ramtouses and Carnabrara into the town where many onlookers, mostly women and children, stood in groups. It was obvious the majority of the male population was working at the building site.

Carnabrara said, "These people are our cousins. We are descendants of the same ancestors. They call themselves Kush, or Nubians. They are the dominant offspring."

They were shown the town of Meroe by one of the tribesmen. It had grown dark when the governor came to greet them.

He reminded Princess Carnabrara that he had met her years before when she accompanied her father on a visit to Egypt. He made both travelers welcome and invited them to stay and share the evening meal with his family. They accepted with pleasure and enjoyed a good meal and friendly conversation with the governor and his large family.

⁘

In the morning, an escort gave them a tour of the two newest pyramids. During their visit, they encountered men riding on horses like the Egyptian traders. This was interesting to Ramtouses. Travel would surely be faster astride these animals, and the ability to carry additional items with them was appealing. But though the horses interested him a great deal, they were no competition to the pyramids.

When they reached a spot where they could oversee the whole construction site, he shouted, "Yow! What on earth is going on?" He turned to their escort in excitement. "This work effort is tremendous." He was awed by the immense and complex construction process.

Their guide described the work being done. He called these steep-sided structures pyramids as Carnabrara had.

**Nubian steep-sided pyramids**

*What a beautiful sight,* thought Ramtouses. They truly were striking, with white marble-finished domes and smooth masonry lining below. The masonry consisted of tremendously huge pieces of cut rock. Ramtouses spread his arms wide open and exclaimed, "I have never seen so many people working together for one project, or structures so enormous. These are simply wondrous."

Utter chaos seemed to rule amongst the hundreds of workers employed with varying tasks and men riding horses trotting from here to there, giving directions in loud voices. In reality, the project was very well organized, and Ramtouses was enthralled with the entire process. It reminded him of the construction methods of the ants he watched as a boy. Neither the guide nor the princess could persuade Ramtouses away from the areas of construction. All day he watched the builders.

His enthusiasm seemed to please Princess Carnabrara. "When the Nubians, our distant relatives, conquered Egypt, they kept their burial sites here, in their homeland. The tombs will be for Pharaoh Shabaka and his queen." She gazed at them. "I have not seen these being built before either. They are, indeed, amazing."

They returned to the city of Meroe, and Carnabrara took Ramtouses to the docks. In the early evening hours, boats arrived and departed. "They travel back and forth between Meroe and Egypt," she said.

The boats were larger than any he had ever seen.

When a smaller boat arrived, Princess Carnabrara recognized it as one of her father's. As soon as the boat docked, one of the men ran up to her and bowed. "Your father sent us to carry you home to Tungal."

They enjoyed an evening meal aboard the boat. The governor brought gifts for King Tasmeria and bid them farewell.

As the boat departed, Ramtouses waved his own farewell to every person along the shoreline.

*I have experienced more of the world beyond Juba in just a few days than most of my fellow tribesmen will in a lifetime.*

⁘

The boat dropped anchor later that night. Princess Carnabrara walked to where Ramtouses lay alone on the deck. She looked down at this man who both irritated and charmed her, then lay close beside him. Looking up at the beautiful stars, they relaxed together with the gentle rock of the boat. She moved closer, until the warmth of his body radiated to hers. At that moment, she felt more connected to him than at any other time.

In a low voice she said, "Ramtouses, I wanted you to see some of the world I have told you about. This is only a very small portion of their kingdom. I do not want to live out my life in the bush. I want to be a part of this world. I hoped if I brought you to see these places you would come to a better understanding of my situation."

⁘

Her voice was soft and gentle. It filled the deepest corners of his mind. He desired more than ever to always be with her.

"I can resettle with you in Egypt. We will have a fine life together, and we will have each other. You will see. I will build you a magnificent home and provide for you."

"Ramtouses," she interrupted. "No, please listen to me. You will be out of place. People do not respect you there. You are not royalty. No one in Egypt cares that you killed a lion. Wealthy, powerful Egyptians will dominate you as if you are nothing. In time you will hate both me and yourself." Her next words were gentler. "You are a stunning man, Ramtouses, and some young woman will find a great husband in you."

The still quiet of the night carried her words to Ramtouses. He ignored them. They created an invisible dance through time and space under the twinkling stars. It seemed an endless performance.

The two were finally rocked to sleep by the gentle movement of the boat.

In the morning, they resumed their journey down the Nile toward Tungal. Upon arriving, Carnabrara told Ramtouses she had a wonderful time and felt as if she knew him better than before.

He thanked her. "It was a most exciting journey."

Carnabrara told him she wanted to advise her father of their safe return and give him the gifts from the governor at Meroe.

On shore they parted ways, moving in opposite directions.

Ramtouses wanted to share all the wonders he discovered with Lozato, and he immediately sought his brother's whereabouts. He found him quickly.

When he finished his story, he said, "The trip was Carnabrara's way of explaining why she would not choose to marry me."

⋅⋮⋅

The following day King Tasmeria summoned Ramtouses.

After they talked of the Nubian pyramids, Ramtouses asked, "The workers labored sorely. Why would any ruler demand such sweat and anguish from their people?"

The king responded. "They need such burial monuments to be remembered forever."

Ramtouses struggled to keep the sadness from his voice. "Princess Carnabrara says the wonders she shared with me are small compared to the great cities of stone and marble statues of Egypt." He held his head low. "That is why she would rather die than be denied her wish to live that life."

"I believed convincing you of her determination was her purpose when she came to me to ask permission for the excursion." The king's voice was gentle.

His tone became more forceful. "Awake, man! What happened to that bold, impudent giant who came before me and swore neither man nor beast would stand between him and the woman he loved?"

Ramtouses raised his head.

The king spoke more gently. "He who would only marry for love is the man I want to marry my daughter. Not some nobleman or prince who cares only for his own greed. Listen to me, Ramtouses, Carnabrara has her dreams, but in truth, I have been waiting for one such as you to awaken her. She sees these places and people with the eyes of a stranger. I have seen their true faces, and they can be like monsters, wanting nothing but power."

Ramtouses stood silent, caught by surprise at what King Tasmeria said.

The king paced. "She sees their respect for me and believes it would be thus with her. But their respect for me is only as plentiful as my gold, silver, precious stones, copper, spices and much more. There are hundreds of beautiful young girls they can have at their calling."

He quieted, and sat.

Ramtouses spirit was renewed. "Thank you, King Tasmeria, for reminding me my purpose here was not to kill a lion, not to be a champion among your people, or a builder of massive monuments. My destiny was to meet your daughter, Princess Carnabrara, and be her companion on the journey from youthful innocence to womanhood.

"I will stand beside her when the sun rises in the morning and sets in the evening, to sweat with her from the work of the day, grow with her in knowledge, laugh when times are good and even mourn with her when life brings sorrow. I am here to lie down with her in the quiet evening. From our seed will come multitudes of bronze men and women, robust in stature, who will dominate and rule all the land."

He spoke with renewed confidence. "I shall win her deepest affection. I will not allow myself to be discouraged or swayed again."

King Tasmeria smiled. He stood and clapped his hands. "These are the words I want to hear!"

He put his hand on his chin then said, "A thought has come to me. This will take a bit of courage on your part but I know you can do it. It is our custom when a dispute or controversy arises between warriors wanting to marry the same woman. It tests the man's love for the woman—a mock battle, fought with the donga stick, between the bridegroom and some of the young woman's family members.

"The bridegroom fights as long as he can. It is not a fair fight. They will all attack him at once. The longer he fights, the deeper is his love—measured by the depth of punishment from the donga sticks he can endure."

Ramtouses looked the king in the eye. "I would endure until my sense left me, bleed my last drop of blood to prove how great is my love for the princess."

⁎⁑⁎

But before any donga-stick fight was prepared, the time came again for the traditional games, and Ramtouses would participate. He finished high in all his entries and won the wrestling match. Only the men's swimming contest remained.

Second in popularity to the women's foot race was the men's swimming race. Urentu, the king's oldest son, heir to the throne, won the competition in the last four tournaments.

The prince stood before his father, his fists raised over his head. "I will win this match and preserve the swimming championship for our royal family."

Thousands of Tungul tribesmen roared on behalf of the prince. His spirits soared.

The excitement surrounding the swimming competition was contagious, and Ramtouses wanted to win this race more than any other event.

Lozato came up behind him and slapped him on the back, "You are the best swimmer I have ever seen. Now prove it to the world."

"I will." Ramtouses never considered his confidence a conceit. He knew in his heart he would win. His declaration was not a boast.

⁘

The swimmers were ferried to the far side of the river where they lined up along a starting position on the riverbank. The course required them to swim the breadth of the great River Nile to the finish location on the Tungul side. A blast from the ram's horn started the race and the swimmers dove in. Over fifty top swimmers raced across the Nile.

Very quickly the distance between the elite swimmers and the rest of the pack widened. The leading group narrowed to twelve swimmers. Of those, Ramtouses and Urentu led the pack.

Princess Carnabrara and her family all shouted with excitement for the prince who pulled ahead for a few moments. It was in the final quarter of the race that Ramtouses burst ahead like a speedy water moccasin. The screams and cheers of the crowd were deafening as he overtook the prince. No one finished even close to him.

Thousands chanted his name as he climbed out of the water. Hundreds mobbed him and a couple men raised him unto their shoulders. Lozato, beaming proudly, was among them.

⁘

Urentu slowly climbed onto the riverbank and watched his people cheer and celebrate the interloper. Feelings of hatred and jealousy grew in him. No one save his family even noticed that he finished second.

It made things worse that his sister Carnabrara prevailed in the women's foot race for the fourth straight time, bringing glory to the family.

After the awards ceremony the next day, a crowd of the spectators gathered around Ramtouses as he held his trophies.

A voice in the crowd shouted, "How did you ever learn to swim like that?"

Urentu burned with rancor.

Ramtouses answered the question. "It all starts in the mind. Even if you have a strong, healthy body, it takes hard work. You cannot excel without determination. You must believe you are the best and let nothing stand between you and your goal. It is the way of all things in life. Hard work and belief in oneself makes a winner."

He turned and made his way through the crowd.

Urentu watched him leave. Princess Carnabrara stood alongside him. She said, "My brother, we will have our day."

Deep in thought, he was too angry to respond.

*How can I extract this thorn from my foot? I will not be second to this interloper.*

She came to her brother's hut a few nights later. "I know a way to make him pay for his arrogance. Ramtouses is to fight a mock battle soon. You must be one of the family members to face him. If you wound him, disable him, there will be doubt he is worthy of a princess of my caliber. Father would change his mind about the marriage."

Urentu nodded slowly. "It is a good plan."

He did not, however, have it in mind to wound the man he now considered his enemy. He planned to kill him.

It would be important to make Ramtouses's death appear unintentional. If the elders discovered his treachery, the royal family would be disgraced and he would be exiled for life.

⁘

On the day of the fight, Ramtouses came out to challenge three of Carnabrara's biggest and strongest brothers, including Urentu. The elders brought the flexible donga sticks to be used for the battle. A sack filled with sand and leaves was tied to one end. Such a weapon was designed to bruise and hurt a man but not to cut or break the skin.

It was a long match. Ramtouses grew tired, but eventually beat two of the three brothers into submission. He continued fighting his last opponent, the oldest prince.

⁜

Lozato stood in the crowd of spectators, watching as the prince and Ramtouses moved around the designated fight area. Early in the fight he noticed a man who stayed in one spot, by some thick tall grass.

*It seems strange that he does not move to better observe the fight.* Lozato kept a subtle watch on him.

⁜

Ramtouses and Urentu moved around the area dodging and attacking each other. They exchanged many blows. After one hard whack, the prince collapsed in some tall thick grass. He lay as if exhausted, feigning an air of defeat. In reality, he purposely fell back to the spot where another brother stood, guarding a hidden donga-stick which contained a heavy stone with sharp edges in its bag. While in the grass he subtly switched sticks.

Ramtouses assumed he, like his two brothers, had given up. Feeling victorious, he turned toward the crowd. Suddenly, Lozato cuffed his mouth and shouted, *"Olamayio!"*

Ramtouses didn't know from where the danger came, but he dropped to his knees as Urentu stumbled over him and fell to the ground. Ramtouses leapt up and struck the prince several times. The prince gave the submission gesture, and the donga-stick fight was over.

⁜

The donga-stick fight left Ramtouses in an abundance of pain with bruises and welts covering his battered body.

Yet six weeks hence, when Carnabrara and Ramtouses had an angry disagreement over the results of the match, Ramtouses offered to face them again.

Five different brothers met him, this time with a more strategic offense. The princes darted back and forth, in and out, around and around, coming at his blind spot, striking him from behind while he faced one of the others. Ramtouses could only compare the strategy to that of a lion defending his kill against a band of starving hyenas.

He withstood the beating at length, but eventually the five overcame him and beat him mercilessly. Throughout it all, Ramtouses did not say a word.

Lozato finally ran from the crowd and pushed the princes away. "That is enough! Don't you see he can no longer defend himself?"

The king signaled his sons to stand down.

Ramtouses was unable to move. One of Carnabrara's brothers helped Lozato and others carry Ramtouses to his hut.

He could barely speak. "Do not lay me down, just set me on the ground." They lowered him to his knees. He leaned against one of the hut support poles.

Three healers came to nurse his battered body. Princess Carnabrara burst into the hut, but Lozato stepped before her. "Why have you come? Haven't you done enough?"

She was upset. "I am sorry. She moved past Lozato and pushed the healers aside. "Let me tend to him."

Ramtouses heard the tremble in his own voice. "Carnabrara."

⁂

She looked at his battered body and shuddered. *Why did he fight so hard! Why can't he see my dream is as strong as his? Why do I even care what he thinks? Yet, I do.*

⁂

Both sadness and anger were heard as she talked to him. "It was just a game. You could halt it at any time. It was expected you would give the signal to end the fight. Ramtouses, all matters become so crucial to you."

He was aware she stayed by his side and tenderly nursed his body long into the night. Her touch was gentle each time she changed the healing leaves covering his bruised body. She returned to his hut early the next morning to help in his recovery. On the fifth day he felt better and began to show good signs of improvement. Carnabrara stopped coming. He missed her.

⁙

Several days later, Carnabrara began receiving flowers and fruit again.

⁘

Four months of Ramtouses's year remained when King Tasmeria sent messengers to Egypt. He requested Pharaoh Shabaka dispatch an advance convoy to Tungal at the end of the year instead of waiting two or three years as was his habit. He made this request because he wanted to travel back to Thebes, the pharaoh's capital city, with the convoy.

He promised Carnabrara if by the end of Ramtouses's allotted year she had not succumbed to his charms, he would arrange an unscheduled trip to Thebes.

In case Pharaoh Shabaka did not agree to the change in schedule, the messenger was instructed to inquire if the pharaoh objected to King Tasmeria organizing his own expedition to Thebes. Tasmeria had no doubt the pharaoh would be delighted to send a convoy to Tungal earlier than planned. Pharaoh Shabaka never shied away from the gold and beautiful stones Tasmeria offered for trade.

The messengers returned a few weeks before the end of Ramtouses's year delivering word that Pharaoh Shabaka of Egypt would not entertain any guests for an indefinite period. The pharaoh's plan was to send for the King of Tungul when other pressing issues were dispatched.

King Tasmeria was surprised and thoroughly disappointed the pharaoh had set aside an opportunity to gain more wealth.

He sent for Ramtouses. "My daughter and I will not depart for Egypt as planned. I am moved by your great devotion to Carnabrara and the efforts you made in the mock battle. It is my decision you shall be allowed to continue your pursuit of the Princess. You have made clear your love for her."

The news delighted Ramtouses. His lively step reflected his cheerfulness as he left the royal compound.

⁌

When Princess Carnabrara heard the news, her disappointment almost caused her to scream.

She asked her father, "What has happened? Why are we not going to Egypt?"

"Shabaka has made his will known. When more pressing matters are cleared up I am sure he will send for us. His love for wealth will ultimately prevail."

"Father, I must go now. I will be deemed too old in a few months. The elite want the youngest, most beautiful women. By the time I am nineteen or twenty, they will look upon me as undesirable." She began to weep.

"This whole thing has erupted in my face. You, the lion, Ramtouses, Pharaoh Shabaka have all made my life miserable. How will my dreams become real? How can I live like this?" She ran from her father's presence, to her hut.

Laying on her sleeping mat, Carnabrara's tears turned to anger. Her ire boiled up and rage took over. Indignation settled in her belly like a stone. She focused all her resentment and fury on Ramtouses.

*If he had never come here, I would be in Egypt now, happily married.* The thought of Kinky Mane gave her pause and a moment of clarity. *No, the lion would still be killing the villagers!*

She rolled over, began to cry again and screamed. "I hate him! Why did he have to pick me? Why will he not leave me be?"

For all the next day her servants, family, and friends stayed away from the princess, and Carnabrara fumed alone. By nightfall her anger still had not abated.

She lay awake, consumed with hateful thoughts of this man from Juba, this Ramtouses.

*He has dedicated his whole life to pursue a love that will never happen. It has been over a year now and his determination has not diminished, not in the slightest. Will he never leave? I must do something so repulsive, so shocking he will never want to see me again. It must be something that will drive him from me.*

In the morning she wore a smile as she rose from the bed. A plan had come to her and she intended to adopt it right away. She quickly prepared to make a trip to the community where Adzua, her look-alike relative lived with her family.

King Tasmeria's brother fathered Adzua in the year of Carnabrara's birth. She was a child conceived with a tribal woman outside his clan family marriage. Though not a member of the royal family or of their clan, Adzua had often played with Carnabrara when they were young. It was often said the two women were much alike in face and form. In recent years, and particularly when Kinky Mane disrupted life in the villages, they stopped visiting each other. Now, Carnabrara needed her relative, and she left to seek her out.

Carnabrara walked the maze of pathways threading through the valley villages and up to villages in the hills. Carnabrara remembered Adzua saying once that she would do "whatever is required of me, no matter the task" to gain recognition within the tribal royal family. *I can use that ambition to my advantage.*

When Princess Carnabrara found Adzua, she led her away from everyone and told her of the plan. Her kindred sister was outraged at Carnabrara's revelation.

Adzua's voice filled with disgust and anger. "I can never do that! What must you think to ask me of such? You are sick of mind and heart."

"Are you satisfied with being only a bastard child of my father's brother? I know you would like nothing more than to become a wife of Urentu. I hold your wish within my grasp."

"Carnabrara, stop it! Stop it! Have you no respect for others? Are there no boundaries you won't cross to get what you want?" Tears flooded Adzua's eyes as she shouted at Carnabrara. "No one is exempt from your treachery." She turned to walk away.

Carnabrara took her by the arm, whispering, "What you desire in this world you must seize when the opportunity presents itself. Life is brief and the prospect closes quickly. Don't sit back and wonder what could have been."

Adzua pulled away and hastened back to her family

Princess Carnabrara returned home disappointed but still hoping her kindred sister would change her mind.

⁙

After a few days, Adzua stood before Princess Carnabrara's hut.

Carnabrara grabbed her by the arms and pulled her in. "Have you changed your mind?"

When Adzua did not respond, Carnabrara assumed she accepted the plan and wrapped both her arms around her kindred sister. "No one shall know of this save you and me. Now, first, you must leave off shearing your head. Wear a covering as it grows and do not come around here. I will come for you in three new moons."

Carnabrara exulted in Adzua's decision. She prepared to live her normal, day-to-day life, interact with Ramtouses, family and friends in a manner they expected of her. But the day of her delivery from this insane oppression was nigh.

⁙

Three new moons passed and one night Princess Carnabrara entered Adzua's hut shortly after the family retired for the night. She gently awakened Adzua.

"We must make our way across the villages to my hut."

They reached her hut unnoticed in the deep dark of the night.

Carnabrara immediately focused on the next step of her plan. "This may take a long time but try to remain calm. Sit still while I work."

Her servant attendants had been sent away for a few days. Now, Carnabrara wove locks from her own cut hair and the hair from a young black goat onto Adzua's new hair growth. She braided her hair also to match Adzua's new look. The transformations took all night. Come morning, they slept soundly all day.

It was evening when Carnabrara sought out Ramtouses.

He was near his hut.

She forced a smile to her face, seductiveness to her voice. "I have thought about our situation and wish to say I am earnestly considering the idea of our marriage."

⁖

Ramtouses was stunned by the news. He took her into his arms and kissed her ever so lightly. Carnabrara responded with energetic passion, jumped into his arms and wrapped her long legs around his waist. They kissed, long and deep. It ended with Ramtouses saying, "How can anyone be as happy as I am now!"

He held her tightly, not wishing to release her. He moved to kiss her again.

Carnabrara pulled back and jumped down. "Not now, Ramtouses. I will come to you tonight."

"Truly?" Ramtouses looked very surprised. "You do not have to do this. We can wait, my beloved."

"I want to," she said." You deserve it after all I put you through. I want to make it up to you starting tonight."

Carnabrara turned to go but stopped. "How do you like the new way I braided my hair?"

Her hair was braided and coiled into concentric circles on top of her head, like a cobra snake curled up prior to an attack.

Before he could answer, she waved and left.

⁖

Princess Carnabrara returned to her hut. She found Adzua weeping.

"I cannot go through with this. I would not know what to do! I tell you, Carnabrara, you have no convictions. You can be cunning and sly when it helps win your goal, but I am not devious. I have very little guile."

"Don't be foolish, Adzua. This is your opportunity also. Have you forgotten?"

"Something like this may be easy for you, Carnabrara, but not for me. I will be too nervous to lay down with him. And, if he touches me, I will be horrified. I may panic and run away! Your plan is insane."

"Quiet," Princess Carnabrara ordered. "Drink this tonic. It will give you courage."

She bathed and perfumed her kindred sister and gave her a sweet herb to chew on to remove the taste and odor of the tonic. The scent of cinnamon floated in the air. Carnabrara smiled. The plan progressed well. She meant to soothe Ramtouses's senses and still provide every indication possible it was she who lay with him.

Carnabrara recalled the story of the elephant's poor eyesight and keen sense of smell as she shaped Adzua's braided and woven hair on top of her head to resemble her own.

*He will notice my natural scent because this is mostly my hair.*

⁺⁘⁺

A quarter-moon lit the way as Carnabrara walked with her kindred sister to a place near Ramtouses's hut.

"Remember, do not say a word," she whispered. "Keep your face down or turned away until the door flap is closed. Just get in the bed and let him do the rest."

⁺⁘⁺

Adzua knew the tonic must have been taking affect because she felt calm, relaxed and more daring than at any time in the past three new moons. She opened the flap just enough to allow a sliver of moonlight into the dark interior.

The way was clear between her and the man stretched out on a sleeping pallet.

Adzua let the flap fall softly into place and plunge the hut into darkness. She gasped and froze, startled for a moment by the total lack of light. She stood motionless, barely breathing, but then the resolve to continue returned. She bent to her hands and knees, and felt her way to the sleeping pallet.

⁙

He had lain unmoving for hours with his eyes closed but totally alert. He heard her enter the hut but did not move. The soft rustle of her clothing whispered sweet promises as she moved to where he lay. He felt the slight pressure of her hands as she touched first his leg, then his side and then lifted the blanket to slip beneath it with him. Ramtouses's breath almost stopped. His heart beat loudly and every nerve in his body reached a point of near combustion.

"I didn't think you would really come." It was a whisper.

She didn't speak but lay still and quiet.

Ramtouses leaned over her and began to kiss her very gently. He wrapped his arms around her and kissed her more intensely. She began to return his kisses.

⁙

Back in her hut, Carnabrara was restless. Unable to lie still, she tossed and turned on her mat. Thoughts of Adzua and Ramtouses in bed raced through her mind, allowing her no peace. *They are loving each other? A pleasure I will never know. Is he really enjoying her? Was I right to do this?*

She did not sleep. Before dawn, she rose and went to Ramtouses's hut and sat there watching, waiting for his morning appearance.

The first rays of sunlight streaked the skies, bringing a new day. Carnabrara nodded off but jerked awake when Ramtouses came out of his hut to fetch fresh water.

She bounded up and ran over to him. With as much intensity as she could muster, Carnabrara whispered a near scream, "Ramtouses, you ass! You could not wait to get your hands on me!" She let her fury fly in his face without disturbing the morning quiet. "You did not even take the time to identify the woman you claim to love so much before slaking your lust in the dark of the night."

⁘

Ramtouses froze, stunned by her anger and baffled beyond belief. He looked first at his hut then at Princess Carnabrara. He gaped at her, his gaze alternating between this woman before him and the entrance of his hut. He did not fully understand what he saw yet somehow knew. He covered his mouth in disbelief.

She stood in front of him, mad as a swarm of bees. She hissed at him violently. "I trusted you would have the sense to know me even in the dark of night. I hate you!" Tears flooded her eyes. "I never want to see you again! You see! You are nothing but an easily-duped, stupid man."

Ramtouses could not say a word. He stood motionless in the early morning air, bewildered and puzzled. All he could ask himself was, *What is happening?*

The woman of his heart stood before him, buzzing with fury, and the woman he held and loved during the night still lay on his bed. At the moment, he did not grasp the tragic truth.

Carnabrara turned away and he watched her walk over to his hut and summon the other woman from inside. She came out, covered in a large dark robe.

Walking away Carnabrara spat, "Go marry a woman as stupid as you. The man I marry will know me at all times, day or night."

Ramtouses felt as if he had been hit in the face without warning. This heart-stopping nightmare left him paralyzed. Comprehension dawned in small, clear segments until a whole picture emerged. It was a well-planned scheme the purpose of which was to break his heart and make him look like a fool before the entire town.

His head lowered and his entire body drooped after realizing who had plotted and schemed against him so cunningly. As the appalling reality overtook him, he withdrew mentally and emotionally.

He returned to his hut and sat on the hardened ground, no longer bewildered but hollow, emptied.

⁜

Lozato came from his nearby hut and found Ramtouses sitting by the entrance. It was obvious something had seriously disturbed his brother. He sat down beside him.

Absolute silence filled the space between them for a long time then Ramtouses spoke so quietly the sounds of insects could be heard over his voice. He told his brother all that happened. When the story ended the two men simply sat there, and again silence filled the space.

Finally, Ramtouses said in a hopeless voice, "What do I do now?"

Lozato looked at his brother as he spoke. "Giraffe legs, I watched you grow from a little bean. You tower above ordinary men. Your name is recognized throughout all the tribes, and thousands you have never even met love you.

"Love is nothing to be ashamed of. It is part of our nature. It must come naturally and cannot be forced upon anyone. No matter how much it hurts, if it does not happen for both partners, you must have the strength to go forward and put it behind you. No one wants to endure such an excruciating experience."

It was quiet once more. Eventually, Ramtouses stood and looked down at Lozato. "Let us go home."

# HEZEKIAH REFORMS
# THE KINGDOM

### 705-703 B.C.E.

King Hezekiah went before the citizens of Jerusalem. He stood on the palace balcony and looked down at the faces of his people filling the courtyard, even spilling out into streets and walkways farther than he could see.

Hezekiah held his hands out, open to the sky. "Citizens of Judah, thank you for your sincere concern during my illness. I strive to be a good king and make our city of Jerusalem a wonderful place to live. We have many new public buildings. We continue to improve food storage capacity for times of famine. An aqueduct now brings fresh water within our beloved city walls. Roads are being rebuilt for more trouble-free travel throughout the city.

"We are grateful for these blessings, but our greater happiness lies in the love of our Almighty God, whom we have neglected for fear of our enemies. On my deathbed our God spoke to me through the prophet Isaiah. He told me I would not die from that illness, but that I will live for a number of years to come and that our LORD will protect us from conquerors.

"He beseeched us, 'Give your total trust to your LORD God and the people of Judah shall be saved.'

Our God is the one God, and to honor Him I proclaim the end of forced idolatrous worship in Judah. I decree all idols shall be removed throughout our land. The freedom to worship the God of our ancestors is returned to all."

With that, Hezekiah withdrew and turned from the balcony. Jubilant cheering and prolonged applause followed him inside.

⁜

King Hezekiah appeared at the next elders' council meeting anticipating controversy over his decree to remove the heathen idols.

He thought it best to address the council. "As I said to the people, all idols will be removed from Judah, first from the LORD's Holy Temple."

The elders' responses were swift and direct. They feared war with the Assyrians.

King Hezekiah reminded them, "When we hold true to the LORD, we are victorious over our enemies. When we abandon Him, we suffer defeat. Why should we abandon Him now? Thousands of our people follow the Law of Moses and worship the one true God. They have been doing so in private."

The elders nervously asked King Hezekiah to reconsider demolishing the idol statues while he negotiated a new pact with Sennacherib. They suggested he could store them.

Hezekiah shook his head. "King Sennacherib has not responded to my wishes regarding a meeting to renew the tribute pact."

He waved his arm acknowledging Judith who indicated she desired to speak.

She stood. "We cannot be half-hearted with our God and commit only to a partial journey of faith. If we put our trust in Him we must believe all the way. We should not say 'As long as we are safe, our LORD is almighty,' and when trouble comes, switch our beliefs to save our own lives."

King Hezekiah understood the fears and concerns of the elders, but he also heard Judith. He concurred fully with the truth of her words. "I am convinced a renewed relationship with the LORD Almighty is at hand."

He went forward with the destruction of all the idols of the Canaanite and Assyrian gods placed in the Temple to appease the Assyrian overlords. He gladly took up leadership of Judah's commitment toward a restored faith in Yahweh. Furthermore, he ordered the celebration of the Passover restored. While this decree brought many long and serious faces to the council membership, it signified the sincerity of Hezekiah's intentions.

The meeting moved to military matters. Hezekiah understood the need for a strong army. Very early in his reign he consulted with his generals and reached full agreement regarding the need to build an authoritarian military as a deterrent to any aggressors throughout the region. To that end, he ordered the recruitment of all young men within Judah.

⁘

The elders' council met more frequently as talk of preparing for possible war came up again and again. The issue of water was also a constant concern. At one meeting an elder spoke of the system used by the old city of Jerusalem which continuously drained water from the Gihon Spring into the Pool of Siloam inside the walls of the city. It was said a tunnel built long ago connected the two.

King Hezekiah tasked his chief engineer, Manasses, to seek evidence of the old water system. If a tunnel system remained intact, perhaps they could modify and upgrade it to supply water for the city again. If not, would it be possible to build a water source through the hard limestone?

They considered other water sources, thirteen in all, from which water could be brought to Jerusalem. They were rejected in favor of Gihon Spring, which was invaluable due to its close location and constant flow of fresh water.

⁘

Manasses came to the conclusion above ground wet spots called *karsts* indicated underground fissures that likely led from one water source to the next. He reported to King Hezekiah this theory of deep cracks and cavities in the limestone hills connecting the Gihon Spring and the Pool of Siloam. His theory supported the idea of an old water source within the city walls. At once, Hezekiah declared a tunnel must be built and authorized unlimited resources to accomplish it. It would be life itself to Jerusalem in the event of an enemy siege.

To penetrate the hard limestone, Judah would need help to forge iron picks and chisels. The valuable smokehouses in Philistia could now be used to serve that end.

⁜

While sitting in her quarters, Judith listed her ideas for the tunnel and brought it to Manasses.

He reviewed the list. "I will be involved in the details of building the tunnel," he said. "You, Judith, display a strong commitment to the project and a sincere concern for the well-being of the workers. Someone must focus on that part of the operation. Are you willing?"

"I am honored to help," Judith said. "I would like to start immediately."

She planned to provide food from her own farms. She determined where the eating area would be. She also addressed the need for a medical center for the inevitable smashed fingers, cuts and bruises.

⁜

The work on the tunnel started at both ends and after a few months became a daily routine. Manasses thanked God for Judith's commitment. She was a great help to him, doing all he asked and more, and never missing even one council meeting.

Manasses developed a device to enable him to hear sounds from deep underground. He worked long hours refining the design. Judith often brought him his evening meal. He called her Rufus, which made her laugh and somehow lightened their load.

*What a wonderful way to end the day. She is marvelous,* he thought, *always working to ensure the tunneling project continues.*

Manasses completed the assembly of the listening device late one evening after Judith brought him the evening meal. It was one of many that would be needed to track and direct the excavating work so far below the ground surface. He came up behind her and placed his hands on her shoulders. "How do you do it? Your life is so full of obligations I see no time left for yourself."

Judith smiled, "Yes, but so much has to be done. You too have long days filled with responsibilities from sunup to sundown."

He turned her to face him and gently kissed her on the forehead.

She looked up at him. "I have no one in my life."

She placed her hands on his waist. He kissed her gently on the lips then, pulling her close to him, he kissed her again more intensely. When the kiss ended, he held her, aware of her rapid breathing.

He whispered beside her ear. "I feel the need to tell you of something I did."

She pulled back and looked at his face. "What was it?"

"Something a man of God should not do."

"Tell me," she said. "Do not leave me guessing."

"I hope you will forgive me. The other morning I came by your quarters to fetch you. No one confronted me. It seems I am there so often, your guards and servants think nothing of my presence. When I entered, I heard the sounds of your bathing. I looked into your bathing area where you stood washing your smooth skin. I never imagined you could be so lovely. Your beauty is all natural—no creams or perfumes, no jewels. You dress in simple robes and do not seek to enhance your loveliness. What a charming surprise to see your natural beauty fully disclosed. You were like a dream. You are a dream, a gift from heaven."

Neither spoke for a long moment. Eventually, she said, "If you find me so beautiful, marry me and have me for yourself. Show me the ways of love. Enter my soul and take from me all the years I have dreamed of the passion of being with a strong man. Teach me wild and unconstrained desire as if each night was our last."

Manasses's surprise at hearing these words left him speechless.

He looked into her eyes and saw his face reflected, he kissed her again, deeper and longer than before. She began to breathe heavily and pushed him away. "Wait."

"I love you, Judith, more than anything. Let us marry, the sooner the better."

She smiled. "Yes! Yes. I love you, Manasses."

"I promise to be a loving husband for all our days."

⁂

Judith shared her happy news with her mother, the king and her friend, Queen Hephzibah. The announcement gave special reason to rejoice, but Judith did not want the focus to be on them.

She said, "We want to be married very soon and it will be a small ceremony."

And so it was that Judith and Manasses married. They left the tunnel work to enjoy some time off from all the project pressures.

In their absence the tunnel work continued per Manasses's strategic instructions. His engineers regularly went into the tunnel to check that all was done to his specifications.

Judith and Manasses returned only a week after the wedding. Judith bloomed with happiness, she sang and danced about and even kissed Manasses lovingly in public. Their obvious joy reflected in the workers attitudes as they rotated in and out of the deepening tunnel with a snappier step and more enthusiasm than usual.

⁘

Judith's first day back at the elders' council meeting found the main topic was now the ever-increasing likelihood of Assyrian aggression. Should warfare come, King Hezekiah considered an agreement with major powers in the area against the common threat. He sent ambassadors to Egypt and Ethiopia to present the idea of an alliance against a potential Assyrian invasion.

Weeks later, the ambassadors returned with officials from Egypt and Ethiopia. Hezekiah called a council meeting at once. Everyone voiced his own opinion, creating a lot of mixed conversation, regarding just how the alliance should work. The Egyptians wanted to control all the forces on the battlefield if war came. Ethiopia wanted Jerusalem to aid them financially. Hezekiah wanted the Egyptians and Ethiopians to move their armies to Jerusalem and set up their bivouac north of the city. This bickering went on for hours. It became obvious no real alliance could be agreed upon at the time. It would take months.

In the year 704 B.C.E. Merodach-baladan proclaimed himself King of Babylonia for a second time. He sent an ambassador to King Hezekiah's court to congratulate him on his recovery from his severe illness. Hezekiah saw this as an opportunity to swing Babylon to his side. He, some military officers, Queen Hephzibah and Judith escorted the visiting party to view the city. King Hezekiah understood the Babylonian objective was to ally with the southern Mediterranean vassal state and strengthen the Babylonians' financial position. An army powerful enough to withstand Assyrian aggression would require a deep war chest.

Merodach-baladan's ambassador spoke before the council. Babylonia proposed a union of the southern Mediterranean states to encourage free trade and prosperity among all the nations, promoting peace throughout the region. Merodach-baladan also proposed stopping the tribute paid to Assyria.

Hezekiah assured the ambassador details would be worked out quickly. With this new development, the king and elders were more confident in severing ties with Assyria. The construction of the tunnel remained a secret from all outsiders, including their neighboring nations.

⁘

The city of Ekron adopted the same policy regarding idols as Jerusalem had and removed all the statues and objects of heathen worship. Governor Padi, appointed by Assyria, opposed such a move. Thousands rallied around the governor's palace and demanded Governor Padi resign and depart the city. He refused and fighting broke out. Padi had only a few hundred troops at his disposal, mostly Ekron citizens who ran away after a short skirmish. The people stormed his palace and brought him out kicking and screaming.

"I will have my revenge. Assyria will punish you all for this with swords and spears."

One of Ekron's first noblemen came forward and pointed to him. "Strip off his opulent clothing. We are poor in our own country and this man has a fortune of jewelry upon his person."

They removed all his garments, placed shackles around his ankles and wrists and gagged him to stop his screaming obscenities. They stood him on a platform in the center of the city and burned down his palace as well as other Assyrian buildings after removing all the booty. The idol statues of heathen gods were smashed into fine rock and used to improve the roads in and around the city.

The citizens of Ekron decided to send the Assyrian governor, Padi, to King Hezekiah to strengthen any coming alliance between Judah and Babylonia. Hezekiah convened his court of elders when the Ekron party entered the city.

They announced: "Ekron has disposed of the filth of Assyria and here is the source. Please take this corrupt soul off our hands and execute him as you see fit."

They brought Padi before King Hezekiah and his council. Someone asked, "What should be done with this man?"

Some shouted, "Burn him."

Others shouted, "Stone him!"

Hezekiah said, "Wait. Wait. Let us hear what he has to say. He has the right to speak for himself." He gestured toward the deposed governor. "Remove the gag from his mouth."

Padi shivered and shook from the cold and could barely say a word. Only a small cloth covered his loins. Murmurings from the room still encouraged the man's death.

Judith stood and asked for the right to speak. She still heard the calls for Padi's death. "Stop it," she stated. "This man has only done what his king has asked him to do."

Approaching the deposed governor, she took a heavy robe from the lap of a robust spectator and placed it around Padi's shoulders.

"Let us think before we act so harshly," she said. "This man may be of some value to us, being an Assyrian governor." She turned briskly and walked back to her seat.

Hezekiah considered her words. "Judith makes a good point. He may be useful to us alive. He is of no use to us if dead."

With that, he ordered Padi locked in a military dungeon for safekeeping.

⁘

King Hezekiah was relieved to have an astute and objective council member to replace the invaluable Merari. He approved of Judith's quick responses to questionable situations and how she handled herself. The elders also valued her input and honored her judgment. Queen Hephzibah took pleasure in Judith's good fortune, which helped bring purpose to her once writhing soul.

# 11

# CONFRONTATION WITH THE VASSAL DISTRICTS

702-701 B.C.E.

The Assyrians broke camp and began the long expedition to reestablish their domination over the rebelling vassal subjects to the south. King Sennacherib took up his position as the representative of the living god Baal to oversee the operations. General Holofernes, the commanding military chief and field marshal, and his mighty army took up their position as the enforcer of Baal's will.

General Holofernes arose with the dawn the first morning of the military campaign.

He spoke to his officers. "Yesterday, our men looked more prepared for revelry rather than war. Assemble one-third of this force. Work them strenuously. Prepare them. Soft soldiers are dead soldiers."

This became his daily pattern. He never failed to find one minor problem or another on which to reprimand the men. He wore a stern and worried look, not the cocky confidence of his former countenance. Other than the reviews and inspections of his men, he secluded himself, also contrary to his previous custom of entertaining his officers. Occasionally, the men saw him in prayer to the gods, something he never did publicly in the past.

The Assyrian army knew Holofernes well. It was clear he had changed, but no one dared say anything. These men had fought with him through knee-high mud smeared red with blood. They were loyal and would follow him to their deaths

⁘

A few weeks' march, brought Holofernes's army to the territory of Sidon. They swooped down over the hills like a giant cloud of locusts. The people of Sidon rejected alliance with the other countries rebelling against Assyria. When they came out to the field to fight the Assyrians, thousands surrendered, and what was expected to be a full-scale battle turned into a few brief skirmishes.

The beauty of the landscape, the farm areas and richness of the soil in this territory so impressed King Sennacherib he made it a new province of Assyria. He installed an Assyrian as King of Sidon and gave him authority over the new province and its many towns.

When Holofernes wanted to divide the women between his men, King Sennacherib came forward and stopped him.

General Holofernes asked his friend, "What is this, my king? Our men have always shared the spoils of war as a reward for victory. The women are the prized gifts."

"Yes, I know," said the king, "but some of these people remain loyal to Nineveh. I do not want them punished along with those who make war against us."

"How can we know who are loyal, and who are not?" asked Holofernes.

"I will go to the high priest and ask who worships our gods. Let those who are faithful bear witness to those in league with the rebellion."

And so it was that thousands found themselves named guilty of treason and turned over to the Assyrians. Holofernes gave the women from this group to his men as spoils of war, but to everyone's surprise, he did not touch a single woman. The remaining faithful population of Sidon was left untouched, able and motivated to contribute to building a new province.

The next part of this campaign would be much more difficult. After another month of preparation, Holofernes moved his Assyrian forces south toward Samaria, the capital city of Israel. They trampled over every town in their path. When the Assyrians reached the border, the entire Israeli army was waiting. Israel had not joined with Judah and its allies due to years of conflict between the two countries. They mounted their own defense, knowing they faced possible defeat fighting the powers of the north alone, as they had many times.

It was evening when Holofernes's army arrived at the border. Rain fell. Holofernes called for his wet and travel weary soldiers to make camp and prepare for the battle the next day.

Holofernes paced inside his tent.

Late into the evening, his officers saw their general stride back and forth. One officer remarked. "The General also talks to himself. What troubles him so intensely?"

No one knew the answer but all were wary when speaking with him.

The next morning the two armies advanced toward each other. When the Israelite army came within range of the strong Assyrian bowmen, Holofernes gave the order to open fire, and a hail of arrows took to flight. The archers of Israel were not yet within their range to return effective fire.

The rain of arrows was unrelenting. The Israelites had to keep their shields overhead, and their archers were unable to return fire in the face of this barrage.

The Assyrian army's battle plan worked with precision. The cavalry galloped upon their opponents with a sea of horsemen just as the last of the arrows fell. When the Assyrian infantry reached the battle, the Israelite army had already sought relief in flight. The Assyrians pursued them throughout the day like a pack of jackals with the scent of blood in their nostrils.

By nightfall the Assyrians had driven them to within a faint view of Samaria. Holofernes halted his march to allow a good night's sleep for his men.

Sunrise found the Israelite camp abandoned. They had fled into the walled city for a desperate last stand. Holofernes brought up the immense battering rams and wheeled siege towers they had constructed in the month following the fall of Sidon.

The sight of these monstrous weapons slowly creaking up to the city walls was enough to terrify all who beheld them. When the battering rams and wheeled towers were in place, the bowmen on the tall towers opened fire, intent on keeping Israelites from the gates while the battering rams were employed. The Assyrians broke down the gates and plowed their way into the once proud city of Samaria. The city fell before nightfall, victim to the overwhelming aggression of the Assyrians.

Israelites suspected of being a part of the rebellion suffered torture and execution. Many of the people were deported to Assyria and became slaves. The remaining Israelite population was scattered by the Assyrians to various locations under their domain while others were relocated to a refugee camp in Israel.

Ekron lay at the gateway to several other territories and had sought help from its allies. They were more fearful of invasion than other vassal states due to their vicious destruction of all temples and statues of Assyrian gods as well as their cruel treatment of the residing Assyrian governor, Padi.

✛

**Example of Assyrian battering ram.**

As the Assyrians devoured everything before them, the Egyptians mobilized their army and marched northeast. They united with the Ethiopian forces with the contingency King Hezekiah's troops would merge with them before they reached Eltekeh.

As his army lay poised to attack Joppa, an unwalled city, General Holofernes received word of the advancing army. He expected to overwhelm the town in one day, but the town had blockades everywhere. It took three days to overcome the last of the Joppa rebels.

This was ample time for the Egyptian and Ethiopian armies to prepare a defense against the Assyrians at Eltekeh.

⁛

King Sennacherib and Holofernes altered their drive to Ekron to face the Egyptians and Ethiopians before more forces joined them.

When the Assyrian forces arrived, the Egyptian and Ethiopian forces were spread out over the plains before Eltekeh, a small town on the Philistia Mediterranean coast. The Assyrians closed ranks with a wall of shields. The two armies faced each other, exchanging brief arrow attacks.

The Egyptian and Ethiopian forces did not wait for a charge from the Assyrians' fine cavalry. Thousands of warriors raced across the fields to clash with the Assyrian front lines. The Assyrian forces threw heavy spears at the swarm bearing down on them.

The heavy spears weighed down the defending armies' shields. The infantrymen abandoned them and continued the attack unprotected, vulnerable to spears and arrows. Thousands of the infantry managed to reach the Assyrian wall of shields, but it held fast. The Egyptians and Ethiopians persevered, pounding the Assyrian fortifications.

They could not break through the stout wall of Assyrian shields the first day. By early evening they retreated, carrying their wounded out of the fighting area. The Assyrians suffered minimal losses.

Realizing their attack plan failed, the Egyptian and Ethiopian forces switched their method of attack on the second day of battle. The Assyrian wall of shields could not be penetrated in a straightforward assault. The new strategy utilized their cavalry in a sweeping charge to the weakest side of the Assyrian forces to break through at that angle. If it worked, this maneuver would draw the Assyrian cavalry away from the area of their target pavis wall.

Like the Assyrians, the Egyptians and Ethiopians had a huge cavalry, thousands of horsemen.

The Assyrian general commanding the cavalry assigned a quarter of his horsemen to protect the pavis wall. The rest moved to meet the charging Egyptian and Ethiopian horsemen who raced toward them from a different angle. Assyria's cavalry met them in a tight, uniform formation. A tremendous battle ensued.

⁙

The second phase of the revised Egyptian and Ethiopian war plan went into effect when the two cavalries met. They brought up the battering ram chariots. This chariot had a long and heavy pole protruding from the front. Preceding their infantry, hundreds of ram-chariots forged ahead to plow their way through the wall of shields. The Assyrian cavalry left to protect the wall wasn't enough to repel the horse drawn ram-chariots, and a number of chariots breached the wall of shields. The Egyptian and Ethiopian foot soldiers pushed through the breach, and furious fighting resulted.

⁙

One mighty man shone like a glittering star. He struck down every Assyrian warrior who came before him. He wore white with gold and silver plating covering his body armor, shield and helmet. An assortment of sparkling adornments reflected the brilliant sunlight. Ostrich feathers encircled his waist like a skirt and sprouted from the top of his helmet in all directions.

Holofernes felt surely this man must be a prince. He leapt from his chariot and entered into the fighting. He sought the man in the elaborate dress, convinced of his royal status.

They met, and their swords rang out. The two men of war danced around each other to gain advantage. Men fell around them trying to protect their leaders at all cost.

As the Assyrians began to gain the upper hand, a second warrior prince, dressed as the first, entered the combat with another large group of warriors.

Holofernes knocked down the man in the golden armor once, then twice. Each time he sprang back on his feet. The third time he fell, Holofernes bent over for the kill, but the prince's sword nearly struck him in the face. As chance would have it, the blow glanced off his shoulder armor. Holofernes backed away surprised by the force and speed of the blow. He recovered in seconds and went at the prince again.

Once again, the prince went to the ground. The second prince intervened at this point with a sudden and staggering whack at Holofernes. Had it landed, the blow might have been fatal, but Holofernes blocked it with his shield. The first warrior got to his feet, and the two princes joined in fighting Holofernes with scores of warriors in battle around them.

⁛

King Sennacherib's chariot driver shouted, "Look, there is General Holofernes in the heat of the battle!"

Sennacherib saw the unbalanced fight and yelled. "Get me there."

The powerful horses surged under the driver's hand and maneuvered through the crowded field filled with men in mortal combat.

At Sennacherib's approach, the Assyrians battled to open a path for him. Within moments, Sennacherib was there and sprang from his chariot to fight alongside Holofernes. The Assyrians blocked the young prince's infantry support.

On equal footing, Holofernes gained the upper hand. He knocked him to the ground and put his foot on the man's throat. Holofernes poised his sword for the mortal blow when King Sennacherib shouted, "Do not kill him. I want him alive."

Beside him, King Sennacherib's opponent was also overcome. Once he successfully disarmed the man, Sennacherib seized the leader from behind around the neck. He removed him from the fighting under the cover of his mighty army.

Holofernes dragged the first prince on the ground while Assyrian soldiers held the man's arms and followed King Sennacherib away from the front.

⁛

The Egyptian and Ethiopian forces were largely defeated due to the capture of their two leaders. They lost their discipline, and the organized plan of attack broke down as they frantically threw themselves at the Assyrian forces, trying to save their leaders.

The Assyrians maintained complete control and composure. The Egyptian and Ethiopian penetration that at first seemed so promising, became a death trap as the Assyrian forces closed in tighter and tighter, compressing their forces within the Assyrian ranks.

Like a lion full from a heavy meal, the Assyrians withdrew from the tiresome battle knowing total victory would be theirs the next morning. They left what little remained of the Egyptian and Ethiopian army to care for their wounded and dead as the day came to a close.

The following morning it was clear the Egyptian and Ethiopian armies had fled during the night.

General Holofernes laughed and smiled, as he looked toward Egypt. "Run, for now. We will come for you later." He joked with his officers, embraced and congratulated them. This victory was key to the campaign. It opened the gateway to all the remaining vassal states leaving no military force yet to face equal to the one they just defeated.

⁎

Holofernes needed to cleanse himself by confessing the evil deed he had nearly committed. That meant going to King Sennacherib's tent to inform him of the aborted attempt he so treacherously made on the king's life. He also wanted to thank the king for helping him in battle.

He thought upon a manner in which to tell King Sennacherib. *He may have me killed when I tell him what I did.*

Holofernes came into the king's tent, his heart heavy with its burden.

The king looked at him. "What is it, Holofernes? Raise your head so I may see your face." After looking into his eyes, Sennacherib said, "Ah, yes. You need not speak. I know what you are thinking. Do not trouble yourself with words. In Nineveh, it came to a test of wills. It is trust and understanding that binds our friendship. Sometimes I feel you do not have complete knowledge of whom you are. Trust in Baal, and you will be all right. I forgive you for what you thought on the terrace that day. Now, go back to your men. We gather tonight to devise a plan of attack on Ekron."

Holofernes's relief was on his face. "Can I at least thank you for fighting by my side today."

The two men embraced. Holofernes clasped Sennacherib's hand. "This day I feel happy and free as I have not for many months."

⁙

The captured princes' lives were spared because of their extreme bravery shown in battle. Sennacherib sent a courier to Egypt demanding a hefty ransom for the safe return of the two men.

⁙

Weeks later, on a wet and dark day, the Assyrians arrived at the unwalled town of Ekron. A heavy mist hung in the air.

Field Commander Holofernes came up the main road and declared to the people of Ekron, "If anyone remains who was loyal to Governor Padi, let him or her leave today. Hasten. Gather your belongings and evacuate now."

There was no movement through the gray, misty air. No one came forward. It seemed most of those who planned to leave had already done so.

With fire in his eyes, King Sennacherib said to Holofernes, "We will storm the city. I have come this great distance for just this day. The insults these people placed upon us and our gods will stand in history forever. We will reward them with a day of damnation that will last equally as long."

Holding his sword high, he ordered, "Take no prisoners. Bear only valuables you can carry as spoils of war. Burn all else and destroy every building standing. I wish this place leveled before my very eyes."

❖

General Holofernes shouted orders to his men. "Hurry. Search and empty all the buildings." He watched as his men descended on the town. To his surprise, arrows and spears started flying from all directions. Door-to-door fighting broke out.

He pushed his men to continue the effort to clear the buildings, but by midday he realized it was a total disaster, and he had lost hundreds of men.

Angry with the situation, he shouted. "Forget about clearing the buildings. Set the town afire."

He and his men watched the fires burn for hours. By morning the fires had cooled a little.

Holofernes ordered. "Go into the town. Search for and slaughter any survivors."

When a new barrage of stones, spears and arrows came down upon his men, he shouted, "What am I seeing here? How can there be so many fighters left alive in this rubble?"

Frustrated and humiliated, Holofernes demanded his officers employ more men but that did little to hasten the end of the battle. He had expected to find no one alive in the burnt out city, yet the army was under heavy attack all day. "Withdraw!" He finally ordered.

He watched his men return to camp after a miserable second day of fighting, dragging their dead and carrying the wounded. *With daybreak, we will exterminate the people of Ekron.*

❖

In preparation for war, the people of Ekron had designed a tunnel system leading from building to building throughout the city. After the fires, many stone buildings remained standing—hundreds of homes, public centers, and trade buildings secretly shared a connection by these tunnels. The tunnels were well vented, and certain areas could be blocked off to avert smoke, which facilitated prolonged stays underground.

The people of Ekron knew the maze well. This allowed them to surprise the Assyrians with unexpected attacks. These sporadic attacks proved successful against the Assyrians and swayed the battle in favor of the citizens of Ekron.

They had a mission. Every man, woman and child fought with bow and arrow, shooting quickly from behind cover of debris or through an open window then disappearing into the tunnel system.

The citizens of Ekron expected to be killed if captured, so they continued to fight to their deaths. They suffered heavy casualties but it came at an extremely high cost to the Assyrians. All who remained in the city accepted the fate of death in exchange for taking with them even one Assyrian soldier.

✛

With hundreds of bodies lying throughout the city, the fighting continued as it had begun. There seemed to be no end to the stealthy attacks.

Early in the confrontation at Ekron, the Assyrian generals agreed upon a plan to surprise their field commander, Holofernes, with a special gift. They ordered their men to capture as many young girls as possible. The Assyrians paid dearly for this special gift. The young girls fought just as hard as the men, and often set themselves up as bait to kill an Assyrian for his efforts. The hatred between these two rivals grew like a disease with no cure in sight.

✛

Holofernes reported to King Sennacherib. "I am astonished at how many fighting men we lost in this town with a population of approximately twenty thousand."

Sennacherib fumed with anger. "Keep the pressure up. They cannot last forever."

⁘

Each day unfolded as the day before—like a ghostly nightmare. The daylight hours began as overcast and gloomy then turned melancholy. Everything seemed damp but without rain. Mist hung heavy in the air, tainted with the smell of blood, a sickening odor to most yet pleasing to the Assyrians soldiers.

Finally, after seven days of door-to-door fighting, they subjugated the last of the Ekron rebels. Those taken alive totaled only about one hundred fifty, including the wounded. During the seven-day destruction of Ekron, the Assyrians lost more men than in the entire Mediterranean campaign.

The one hundred fifty prisoners who survived the battle received brutal treatment by their captors. On the ninth day at Ekron, the prisoners were forced to dig two large trenches to dispose of their dead. The majority of the prisoners eventually met death through torture. The Assyrians bled or skinned them, trying to force them to pray to Baal for forgiveness and pledge loyalty to him. For the children, death came quickly by the sword. Older women burned to death.

⁘

King Sennacherib stood before Holofernes. "There will be no prisoners or slaves."

General Holofernes agreed. He spoke to his officers. "The few surviving men shall receive the maximum penalty. Impale them alive on tall poles throughout the city where the statues of our gods once stood. Let the trenches remain uncovered so the rotting corpses of Ekron will be open to animals and birds of prey and can be seen by all who pass."

⋅⊹⋅

A prolonged reconnaissance found no one in the city of Ekron left alive. The entire population was annihilated with the exception of nineteen young girls, captured through the course of the seven-day battle and saved for General Holofernes's entertainment. They alone escaped with their lives.

Holofernes ordered every building not already destroyed leveled, stone by stone. The Assyrians took seven days off to burn their own dead and pay homage to Baal. They built a huge statue of Baal standing the height of seven men. Its head was like that of King Sennacherib, the trunk and body of a lion with wings of an eagle. They placed the statue on the main road leading into Ekron. They cleared the road of all rubble and restored it for a long distance leading up to the city and a shorter distance into the city.

The level of death and destruction in Ekron testified to Assyria's capacity for diabolical brutality and ruthlessness. This was, beyond a doubt, their most horrendous performance.

They gave the glory to Baal.

⋅⊹⋅

The generals presented Holofernes with his gift of young girls. He expressed his pleasure and had a girl brought to him each night, beginning with the virgins—the darker complexioed girls first then the ligher-skinned girls. After fulfilling his cravings, he sent most of them to his officers who passed them around and made certain they received proper care and ate well. None faced death. The only Ekron survivors disappeared into Assyrian history. And so it came to be that Holofernes returned to his old self.

# 12

# THE SEIGE OF JERUSALEM

## 701 B.C.E.

Jerusalem, that great city in Judah, worked feverishly to prepare for war against Assyria. Work continued on the tunnel that King Hezekiah had declared must be dug to provide the city with water. His chief engineer, Manasses, reported completion would take a few more months, but no more than five. That good news moved the council to the next agenda item.

King Merodach-baladan of Babylonia had not responded to King Hezekiah's offered alliance between Babylonia and Judah. Nor had the Egyptians and Ethiopians consented to meet again with Judah regarding the same issue. Hezekiah sent another group of ambassadors to Egypt, urging them to join in council with Judah to discuss the Assyrian threat.

⁘

Judith and Manasses walked the tunnel excavation sites reviewing details of the project when a boy approached them.

"Judith, you are needed at once. The council is called to an emergency session. Hurry."

They went straightaway to the court, Manasses to the observation area and Judith to her council seat. The other elders were already present.

King Hezekiah came to the head of the table. He looked grim. His eyes scanned the council membership and those seated in the observation area. "I hoped King Merodach-baladan would have returned my request for a meeting, but that will not happen now. As I stand here the Assyrian army is invading Babylonia. War now exists between those two nations. Our hope of a peaceful settlement is blowing in the wind, like a puff of smoke."

The hall grew quiet. No one seemed to even breathe. The room was still, as if everyone had lost the capacity to move.

The king went to the window and looked out. "Even though we had dreams of a brighter future, we all knew this could happen."

The meeting ended. There was nothing further to be said at the time, no questions to be asked. Another war loomed before them. The history of Judah was written in the blood of its many wars.

⁘

One worry stubbornly wiggled its way into every person's mind if the Assyrians found victory in Babylonia, all hell would burst forth in the Mediterranean south.

Work in the tunnel became more intense.

Manasses and his engineers used his newly designed instrument to monitor the progression of the tunnel excavation. This instrument was cone-shaped with a long tube inside that extended down into the *karst*. The engineer placed his ear over the smaller opening of the cone, and the device amplified sounds deep from within the limestone.

It worked so well the team had no problem following the direction of the excavation and could suggest corrections based upon what they heard. The tunnel did not connect the Pool of Siloam and the Gihon Spring, the two starting points, in a straight line. It took many turns as the digging from both ends followed existing fissures. In general, each team headed toward the other just as Manasses had expected.

⁘

**Hezekiah's tunnel as it looks today**

When King Hezekiah received word the Egyptians and Ethiopians would arrive in Jerusalem in a few days, he immediately invited leaders from Ekron, Syria and Philistia to be present as well. The urgent discussion centered on what should be done if the Assyrians defeated Babylonia and marched south, a likely scenario.

Egypt's huge army had to be mobilized and moved the greater distance. They wanted compensation from Ekron and Judah to help cover the costs of such an ambitious maneuver. Hezekiah argued the Assyrians had not yet won the war. His position was that King Merodach-baladan had shown himself to be a wise and courageous leader who could find a way to win.

In the end, they agreed to continue to prepare for the worst, but wait and not move the armies prematurely. Ekron and Judah agreed to help finance the recruitment of armies in Egypt and Ethiopia, including a bivouac area made available by Philistia when the time came.

⁙

Deep in the tunnel, light became a challenge. Manasses and his engineers resolved the issue by reflecting light off large, shiny sheets of silver set up at various angles allowing the work to continue.

Manasses worked on the steep side of the hill. He pulled away from the cone device as a low rumble caused him to look up. *Earthquake?* His heart caught in his throat. They had worked so hard. *The tunnel. Oh, no.* Beneath him the ground shifted, and he was thrown off balance. Above him, a few skittering rocks became a thunder of boulders that crashed onto his head and shoulders.

In the medical area, Judith heard the rumble and felt the quivering earth. She thought little of it until they received word of twelve injured men above the dig site. She dropped what she was doing and rushed to where Manasses had been working. She knew when she saw him the head injuries were critical. She dropped to her knees, clinging to his hand and to blind hope, but his injuries were too severe. While Judith knelt by his side and held his hand, Manasses quietly died.

Again, sorrow tore at Judith's heart. She wept openly. The joy and vigor of life seeped out of her body with each tear.

"Why?" she asked. "Why was I given the chance to be happy only to have it snatched away so quickly?"

Judith's marriage lasted six months and four days.

The city's entire population mourned the loss of Manasses. Work on the tunnel stopped for a day so people could attend the burial. The other eleven men recovered from their wounds and bruises.

⟡

Judith emerged from the death of her husband determined to overcome the emotional devastation and personal wreckage inflicted on her. Once again, she was burdened with the heavy grief that left her mired for months after her father's death. But this time she would not succumb to it. She resolved to place her faith and confidence in Yahweh. She would move forward with whatever plan God had for her and embrace the undiscovered reason for her existence.

Following the burial, she displayed few signs of mourning. She spoke out boldly and expressed her renewed trust and faith in Yahweh. She occupied herself with the council meetings and the completion of the tunnel project on Manasses's behalf.

The tunnel breakthrough had been expected for a few days, and it came with great shouting and cheering when the two crews stretched their arms through the opening and shook hands. The king viewed the project as a wonderful success, especially when fresh water flowed from the tunnel into the Pool of Siloam. He ordered a celebration honoring the workers for a job well done.

⟡

The time came for the elders' council to discuss plans for the Passover celebration. It was during this meeting that a messenger interrupted with a message for the king.

Hezekiah read it aloud to the council. "The Assyrians have defeated the Merodach-baladan forces."

The elders had held little confidence in a Babylonian victory so the bad news came as no surprise. There was no reason to abandon the Passover plans.

King Hezekiah ordered all the priests of his father's Canaanite sects be removed from the Temple of Solomon. He recruited a number of Levite priests to consecrate and sanctify themselves and the Temple for the upcoming Passover.

Passover had to be attended by members from all twelve tribes. King Hezekiah sent a message to Israel inviting the ten tribes of the northern kingdom of Israel to join Judah in commemoration of the Passover and the week-long feast of unleavened bread. The king of Israel scorned the idea but did not interfere with those of the northern tribes who wanted to celebrate the Passover once more. A multitude of people made the journey down to Jerusalem in response to King Hezekiah's invitation.

Their long journey south made it impossible to observe Passover on schedule so Hezekiah cited an ancient law. If the Passover ceremony could not be held on the appointed date, it could be observed one month later to the day. King Hezekiah and the elders invoked this law on behalf of the entire nation and all of Yahweh's people who needed to travel from afar.

It was a great congregation that gathered at Jerusalem in keeping with observance of the Passover, an exciting time for the people of Judah and the remnants of Israel. The Israelite tribes from the north had been unable to observe the ritual preparations due to their journey and lack of time. Contrary to what was written, they were granted permission to eat the Passover feast. Their hosts in Jerusalem all prayed to the God of Israel to provide atonement for everyone who prepared his heart, even though he did not cleanse according to the purification of the sanctuary. The God of Israel heard their prayers and healed those people.

Hezekiah ordered a great sin offering of seven bullocks, seven rams, seven lambs and seven he goats. He encouraged all the people to bring their own sacrifices. The people of Judah and the Israelite guests brought a thousand bullocks and seven thousand sheep, so many that the priests could not handle the workload. Hezekiah directed the priests to build storehouses to keep the livestock for no lamb could be killed until the Passover day.

On the appointed day, Levitical priests sacrificed the Passover lamb and observance of the weeklong feast of unleavened bread continued each day. The public celebrated so intensely the whole assembly agreed to keep the feast another seven days.

After the Passover, King Hezekiah sent most of the local people home with instructions to continue combing the land to destroy all the pagan shrines. He included orders to destroy shrines built for the one LORD God as the law forbade worship in local shrines, requiring pilgrimage to Jerusalem instead.

⁘

Many Israelites of the ten northern tribes feared the return trip to their homes because the threat of war was in the air. King Hezekiah did not insist they leave Jerusalem. Rather, he opened the next elders' council gathering with the question, "What should we do concerning the Israelites who attended the Passover and now fear to return home?"

The elders wanted them to stay but realized the already over-crowded city could not handle such an increase in population. In addition, many people from local communities throughout Judah sought to stay in Jerusalem.

An elder said, "If war comes, the new faithful could be useful."

Judith added, "There is now enough water for all with the new tunnel."

King Hezekiah took the thought a step further. "All who want to stay will work for their keep. The young men will be called to the military and train with the army. A new outer wall will be built to enlarge our boundary, and there shall then be room for all to live within the city walls."

Thus, the order of the day called for all the new people to join the workforce, and they did so with enthusiasm. Engineers hurriedly drew plans for a new wall, larger and stronger than any ever built in Judah.

**Remains of broad wall at Jerusalem, constructed prior to the 701 B.C.E. siege**

At another council meeting, Judith took the floor. "Hear me, my king and council members. We have praised ourselves for cleansing our city and our lives of all the influences of paganism. We have broken down the idols, and we no longer worship the pagan gods. All shrines have been destroyed. Still, one idol remains inside the Temple. It is the Nehushtan, the serpentine bronze statue Moses created to heal those who were bitten due to the infestation of poisonous serpents during the wandering in the wilderness. It remains in the Temple court where the priests placed it, worshipped as the Canaanite snake god. There are those who see it as an idol and burn incense to it to cure snake bites. Why does it yet remain in our midst?"

"Bring the Nehushtan to me." King Hezekiah ordered.

While the council waited, Judith and four palace guards went to recover it from the Temple. She returned holding the Nehushtan high over her head with both hands and handed it to the king. He took it and waved it back and forth in front of the elders then slammed it down to the marble floor. A large piece broke off. He picked it up and thrust it to the floor again and again until only a short curl of the original bronze snake remained.

The King said, "We will suffer no reminders of idolatry in our kingdom again."

⁜

Progress on the new wall moved at a frenzied pace for the next five months.

A messenger arrived requesting an audience with King Hezekiah during a council session.

After listening, the king stood. "The Assyrians mighty veteran army is now encamped at Sidon." He folded his hands behind his back and walked to the window. Around the room every face was grim. This marked the beginning of King Sennacherib's campaign to the south.

The King turned to face them. "Every able man and woman will join the labor force. The new wall must be completed, quickly."

⁜

Within days the king sent ambassadors to Ethiopia and Egypt. Judah would contribute additional funds to begin moving their armies north. He committed Ekron to a similar donation.

The Egyptians and Ethiopians had gathered thousands of men and trained them day and night preparing for war. The Egyptian Pharaoh Shabaka, of Kush descent, placed his son in command of his Egyptian army. His Ethiopian nephew commanded the Ethiopian forces. Both armies were well

175

equipped and well paid, due in no small part to the war chests of Judah and Ekron.

By the time the ambassadors returned to Jerusalem, King Sennacherib's notorious Field General Holofernes had overrun scores of towns. At least a hundred more lay in his path. Hezekiah's spies reported the Assyrian drive now swung toward the Israelite border.

Thousands from the north took flight, seeking refuge in Judah.

King Hezekiah ordered his army to turn them away from Jerusalem. The city was already too crowded. The military personnel diverted the refugees to Lachish, another well-fortified walled city two day's march southwest of Jerusalem.

Every day he received news of the Assyrian army's advance. Holofernes's ability to maneuver such a huge body of men across vast distances so swiftly astounded Hezekiah.

⁘

The Egyptian Pharaoh Shabaka sent word his armies broke camp to head north and expected Judah's army to join them before they reached the flatland leading into Eltekeh.

King Sennacherib and the veteran Assyrian army marched on Samaria after defeating the Israelite army in only two days of fearless fighting.

King Hezekiah sent a message to the Egyptian and Ethiopian armies asking them to get there with all speed. *Have I waited too long to send for them? Should I have requested the Egyptians and Ethiopians move their armies to the north months ago to bivouac on the plains of Judah? Hindsight is worth little*, he thought.

⁘

The new city wall neared completion. Every effort was made to finish it before the arrival of the enemy army, including demolishing houses to provide bricks.

The elders, the King, his wife and Judith went to inspect the completed effort. At the entrance stood a huge bronze gate like none other ever built. Tall twin towers rose on either side of the gate. They stood on the walkway above the gate spanning the distance between the towers.

Hezekiah said, "These walls are strong, well-built. Surely they will protect the people of Jerusalem with absolute success!"

Judith and Queen Hephzibah left the walkway and climbed to the top of one tower. The King followed them. When they reached the top and looked out to the horizon, Judith threw her hands to her breasts. The queen gasped and covered her mouth. "This is a breathtaking view," she said.

The king reached the landing and looked out over fields beyond Jerusalem. "I always knew our countryside was beautiful, but from up here, it is magnificent to behold."

Everyone was quiet.

The sloping landscape was covered with grass. It looked perfectly level in all directions for as far as the eye could see. Patches of wild flowers randomly dotted the giant field, creating a scene of color as brilliant as a peacock's tail. There were few trees. The shrubbery lining the road leading to the gate all appeared well-groomed.

Others who joined them were in awe of the pastoral scenery. They watched the sky catch fire as the sun lowered toward the horizon. It seemed to kiss the earth. The bright reddened sun slowly slipped below the horizon, colors melting together into darkness. Judith could not look away from the color show. She stood mesmerized by its beauty, etching the image into her mind's eye to always remember the glory of Yahweh's creation.

As the King and his party made their way back to the council hall, a messenger stopped them with the news that Samaria, the capital of Israel, had fallen. This was difficult for them to hear. The fall of Israel carried deep meaning for the people of Judah. Through many wars and years of strife, the two countries shared a common heritage that might now be lost forever.

⋅⋅⋅

He prayed there was enough time for the Egyptian and Ethiopian armies to reach Philistia before the Assyrians continued their march south.

Judah's army was prepared to march to the meeting place in Philistia when King Hezekiah received a report informing him the Egyptian and Ethiopian forces were still three days away. A similar report notified him the Assyrians had broken camp and were on the move to the territory of Joppa.

Hezekiah's next move was critical. Should he move his army to the agreed meeting point or keep them in Jerusalem? If Sennacherib's army overran Joppa, there was no way to know in which direction the Assyrians would march next. They might go to Ekron. If so, the three armies would have time to combine and stand against them. But they might move against Lachish or Jerusalem itself. Without their army, the two cities would be without defense.

He convened the elders' council to hear their voice on this matter.

Judith stood immediately. "The Assyrians have demonstrated the great speed of their mighty war machine, and their next objective is yet unknown. Our LORD God is with us. Let our troops stay and defend our city in His name."

The King said, "If the Assyrians march on Ekron, the Egyptians and Ethiopians will have time to meet them. Their armies could deliver a crushing blow or at least weaken the Assyrian forces. In such an event, we can fight on even ground with their remaining forces."

It was decided the army of Judah would remain to defend Lachish and Jerusalem. The king sent word to the Egyptian forces that the Assyrians' proximity made it unwise to leave their cities unprotected at this late time.

⋅⋅⋅

The forces defending Joppa held out three days against the Assyrians, giving the Egyptian and Ethiopian forces time to flood into Philistia.

⁙

King Hezekiah sent Judith and all his council members a message saying the Assyrians had engaged the Egyptian and Ethiopian armies and there would be no governing elders' council meeting until he received word regarding the outcome of the battle.

It was only a few days later when King Hezekiah called an urgent session. The grim expression on his face when he entered the council hall left little doubt as to the news.

"The Egyptian and Ethiopian armies were utterly annihilated at Eltekeh in Philistia, while the Assyrians forces suffered only minor losses. They have shown no weakness. General Holofernes is now marching toward Ekron." He looked around the council. "This is not the end of our world. We have new walls, thousands more people to fight and plenty of fresh water and food stores."

⁙

In less than ten days the Assyrians moved against Ekron. After a week, it was reported Ekron had not yet been taken, that hostilities continued, but then a message arrived from King Sennacherib himself.

Hezekiah read the note to the council. "Ekron has fallen. Jerusalem will be next. I will burn your fine city to ashes then I will campaign against the homelands of Egypt and Ethiopia for their part in the senseless rebellion. I will reclaim the empire given to my nation by Baal."

The elders jumped to their feet, all shouting at once. Judith sat still with her hands on her lap. King Hezekiah quieted everyone and regained control of the meeting. "I will send an emissary to King Sennacherib requesting he negotiate a new agreement."

⁘

After only a day, word arrived from the Assyrian king.

Once again King Hezekiah read King Sennacherib's response to the elders. "To spare Jerusalem and Lachish, I now demand tribute ten times greater than before."

Pandemonium broke out.

"Pay the tribute," came the cry from most. "Save the city."

But Judith banged her fist on the table. "No! No! No!"

King Hezekiah raised his arms. The room quieted.

Judith stood and faced the council. "King Sennacherib will never let us live. He will do to our beloved city as he did to Ekron. He hates us and our faith and will never leave until we are all dead." She brought her hands together in supplication. "Let us have faith in the LORD. He will save us."

The mortal fear in the room blocked all thought save paying the tribute. The shouting resumed and Judith sat.

*They are more willing to risk their lives on the word of an enemy king than to put their trust in our God*, thought Judith.

⁘

With the Assyrian monarch and his forces at Jerusalem's doorstep, King Hezekiah agreed with the elders. He sent word back to King Sennacherib the tribute would be paid. Accordingly, he ordered all the wealth of the city to be gathered up to pay the tribute. They collected eight hundred talents of silver and thirty talents of gold. Hezekiah added all the silver remaining in the house of the most-high LORD and in the treasures of the king himself. The gold from the doors of the Temple of the LORD and from the pillars of his palace was severed and added to the fortune. To show his sincerity, Hezekiah accompanied this treasure with bags of precious stones, vats of antimony, lovely palace women, musicians and singers, precious woods, couches inlaid with ivory and elephant hides. He even sent his two eldest daughters as part of the spoil. It was all transported to King Sennacherib. Hezekiah also released the former governor of Ekron, Padi, who had so pleased Sennacherib with his loyalty, and returned him to his people. It was truly a king's ransom paid to Sennacherib in exchange for the safety of Jerusalem and Lachish.

⁘

These negotiations occurred while the Assyrian army rested for seven days and mourned their dead after the furious battle at Ekron.

Holofernes went to Sennacherib, and the two watched as the parade of gifts arrived on pack mules.

He said, "We have taken forty-six communities of Judah. Only Jerusalem and Lachish remain. When do we march?"

King Sennacherib answered, "I promised to withdraw from these cities. I would keep my promise, but Baal will not forgive them for the insults they placed upon him before the entire world and all the generations to come." He looked in the direction of Jerusalem. "I will make them bow down to Baal and erect a mighty statue of him before I enslave the whole city and impale the rebellious leaders, starting at Lachish. We will divide the army. I will go to Lachish and destroy that place. You will lay siege on Jerusalem. Take Ahikar with you to deliver my message to them publicly in front of their walls in their own language. I will join you there after my work is done at Lachish."

General Holofernes and King Sennacherib spent a peaceful evening with Governor Padi consoling him after his terrible ordeal. Sennacherib promised to rebuild the city and seat Padi as governor of the entire territory, not just the city of Ekron and repopulate the region with newcomers.

⁘

Without the certainty that the Assyrians would withdraw, King Hezekiah continued defense preparations. He issued an order that affected all water sources within a day's travel of the city. "We will plug and block up all the old wells in the countryside to deprive the attacking armies of water."

181

Judith's mother gathered her valuables, and she and hundreds of field workers crowded through the gates of Jerusalem, fearing the worst. The people carried with them whatever they could salvage. Judith burned her fields, holding no trust in Sennacherib's promise. Other farmers followed her lead and set fire to their fields of grain, burning everything that might possibly benefit the enemy.

⁂

King Sennacherib's civilian guards escorted the tribute of King Hezekiah back to Nineveh. Governor Padi accompanied them for rest and recuperation. Sennacherib had not heard from Pharaoh Shabaka regarding ransom payment for the two captured princes. With no patience to wait further, he told the two young princes, "Your dear Pharaoh, who is little more than a slattern swine, will not pay the sum required to insure your return to Egypt. I will keep my promise not to kill or make you slaves. But neither can I give you freedom. You will reside in Nineveh, serving the noble women who might be well entertained by black men."

They, too, joined the party returning to Assyria's golden capital.

⁂

King Hezekiah asked the prophet Isaiah to take shelter in the city. The people of Judah needed their prophet among them during these trying times. Isaiah accepted and led his band of followers through the city gates.

⁂

Judith was in her palace quarters when an officer came to her. "King Hezekiah requests your presence at the new wall."

She put aside her evening meal and ran to mount the chariot waiting outside.

At the wall she climbed a ladder to one of the two tall towers where she joined several high-ranking officers, the King and the Queen. From that height, she looked out over the plain to what appeared to be a thin layer of dust above the horizon against the early evening sky.

A sound from far off in the distance carried on the wind, barely heard, weak and difficult to identify. Horns? Drums? As she listened, it grew louder, echoing off the faraway hills.

The cloud of dust hovered above the horizon, larger now. As both the sounds and cloud grew, Judith began to see tiny images of horses and men covering the entire distance along the western horizon, stretching to the northern horizon facing the city.

One of the officers cried out, "Almighty God, please stand by us in our hour of need."

Then there was silence as they watched a horde of soldiers, horses and war machines grow larger and larger. The singing of an Assyrian war cry reached their horrified ears. It continued as the Assyrians approached the walls of Jerusalem and set up camp just beyond the range of an arrow's flight.

⁘

*This is our beautiful land, so exquisitely formed and touched with the bold and delicate colors of flowers,* Judith thought. *Now it will become wounded and scarred. Decay approaches as a giant, treacherous serpent to swallow the beauty of these fields, then regurgitate it as waste.*

That evening the army's campfires dotted the landscape far off into the dark of night, as if an extension of the heavens. The flickering of the firelight looked so similar to the twinkling of the stars one could not tell where the stars ended and the fires began.

# THE AGONY
# OF RAMTOUSES

702 B.C.E.

T he two men packed their belongings. Since Lozato had moved his wife and children to Tungal, it took an extra day to prepare for the trip to Juba. Without a word to a single soul, Ramtouses and company quietly departed in the early morning hours of the third day after the second darkest day of Ramtouses's life.

Ramtouses wondered aloud to his brother. "What do you think they will say? Maybe they will throw stones at me for running out on Lizoka like I did."

Lozato did not know what lay ahead for them but he attempted to ease his brother's mind. "People have short memories of the mistakes their heroes make," he said.

That did little to lighten Ramtouses's worry.

⁘

The return took longer than the outbound journey due to traveling with Lozato's family. When they finally approached Juba territory, it was midday. They stopped to rest on a low hill overlooking their home village before going down to greet and face the people.

"Ah!" Ramtouses said. "It looks bigger than when we left." He felt no hurry to move, but they eventually started down.

A young village boy recognized him and yelled, "That's Ramtouses!" The boy's eyes grew large, and he jumped with excitement then turned and ran into the village. "Ramtouses is coming. Ramtouses is home!"

People came, first a few, then more, and in a short time it looked as if the entire village joined in a race up the hill to meet them. They shouted his name. Some called him, "Lion-slayer."

They danced around him, reaching out to touch him.

Tears filled his eyes. He lost the strength to stand and collapsed in their arms, so moved was he by their show of love.

Two of the village leaders raised him to their shoulders, carried him down the hill and around the village. The drums began to *talk,* and the news traveled everywhere, even so far as Tungal.

When the excitement subsided, and Lozato settled into his old hut with his wife and children, one of the elders came to them. "We are proud it was a son of our small village who saved Tungal from the killing monster lion when others failed at the task." He pointed to a nearby hut. "You can sleep there for as long as you need, Ramtouses. Tonight we sing and dance in your honor."

The announcement humbled Ramtouses and he started to give his version of the story when Lozato nudged him, thanking the elders for their kindness. Then, taking his brother by the arm, Lozato led him away.

"Do not spoil your people's happiness. You did kill the lion and saved many lives. That is what matters to them. You do not need to concern them with more than that."

⁘

The celebration brought happiness to the entire area. Many people came to Juba from nearby villages.

Ramtouses's second brother, Baako, who had participated with him in the same lion hunt, approached him when most of the eating, singing and dancing had ended.

"Ramtouses," he said. "I ask you to speak with Lizoka. I love this woman and took her as a second wife after you left.

It would gladden my heart to see you and Lizoka resolve the issues between you."

"I will speak with Lizoka," Ramtouses said. "It is reasonable you ask this of me for I did abandon her and I wish for no hard feelings. You are my brother, and I respect you. Can we meet yet tonight?"

And so they agreed to a meeting.

He stood. "Listen, everyone."

The crowd turned toward him.

"I am wonderfully surprised and happy. You have all shown me love. I feared you would be angry with me because of my sudden departure, but you have welcomed me back home. You have reminded me of the power of love, of family and home. I will never forget. Thank you. You are my people, whom I cherish."

He nodded and sat.

*

The moon was full as Ramtouses walked to the hut the villagers had selected for him. Lizoka walked toward him, swaying as she moved. He quickly saw the reason. Her swollen belly foretold the eminent birth of the child she carried. Ramtouses felt genuine joy for Lizoka and Baako. He moved the entrance cover aside as she entered then lit a small fire-torch near the open hut entrance. Through the opening, they could see the moon low in the eastern sky.

They sat quiet for a long, awkward moment. Ramtouses finally said, "I abandoned you. It was an unforgivable action, and I am sorry. My heart was full of confusion that morning."

He spoke of the dream that filled him with a force stronger than anything he had ever encountered but which still puzzled him. "It led to horrible disaster in my life. I do not return as a hero, Lizoka. As one who was blind and deaf, I pursued a love that never existed for me. I left Tungal rather than face the excruciating pain of embarrassment.

Lizoka's voice carried a gentleness that reminded him of his mother. "Many people, fathers, mothers and even children, live today because of your courage in facing the killer lion. You shall always be the hero of their village. You are my hero also and my first love. I will always love you. My husband knows this to be true, but his love is honest and his devotion to me deep." She smiled. "I carry his child, and I will never do anything to hurt him."

Lizoka offered his mother's land back but Ramtouses refused to take it. "I will clear some land for myself and build a farm. My brothers have already offered some animals to help."

"You plan to make your home here for always?"

"This is my home. It is where I will be."

They talked for a while longer. When Lizoka readied to leave, she wished him good fortune, put her arms around him and kissed him softly on the lips. "Goodbye, Ramtouses."

⁑

Ramtouses and Lozato learned their brother had died. They missed the burial rites by little more than one week. Both felt very bad about his death.

*Losing my dignity seemed so overwhelming,* thought Ramtouses. *I should remember others have difficulties as well, like my brother's wife and children who must now go on without him.*

Ancient tribal custom indicated that a widow became the wife of the next younger brother of her deceased husband. If the husband had no brother, the widow would live alone and help in the raising of orphans, just as the village widow woman raised Ramtouses after his mother died.

The family gathered to determine the widow's future. The brother next in line had no means to support a second wife so the next brother accepted the obligation.

The gathering gave the family an opportunity to welcome Lozato and Ramtouses back to their home.

❖

One morning soon after Ramtouses departed Tungal, Carnabrara awakened and stretched her arms. She said to her serving attendant, "Go out and bring in the fruit."

The young attendant hesitated then said, "You remember. He has not been seen in the village for quite a few days now."

Sitting up, Carnabrara remembered all that had happened. "Oh, yes."

She stood and walked to the doorway, looking out where Ramtouses always set the basket of fresh picked fruit. An odd, hollow feeling pulsed through her. She shook her head, smiled slightly then withdrew Unsure why she did so.

Princess Carnabrara sought her kindred sister Adzua. "How was he?" she asked.

Adzua turned away. Carnabrara grabbed her arm and repeated the question.

"Leave me. I never want to speak to you again."

Carnabrara insisted. "Tell me."

"Go away. You are evil!"

Carnabrara persisted. "I have to know. Tell me."

"You are disgusting, one deranged soul, like a rabid animal."

With those words, Carnabrara slapped Adzua's face.

Adzua wept. "I do not know what you want from me! He was a sweet and gentle man with a ferocious appetite for love. If I had him I would have never treated him as you did. I would have loved him forever." She looked Carnabrara straight in the eyes. A fierce anger seemed to rise in her. "Will I ever be free of this shame? I am so sorry I was a part of your treachery."

Carnabrara turned from her, disgusted, and dismissed her kindred sister with a wave of her hand.

She made her way back to her abode.

❖

From then on, wherever Princess Carnabrara went in the village, she commented to anyone who would listen, "Yes. It was I who got rid of Ramtouses. He was a thorn in my foot that I had to extract, as my brother might say."

People asked her, "Why did you do such a thing?"

They spoke well of him, with respect and sincerity.

"Ramtouses, he was a good man."

"Ramtouses was always ready to help me."

"I miss Ramtouses."

She did not enjoy hearing their comments.

Her father, King Tasmeria, summoned her. "What did you do that persuaded him to leave?"

Carnabrara only remarked, "This is my secret, and I will tell no one."

Her father shook his head. "Ramtouses is a remarkable young man. I have come to love him as my own son."

Carnabrara flipped her hand in the air and walked away.

A few days later Urentu said, "I understand it was you who caused him to leave. I think you and I are the only ones glad he is gone."

Carnabrara nodded, relieved when he changed the subject.

"I saw you with our kindred sister Adzua recently. I have looked upon her with favor. When you saw her, did you speak of me? I have thought her interests would lie in a man with no wives. I have two wives already."

Carnabrara confidently answered, "Yes, I talked to her about you," she pinched his cheek and smiled, "and to the contrary, she is most interested. In truth, she wishes you to call on her."

Carnabrara walked away, then turned back. "It would be well if you told her it was I who suggested you to go to her."

⁘

Sleep eluded Carnabrara most nights. She began having dreams that interrupted her precious few hours of rest but which she could not remember when daylight finally arrived.

She embarrassed herself at a new moon celebration dancing shamefully at the ceremony, causing the king to end the activities. The drums were silenced. All stopped dancing. All, that is, save Princess Carnabrara. She kept pulling at the tribesmen to continue dancing, but no one would respond.

Eventually, she turned and ran to her hut, threw herself on her sleeping pallet and began to sob. Her attendants asked if they could help, only to be ordered, "Get out! And let no one in here."

Carnabrara wept until she finally went to sleep.

That night she had a horrible nightmare. She and Adzua both lay in bed with Ramtouses. He climbed on top of her, kissing her, but then Adzua pulled him to her. He kissed Adzua. Carnabrara angrily pulled him back. And so it went, this fitful wrenching of the man, until Carnabrara pulled Ramtouses to herself and, in a fit of anger, punched Adzua in the face. "I will mutilate you! I will tear off your face and no man will want you!"

She and Adzua fought, until they rolled out of bed. Carnabrara woke up hitting, scratching and screaming. She lay on the floor of her hut, feeling sore, disconcerted and fully awake.

Tormented, she called aloud to him. "Ramtouses, what have I done? I am so sorry. I am so sorry for what I have done. Please come back. Please forgive me. Oh, please."

⁕

Morning came and the two attendants debated the safety of entering the hut. They heard her speaking, and one peered inside her sleeping space. Seeing Princess Carnabrara covered with scratches and bleeding, she hurried to inform the king.

⁕

Carnabrara's body hurt all over. Shame and sorrow lay on her like heavy rocks, leaving her exhausted. She rolled up next to the bed.

King Tasmeria entered her hut and asked her to come to him. She moved slowly toward her father.

Even her speech was faint and slow. "The charade is over. I am fooling no one. The truth is I love Ramtouses." She laid her head on her father's shoulder. "Father, I had a nightmare, a reflection of how I hate myself for what I have done."

The king sent the attending girls to go fetch the tribal healers. When the healers came, Carnabrara moved onto the pallet to allow them to treat her wounds.

She turned to the king. "Father, I beg you to organize a convoy to escort me to Juba. I must go and search for him. I will wither without the love of Ramtouses to make me whole. "

⁕

Early that evening she worked with her attendants to prepare for the journey. She moved without vigor. Her emotions remained sorrowful, and shame clung to her spirit.

On the second morning after her most recent nightmare the caravan began its journey to Juba. Princess Carnabrara's family came out to wish her farewell.

King Tasmeria wished his daughter a successful journey. "You are the jewel of my life. There is nothing I place above you in my heart. Please come back to me safely with your aspirations fulfilled."

She was still waving as the village disappeared behind her caravan. The trip was uneventful and progressed so smoothly they neared Juba territory in thirty days.

Only Carnabrara could hear the throb of her heart as they approached Juba. Several senior warriors came to greet them. She expressed the desire to see Ramtouses and was escorted to their village.

⁕

One of the warriors called to Lozato.

When he turned and saw Princess Carnabrara with the traveling group, he reacted with great surprise welcomed her with a big embrace.

Carnabrara did not seem to know what to say to him. "I can think of nothing but my great need to see Ramtouses. Please, will you take me to him?"

"Yes," Lozato answered. "I will, happily."

She left her caravan behind and walked with Lozato.

As they walked, she asked, "Do you think he will still want me?" Before he could answer, she said, "I don't care. He will have to kill me to keep me away. I would rather die by his hand than live without him."

Lozato stared at her, astonished. He shook his head. *If I had not heard this from her mouth, I would never have believed it.*

Ramtouses was not at his farm or at any of his several favorite forest locations Lozato knew about. They spent most of the day looking for him. Lozato decided they should wait at his abode, but then remembered one more spot Ramtouses had once mentioned. "Hippopotami! He spoke to me of a place where hippopotami had to defend themselves against crocodiles in their water space."

Still, they did not see him there. Lozato was about to call out when they spotted him sitting on a low cliff, overlooking the river below. He did not see them yet, but Princess Carnabrara screamed, "Ramtouses!" and broke into a run.

Lozato stared after her. It was as if she found new energy deep within.

❖

Ramtouses climbed to his feet but said nothing. He never looked away as she scrambled up the slope then ran to him, still screaming his name.

When she reached where he stood, she punched his chest with her fists, over and over. He caught hold of her arms.

She wept loudly.

"Why have you done this to me? I love you. I love you! Ramtouses, please forgive me." She freed her hands, wrapped her arms around his waist and held him. Then she slowly slid down to her knees with her arms around his legs.

Ramtouses still said nothing. He knew her pain but no words could describe it or even speak to it. Love hurt deeply.

Her cries continued. "Do with me whatever you want. I will never leave you." Tears covered her face. She trembled all over and pressed the side of her head against his thighs. The weeping persisted.

⁕

Lozato watched their silhouettes come together against the red evening sky. He turned and walked away, feeling relieved. The pain within the two of them had come to fruition, and now they would finally be one.

⁕

Ramtouses bent and pried Carnabrara from his legs. He lifted her and carried her away in his arms. Still, he said nothing. She put her arms around his neck and laid her head against his chest. The loud cries subsided into soft whimpers as he carried her.

"I am here with you, my love. There is nothing to forgive." He kissed the tears on her cheeks.

She turned her face toward him and looked into his eyes. "I love you, Ramtouses. I will love you for all eternity."

He carried her to his hut. The rest of the evening and into the next morning, they never left it.

⁕

Eventually, he came out to tend the animals and fetch fresh water for Carnabrara. A little later, he came out again, started a fire, boiled some eggs, gathered fresh fruit and milked the goat.

Lozato's young son walked over in the afternoon hours to inform them that Ramtouses's brothers and sisters planned to meet at Lozato's abode to greet Carnabrara. Ramtouses agreed

193

and disappeared once more into his hut until early evening when they both came out to go and meet Ramtouses's siblings.

Word came the village elders planned a feast the next day in honor of the guests from the land of Tungul. It was their wish to meet Princess Carnabrara.

In the morning, at Carnabrara's suggestion, Ramtouses brought her serving attendants and the rest of Carnabrara's things to his abode. She chose to wear her formal clothing. The drums had broadcast their arrival, and leaders from nearby villages came to join the gathering, eager and delighted to see this princess from the great kingdom of Tungul. None had ever ventured as far away as Tungul and they came out of high curiosity.

⁘

No one in the village could take their eyes from the Princess. She was different from any woman they had ever seen and had an exotic appeal. No woman in Juba grew her hair to such a length, almost to her waist. She wore no ornaments or decorations, no rings or piercings, and her smooth skin bore no markings. Her breasts pointed straight out, large but not overly so for her body shape. She had a beautiful face with large eyes and full lips. Her long neck rose perfectly between straight shoulders. She stood tall, with a small waist and long, shapely legs.

Carnabrara's loose fitting dress was the color of berry juice, falling to just above her ankles. Though not transparent, it was lightweight and thin. When the wind blew it against her, the full outline of her body was discernible.

The village leaders and elders invited Carnabrara and Ramtouses to sit with them. Excitement glowed on every face. Many people asked her questions about her family and the nation of Tungul. Ramtouses felt extremely proud of Carnabrara. The people of Juba and the visitors from neighboring villages bowed down to her throughout the evening. After the dinner the talk continued with Carnabrara and the village elders. The many questions seemed to have no end and after quite some time Ramtouses moved her over to where many of the village women waited to meet her.

A large crowd had gathered and only a few at a time could get near her. They all seemed to want to touch her hair and skin and talk with her. She stayed late into the evening. Carnabrara was gracious and receptive to them all, giving them the attention they wanted. She did not rush her conversations with them and accepted the flattery and fawning over her hair and skin with grace.

Eventually, Ramtouses led her away and back to his farm.

For two weeks he escorted her everywhere as visitors from nearby communities continued to come to see her. She had not sojourned on a diplomatic adventure, yet she turned no one away. For the first time in her life, she felt like a royal princess.

⁙

Ramtouses informed the village that he and Princess Carnabrara, along with his brother Lozato and his family, would soon move back to Tungal. The one person among all the villagers who had not met Carnabrara was Lizoka, and she wanted a face-to-face meeting.

They reached Lizoka's hut and Princess Carnabrara called out first, asking if she might enter. Ramtouses opened the door covering for the Princess to enter, and then he waited outside alone.

*At least there is no shouting*, he thought.

In fact, the two women, who each loved Ramtouses, oohed and aahed over Lizoka's baby. They recognized each other's love for this man called "Lion Killer," and they talked of the roles they played in his life.

When Carnabrara returned to Ramtouses, she threw her arms around his neck. "What power brought you to me I do not know, but I am forever grateful for its influence on you. After seeing and meeting all these wonderful people who care so much for you, I know you are the love of my life."

⁘

The traveling party started across the open fields. Nearly the whole village came to see them off.

*This is a lovely village*, Carnabrara thought. *It is the people who make it so lovely.*

She turned to Ramtouses. "Until I visited Juba I really did not understand the meaning of nobility and the distinguishing role of a princess," she said. "It is so much more than just being the daughter of a king."

⁘

As they approached the Tungal villages, King Tasmeria received word of their coming and hurried out with the villagers to meet them.

After greeting them all, the king said to Ramtouses, "You see, it is not that easy to keep Tungal out of your mouth after you have smelled the aroma. She is like a delicious food."

Ramtouses agreed.

Tasmeria hugged and kissed his daughter. "Oh my child, I love you so much. At last, you two are together. Now my heart will be at ease."

He restrained the villagers from gathering around Ramtouses and Princess Carnabrara this first day back in Tungal. The villagers had cared for their living spaces in their absence, and they retired there to rest and prepare for the private family gathering that evening. The two were separated for the first time since their reunion.

Escorts came for Ramtouses, Lozato and his family. It was not a big celebration, just a happy social mingling of the two families. The king's finest livestock became a wonderful meal.

⁘

Ramtouses and Carnabrara agreed to wed on the third new moon. When Ramtouses had left his farm to return to Juba, the elders held his land on orders from the king. Now, he negotiated the cost of the care and upkeep, and accrued more land befitting a man of his new stature. He also increased his involvement with the tribesmen of his age group.

Carnabrara filled her days with preparations for the coming ceremony. After the announcement of their pending marriage, hundreds of young virgins chased after Princess Carnabrara hoping to be selected as a member of her reed dance festivities.

The reed dance would begin seven days before the wedding and continue until the night of the new moon and the marriage. It was performed by young virgins who might be picked for marriage during the same ceremony. This ancient ritual was how the people of Tungul paired their young people, unlike the people of Juba.

Virgins chosen for the reed dance ceremony were required to locate and harvest grass reeds growing wild in swamps or marshes. Reeds grown domestically cannot be used.

As the highest ranked woman to be married at the selected new moon, Princess Carnabrara was queen of the ceremony. It was her honor to select the girls for the dance. She took the task to heart, considering every young girl who came before her. Hopeful girls constantly surrounded her, and Ramtouses could not be with her as he wished.

The virgins selected for the ceremony were stamped with a dot of yellow dye on the inside of their wrist. Their virginity would be verified the day of the festivities to ensure the purity of the ritual.

⁑

Princess Carnabrara raced to Ramtouses. She was overjoyed!

"I have learned of an elderly woman who can lead me to golden reeds, the most prized. We know of them, but no one in our village has ever seen them. They guarantee longevity and a fruitful life of happiness. They are giants, well over three times the height of a man."

Ramtouses answered. "We have been here only seven days. Are we planning on leaving right away?"

"No, my love, you cannot go. It would bring ill fortune. The ritual would be tainted. Don't worry. I will leave seven days before the next new moon. That will give me twenty-eight days to find them and return in time. I love you, Ramtouses. There is nothing that will keep me from you. Some of my father's finest warriors will escort us."

She threw her arms around him.

⁂

Ramtouses cherished each day with her and secretly dreaded the time she would be away searching for the golden reeds. *Four weeks will pass slowly without her,* he thought.

The King came to Ramtouses a few days before the reed search party planned to leave.

"Ramtouses, I know you do not want Carnabrara to leave. Let me ease your mind. She has in her company nearly one hundred young girls and she will be responsible for them. These young virgins come from many different villages near here. I will send seventy of my best warriors with them. Do not worry for their safety."

⁂

The day the party of reed hunters broke camp, Ramtouses came to the elder woman who knew of the reed location and asked, "How is it you are the only one who knows of these reeds?" He looked her in the eyes. "Can you be sure where to find them?"

"I have not seen them myself. People from a village near my village have said at different times they saw them. Their tribe does not perform this ritual so they do not seek them, only talk of seeing them. When I heard from the drums about

198

the princess' wedding plans, I thought she would like to know about the golden reeds. Her people believe in this tradition of the reeds."

Carnabrara walked up at that moment and began to cry. The old woman smiled then turned away.

"I am so sorry to leave you, Ramtouses." She buried her face in his chest then raised her head and kissed him all over his neck and face. "Nothing, nothing will ever diminish our love, I will love you forever."

⁂

As the convoy departed, Ramtouses stood beside King Tasmeria. Both were quiet and downcast.

The group ferried across the Nile and slowly disappeared in the distance.

"Why are these reeds so important? Why would they travel so far to bring them here?" Ramtouses spoke so quietly that the king had to turn and look at him. The young man looked forlorn and the king saw his own feelings reflected in Ramtouses' gloomy expression.

He said, "The golden reeds symbolize the power that is vested in nature. They reflect a deep spiritual connection with nature. The elders have told the story through the multitude of generations of our original ancestor who emerged from a bed of golden reeds, mated with the native virgin girls he found dancing in the wild, and created humankind."

Ramtouses said, "That explains some of the mystery. Still, why is it I am feeling so lonely? I have never felt like this before."

⁂

After five days the convoy came to the elderly woman's village where they were told the village nearest to the reed sightings was another ten miles north in the country of Ethiopia.

They camped for the night and journeyed on in the morning.

The people in the small Ethiopian village looked like them but dressed in different styles of clothing and spoke a slightly different dialect.

Carnabrara inquired as to the reeds, announcing herself as Princess of Tungul. The villagers said golden reeds could be found in a swampy marsh about a day's walk north. The villagers were honored. Not every day did a princess visit and they joyously broadcast her arrival throughout the country.

Several tribesmen agreed to guide them into the unfamiliar swamps.

Their search for the reeds began early the next morning. Due to heat, humidity, bugs and swampy grounds, each day was an agonizing adventure. They searched four days without success.

On the fifth morning, one of the guides yelled, "Look!"

He jumped excitedly and pointed toward some tall grasses growing in the swampy area far to his right. "Are those the reeds we're looking for?"

The older woman came forward, looked and shouted, "Princess Carnabrara, there they are."

Carnabrara ran to see the rare golden reeds she had only heard about in the tribal stories. They stood tall, some even taller than the swamp trees. The sun angled down on the reeds, making them appear a brilliant gold.

A soft breeze blew just strongly enough to keep the reeds waving gracefully back and forth. "They are beautiful." She spoke softly. The gentle flowing movement mesmerized Carnabrara.

Princess Carnabrara was thrilled they had finally found the precious golden reeds. Tears filled her eyes and trickled down her cheeks.

"Now I understand why the golden reeds are sacred," she said.

⁙

Excitement riddled the air as the young women waded through the watery marsh toward the golden reeds. The men were not allowed to even come near the plants. They retreated back away while the girls went to work cutting the long reed stalks.

Princess Carnabrara stood beside the elderly woman as each girl cut down one plant from the thick wall of reeds. Then the girls cut their reeds into four or five sections.

The virgins rubbed the sap that ran out all over their bodies and onto their tongues to taste and swallow. They kept to themselves, as if quarantined. If someone touched a virgin's reed, the spell was broken, and she could not continue in the ritual. They sang a tribal song of happiness as they made their way back to the Ethiopian village.

**Giant golden reeds**

A number of days earlier, in Egypt, evil and fear filled the air. The Egyptians and Ethiopians were terrified of being overrun by the Assyrian army in the wake of Judah's anticipated destruction.

Pharaoh Shabaka spent many hours analyzing the situation. He could think of no way to combat the Assyrians as he paced the palace floors. *We need allies,* he thought, *but who is there around us willing to fight and die with us?*

He considered the large population of Africans surrounding Egypt. Could they be recruited? What argument could he use to entice his cousins, the Nubian tribes to the south and west, to join in the battle against Assyria?

*Only a strong motivation would convince them to fight. If the people of Tungul will muster an army of mercenaries to aid Egypt during her hour of need, there is a possibility we could prevail.*

He convened a meeting with his trusted leaders of the Royal Guard who came prepared to report all recent activities involving their African neighbors.

At the meeting, officer after officer spoke of trade activities, hunting parties, minor skirmishes between neighboring tribes but nothing of use to the pharaoh. He began to feel desperate.

A message had arrived from King Sennacherib demanding a grand ransom for his two princes. He read the note to the officers at the meeting then said, "If we paid this ransom, we leave ourselves at the mercy of the marching Assyrians. This is a matter of saving our nation. Our two princes must be sacrificed in order to build a new army as fast as we can."

It was a difficult decision to make but everyone knew their Pharaoh had no other alternative. He did what had to be done.

He ended the meeting instructing all to return the following afternoon to resume the discussion of a handsome remuneration to mercenaries joining Egypt's forces. Before the room emptied, a young officer recently returned from duty in Ethiopia spoke up.

"This may mean little, but it is news from the area south of Egypt. A drum message told of a princess from Tungul traveling in the western regions of Ethiopia in search of golden reeds for her wedding ceremony."

Pharaoh Shabaka thanked the young officer as the words *Princess of Tungul in Ethiopia* echoed through his mind. An idea began to grow, and the more he considered it, the more it appeared to be the only way to gain an ally.

*Could this be the motivating factor I need to enlist them as mercenaries? They place high value on their children—as they should,* he thought.

He knew of the traditional reed ceremony. He also knew of the deep-rooted dread of the malevolent Ell, two beliefs profoundly embedded in the culture of Tungul. The reeds and the fearsome Ell, the solution to his dilemma looked more and more promising.

⊹

The first phase of the plan required a third of his royal guard to head for Ethiopia and locate the Tungul party searching for the golden reeds. The Royal Guard comprised an army of warriors sworn to protect the capital city of Thebes with their lives. They received their orders from no one save the pharaoh.

Seven thousand warriors sped on horseback to the small village where they thought the princess might be camped. The timing of this mission was critical. They had to reach the Tungul Princess and her party before they returned home. Upon arrival at the village, they discovered the princess and her party found the reeds, spent the night and departed on their return trip home that very day. They had a half-day start on the Egyptians who were confident the distance could easily be made up.

The success of their mission depended upon secrecy. To ensure no one would reveal the Egyptian presence in the area, they slaughtered everyone in the village.

⊹

Princess Carnabrara and her party traveled slowly. The Egyptians found them well before the setting of the sun. By morning the Royal Egyptian guard had them surrounded and fighting broke out.

After an intense and bloody battle, all seventy of the Tungul warriors were dead. Not one tribesman was left to tell what happened. The elder woman who had led them to the reeds also met her death. The young virgins were held as prisoners and spared execution. Pharaoh Shabaka ordered none of the young virgins were to be abused in any way. The entire group was to be brought back to Thebes unharmed. This directive made it especially clear that Princess Carnabrara be respected and treated as royalty.

Carnabrara's intense desire to escape made it difficult to contain her. At every possible opportunity she desperately attempted to flee her captors. She shouted continuous obscenities and threats at the Egyptian soldiers.

"What do you think you are doing? My father will kill you all! Let me go, you murderers. I curse you all. Let my girls go."

The Egyptians provided fresh garments to the virgins. When they tried to disrobe Carnabrara and dress her in royal Egyptian garments, she snatched a knife off one Royal guard and stabbed him to death. It took three attempts to successfully redress her.

She asked to be allowed privacy to urinate and stabbed one of the escorting guards in the throat with a tree branch. When she convinced the leaders to allow the women to bathe in a nearby river, she lured a guard into the water and hit him on the head with a rock. Struck unconscious, he drowned. A number of other incidents when she attempted to win her freedom also failed, but Princess Carnabrara inflicted a lot of damage on her captors.

Because of Pharaoh's directive, the guards could not fight back, but after she killed or seriously wounded several guards, it was clear the order could not be met. They restrained her with shackles and set her on a horse. They told her the horse would bite off her face if she jumped from his back.

Carnabrara had never ridden a horse and knew nothing of their nature. She made no serious escape attempts for the rest of the journey to Thebes.

∘⋅∘

The second phase of Pharaoh Shabaka's deception required two of his most trusted officers, Baduga and the Ethiopian, Taharga, to lead two hundred of the Royal Guard detachment to Tungul while the others returned with their captives to Egypt. Baduga and Taharga were both highly skilled scouts. They knew the territory of Tungul well and were loyal to their Pharaoh.

After the slaughter of the Tungul warriors, they smeared the clothing of Princess Carnabrara, the virgins, and the warriors with the blood of the slain warriors. They took the clothing along with some of the golden reeds with them.

Pharaoh Shabaka charged the two officers tell a tale of evil, a gruesome tale of how the people from Ell had struck down thousands of Egyptians and Ethiopians and the entire golden reed search party. The Ell ravished all the lands of the north. They raped, mutilated and killed everyone in sight. It had to be a tale of horror.

To support the lie, Pharaoh Shabaka cut out the tongues and put out the eyes of two Assyrian spies captured before the battle at Eltekeh. They were sent with Baduga and Taharga to prove their tale true.

Baduga and Taharga's story must be convincing, one that would inflame the Tungul soul to the very core, leaving no doubt that they would be motivated into mobilizing a massive mercenary force to join Egypt in her fight against the fiendish Ell. But in reality, they would fight the Assyrians.

∘⋅∘

Baduga, Taharga, and the Egyptian Royal Guards neared the town of Tungal. The closer they drew, the more senior

205

warriors appeared. Before they reached the village, a large number of warriors stopped them.

Baduga asked to speak to the King of the Tungul nation regarding the golden reed seekers. A messenger was sent to King Tasmeria.

The drums began to beat, and soon everyone in the area knew strangers had come to their villages. The two scouts, Baduga and Taharga, were brought to the main village of Tungal while the rest of the travelers remained guarded by the Tungal warriors.

King Tasmeria hurried to meet them. Ramtouses also heard the drums and rushed with hundreds of other villagers to learn what information these strangers had concerning their loved ones traveling in the golden reed convoy.

When the king reached them, he called out, "Where is the princess?"

Ramtouses burst upon them. "Where is Princess Carnabrara?" He charged the two men and had to be restrained.

King Tasmeria asked again, "Where are my Tungul children?"

Baduga turned and pointed to the north. "The sons of Ell have materialized as humans. A wave of them came from the north without warning. They raped, devoured and killed thousands of my Egyptian people."

The Ethiopian, Taharga, spoke up. "And thousands of my people also.

"While burying our dead, we discovered the bodies of your people who were caught up in this tragedy. They were partially devoured and mutilated so badly we could not carry them back to you. One female had very long hair. We suspect she was your princess."

Ramtouses screamed. "I do not believe you. It cannot be true. I will kill you both with my bare hands."

The warriors had to continually restrain Ramtouses.

Baduga and Taharga signaled for the mules to be brought forward with the bloody clothes bundled on their backs. They opened the bundles for the Tungal people to see.

Carnabrara's clothing was among the many bloody articles. Ramtouses saw them and knew they belonged to his beloved Carnabrara. He grabbed her garment, wrapped it in his arms, and wept. He fell to his knees, rocking back and forth. A moan was born from deep in his soul, the torment of which silenced all sound around him.

"Why did I let this happen?" He looked up at the messengers. "How can I know it was the sons of Ell? No one has ever seen them. It could have been anyone, even you."

Baduga spoke again. "I have brought proof. As the Ell fled back to the north in disorderly haste, these two got separated from their party and we captured them."

He ordered the two hooded prisoners brought forward and removed the hoods. When the people of Tungal saw them, their eyes grew large. They tried to get closer but were held back by the senior warriors. They groaned in disbelief and amazement. Ramtouses himself could not process what he saw and heard. Bewildered and confused, his mind shutdown. He was beyond words.

King Tasmeria walked up to the prisoners and touched their skin. He pulled at the long hair on their heads and chins. The people of Tungal had never seen beings with such pale skin and straight, stringy hair with long beards.

"The Ell will surely return to overrun Egypt and Ethiopia and venture south to your homeland. They kill as they go. Alone we cannot possibly destroy them. If you join with us, together we have a chance." Baduga's voice was strong and could be heard far out into the crowd.

Taharga spoke. "The Ell have established a kingdom on earth that threatens all our existence. They must be stopped."

Ramtouses regained control and walked slowly over to the prisoners. His face was covered in tears. Carnabrara's clothing was still clutched in his arms. He studied them from head to foot.

Ramtouses's loss reflected in his voice as he spoke in a low tone, slowly and without inflection. The total lack of nuance gave his words more depth than any shouting or gesturing or show of emotion might convey.

"I could easily kill these two but that would not bring back my dearest Carnabrara. She has been violently ripped from my heart for the rest of my earthly life."

He handed the bloody garments to King Tasmeria and ran off toward the forest.

The king watched the young man disappear in the crowd then he turned and spoke to the villagers.

"Take the garments of your family member, if you recognize them. We will have a ceremony to bury these items tomorrow. There will be a two-day mourning period in honor of our lost family members then we will consider what should be done to those who wrought these terrible acts against our people."

He sent the strangers to a bivouac area near the villages. The drums announced the horrible deeds throughout the land. Tungul's sorrow echoed in every rumble and boom of the drums. All day and late into the night, news of the tragedy spread throughout the land.

When King Tasmeria finally returned to his hut, grief overcame him, and he wept without restraint.

# BUILDING AN ARMY

702 B.C.E.

amtouses walked for hours. As he regained control of his emotions and thoughts he wiped away tears then he wept again. His feet moved without direction. Once enthralled by the signs of life all around, he now felt a keen disconnection walking—as if he had no substance, as if he were invisible.

Without his love, without her, there was no him.

At some point he stopped walking. A small creek provided refuge, a place apart from the activities of life in the woods. He slid down against a large boulder and sat quietly, listening to the steady flow of water over and through the rocks and pebbles. The unending rhythm soothed his aching soul and eased his damaged heart.

A new sound interrupted the peaceful water harmony. Irritated by the disruption of his solitude, he rose to investigate. He recognized the slurps and mews of young cubs with their mother. He dared not move closer. Cats protected their territory and young from all outsiders with a fierce determination.

He returned to his boulder and sat again, the sharp pain of his loss returned. He pondered his position in life without Carnabrara. *What remains for me now?*

Later that evening, the mother leopard left her cubs to hunt for food. As she disappeared into the night, Ramtouses became aware of sounds of distress coming from the den. He rose and moved closer. A large asp was attacking the young cubs. He ran toward the den, picking up a fallen tree branch along the way. It could be used to chase away the snake. By the time he reached the den the reptile had left, but not before killing the kittens and possibly devouring a few. He quickly turned and left.

Moments later he heard the mother leopard crash through the foliage somehow alerted to the danger. It was, of course, too late. When she smelled and pawed the cubs and knew for certain they were gone, she curled up, pulled her legs and feet close to her body, and began to mewl loudly.

Ramtouses knew her agony well. His own wailing was internal. Soon the mother leopard started to hiss and growl. She got up and began to sniff the ground until she appeared to pick out the scent of the villain. She padded silently, following the trail.

Ramtouses heard her snuffles then watched her movements against the varying shades of night. He trailed her. The leopard came upon the murderous reptile and sprang upon it. The asp fought for its life, but in the end the large cat tore it apart.

Her victory lasted only a short while. The snake had struck her several times. She went down within minutes and began a slow death. Ramtouses had no fear of the dying leopard. He sat beside her and stroked her head as she died.

*She has no purpose anymore,* thought Ramtouses. *She has satisfied her desire for revenge upon the one that destroyed her family.*

He no longer wept tears of sorrow. His emotions turned to anger and hatred as he thought of this female leopard that gave her life in retaliation against an enemy that meant certain death.

Ramtouses stayed with the leopard that night. Upon awakening in the morning he felt a sense of purpose as strong as when he first experienced that fateful dream so many moons past.

*I must return to Tungal.*

With each step a change occurred in his mind and body, a metamorphosis that hardened and strengthened him. He strode from the woods and crossed the fields leading into the village. He felt it surge through him, from him, not transforming him so much as making him more, more than the kind and loving person Carnabrara had known.

The new Ramtouses grew rigid with a potent rage, a warrior bent on retaliation.

He returned to his hut and prepared himself for the burial of his beloved.

He stood beside King Tasmeria when they placed Princess Carnabrara's clothing in the ground at the royal family's gravesite.

The drums continued a loud angry beat sending their message all across the Northern territories.

⁘

King Tasmeria held a meeting to determine what could be done to counter this brutal massacre of their people.

Baduga spoke first. "The progeny of Ell live far to the north. They find our blood delicious, sex with our women satisfying. Their goal is to kill us all and deliver our souls to their father in Ell to be tormented forever."

The Ethiopian officer added, "We must fight them in the north before they re-mobilize and charge down upon us again, when we are not aware of their coming."

"It will take months to gather a large army, train and march them to the far north," Tasmeria said. "I am leaving the entire enterprise to my new military chief and authority, Ramtouses."

None of the king's sons objected to their father's choice. They wanted revenge and believed Ramtouses was the best choice to lead men in battle. His name would stimulate recruitment of fighters since the deeds of Ramtouses were known throughout the land.

Baduga said, "It could be months before they strike again, but if we sit back and do nothing we will be at their mercy when they come."

"King Tasmeria, Pharaoh Shabaka is gathering a massive army to repel the blood-craving Ell. He requests you send mercenaries and he promises you will be handsomely compensated if you join the excursion under the Egyptian command."

Ramtouses heard enough. "I will raise an army myself and lead them to the homeland of the murderers. They will be slaughtered as they slaughtered our innocent loved ones. We will not be in service as mercenaries for Pharaoh Shabaka. The pharaoh fights for Egypt, we will fight for revenge, for the anguish they caused us to suffer and to prevent further malevolent crimes at our expense."

When the meeting ended, Ramtouses and King Tasmeria discussed where the army would live and train. The king arranged to have a huge field cleared of trees on the far side of the Nile across from the Tungal community. Meanwhile, Ramtouses had the drums deliver a message that King Tasmeria demanded all able young tribesmen of Tungul make themselves ready for war and be accounted for at Tungal to avenge the crimes against their people. Thousands answered the call.

When the fighting men of Tungul and surrounding areas gathered, Baduga and Taharga warned more men were needed to assure victory. Ramtouses knew of the drought stricken areas and decided many thousands more might join their crusade against the Ell if offered futher encouragement. So the drums gave voice to a second message and sent it throughout the entire territory, offering food and livestock to those farther away in drought stricken areas. It asked brave warriors to come forth and be recruited in Ramtouses's crusade against the killers from Ell.

The drums pounded the new message long into the night and started up early in the morning, day after day. The response was great and Ramtouses assembled a large army. So great, that King Tasmeria had to clear more forest for use as bivouac and training grounds.

Tasmeria felt concerned that the gift of grain and livestock might not be a viable promise. All the men would not survive. Some would perish in the march to the battle site and even more would be killed in the battle.

*It is a harsh reality*, the king thought, *but it will still be an enormous obligation. Will I alone be able to compensate them all?*

Ramtouses was aware King Tasmeria had realized the financial extent of the undertaking to feed, shelter, clothe and equip the army now amassed and which would continue to grow. In addition, he had to make true on the promise of food and farm animals as a reward. Seeing the worry on Tasmeria's face, Ramtouses was compelled to offer encouragement.

In a quiet voice he said, "A man who is pure at heart stands as a giant among egocentrics. Better to lose all your wealth on earth than to walk the length of a lifetime with a shattered heart."

With compassion, the king answered Ramtouses, "Oh, my son, how greatly you loved my daughter!"

⁙

The fighting men who came trusted the word of Ramtouses and believed in the promise of food and livestock. The officers from Egypt and Ethiopia expressed their astonishment at the crowds of would-be warriors coming into Tungal. Although Ramtouses had stated his purpose to lead his own army, the emissaries from the pharaoh were convinced their military prowess was greater than his. They went to Ramtouses and asked if they could lead his men in battle.

Ramtouses rejected the idea. "These men will not follow people they do not know or have faith in. However, I will consider you and your men to serve as scouts, military advisers and organizers for our army."

The Egyptians and Ethiopians accepted his offer without further debate.

Ramtouses said, "I seek nothing for my efforts in fighting the Ell. I only want vengeance for the slash ripped across my heart forever and the satisfaction of freeing the earth of these evil beings. But King Tasmeria has the burden of financing the entire operation himself. It is fitting Egypt share in this responsibility. Please see to it that the mercenary fees come to King Tasmeria so he can distribute the payment among the fighting warriors' families."

Baduga composed a list of items to be included in the payment. He sent this information with the attachment of military personnel returning to his homeland. Baduga told King Tasmeria all these supplies and gifts would arrive before any man left for battle.

Tasmeria placed his arm around Ramtouses shoulders. "You are more than a son to me. There is never an immoral word uttered from your lips. As for Pharaoh Shabaka, he is an honest man as long as there is something for him to gain. I know him well and believe he will hold true to his offer to support us in our critical hour."

※

Ramtouses contemplated the huge task ahead, considering every phase of the coming war effort.

*When we go to war with the Ell, we need to understand all there is to know about them. I need more information.*

He asked the two officers, Baduga and Taharga, to give him a detailed description of all they knew concerning the Ell method of fighting. They explained to Ramtouses what to expect from these murderers, and Ramtouses listened intently. Even with all the men he had recruited, the situation looked grim. The outcome could depend heavily on the size of the Ell forces. The pharaoh's officers expected the worst, fearing the tribal warriors would face a massive, well-trained and fully equipped Ell army.

After much thought, Ramtouses revealed his plan to counter any advantage the Ell might have. He meant to outwit the enemy. He planned to reverse everything the Ell knew about war and surprise them with elements of fighting unlike any they ever faced.

All he learned from the time he studied life in the forest, he remembered, and he believed some of those strategies might work on the battlefields, especially if the enemy was caught by surprise.

The two officers were skeptical such untried tactics could be successfully implemented against the mighty world-class army they soon would face.

But though Baduga and Taharga expressed doubt, they admitted they also felt some optimism, a ray of hope that grew brighter as Ramtouses told them more.

Baduga and Taharga told Ramtouses the Ell performed their savagery and brutality in daylight. Lions held an advantage over their prey when they hunted and attacked at night. Right away Ramtouses began training his men at night and had them sleep during the day to acclimate them to nighttime activities. Forty nights of this training should sufficiently hone their night-fighting skills.

He devised a way to employ sounds to intimidate the enemy. Certain species of birds made annoying sounds to irritate their would-be rivals for food. Families or groups of monkeys screamed in high voices to annoy large cats that stalked them as prey.

The men of Ramtouses's army practiced different sounds at high pitch and low pitch to determine which proved more effective against an enemy warrior. When they found a shrill sound they could maintain for a long period of time, they practiced it nightly. Many villagers complained of the high-pitched noise.

That sound emanating from thousands of men confirmed their choice because of its ability to disrupt and confuse.

Ramtouses also devoted his attention to the weapons they would use in the coming battles. He selected swords, arrows, darts and spears, all typical weapons, and to maximize the use of these, he introduced two types of poison long used in war by the Nubian tribesmen. Many of the thousands of would-be warriors gathered at Tungal already knew of these poisons, but were unaware how to obtain or prepare them or safely store them. Ramtouses asked those who understood the preparation and handling of the poisonous fluid and powder to teach the villagers.

The poison for the arrows, made from the milkweed plant, caused a quick death from heart seizure. The slightest contact with blood would be fatal. The poison used on the darts came from the skin of the frogs and was strong enough to take down an elephant.

Ramtouses consulted his Ethiopian and Egyptian advisors for information regarding the enemy's location and the terrain through which this massive body of men would travel to reach them.

The shortest route only offered two supply points—one before crossing the Red Sea and a second at an oasis. They advised there would be much time spent in the desert and warned him of the dangers of low morale and anxiety. Efforts to maintain order could become difficult and possibly lead to mass desertion.

Ramtouses planned to deliver a departure speech on the first evening of the journey and inform the army of the hardship involved in such a long trip.

He grew confident after seeing the progress the warriors made over the last thirty-nine days. They had the capabilities of a full-scale military operation plus tricks and schemes perfectly timed to deceive and gain victory over the progeny of Ell.

A few days later a convoy of mules arrived, loaded with supplies for the fighting force and their families as agreed upon with the pharaoh. The Egyptians kept their word in that their share of the payment arrived prior to departure. King Tasmeria responded with calm relief and felt grateful as the long line of mules came into Tungal. He knew the warriors preparing to depart also experienced gratitude and confidence in seeing that King Tasmeria and the Egyptians supported them in this perilous, almost unimaginable adventure.

Aside from the family gifts, each warrior received personal equipment he would need in war—his own water skin, imperishable foods, added weapons, a blanket for cover, and a waistband to carry the supplies. During the previous two weeks, representatives from many of the tribesmen's villages came to receive payment for the families.

⁘

Ramtouses sat alone the night prior to departure. He considered the possible consequences of this huge undertaking and it nearly took his breath away.

*At some point,* he thought, *this venture will cause the death of many fine men. I am responsible for this move to avenge. Will I be able to live with that knowledge?*

His conclusion was swift. *Yes, this has to be done so humankind will not be doomed to death at the hands of the Ell.*

Ramtouses visualized Carnabrara as he fondled the lion's mane necklace she made for him. He kept it with him at all times and would wear it during the war. So it would not hinder his movement, he had a weaver sew it onto his large waistband.

⁘

On the day of departure, the day of his speech, two platforms were erected beside each other. One was for Ramtouses, the other for the two Ell prisoners. He expected, with this huge multitude of many tongues and dialects, communication would be a problem. He formulated a system to reach the entire congregation with the use of relay stations where interpreters and hand translators would deliver his words to those who did not speak or understand his dialogue and to those who stood too far away to hear his voice.

Ramtouses climbed to the top of the podium and looked out over the multitude of proud warriors filling his field of vision in all directions. He took a deep breath, filled with pride and a great sense of confidence.

*How did all this happen? Yesterday I was brokenhearted. Today I stand before what could be the most powerful army in the world. My words must feed the fire and wet the thirst of vengeance in the heart of every warrior before me.*

The army numbered close to four hundred thousand fighting tribesmen. The responsibility for their well-being nearly overwhelmed him. He acknowledged King Tasmeria, and bowed down to him.

"Thank you, King Tasmeria, for your commitment to make this day possible."

A thunderous roar erupted as all the warriors gave homage to the king. Ramtouses waited to speak until he could be heard again.

"The agonizing pain felt by so many at the loss of our loved ones shall not go unavenged. Nor can the progeny of Ell be allowed to continue their vehemence against humankind. They must be stopped. We will show the world that the men of the bush are the most fierce produced by Mother Earth."

Another roar arose from the army, echoed by the many villagers congregated on the training grounds. Ramtouses allowed the wave of response to end before continuing.

"Thousands of you came from villages far away. You have endured many hardships prior to joining us, failing crops due to lack of water, too little food for your loved ones. The Ell have cursed your lands for generations turning away the rains, leaving our crops and us thirsty.

Ramtouses waited briefly. Silence fell across the crowd before him.

"Let me tell you a story of survival. When a water buffalo discovers the presence of a lion, his natural instinct is to alert the other bulls in the herd and the alert is followed by a quick attack. They do not want the lion to have an opportunity to survey the herd for the purpose of finding weak links, the old, the young, or the less fit. The bulls want to drive it away or kill the lion, if possible. Protecting the group is what makes the herd strong. If the young become victims of predators, the future of the herd is weakened and eventually the herd will die. No member of the water buffalo herd is left unprotected, at the mercy of the lions. Survival totally depends on their ability to protect themselves as a whole and moving at once to that end.

"We must act as if we are the bull water buffalos, defending our homeland while we are joined together as one mighty force. If we divide into smaller families in our home village, we become like the old, the young or even the weak. The invaders from Ell will be as the lions and come in to devour and destroy our very existence, picking the smaller and more vulnerable targets first.

"Today we have mobilized a magnificent army, superior to any military might the earth has ever given birth to. Why? Because the diabolical sons of Ell have burst forth through a corrupt branch of nature. They are bent on the destruction of all mankind. For generations our ancestors foretold of the day the people of evil Ell would show themselves and attempt to carry away our souls to the pit of Ell to torment forever. Our goal is to relieve the Mother of Life of this unfortunate error and bring about the unblemished progression of life as it was intended.

"Remember your training. Though you may have hated the strenuous work, it may be your savior on the battlefield. The journey itself is also our enemy. The elements will fight us in every way to break our spirit. Once our spirit is broken, we become disorientated and lose our will to fight and win. I will be with you at all times pulling you from the forces of nature that want to destroy you. In the desert we will face sand storms, a blazing sun, and water will become a problem. When these dreadful times fall upon us, and our morale reaches rock bottom, I want every warrior to have images of the sons of Ell etched and burned into his memory down to the bottom of his soul. We shall not forget our objective during these trying times."

The Ell prisoners were led to the lower stand. They had been kept in captivity but were not abused. They had been thoroughly cleansed from head to foot so their pale skin would not be tarnished with dirt. A large cloth covered them. Ramtouses jumped from the higher stand, grabbed the cloth and jerked it away so all could see what was hidden underneath.

"Here are the Ell in their flesh." He shouted the words and then stood quiet. The tribesmen gathered directly before him gasped when Ramtouses ripped away the cloth.

"Every warrior shall move in procession past this stand. Burn this image into your mind. This is the enemy who is out there waiting to kill us and drink our blood."

The tribesmen gazed in awe as they filed past the prisoners. Their murmurings echoed their surprise

"I have never seen such pale creatures. Hideous."

"They are strange to my eyes."

"Truly these are the Ell."

Ramtouses praised his men as he departed the podium. Some cheered him, others were in a state of near hysteria overcome with newly found hatred of what they saw when they looked upon the two prisoners.

After the viewing, the army massed together to move out.

King Tasmeria stood alone with his back to the setting sun. The thousands of men who passed before him were reddened by the sun's reflection. As the light of day dimmed to total darkness, the last of the men disappeared into the night. The king thought of his sons of warrior status and of all the young men throughout the territory, including Ramtouses. They had all walked past him.

*Will I ever see them again? When they find the men of Ell, will they be victorious over them?*

His thoughts shifted to optimism and the goodness in their purpose.

*Of course! These mighty warriors will win over any opposition.*

Still, the nagging question remained. Could he be certain? Only the future would tell the tale. What he did know, above all, this day would change the history of his world forever.

# 15

# DAMNED ENVIRONMENT

### 701 B.C.E.

The tribesmen enjoyed high spirits as they made their way northeast. Ramtouses sent scouts ahead to inform villagers in their path that the army would pass through their boundaries during the night, and they should not be alarmed. He specifically warned them not to use the drums to pass on news of their travel as it would endanger the troops.

Several days later they reached the Red Sea where they were to meet an Ethiopian supply caravan. Early the next morning, camels and mules were seen moving toward the arranged meeting point. Over a thousand camels carrying extra water for Ramtouses's army and five hundred additional pack mules loaded with more water, food and metal-headed arrows.

The tribesmen took possession of the additional animals but kept the mules that carried the sealed jugs filled with poisons separated from the other pack animals as a safety measure. The shift of supplies went smoothly and a few hours after the arrival of the new provisions, Ramtouses's men settled in for their day of rest.

⁘

Ramtouses stood looking at the western arm of the Red Sea. A cool sea breeze washed over him. *This body of water is larger than I first envisioned. I can barely see to the other side*. Though Baduga told him the water ran shallow at this point, he now suspected that crossing the water with four hundred thousand men and hundreds of animals laden with supplies might be a greater task than they originally believed. The water was shallow but too deep to guarantee the safe transport of their critical supplies on the backs of mules. Ramtouses changed his mind. They would cross the water in daylight hours rather than night.

The men rested a few hours then spent the remainder of the day collecting wood to build several hundred rafts for transporting weapons and supplies. Breaking their rest cycle, they worked late into the night then slept until morning. Before noon they began to cross a shallow section of the Red Sea separating Upper Egypt from the Sinai Desert.

They tied the animals together, forming long lines. The vast majority of the warriors could walk the entire distance since the deepest part of the water measured about chest high. By late afternoon, while the sun still shone above them, the last of the tribesmen army made their way onto dry land at the edge of the Sinai Desert. They slept in the wet sand along the eastern shore and, come late evening, the huge army of warriors arose to face their first opponent, the environment.

The desert crossing proved to be much more challenging than Ramtouses had expected. The warriors were exhausted by early morning after the first fast-paced night and looked forward to a day of rest. The sun did not cooperate. Temperatures rose fiercely hot, and no one slept well. The lean-to tents made with the Egyptian blankets resulted in little protection. Thus it went for the next four days, and their pace slowed more each night.

On the fourth day, they lost over a hundred men when they unknowingly bedded down next to a snake den. The snake bites were deadly, and Ramtouses could only offer brief words of comfort to the dying men. The next day several hundred warriors came to him wanting to turn back. He pleaded with them to stay the course with the army. Turning back was not an option.

"We are much closer to the oasis than to the sea where we started," he said. "Anyone who turns back now will perish in the hot sun."

Many decided to stay but others took their share of supplies and left.

The heat continued to beat down, and sleep under the relentless sun escaped them. They should have reached the oasis within nine nights. By the tenth night, Ramtouses grew increasingly concerned when the men began to have delusions, and some of the warriors wandered off, to be swallowed by the desert night.

During the eleventh night, more men wandered away. The water supply neared depletion. He feared losing the whole army. The water skins were partially filled one last time, and each unit leader stressed to his men it was critically important each man use his water a little at a time.

By evening, when the march resumed, no one showed any sign of vigor. Physical and mental lethargy ruled. They wasted nothing on movement that did not carry them forward, and, fortunately, the majority wandered slowly in the desired direction.

The stars witnessed a throng of men barely moving. By midnight most of the men looked nearly dead.

Ramtouses screamed at them until his voice grew hoarse. "Get up. Start walking. Keep walking! This is the last night. We will make it. Keep walking!"

Baduga scouted ahead of the army and before the morning hour, Ramtouses heard him shouting and saw him waving his arm. "Over here. Over here."

The scout had found the oasis.

"Pass the word along. We have made it to the oasis."

Ramtouses staggered his way over to the vegetated island refuge in the middle of nowhere and sat down. *Can it be real? Have we finally reached the meeting place?*

"This is the meeting place," Baduga said.

Ramtouses looked around, but all he saw were gray-green desert palm trees and bushes surrounded by limestone rock and near-white desert sand. "Where is the caravan?"

The men of war had reached the meeting point, but the Egyptians were not there with the desperately needed water and food. Ramtouses and Baduga felt bereft and utterly stunned to discover no supply caravan had arrived. The tribesmen were near death from severe dehydration. They would be devastated when they realized there was no supply caravan to rescue them.

The desert palms scattered here and there along with many scraggly bushes were by no means enough shelter for his large army. However, the crucial worry was water, not shelter.

Ramtouses and his army began the slow slide into despair. At the onset of this campaign his army was a multitude of thousands of courageous fighting men. Now they were fatigued beyond comprehension, thirsty, hungry and sand covered—a disorganized group of bewildered nomads all near collapse. Still, his unit leaders struggled to maintain order, and the tribesmen tried to cooperate. Those suffering most from dehydration were brought under the trees and shrubbery to shelter them from the glaring sun.

Ramtouses dropped to his knees, his head hung low. His brothers, the leaders, and tribesmen surrounded him, hoping to hear some words of hope. Ramtouses wept silently, but no tears wet the hot sand beneath him.

*What have I done? I have led these people to a perilous state. Am I totally mad? I have poured my immortal sickness, this fierce drive for revenge, upon so many souls desperate for hope and a better life. Does my frantic torment have no end? Must I drag everyone down with my sorrow?*

Slowly, he raised his head and looked into the sad eyes of those around him. They all seemed to speak at once. "What shall we do, Ramtouses? What shall we do?"

He closed his eyes and tried to look into his soul. He searched the depths of his heart for even a morsel of purpose, for just one reason to survive. And, there, tucked in the recesses of memory, he recalled the words his beloved Carnabrara spoke to him: "I love you, Ramtouses. I will love you for all eternity."

He opened his eyes slowly. He did have purpose.

"We all have purpose," he said with confidence. "I want all the translators here before me at once."

At that, the people who represented the different tribes came forward, and he directed his words to them.

"Locate yourselves around this oasis so my words can be passed along. Do as we did in our town of Tungal."

The translators and leaders situated themselves so they could hear him speak then pass it on. Ramtouses stood alone with his hands folded behind him. The Egyptian blanket hung from his head, falling down to cover his neck and back, giving small protection from the sun. After a time one of his brothers reported that all were ready. He climbed a hill of sand nearby, held his hands out and spoke.

"What can I tell a man who has no water or food? Do I have magical powers? Can I command the pain in his stomach to go away? What can I tell a man who has blistered and swollen feet? Take another step, even if you fall down from exhaustion and dehydration? Are you all waiting for me to say something profound?"

His voice grew louder. "I told everyone here the war against the elements would be the first battle we fought. This world we live in, the total environment wants to destroy us. Every day of our lives is a battle against the forces of nature. We will all die someday. Even so, there are times we have an alternative in this conflict. Today is one of those times."

He shouted into the dry, hot air.

"Will environment be our damnation? Let us change the course of history together by surviving just one more night.

"Let me see a raised fist from all who are with me, who will endure the battle against the elements of nature one more night and create a path for our future just by staying alive for one more night!"

The weakened condition of the men made raising their arms difficult, but as his last words carried from man to man, translator to translator, a sea of fists slowly undulated above the heads of thousands.

Behind the desperate army, an ominous wall of sand appeared near the horizon. For the first time since they entered the desert, the sun's rays darkened. The early morning skies were heavy and appeared to carry the mightiest of all storms, plowing toward them at an astonishing speed.

"Brave men, cover yourselves," Ramtouses shouted. "Endure whatever powers of nature challenge us. You will survive. I tell you, you will survive!"

He could no longer stand on the hill because of the high winds. He stepped down to his waiting brothers, and they covered up quickly with blankets. Nature roared over and above them, blowing the desert sands over the massive army, burying them, hiding them, giving them one last day of desert terror.

⁛

Ramtouses awoke late in the day. He lay still with his eyes closed, and allowed the memory of their arrival at the lonely oasis ebb slowly into his mind. Visions of his suffering men floated across his still closed eyelids. In the silence he realized the storm had subsided.

A strange, far away sound repeated, again and again. Ramtouses guessed it could only be an animal's cry. He uncovered himself, shaking away the sand that totally covered him.

Sitting up and looking around, he saw sand, mounds and hills of sand, some small and others larger. He could not see his army. An immense blanket of sand covered and camouflaged everything but the trees. A soft breeze blew across his face and slightly stirred the mounds of sand, whipping up small sand devils. The blue sky sat as a dome over the desert, and amazingly, the sun did not burn nearly as hot as it had the past twelve days. The storm had brought about a change in the weather.

The strange sound came again from off in the distance. Around him, the sand mounds began to move, and one by one his men emerged. More and more of the warriors awoke in the darkness of their sand covered blankets and dug their way out to the light.

Ramtouses looked westward. It clearly was the sound of animals.

He saw them, camels emerging over a large hill in the distance. Hundreds, then thousands of his men were now up and looking to the west. Excitement erupted in rough, throaty cries of joy. Certainly it was not a mirage but the caravan of supplies making its slow yet steady journey to the oasis.

Ramtouses's chest heaved with gratitude. He had led his men to this brink of despair, where they might all perish. The burden of that reality was tremendous. Yet, help arrived.

"Oh, we are saved," he cried out. "Oh, Carnabrara, I never lost my faith in our love."

As weak as they were, the men attempted to dance in celebration. Many could not get to their feet but waved hands and smiled with joy.

Ramtouses instructed his leaders to inform the men to stay where they were and wait for the caravan. To avoid mass confusion over the distribution of supplies, he assured them everyone would receive equal portions of water and food in the usual systematic manner.

Because of their extreme dehydration, small amounts of water were first distributed to everyone. Within the hour, a second portion of water reached the out-stretched hands of those most weakened. The tribesmen showed remarkable patience and cooperation with the distribution system as they slowly regained health and energy.

They had beaten their first opponent, the environment, and the men credited Ramtouses's leadership. They loved, trusted and respected him more than ever.

⁙

The fifth night after the supplies arrived, they had recovered strength and vigor. They felt refreshed and ready to continue their journey. All supplies not carried by the warriors were packed and transferred to the fresher mules, including the sealed jugs filled with poisons. The camels returned with the caravan to Egypt, and the army moved out.

On the second night after leaving the oasis, the sand and rocky areas slowly diminished. Vegetation increased. The change from sand and rock to dirt felt good beneath their feet.

Though relieved to leave the desert behind, the tribesmen remained somewhat disconsolate. They wanted more daylight and Ramtouses recognized the need for sunlight so he changed the pattern of their sleep to waking cycle in the hope their morale would improve. Where the army had been traveling all night and sleeping all day, they now walked from midnight to noon, and rested and slept from noon to midnight. He also directed the tribal leaders to take a census of all remaining forces.

The census count result deeply saddened Ramtouses when he learned they could not account for nearly one hundred thousand men. They knew the various explanations for the missing men, but Ramtouses grieved their deaths. He called for a day of mourning.

He talked with his brothers, saying, "I feel terrible about the men we have lost. I expected the desert trip to take a heavy

229

toll, but this is surprisingly greater than I projected." Though troubled by the terrible loss, he knew they could not expend any more thought on this terrible loss, so he pushed beyond the sorrow to the here and now.

"We must look at the positive result. More than three hundred thousand of our fellow tribesmen did survive and are physically able to go to war. The strongest have survived."

.⋅⋅.

That morning they entered Southern Philistia and noticed the changing landscape was substantially more welcoming than that of the past two days' march. Baduga informed Ramtouses the army had emerged into a land of plenty. That evening it began to rain—a welcome sight.

.⋅⋅.

The Egyptian and Ethiopian advisers and guides knew the area well and purposely led Ramtouses north near the Mediterranean coast to the town of Ekron. No one knew for certain what they would find at Ekron. But one thing the advisors knew beyond all doubt, the Assyrian army was merciless.

At midnight, with the men prepared for the next day's journey, Baduga warned Ramtouses that a city which suffered an attack by the enemy would be in full view by sunrise. He suggested that Ramtouses inform the tribesmen of what they might see because he expected a horrid sight of death and destruction.

The morning arrived melancholy and gloomy, a heavily overcast day. Perhaps the warning from Baduga predestined the bleakness. The hot and muggy air seemed out of place for so early in the day, and the men were tired. They had traveled without stop since midnight over a series of long, low rolling hills.

"This is the place," Baduga said to Ramtouses. "This road will take us directly into the city over the low hills ahead."

Ramtouses commanded the military leaders to stop their forces while he and a few others investigated the remains of this once thriving city that lay over the next hill.

Reaching the hilltop, Ramtouses looked down and immediately noticed an enormous statue standing in the distance, in the middle of the road. The figure stood tall and mighty. It captured his attention and refused to release him. His eyes grew large staring at it. It seemed to guard what lay beyond, and Ramtouses was mystified. Why did it block the road that led into a burnt-out village?

Whatever it represented, Ramtouses and the men with him felt very uneasy in its presence. They cautiously descended the hill. A rancid stench filled the air. When they neared the sculpture, Ramtouses instructed his men not to touch it. Something malevolent radiated from it.

Its eyes were polished emeralds and seemed to follow the movements of the men below. It had the head of a king with a high crown and wore armor covering its torso. The lower body looked like a muscular lion. It had wings spread wide like a giant eagle settling to its perch after flight. Baduga and Taharga warned that this image symbolized the Ell god, the keeper of the Ell progeny.

Dark red-black stains covered its base and feet.

Taharga said, "This must be the blood of the Ekron citizens. The Ell god has trampled over the city."

A cold chill rippled through Ramtouses's body as he and the company of men with him walked past the statue toward the devastated city of Ekron. They came upon two huge trenches by the road near the entrance of the city where hundreds of skulls and skeletons were stacked upon each other.

Seeing such destruction of life, he said, "Lozato, have the entire army brought up. Let every man see the work of the enemy we have come to annihilate."

Upon entering Ekron, they saw more skeletons impaled on long poles and displayed along the streets. Rubble was piled

**Statue of Assyrian god, Baal**

wherever they looked. All structures had tumbled or burned down to the ground. Bones lay scattered everywhere, rotted corpses remained where the people fell, many with small skulls, indicating the slaughter of children, many half eaten by animals and birds, and possibly the Ell.

All the tribesmen viewed the statue closely as they moved over the hilltop and down the road leading to a once proud center of population and trade, the city of Ekron. They were appalled at seeing the huge statue, its feet soaked in human blood. Then the trenches of death came into view. As the day progressed, the evidence of the horrors committed upon this town lingered in the minds of Ramtouses's army.

The tribesmen were stunned by what they saw. Death was not a stranger to them, but they had never seen this amount of destruction and desecration. It was immense. The impaled men hung on tall shafts. No flesh remained. Only bones held together with taut dried tendon ropes and tattered bits of cloth moving slightly in the breeze still hung on the poles. They had become like flagpoles for this city of death.

Ramtouses gave orders to fill the trenches outside the city with all the corpses they found. Another trench had to be dug as the body count reached high into the thousands. They covered the trenches, and the dead at Ekron finally received burial by the hands of an army of tribesmen. It was well past midday before the army bedded down.

⁘

Two days after arriving at the city of death, Ramtouses led his army away from it to a nearby river where he and all his men bathed, attempting to cleanse their bodies and minds of the horrors of Ekron.

He laid his hand on Baduga's back. "We needed to see that. No matter how jolting. It has reinforced the fact that these people must be stopped."

⁘

The men began to show signs of unease. The atrocities of Ekron still pressed fresh in their minds, a memory not quickly dispelled.

They asked questions. "Where are these people from Ell? Maybe they will find us first and do to us as they did to the people of Ekron."

Thoughts of that wicked statue persisted. They spoke of its grotesqueness and how its eyes watched them, plotting to curse or cast evil spells upon them.

Other questions needed answers. "How can we know how many of them there are?"

"We are so far away from home. Will we ever see our own people again?"

The army needed to be revitalized, their morale lifted. The next night would be the new moon celebration back in Tungul. Ramtouses's tribesmen loved the festivities, and such a diversion would benefit all his men.

He ordered a halt to the march and declared a two-day rest including the new moon ceremony, a feast and war dance. Hunters went out to catch fresh meat and fish. Others prepared dance costumes. The mood among the tribesmen began to improve.

⁙

Ramtouses said to his brothers, "I want to see this country around us to determine if there is any human life nearby."

He instructed Lozato to command the army while he, two brothers and a few others left to search for signs of other humans. Baduga and Taharga accompanied them to translate should any people be found.

They walked for several hours before coming upon a cultivated field. They followed the field a short distant before seeing a small house then a few more a little farther up. An old man came out.

Ramtouses spoke to the others with him, "Check all the huts here. If anyone is in them, bring them out."

The old man questioned. "Are you here to kill me?" The old man shook as he spoke.

Ramtouses turned to Taharga, "Tell this man we mean him no harm." Taharga relayed the words.

"Who are you people? Why are you here?"

Taharga ignored the old man's questions. "Who else is here with you?"

"Only the children and I are left here. All the others have gone to Ekron to fight the Assyrians. We have not seen another living soul."

Taharga relayed the answer to Ramtouses and, after a short pause, he spoke again to the old man.

"We are not Assyrians, nor people from Ell." Taharga was aware the old man knew the Assyrians but nothing of the Ell, while Ramtouses and his men knew the Ell but nothing of the Assyrians.

*It is a huge game I play.* Taharga thought he would happily end the charade, if only he could.

Soon after he finished speaking, the tribesmen returned from their search of the few abodes. They came forward with seven small children, and two women, one the elderly wife of the old man.

Ramtouses looked at the frightened faces of the children and then back to his men.

"Did anyone bring along food? If so, give it to these children." The men gathered up the food they carried and gave it to the children.

"They may not know it yet, but they are orphans," Ramtouses said.

They left without speaking of the slaughter or that no one would be coming back from Ekron.

They returned to their camps. As they neared, the unmistakable aroma of wild goat and deer roasting over the fires filled the air. They hurried to ready themselves for the evening activities.

Ramtouses had sent sentries out a day's walk radius around their encampment to ensure no enemy was nearby during the time of the festivities. The army split into hundreds of smaller groups, each representing a tribe or village and their unique customs and traditions. They performed the war dance as ritually practiced by their people and in exclusive colorful dress, as close to the tribe as circumstances allowed. The dancers represented their ancient warrior ancestors.

The festival lasted late into the night. No drums were beaten that night for sound would carry far. They kept the beat with their feet and sang softly, almost beneath their breath. But the excitement of the near silent festival still filled the hearts of the thousands of warriors.

By the next midnight, when camp had to be broken and the march resumed, their spirit was rejuvenated. They marched and rested in the thick bushes and trees for one more night and day without interruption.

⁑

The scouts and guides knew the trail the Assyrian army had taken to Jerusalem. They intended to use a more direct route along a small river. The low ground would offer more camouflage for the massive army of tribesmen.

At noontime the men prepared their equipment for the coming night's march then settled in for their sleep period. They awoke near midnight. Just as they were about to break camp, the forward Egyptian scout returned with information they all had waited so very long to hear. The Ell camps had been located. Ramtouses's heart beat fast, and he bit down hard. He felt great relief at the news.

"Draw me a map," he commanded.

The scout took a stick and drew a map on the ground showing the position of the Ell's main forces and some of the smaller campsites in relationship to their location. Ramtouses increased the number of scouts, including some excellent tribal trackers and surveyors. Under the sliver of moon high in the sky, the new scouts examined the map and found points from where they could observe the Ell activities the best.

Ramtouses doled out instructions. "Bring information as to how we can approach this conglomerate of military might without being seen until we want to be seen. I also require details as to how many sentries and patrols guard the enemy locations."

⸭

They came back reporting few to no sentries on guard around the Ell camp. It seemed to Ramtouses the confident and fearless Ell army posted no sentries because they believed no military existed they should be forewarned about.

Ramtouses was surprised and thought this careless of the Ell. The scouting information allowed him to map out the terrain and determine a pathway that would camouflage them.

## 16

# THE TALES AND DEEDS OF AHIKAR

### 701 B.C.E.

After seeing the mighty Assyrian army at his doorstep, King Hezekiah abandoned all hope for peace. A great grief enveloped him. He retreated from the main gate to his chambers, tore off his clothes and covered himself with sackcloth, signifying his sorrow and contrition. He went into the house of Yahweh and fell to his knees, weeping. He slid to the floor and lay fully prostrate before his God, crying, "Oh, my LORD, what have I done?"

Hezekiah believed the enemy boasted arrogantly within their camps of how they deceived him and denuded him of all his treasures. He felt taunted by their antagonistic behavior.

"Again, my God, I have shown so little faith. I have given away all the wealth of the city. My grievous errors will bring much sorrow to my people. My soul is crushed to near unbearable depths by this terrible weight. I humiliated You exceedingly with my shameful deeds. I do not deserve Your love. Oh, my God, I have failed You."

King Hezekiah lay on the cold stone for hours.

⁌

The God of Israel heard His servant, Hezekiah, and sent the prophet Isaiah to him. Isaiah found the king lying on the Temple floor.

238

⁖

Isaiah spoke to the king. "Fear not. Get up, King Hezekiah, and hear my words."

Hezekiah rose to his feet burdened with despair.

"The LORD God of Israel, has sent me to you with this message. 'The virgin, the daughter of Zion, has despised me, laughed me to scorn. The daughters of Jerusalem have shaken their heads at Me. Whom have My people reproached and blasphemed? Against whom have they exalted their voices, and lifted up shiny eyes on high, even to the Holy One of Israel? Have you not heard of long ago how I lay to waste fenced cities into ruinous heaps? Beware, for I know your abode, and your going out and your coming in, and your rage against me. And the tumult is come up into My ears. Still, I will not withdraw from the remnant that has escaped the house of Judah. They shall yet again take root downward and bear fruit upward.'"

Silence filled the Temple until Hezekiah spoke in a weak, repentant voice. "In seeking a bid for independence for my people, my efforts have brought about these days of trouble and rebuke. It is like the child that comes to birth but lacks the strength for delivery from the womb."

The prophet Isaiah said, "Fret not, for the God of Israel has said, concerning the king of Assyria. 'He shall not come into this city. By the way that he came, by the same way shall he return. I will defend this city to save it for My own sake, and for My servant David's sake. I, your LORD, will send at night an angel who will smite the camps of the Assyrians, one hundred four-score and five-thousand, and when you rise early in the morning behold, they will be all dead corpses.'"

Isaiah continued, "Go home, speak with confidence to your people, and have faith in God. He will keep them safe from their enemies."

King Hezekiah removed himself from the Temple. He walked through the streets and no one recognized him. Secretly, he reentered the palace.

⁜

King Sennacherib of Assyria sent his Supreme Field General Holofernes with a large army from Ekron to King Hezekiah at Jerusalem. The Field Commander said to his interpreter, Ahikar, "Go to King Hezekiah and deliver King Sennacherib's message how he accepts his gifts with gratitude, but Baal will only be glorified with revenge for the insults placed upon him."

⁜

The following morning a messenger came to King Hezekiah's chambers. "An emissary has come from the Assyrians. He calls for the king to grant him audience."

Hezekiah and the elders' council convened at the central gates. The man waiting there was finely dressed, with a proud erect stance.

"I am King Hezekiah. What is it you want of me?"

The man spoke in the language of Judah. "I am here to deliver a message to you from the Emperor of Nations."

⁜

Ahikar stood within shouting distance from the towering walls of Jerusalem, on a platform with a podium built by the Assyrians, looking up at King Hezekiah. He knew the power of the Assyrian fighting machine, and he believed Judah had no chance in the coming conflict with Assyria. He hoped Hezekiah would make homage to great Sennacherib's demands even though to do so would be terribly humiliating, and the king's world would totally come to an end.

Ahikar believed the king had to ask himself if it was better to fight and risk the chance of what could be complete annihilation, or to admit defeat and stay alive in misery.

He shouted, "This is what the Lord of Nations, Sennacherib of Assyria, has said. 'Upon what do you base this confidence of yours? You believe you have strategy and military strength but these are empty thoughts. Are they not? Come now and make a bargain with Baal, god over all the Assyrian empire. Lay down your arms. Open your gates. Restore Baal to his rightful place back in your temples.'

"I quote the words of my lord, King Sennacherib. 'If you continue your obstinacy against Baal, I, King Sennacherib, have commanded Chief General Holofernes to attack and destroy this place and leave nothing standing. I tell you the truth. I, Sennacherib, was told by Baal, my god, to march against this country and leave it a desolate place for all times, and to revenge the insult placed upon him when his idols were thrown out of the Temple into the streets.'"

⁕

As Ahikar talked, several of the leaders standing around King Hezekiah began to ask one another if they knew this man who spoke.

"Is he not of Hebrew descent? He speaks our language as if born in to it."

"Agh! How can it be so? He has come forward to speak for this massive Assyrian army here today. How can it be that he is Hebrew?"

The men and women on the Jerusalem wall felt humiliated listening to a man they suspected to be one of their own.

"Look now, you are dependent upon Egypt, that splintered reed of a staff, which pierces a man's hand and wounds him if he leans on it. Such is Pharaoh, king of Egypt, to all who depend on him. And, if you say to King Sennacherib, 'We are depending on Baal, the lord and god of Assyria.' Then I ask you this. Isn't he the one whose high places and altars you, Hezekiah, did remove, saying to Judah and Jerusalem, 'You will not worship this god?'

"Baal has not forgotten the crimes committed against him. Do you think of Baal as a sometimes god you can worship only when you see fit? If you see him as such, so also does he see you."

241

In conclusion Ahikar said, "Open your gates today for General Holofernes, and he will spare your city if Baal is appeased with the restoration of your worship. If the gates remain closed after the sun sets, we will not offer another opportunity and you will be destroyed."

At that, Ahikar bowed and removed himself from their presence.

⁖

Ahikar reported to Holofernes after he delivered the message. When the gates remained closed come sunset, Holofernes showed no surprise.

Scouts had reported that Hezekiah blocked off all water sources in the immediate area. The nearest river supplying water was a small one a day's journey away. He concluded that King Hezekiah made this move strategically to deny Sennacherib's army fresh water. To do that, Hezekiah would have a store of water. It wouldn't last forever, and Holofernes felt comfortable with the notion of a siege. His army was content to wait knowing it would be just a matter of time before the citizens of Jerusalem came crawling on their knees. Intense thirst made people crumble.

"We do not have to act at this time. We will wait until their stored water supply has run out, and their tongues swell in their mouths, and their urine is at a dribble."

⁖

Sixty days passed, and Holofernes wondered if his plan was working. He called some of his officers and leaders together to discuss the situation. Ahikar also attended the meeting.

"I considered mounting an attack to see what kind of resistance the people of Jerusalem would give us," Commander Holofernes said, "but I have now decided to refrain from that idea in favor of executing more patience. We will break their spirit and faith in their god and show them the unquestionable power of the mighty Assyrian army. I also want the King Sennacherib here to see our triumph."

Earlier in the siege he had ordered the construction of an enormous high siege ramp, the height of five men, and a battering ram, consisting of more than thirteen thousand pounds of stone and mortar.

"It is time to intimidate and further demoralize the people of Judah," Holofernes told his officers. "We will locate this siege ramp at the southern end of the city where anyone on the high walls will see it and be reminded of our superiority and authority."

His officers agreed with the plan.

Ahikar stood. "Lord Holofernes, may I offer an opinion?"

Holofernes gave his consent and Ahikar continued speaking. "Let the truth concerning these people come from my mouth. Their ancestors knew the God of heaven, who was with them as they sojourned in the land of Canaan where they dwelled and increased with gold and silver and with very much livestock. But when a famine covered all the land of Canaan, they went down into Egypt and sojourned there. While they were there, they became numerous and became a great multitude so that one could not number their nation. Therefore, the king of Egypt rose up against them, dealt severely with them, and brought them low, enslaving them to labor in brick production.

"Then they cried unto their Lord, and He smote all the land of Egypt with incurable plagues until the Egyptians cast them from their sight. And their Lord dried the Red Sea before them and brought them to Mount Sinai. And they cast forth before them all the people of this land and possessed all the hill country and built this kingdom. In time they divided into two nations. The people of one nation, as they had done in the past, turned their backs on the face of the Lord and He stood back when their enemies came in upon them and defeated them very sore in battle. They were led captive into a land that was not theirs.

"The other nation returned to their God where their sanctuary lies. If their God comes to the aid of His people as He has done in the past, it may be an error to attack them. Their LORD God is mighty and if He defends them and does battle for them, we become a reproach before the entire world."

⁘

After Ahikar ended his remarks, the Assyrian officers stared at him totally appalled. They looked at one another in shock. They murmured, "Will General Holofernes kill him?"

⁘

Holofernes yelled, "Get out of my sight, everyone, but Ahikar." He looked at Ahikar with fire in his eyes. He trembled with rage, and the anger within him grew to an absolutely furious state.

"Have your wits left you?" He screamed at Ahikar. "How dare you insult King Sennacherib's magnificent army and his god? Sennacherib loves you as a brother. He has placed his trust in you. For that you do this to him? Why have you destroyed the companionship we three have known our whole lives? This time, Ahikar, you go too far. You have committed blasphemy before Baal and my entire army for the sake of these obscure, primitive people."

Holofernes calmed himself. "Ahikar, tell me the reason for doing such a thing to your king who has done so much for you?"

Ahikar answered, "When addressing King Hezekiah and the people of Judah, I remembered the God of Israel and how mighty He is. At that moment, a cold chilling fright came over me as never before."

Holofernes shook his head in disbelief. "I cannot allow you to live after a crime such as this. The men will see me as unworthy of their loyalty. I will lose the pride of my army."

⁘

Ahikar thought fast. He remembered Holofernes's love for beautiful women.

"Wait," he said. "There is something else I must tell you. While at the wall, I saw a woman of imposing beauty. She had fiery red hair and was absolutely stunning to behold. She wore a giant halo of hair arched from one ear to the other ear. It was braided into a unique and intricate pattern. Her white clothing hung full length down to her ankles, and the material shown brilliantly like jewelry. It sparkled with every move it made.

"She approached me and I felt peaceful in her presence. My eyes were unable to turn away. I was compelled to reach out to her, but my hand was not able to touch her through the glittering gown.

"She whispered in my ear. 'Go to your leader and tell him I will come to him soon to prophesy his future. Whether it be good or evil, he will be wise to listen.' I did not know if she was real or not. No one else gave an account of seeing her. That is why I did not tell you until now."

Holofernes's eyes grew tight. "You are mad!" The fury on his face faded, but the aversion to Ahikar remained evident. "I won't have you killed for the sake of my great King Sennacherib and because of your madness."

General Holofernes called for his orderlies to take Ahikar outside. He ordered his captain and a detachment of soldiers to take the insolent man to the platform from which he spoke a few months earlier and bind him beneath the walls of Jerusalem.

In his anger, Holofernes said, "Let him suffer the inevitable fate of these people he defends when their city falls to our mighty Assyrian forces. That is, if they don't kill him outright."

❖

Most of the soldiers hated Ahikar. He was not an Assyrian, yet he received many more privileges. He was thrown to the ground, kicked and struck in the face. They yelled, "We will take you back to your kind. You do not deserve the honor of being an Assyrian. You are a traitor."

They placed a long, straight timber against the platform, bound Ahikar's arms and feet to it and faced him toward the city gates.

⁘

The Hebrew guards on the wall could only look upon the scene in wonder. They immediately notified King Hezekiah of the strange event. The king summoned his council members and military leaders, and once again they came with him to the walkway above the gates.

Hezekiah saw a man bound to a long pole against the speaker's stand. *Isn't he the same individual who boastfully spoke of the destruction of Jerusalem just a few months earlier?* The scene was puzzling.

The King shouted, "Are you not the same person who declared Judah was doomed?"

"Yes, I am he."

"Are you not an Israelite?"

Again the answer came. "Yes, I am."

King Hezekiah asked, "What has happened in just this short time for you to have lost favor?"

"I do not know what overcame me. It was as if the God of our ancestors controlled the words flowing from my mouth. I said the God of Israel was almighty and could annihilate any force including the powerful Assyrian armies."

Ahikar's answer provoked thought.

*Hmmm, that's interesting.*

Hezekiah turned to his elders. "What shall we do with him?"

There were those who feared this was an Assyrian ruse. Others saw a chance to gain knowledge of the Assyrian forces.

King Hezekiah chose to bring Ahikar into the city and interrogate him before the council of the elders. They locked him in the same dungeon where Padi, governor of Ekron, had been imprisoned.

246

❖

The following day the council met to interrogate the prisoner. Spectators overflowed the assembly hall. Guards brought Ahikar in, shackled and chained, and King Hezekiah asked him what he had to say on his own behalf.

Ahikar held his gaze upon the floor, looking at no one.

"I am a condemned man. I have been loved and trusted by the highest of men in the Assyrian world. I was cupbearer to the great King Sennacherib and tutor of his son. I had everything a man could ask for, but because I fear the God of Israel, I have lost all.

"I am a descendant of the tribe of Naphthali, which converted to the worship of Baal. In the day Israel was overthrown by Shalmaneser and Sargon II, my family was not given the heavy burdens as the others tribes because of their faith. I became a servant to the royal family, and the boy Sennacherib befriended me."

"So how did you become a man of such nobility from being a servant?" the king asked.

"As I said, Prince Sennacherib favored me. I was allowed to be educated in the Assyrian culture. I became a scribe for Sennacherib, and even earned an income to purchase an estate, precious stones and fine clothing."

A council member spoke, "And you say the LORD is responsible for your demise?"

"Yes, because of my fear of the God of Israel, I was labeled a blasphemer and traitor then thrown out of the Assyrian camps."

"Why did they not just kill you? Why did they bring you here?"

It was a woman's voice. Ahikar raised his head. He was unaccustomed to hearing the voice of a woman in a court of judgment. When he saw his mouth fell open in utter amazement. He stared at her as his heart raced in alarm. He clapped his hands to the sides of his head and held them there, trying desperately to still the tremors that seemed to overcome him.

⁘

Judith started and drew back at the man's strange reaction to her.

*Why is he so distraught? What disturbed him so? Is it the sight of me, or my questions?*

"What is your problem? Why do you stare? Have you never seen a noblewoman before?"

He moaned and dropped to his knees then shouted, "Oh, blessed be the Lord, the God of all creation." He slowly focused on Judith. "I had a vision of a woman whose countenance was like that of an angel. I spoke of her to the mighty General Holofernes. She was a seer. I had no thought this woman actually existed until I saw you."

"What woman do you speak of?" Judith interrupted the man. He held his gaze on her, and crawled toward her on his hands and knees.

"She is the beautiful angel with fiery red hair who will come to Holofernes and foretell his future." Ahikar's voice was a low murmur as though he spoke to himself.

Judith could barely hear him, so she moved closer. "What did you say?"

"I made up a fable to save my life." Then he retold the story.

⁘

When he was finished, he grew quiet. His words must seem ridiculous to this court. *I tell such a strange tale, yet here stands this woman with fiery red hair. What does it all mean?*

"Go on. Then what?"

He began again. "The general was perplexed by the story and thought me mad. In Assyria, one who is declared mad is exiled for life. It is their way to forever torment the poor soul."

The woman's voice sounded irritated. "How can anyone believe such a story? You fashioned it just now, after seeing my red hair! Didn't you?"

"To what avail?" cried Ahikar. "What can I gain from a story like this? I am here because the General of the Assyrian armies loves beautiful women, and I wanted to save my life. This story was the first thing that came to my mind."

King Hezekiah interrupted. "How long have you been with the Assyrian army?"

"I have been with these men from the beginning. I know their fighting strategies and military secrets."

"Take him out," Hezekiah ordered. "I have heard enough for today."

From the moment he first saw her Ahikar never looked away from Judith.

⁂

Judith refused to make further eye contact and turned away as the soldiers led him out.

With Ahikar no longer in their presence, the king looked at his council members. "What are we to think of this? Is this man one of the biggest liars we have ever heard? Or, is he telling the truth?"

The council members held mixed opinions on the prisoner's statements, but one direction of thought prevailed—Ahikar should not be put to death, and their military should evaluate his knowledge of the Assyrian war machine.

"What about the angel with the fiery red hair? That was very convincing." The king looked thoughtful, but the council members gave no response to his question. They sensed it to be more of a comment than a serious question.

When the meeting adjourned, Judith addressed the king. "Do you want to learn more about this General Holofernes and the angel with the fiery red hair?"

The king was as curious as she. "The two of us will interrogate the man in my chambers tomorrow."

⁂

The following afternoon prison guards led Ahikar into the king's chambers. He hung his head as he had during the council meeting.

THE BLACK ANGEL OF THE LORD

"You have not yet killed me. Is it because you think I can help your war with the Assyrians? I want to be of service in any way I can. Please, allow me to prove my worth to you."

"How can we know you are not some kind of Assyrian snare? We have knowledge of Sennacherib's deceptive ways."

"If you think the Assyrians sent me as a form of trickery, you are profoundly mistaken. They see themselves as a bold, arrogant fighting machine, a veteran army that has known only victories. They do not see you as an equal opponent. They do not need any deceptions or unique strategies to overwhelm you. To them you are inferior, hiding behind your walls, depending upon some feeble god to save you."

"Enough!" The man's words angered Hezekiah. "However, your point is well-taken. What about their capability of knocking down our gates?"

"Your walls and gates are the best I have ever seen. I do not believe their battering rams will knock down your gates at this time, even though General Holofernes has just built a new battering ram, which he displays in the road before your gates." Ahikar paused in thought for a moment, and then continued. "King Sennacherib has taken half his army to your city of Lachish to bring down the huge walls of that city. Holofernes commands the forces encamped here. They are in no hurry to attack this city, but after King Sennacherib has sacked Lachish and arrives here things could change dramatically."

King Hezekiah stopped the man from speaking more. Lifting his hand toward the prisoner, he said, "Guards, take him away. Clothe him, and have someone attend his wounds. Get him decent living quarters in the military area. Two guards shall be assigned to him at all times. Bring him back here tomorrow, looking like an Israelite."

The king turned to Judith. "After we have interviewed him tomorrow, we will turn him over to the military. We shall see if his knowledge of the Assyrians can help in any way."

⁙

250

The following afternoon Ahikar returned to the king's chambers under guard. His face looked better and he wore respectable clothing chosen by Hezekiah himself.

"Now you look more presentable to a royal court," the king said.

Judith immediately began to question Ahikar this time. "Tell me more of this Holofernes."

"He is a giant among men. He has but one weakness, his love for women."

"How can you be so sure of this?"

"I have known him many years, since childhood," Ahikar said. "Each time he found himself in a dilemma, it was due to his affairs with women."

"Exactly what did you tell him about this seer?"

⁘

*Why would this woman focus on the concocted tale?* Something stirred within him, something similar to the feeling he experienced while telling Holofernes of the imaginary seer, as if he were not in control of his own words. He told her word for word.

"What did this 'giant among men' say other than to exile you?"

"He quieted," Ahikar said. "As I hoped he would. My thought was he would be more lenient. He was. I feared he would cut off my head where I stood if not for the tale I related."

"Do you think he would believe me to be that woman?"

"It would not take much for you to be that seer. That is what overcame me when I first saw you."

Judith eyed him closely as he spoke. She asked no more questions of him.

⁘

King Hezekiah had listened to the exchange of questions and answers between Judith and Ahikar. He found it intriguing that Judith showed a special interest in the conversation

Ahikar had with Holofernes. He made a few more inquires of Ahikar before the guards removed him.

⁘

All that evening Judith stayed to herself. She reviewed the story of the woman seer with the fiery red hair over and over. Slowly an elaborate scheme came to her. She contemplated it from every angle.

*I think I have it. This idea might work, but I need to know one more thing before I can be sure.*

She left her quarters and made her way to Ahikar's room.

She had one question to ask of him. "What is Holofernes's mannerism when it comes to women of royalty, other than Assyrian women? Does he show them respect?"

He answered her question directly. "A beautiful woman such as you can easily touch his heart. Once that happens, any woman of royalty can expect courteous consideration. She will be treated as equal to an Assyrian noblewoman."

Judith nodded and quickly departed.

The following day she went to King Hezekiah with her plan to deceive and manipulate the Assyrian hero. She told the king that preparation and execution of the scheme had to be meticulous to the finest detail.

"This will prove to be a game of life and death with the Lord God as overseer," she said.

Hezekiah listened and reluctantly gave her the go-ahead for her plan. "You shall return when you have gathered every detail and reveal all to me. As yet I am undecided. If I do not believe it will work, I have the option to change my mind. After all, this plan would carry you outside the city gates. That is perilous."

⁘

After a week, Judith had Ahikar brought to her quarters in the palace. His appearance had improved. His face was less swollen, the bruises lighter. "I require your help to convince General Holofernes I am the woman seer you spoke of to him.

"Why would you do that? Even if we did deceive him, your life would be over. He would never allow you to return!"

Judith spoke resolutely. "What value is one life when a whole nation is on the brink of destruction?"

She went on to say she needed to learn to speak the Assyrian language.

"I need to know as well all about Holofernes, his personality and character. Is he faithful to his god? What does he like? What does he dislike? What are his favorite foods? What makes him angry or happy? Does he enjoy his wine? What does he favor to pass his leisure?"

Ahikar saw how determined she was. He knew she could not succeed without him, and he agreed to assist her.

※

With the king's permission, Judith had Ahikar moved closer to the palace. She financed all his expenses including his clothing and food. His life became more comfortable although guards remained with him. Each day they escorted him to Judith's rooms in the early afternoon, and returned him to his room at whatever time their sessions ended.

Ahikar tutored Judith in the Assyrian language, impressed with her quick mind and tongue and easy grasp of the words. He also taught her the culture and behaviors of Assyrian upper-class women. He enjoyed every hour they spent as tutor and student from the very beginning.

"Though it was a vision I fabricated in my panic, I remember my words to General Holofernes perfectly," he said. He gave testimony to those words frequently so she would know the tale as if it were her own. Through the weeks they discussed every facet of Judith's plan. He answered all her questions and tried to prepare her in every way he could think helpful.

She said, "I must be articulate in Holofernes's language and completely believable when I tell him why he should not destroy the city. Phrases like 'the wealth of the city has already been given,' and 'there is nothing of value to gain' must flow smoothly off my tongue."

❖

The entire plan rested upon how General Holofernes received the prophecy.

"If Holofernes is perturbed by these words of wisdom coming from my charming mouth, he should convince the great King Sennacherib to move on to finer pastures, perhaps in Egypt and Ethiopia with a much stronger force at his command."

In case he did not withdraw from Jerusalem's walls, she needed an alternate strategy. Her first thought involved the use of poison, but she changed her mind.

"Ahikar, we have no poison in Judah that would kill a man before he could call for help. If I spiked his wine with a potion that gently lulled him to sleep, should someone come into the tent, they would think he drank too much wine."

"That might work," Ahikar said. "But his attention must be drawn away from his drink so you could slip the sleeping potion into his goblet."

Judith thought for a while. "I will dance for him in an especially sensual and alluring gown."

"It would have to be very sensuous," Ahikar said, "made of a delicate fabric one can see through, if possible."

He averted his eyes. He was obviously uncomfortable speaking of such things with her. Judith sensed his uneasiness and tried to ease his mind.

"Ahikar, you are right about the sexual desire. Do not fear you will insult me with your suggestions no matter how flagrant. We must determine the best approach to accomplish our task."

She turned their attention now to the dress she would wear when first meeting the Assyrians. "You said it was long, down to my ankles, right? And it must sparkle and shine brightly as I move."

"Judith, it was covered with brilliant jewels that reflected the sunlight as she walked," he said. "It will be very difficult to make such an extravagant garment."

"Yes, but I do not worry about the expense. I have the means, and my servants are creative and highly skilled."

⁘

True to her word, Judith's dressmakers worked together to design and create an absolutely beautiful gown. Glittering jewels twinkled and shimmered on soft white fabric. The dress moved seductively as Judith walked around her living space. Truly, it dazzled everyone, even the dressmakers who designed the gorgeous gown.

"You are she. It is as if my vision has been given life!" Ahikar could barely speak.

He was deeply affected by how she brought to life the fable he made up. She gave flesh and blood to his story and made it powerful with her willing self-sacrifice for her people.

Ahikar felt a rushing flow of admiration and respect for Judith, this lovely, red-headed woman. It consumed his heart and he knew she meant more to him than any woman he had known or would ever know.

That evening, when he went back to his quarters, Ahikar had no thought other than of Judith.

⁘

As the weeks went by, Ahikar was given more freedom to move about without his guards. Each day after her noon meal, he went to Judith and worked meticulously with her, transforming the Hebrew noblewoman into an Assyrian noblewoman with the soul of a seer. Almost four months passed. With each passing day, time became more precious for it might be the last before implementing the plan.

⁘

One day, after entering Judith's quarters, he stood by the large window that looked out upon the city. Sunlight beamed through the open space. He looked to where Judith sat in a chair by the window. The rays of the sun reflected off her light olive skin. He could just make out a loose sprinkle of soft freckles across her forehead and cheeks. Her deep red hair hung down to her hips. It grew thick and full. She had a womanly figure with long shapely legs. Her face remained that of a young girl, innocent and free of guile.

*She is so sweet and beautiful,* he thought. *A man like Holofernes would kill for her. She has a light about her that draws anyone who sees her.*

Ahikar did not want the moment to pass.

*I am content to stand here forever, just watching this beautiful woman.*

He believed her to be a virtuous woman but neither naive nor ignorant of the abundance of evil in the world. She was about to take on the ultimate challenge of her life—to bring Assyria to its feet. She lifted her eyes to Ahikar's face and he looked away so as not to be staring at her.

"You are as ready as you will ever be. I have helped you become Holofernes's most favored dream or his most feared nightmare. You should have no trouble communicating with any of the Assyrians. Still, I must warn you. If it does not go as planned, this man can crush you with his bare hands." Ahikar spoke in earnest.

"I know this. Ahikar, I put my trust in God Almighty. He is the light of the world, not Holofernes."

"You are valiant," he said. "Still, I am concerned about your well-being."

⁘

Over time, Judith grew comfortable with Ahikar and invited him to share evening meals with her and her mother. At these times, they set aside preparations for Judith's mission.

He related bits and pieces of his life whenever the opportunity arose, and Judith easily reciprocated with tales of her own life saga.

He longed to ask her many more questions. How had she become a member of the elders' council? But he put these things aside in order to thoroughly prepare her for the coming task.

He fervently wished she would abandon this dangerous plan, yet she remained resolute. And Ahikar realized the critical importance of his role in all of this preparation.

Ahikar said, "I have been treated with respect. King Hezekiah has entrusted me with the most important task of my life, preparing you for the most important task of your life." He hesitated before continuing. "I wish to adopt your Hebrew faith."

Judith was happy to hear those words but she quietly hid her joy.

He met with the priests and disclosed his desire to be cleansed and made worthy in the sight of the LORD, to be a true Hebrew.

⁘

Judith hosted a dinner to celebrate Ahikar's conversion. During the dinner one of the guests, a council member, granted Ahikar's burning desire to know of how Judith became a council member. He told the story of Judith's daring willingness to challenge the priests of the heathen gods and do battle for what she believed right in the eyes of almighty God.

The man's words pleased Ahikar greatly, and later that night he asked himself what he would be without her. This woman had come into his life so unpredictably and became everything to him.

*I know that I love her. Hopefully I can persuade her not to go out to the Assyrian camps. I will go to her tomorrow and ask her to change her mind.*

He slept little that night.

•⊹•

When Ahikar came to the palace at his usual time, Judith was deep in thought. She had spent the morning trying to envision the seer's hairstyle as Ahikar had described to her. Constructing a huge circle, arching from one ear to the other across her head, a web of red hair filling in the circle would be a challenging design. But she trusted her skillful hair stylists would be able to make her hair look like Ahikar had outlined.

He had drawn a sketch of how the hair should look and the stylist followed it down to the last detail. Judith devoted the entire day to instructing the stylists and reviewing the shape of the hair design. Her servants worked diligently with great patience and after many attempts with the most dexterous handiwork, they validated her confidence in them. The style looked just as Ahikar had sketched the seer's hair.

When Ahikar saw them hard at work, he said nothing. He only watched. Their ability to convert his drawings into an actual hair design with amazing accuracy astounded him. It took most of the day to accomplish this. Judith realized that they would have to maintain the hair daily. She had no knowledge when she would have to implement her plan, but she did know it was unlikely there would be enough time to recreate the hair style once the moment arrived.

Because of the excitement over the hair design, Ahikar knew he would not be able to declare his feelings for Judith that day. Nor could he ask her to reconsider her plans.

When he returned to his room that evening he was filled with discontent, mentally punishing himself for not saying what he felt in his heart. He flopped across the bed and folded his hands beneath his head. Eventually, Ahikar found sleep.

# 17

# THE ECLIPSE

## 701 B.C.E.

G eneral Holofernes sent a message to King Sennacherib concerning Ahikar's treason and informed the king of the exile. He included a brief account of Ahikar's insanity and ended with his own assessment that this war with the Hebrews had become too much for Ahikar.

"I think his better judgment was affected," he wrote. "Ahikar committed these crimes in front of my officers and men. If he had spoken these words in private, I would have left him for your judgment."

Sennacherib was confounded. He failed to understand Ahikar's behavior. It left him in disbelief. He thought their friendship was unshakeable. He knew Holofernes would never lie about anything like this and wondered what could have happened to Ahikar.

⁘

The city of Lachish clung to the slope of a giant hill, much like Jerusalem. Due to the sharp incline in the approach to the city, Sennacherib's men were not able to use the battering ram as effectively as they had done in the past. The people of Lachish poured hot tar on the battering ram personnel, burning them and making footing impossible on the steep incline.

Another problem that impeded the Assyrian attack was the presence of large boulders scattered throughout the landscape before the walls. They created an obstacle course that ruled out use of the siege ramps. Assyrian soldiers, sent in to clear a path for the towers, met with a deluge of arrows streaming down on them.

Daily, King Sennacherib had thousands of men bombard the city with flaming arrows, hoping to force them to use their precious water to stop the city blazes.

While there was no sure way to attack Lachish, the shortage of water became evident six months into Sennacherib's siege. Their defense began to show signs of weakening.

King Sennacherib realized this and increased efforts to batter down the gates and remove the boulders blocking the siege ramps. The ramming of the gates still did not yield entrance, but the Assyrians eventually cleared enough boulders for the four huge siege ramps to reach the walls. The soldiers raced up and over the protecting impediments of Lachish. Thousands of them pouring profusely into the once thriving but rebellious city. They overwhelmed the occupants and sacked the city. The majority of the population was taken into slavery but thousands were executed.

Sennacherib sent word of the victory to Holofernes, informing him they would join his forces in fourteen days.

The king was anxious to merge the two halves of his army as well as to learn more regarding Ahikar's behavior prior to his treason. King Sennacherib was irritatingly perplexed. He prided himself on knowing the people in his close circle better than they perhaps knew themselves. Why would Ahikar betray him as he did?

⁂

Four months had passed since Holofernes exiled Ahikar and he had made no effort to attack Jerusalem, but had employed mental games to intimidate and taunt the city's population.

When Holofernes received the message from Sennacherib, he returned word they should bring all the water they could carry. He considered mounting an attack to test Judah's strength against his military might and to determine if the water shortage within the city had yet affected their fighting ability. After giving the situation more thought, he decided against the attack.

He said to his officers, "King Sennacherib is coming, and when he gets here, we will be ready to show him a great victory as he has accomplished at Lachish. We will not attack until then, so he can take pleasure in the triumph."

The Assyrian soldiers celebrated. They sang and beat their drums with the news of the victory at Lachish and the coming of King Sennacherib.

⁕

Ahikar said to King Hezekiah, "They are beating the drums and singing a cry for war. An attack will be coming soon. This can also mean King Sennacherib has found victory at Lachish. The rest of the Assyrian army may soon make its presence known here at Jerusalem."

When the king heard Ahikar's interpretation of the raucous coming from the Assyrian camps, he called upon his military officers to double the manpower assigned to the city walls. The troops were ready. Food and water had been rationed in a way to assure they stayed reasonably fit and in shape for battle. The entire city participated in the defense of Jerusalem. Everyone knew his or her duties.

⁕

Holofernes removed the weapons display from the road. He told his officers, "The next time the Hebrews see this monstrous battering ram and the siege ramps, they will be used to vanquish their city."

⁕

At the same time, King Hezekiah held a council meeting. Ahikar was one of the few spectators as most of the citizens were at their assigned post or duty.

⁘

"This will be a short meeting and maybe our last. I believe Lachish has fallen. Their fight was a gallant one and very remarkable. Against difficult odds, they held on for six months in the face of an overpowering enemy and a limited supply of water."

Loud drum beating and boastful singing from the Assyrian camps remained a constant background noise as King Hezekiah spoke.

"When we return to our duties, pass the word to pray for those who have lost their lives or are now in slavery. We, the people of Jerusalem, are just as strong as our brothers of Lachish. For months Holofernes has threatened us with the presence of his fierce war machines, yet we have persevered because our faith in our LORD is strong. As it stands today, water is not a problem for us, thanks to the will of God. They may believe we are short of water as in Lachish, but that is not the case."

He wiped the sweat from his brow. "We are prepared to drive the idol-worshippers from our gates. We will fight with all our might, for as long as it takes. The true God Himself has told me, through His prophet Isaiah, that not one of these Assyrians will enter His holy city."

The meeting ended.

Judith informed Hezekiah her scheme was ready for action.

They walked together to the palace where they could speak in private and Hezekiah had the opportunity to ask about her rather bizarre new hairstyle. He had noticed it the moment she took her seat at the council meeting. Who did not? Everyone looked surprised and curious at such a sight, but no one ventured to say anything at the meeting.

"Do you think it becomes me?" she asked.

"Yes. And may I add I have never seen anything quite like it before!"

When they arrived at the palace, Judith told Hezekiah some of the plan details.

"This hairdressing and the dress created expressly for my purpose match Ahikar's description of the seer."

She went over what she planned to tell Holofernes, as well as what she would do if her first plan failed. She asked to leave immediately to implement the scheme.

"There is no way I can allow you to leave right now. I must think this through before I make a final decision on something like this. Are you not afraid to venture into the teeth of monsters like these people? And how can I believe what Ahikar says of Holofernes's feelings? A man's feelings for a woman can change from one day to the next. After all, we are at war! This General Holofernes smells blood. He wants to win the war above all else. I just cannot let you go out there. It is as if I am throwing you to the wolves!"

Judith looked into the king's eyes. "I love the God of Israel more than anything. I am but a tool of His desire. I trust the faith I have in the Lord. He will be with me every step of the way."

King Hezekiah shook his head. "I hate the position you put me in. You must wait a few more days. I need time."

Before Judith removed herself from the king's presence she cried out. "We have no time! Do you not hear the cries of their army echoing the rhythm of war continuously?"

After she left him, King Hezekiah began to pray.

⁘

Judith sent for Ahikar as soon as she returned to her rooms and told him of the king's decision to wait. Ahikar secretly agreed with the king. He feared if she left he would never see her again and felt responsible for this situation.

When Ahikar said nothing, she said. "We do not have a choice. If there is any chance my sacrifice will save the city, we must take it."

⁘

Ramtouses informed his leaders that war could begin as early as in three or four nights. Later that same morning his tribesmen scouts returned after most of the men had bedded down for a much-needed rest.

A map was drawn on the ground to show two enormous divisions of Ell fighters, one moving toward the other to combine into one mighty army. This was good news. Fighting on two fronts would be difficult. This meant the Ell forces would be together in one body when Ramtouses attacked.

The scouts were sent out again to gather more comprehensive information about the landscape and best routes for Ramtouses's massive army to approach the Ell camps without detection.

Their reports determined the location of a small river that would bring them within a night's march of the Ell camps. It was a long night's march to the river.

The river was a stone's throw with an abundance of thick grass as tall as a man on either bank. They would use the grass to their advantage. Many of his men slept along the bank while the rest took to the fields bordering the shallow river.

They moved on that evening along the banks of the river away from troublesome water bugs.

The scouts returned early in the morning with news of an Ell patrol half a morning's walk upriver. If the river served as a water source for the Ell army, it could be the last opportunity to get water. Accordingly, Ramtouses intended his men to carry as much water with them as possible when they left the river.

It made sense the Ell would post a permanent guard to protect their only water source as patrols came and went collecting it for the large army.

He dispatched additional scouts to monitor the shift changes. He needed to know if they killed the Ell patrol how long they would have before the replacement patrol arrived to discover them missing.

Three nights passed before the scouts returned reporting the watch had just changed. The new arrivals brought over a hundred camels with them, loaded them with fresh water then sent the previous shift away with the camels.

Ramtouses could now move his forces to the location where the Ell collected their water. That position would be vital for their descent upon the enemy camps. They would kill the newly arrived guards, every one. None could be allowed to escape and warn others of their presence.

Early that evening the tribesmen silently surrounded the water patrol and put down the men with blow darts. They quickly disposed of the bodies to prevent attracting buzzards and inadvertently alerting the enemy of their presence.

They stripped the slain men, cut up the bodies, fed them to a herd of wild pigs that had followed the army for scraps and buried any remaining traces of them. They looked much like the prisoners seen in Tungal, pale with long stringy hair and beards.

The army refilled their water supplies and moved out. The scouts had reported a sparsely wooded area large enough to conceal Ramtouses's army. They should be there before morning.

⁘

The ranks of Holofernes's army, in full armor, stood in formation creating a wide avenue through which King Sennacherib marched his army into the camps of their comrades. It was well over two weeks since they departed Lachish. The sound of beating drums and soldiers singing the Assyrian cry of war filled the air as King Sennacherib rode on a white chariot with four golden horses. His clothing matched the colors of his chariot and horses.

He rode straight up to Holofernes, climbed down and stood ramrod straight while Holofernes knelt to one knee. The king put out his hand and Holofernes kissed it, then the entire military horde called out King Sennacherib's name with a mighty roar.

Holofernes's quarters were set upon a mound nearly the height of a man above the normal plane. His tent faced Jerusalem, giving him an excellent view of the walls and gates of the city. They situated King Sennacherib's living space on another mound near the center of this massive force so when the battle began he could observe the whole war effort in front of him.

General Holofernes was anxious to review the war plans with the king and immediately escorted Sennacherib and his personal attendants to his large tent. "The troops are full of vigor, eager to engage the enemy. We attack in two days. Those who fought with you at Lachish will be rested by then, too."

Sennacherib listened, nodding. Finally he said, "Enough of war. Tell me of Ahikar's insolence. Tell me everything. Withhold no detail."

Holofernes related the incident. Sennacherib did not interrupt his general. His eyes never left Holofernes's face.

Holofernes concluded, "I had no choice. I could not let him reside in camp when he is of the mind the god of Judah will be victorious over us. The words he uttered are blasphemous, and the men know it should not go unpunished. It is a disgrace to those who died in the name of Baal."

Sennacherib bowed his head. He remained silent. Finally, he asked, "Why would he do that to me?"

The king looked distressed for a moment, and then he took a deep breath. "I believe he was driven by a desire to spare his own people the wrath of Baal. But how could he believe Baal would allow such blasphemy to go unpunished? I wonder if he is happier with his own people than with me and the wealth and position he was afforded at my pleasure."

The king straightened and shook himself. "So it will be. He will die. I will see his face once again and then he must die before me. Let the men know that when the city is taken, anyone who brings Ahikar alive to me will receive a rich reward by my hand."

Ramtouses and his men arrived at the wooded area the following morning, and just as the scouts had detailed, the entire army found concealment between and behind the many tall bushes and scrub trees.

Ramtouses climbed a sturdy tree. From that vantage point, he could barely discern the encampment of the men from Ell. Taharga and Baduga returned from their own survey of the enemy camp and reported the location of each unit. No one slept until the scouts finished outlining the strengths of the Ell military.

They drew another map on the ground that showed where the cavalry made camp at the southwest perimeter, away from the walls. It was the logical placement as horses had to be in an open area where a gallop could be achieved. The riders camped nearby for quick access to the horses. Now that Ramtouses knew their precise location, he could finalize his plan for the dart men to attack the cavalry first.

The next sketch in the dirt marked the tall shield bearers, Ramtouses's target for the second group of dart men. He showed the leaders of his dart men where they would approach and attack the cavalry and the tall shield bearers. Three-quarters of the dart men would strike down as many of the cavalry as possible. The cavalry drew the larger group because they represented by far the most danger to the tribesmen. His warriors had no matching horsemen to set against the enemies' force of men on horseback. The success of the dart men's operation was crucial to the overall battle.

Ramtouses wondered how his army of warriors could move to a position just beyond the dart men's attack. They would be needed to provide support for the dart men once the attackers were discovered. Even though the grass stood as tall as most men in many places, it would require both providence and caution to move so many men in that close without being seen. Ramtouses retired thinking the battle could start as soon as the next night.

❖

It was morning in Jerusalem. King Hezekiah forewent his chariot and walked to the main gate. What would the Assyrians be up to now that their king had joined them? An attack could come at any time.

Suddenly, a young boy ran past his guards and up to him.

"My king, where do you need me to fight?" the boy asked. He raised his arm with a small sword in his hand.

One of the guards grabbed him but Hezekiah said, "Let him go."

Looking down to the child, he asked, "How old are you?"

The boy answered him with a serious look upon his face. "I am nine, but will kill many Assyrians for the sake of my people and you, great king. The LORD is with us."

Hezekiah pulled the boy close to his side. He stood still, holding him. *Who am I to judge? Even a child has more faith than I do! How can I say whom God has chosen to save our people! When the fighting starts, children, just like this one, will be fighting to save their lives.*

He told the boy to go home. "When the time comes, you will know to fight."

The king turned and went back to the palace, directly to Judith's quarters.

❖

Judith was in her quarters with her handmaidens practicing the dance they expected to perform before Holofernes.

She heard her name called and turned to find King Hezekiah watching.

"Yes, my king," she answered, "we are preparing a dance for Holofernes. Should you determine my maids and I are going, I wish to be ready."

The king listened then said, "You do not look like yourself with this hair."

She merely nodded.

Hezekiah stood still, as if he waited for direction. He looked at Judith and her maids but appeared to not see them. Judith stood still also, and waited patiently for her king, not knowing what he would say or do.

"You have been in my thoughts," he said. "Who am I to decide what the LORD wants? You have shown tremendous faith. I will not stand in the way of anyone who has enough faith in our God to put their life in his hands. If it is the will of the LORD, so it will be. Carry on with your plan. When you are ready for the gates to be opened, I will inform the guards."

Judith bowed. "Thank you, my king."

King Hezekiah departed. Judith and her maids continued with their dance recital.

❖

Holofernes's army moved all five siege ramps into combat position and brought the battering ram to the road leading to the main gate. Holofernes sent word to King Sennacherib that the battle would begin tomorrow.

He arose in the early morning hours. A soft rain had begun before dawn and by daybreak heavy clouds rolled in, the light rain became heavier. By midmorning the winds picked up. Thunder and lightning prevailed. The lightning flared into blinding light as it flashed across the darkened morning sky.

❖

Ahikar awakened a number of times throughout the night and could smell a hint of rain in the air. Now, the early morning skies appeared somewhat darkened and the hint of rain became a reality. He went to Judith's quarters.

"Oh, Ahikar, I am so glad you are here. I have permission to proceed. I would have left today but this storm has made it impossible. My dress would be ruined and have no sparkle. My hair would collapse. I cannot leave on a rainy day."

Ahikar stood and listened, waiting until she finished. "I do not wish you to go. Please, Judith, will you reconsider?"

⁙

Judith looked at his sad face. "What is this? You know I have to go. What has come over you?"

"Judith," he whispered. "Will you make me say it? I love you. I truly love you with all my heart."

Judith was not surprised to hear his declaration. "Ahikar, I have been confused all my life when it comes to men, not knowing if their pledges were for the person I am or for my inheritance. You are the second man I believe who has loved me for who I am, not for my wealth. Yes, I care for you also, but I am destined to another fate."

"Judith, perhaps I created the tale merely to gain your confidence. Perhaps it was nothing more than a way to be freed from the dungeon and have pleasant quarters, clothing, good food and such."

"It matters not. It is too late. I will go anyway." She considered what he said. "Why did Holofernes not kill you? You said something to save your life. You used his weakness, his love of women. You softened his heart. That had to be the only way you could have escaped that situation. This same weakness is what I shall focus on when I deceive Holofernes."

"I beg you, do not go." Ahikar's voice was a whisper. "If this man turns against you..." He seemed to choke on his own words. He swallowed and breathed deeply, trying to quiet the fear he felt for Judith.

"Remember, these people see themselves as superior over all others in the world. He could despise you and feed you to the men who serve him, men who are as hungry dogs."

"Ahikar, tell me, which is better—for me to die in their camps raped and beaten to death or to wait until Holofernes and his men sack the city and rape and beat me to death at the time of their choosing?"

Judith said no more. He took her in his arms and held her tightly. He kissed her, and she knew all the love in his heart. She did not resist, but once he released her she said, "If only these troubled days were different, our life together would hold much promise. Ahikar, I am very sorry it will never happen for us now. As much as I care for you, I will not refrain from my commitment."

⁙

He held her close and both were quiet. Standing near the window, they watched the storm outside. The storm inside Ahikar's heart was gently muted, although her words did little to allay the spears of fear lodged there.

⁙

Judith allowed the warmth of his embrace to flood her body and soul with a tranquility she had not known for a long time.

⁙

Ramtouses believed that many of his men would die in the coming battle and he felt the need to assure them that their lives would not be lost in vain. This could well be his last opportunity to address the entire formation of warriors.

"We must remain quiet for we are close to the enemy. There will be no shouting or cheering as in the past." The leaders setup relay stations to insure everyone heard the message, and then informed Ramtouses once all was readied.

As he did not stand on an elevated platform, only a few hundred of his three hundred thousand men could see him. The gravity of their situation was not lost to the men, and they needed to hear his words. He scanned his audience, looking at them with a focus so intense it seemed to meld his mind with theirs.

⁙

The tribesmen near him saw a self-assured man who held his head high. His garment bore no special markings. He wore no headgear or decoration proclaiming superior status. He started to speak.

271

"Loyal and brave tribesmen, I am filled with admiration for you all. I am proud of each of you for the discipline and respect you have shown. You have made yourselves into a remarkable army. I will always be honored to say I was a part of it. Tomorrow night we will stop the people of Ell who killed our loved ones and who vow to destroy the rest of us. We will make our world a better place to live. Some of us will not see the sunrise. The agony of death will close our eyes. However, do not let the fear of death overpower your hearts and minds."

Ramtouses held his hands out toward his men, moving his arms from one side of the camp to the other, encompassing all. The relays followed his movements.

"Life forever progresses. Humans are the tallest in the expansion of creation here on earth. Today, we find ourselves at the early stages of this process. Each generation will strive for perfection through countless trials and errors. As time marches on, humankind will choose the path of righteousness as opposed to evil and treachery—once the world is free of the Ell."

Ramtouses wiped the sweat from his brow and stretched his tall frame. He turned from side to side, facing his army. Pointing randomly, he said, "You, you, and you, yes, each of you. We fight this battle to insure life for those future children. The anguish we know tonight will become one of many cries in the night, one of many twists in the road for mankind as he journeys into the unknown.

"Humankind will solve the imperfections of nature. Obstacles, no matter what they may be, will no longer impede our journey.

"Listen to my words. Before the sun and moon grow weary from their travels across the sky, humankind will escape the hard circumstances of life, including death, and complete one of nature's many goals of creation."

He banged his fist into the palm of his other hand, looked fiercely at his army, and spoke with confidence.

"Children of future generations will be perfectly sane of mind and physically healthy in body, and will be able to appreciate complete happiness knowing what was required of their ancestors to obtain it.

"Existence will not cease for the ones who know death, whose souls no longer walk among the living on the morning after battle.

"After all of this has come to pass, humans of the future will remember those of us who sleep here in this field and every other field where death has caught us. Our offspring will capture our souls as we would harvest wheat from the fields and deliver us into their kingdom. They will welcome us as their ancestors and show us the ways of eternal peace and happiness.

"Fight! Fight with all your strength so we can return home with victory, and the stories of our triumph will be told to our children for generations. Remember, I will fight with all my might right there by your side. If we die here in battle, our deaths will not be in vain. I love each of you and hope the best for us all."

Ramtouses finished speaking. He stepped back and Lozato came forward. He raised his clenched fist high into the air. "Let us confirm our agreement," he said. "Show your fellow tribesmen that you will follow Ramtouses's command."

Immediately fists lifted to the sky, one wave followed by another then another as the message carried from station to station. The raised fists punched the air up and down, all in silence in a powerful demonstration of unity. They belonged to a grand design, and the end of it brought a new beginning for all.

Ramtouses was humbled. Though charged with excitement at the moment, he was not thrilled. After tomorrow night thousands of these brave and loyal men would be dead.

❖

They did not sleep much that day. Lightning and thunder dominated the sky, and the high bush terrain provided little shelter from the rain. Baduga came to Ramtouses early that afternoon to relay some important information. The rain had subsided but not stopped.

"The father of the Ell has unlimited power. His foremost weapon is the thunderbolt. Whenever he is angry, he dominates all with his thunderbolt. Whenever he shows his rage, the people of Ell seek shelter and pay homage to him."

Ramtouses considered it. "If this is true, the people of Ell are in their tents hiding from the wrath of their god.

*This could be the time to move to our attack positions.* He ordered the army to make ready to move out into the wet grass. They cut the tall grass and tied it to their arms, bodies and head as camouflage.

With plenty of daylight hours left, the forces of dart men and archers who would use the poisons in their attack carefully filled their pouches with toxin.

The army moved forward with their camouflaged covering. They lowered themselves into a crouching position to stay as hidden as possible. Each followed the trail of the person in front of him, careful to keep the disruption of the tall grasses about them to a minimum.

Thunder still boomed and lightning danced across the skies, but the rainfall had lessened.

The warriors dropped down to crawl the final stretch. By early evening they arrived at the point Ramtouses had chosen for them to bivouac before the attack. The storm cleared. The night was calm. Just as Baduga had predicted, they saw no sign of life in the camps of the children of Ell.

Ramtouses's men were in combat position, which meant they would spend the rest of the night and daylight of the following day laying low in the grass.

⁘

Earlier King Sennacherib addressed his army. "Baal is doing his work in the skies. Let us all pay homage to him. Go now to your tents and worship him."

Following his words, a bright bolt of lightning flashed across the sky. A few moments later, the loud roar of thunder erupted. The Assyrians retreated to their tents. Again and again the lightning flashed across their campsites. The rain drizzled. The thundering echoes from the tall hills around them multiplied the alarming drama.

The following morning, the men arose full of life. Holofernes met with his high-ranking officers to discuss their late morning attack plan.

King Sennacherib sent word to hold the war effort until he finished his rites of worship for Baal. The day seemed ordinary. No clouds lingered from the soaking rain. The men expected a bright and sunny day as they prepared for battle.

⁕

As usual, the Assyrian troops lined up for the meal at midday. The men began to notice something strange in the sky. Puzzled, the troops watched the heavens.

"What is this?" they asked each other.

No one knew.

"The sun has dimmed."

They began pointing and crying out in horror. "Look! Look!"

It was not an hallucination. The whole camp became spectators, trying to figure out what evil curse had been cast upon them.

King Sennacherib came out of his tent and looked up in absolute disbelief. *Is this more of Baal's displeasure? Will this end with their destruction or ours?* Have pity on your servants, oh Baal, we will appease your anger.

Holofernes stood on his mound with arms akimbo as he looked into the sky with wonder. A huge black shadow covered the entire field behind them from the far south to the far north.

It raced toward them. The sight shocked him—a shadow blacking out everything in its path.

He shaded his eyes as he watched the sun. He had no doubt this horror encompassed his entire military force. The crescent of sunlight narrowed until it shrank to a speck of brilliant light. Then, suddenly, there was no light at all. It blinked out and disappeared, startling him.

The dark shadow racing along the ground overtook the entire Assyrian campsite and thrust it into complete and utter darkness.

Chaos broke out. Food spilled to the ground as thousands of brave Assyrians fell to the ground, covering their heads, while others ran to their tents.

King Sennacherib slowly retreated into his tent.

Holofernes's heart beat rapidly, but he remained standing, overcome with curiosity and amazement.

The Assyrian congregation prayed to Baal. Some thought the Hebrew god had come to destroy them. Panic stricken, they cowered. And then, the sun slowly began to give its light again and the huge shadow could be seen moving quickly away from their camps.

*Could this be a curse?* The Assyrians puzzled over what had just occurred. The mystery caused extreme anxiety for many as they slowly climbed to their hands and knees and continued to pray to Baal.

To Holofernes, it was obvious war was not going to happen today. *This was a very bad omen. Best to make the day one of worship for all.*

In the dawning hours of the same morning, Ramtouses and his men prepared for sleep. Periodically each unit made a series of small movements to stretch their muscles and maintain physical readiness.

**Diamond Ring Eclipse**

As noontime approached most of the men slept, but some were awake and saw the sky begin to darken. They woke those who slept and soon all the tribesmen shaded their eyes against the very bright but disappearing sun. A shadow raced toward them, covering the land like a gigantic blanket.

Ramtouses watched the event in astonishment. He could not look away from the colossal wall of darkness rushing majestically toward him and his army. The shadow engulfed them and fear of this unknown event overcame them. They trembled as they lay in the tall grass.

Ramtouses looked up at the sun, screening the brilliant light through his fingers. Strangely, the sunlight seemed to be ever so slowly overcome by a darkening. *How can this be?* The sun slowly disappeared behind a black disk. He stared in disbelief. Would the sky ever return to normal?

He looked toward the horizon. In every direction a sliver of scattered light created a reddish glow and unusual shadow effects. A quick and distinct drop in temperature was noticed. He looked to the sky again and saw the stars. He recognized many of them, as if old friends. Plants and animals around them reacted as if it were nighttime. Birds stopped singing and went to roost. Daytime flower blossoms began to close. Bees became disoriented and stopped flying. All of nature seemed to be still and quiet.

After only a short while, just when everyone expected the end of the world to come, a sliver of light suddenly emerged and, exactly as it had vanished, the sun began to reappear. The skies brightened until the sun, a great disk of light, shone as if nothing had happened. Waves of relief floated over Ramtouses's entire army.

The strange event came at a critical time in Ramtouses's battle plans and could easily become devastating to his warriors' state of mind. He had to turn this episode into a favorable one for his plans of attack.

There was no time to regroup. His army was in a crisis of hysteria in the middle of an open field before an enemy that could lacerate every segment of their flesh. Ramtouses gathered his leaders before him.

"Pass the word. The sign to attack has been given. The people of Ell are all frightened and have run to hide in their tents. Our ancestors have given us the sign of victory by taking the light of day and returning it. Let us show the ancestors we understand by preparing our bodies for the fight. The war will begin as soon as the night is dark black. We all know our roles in this battle. Let us perform well."

The assembly of warriors smeared themselves with war paint carried in pouches on their waistbands. Body paint was a traditional prebattle ritual practiced by their ancestors for generations. If a warrior died in battle, his ancestors would know him by the paint markings he wore. Each tribesman decorated his partner with colors of black, red and white. Black was for life. The color red symbolized war. White signified their spirits. The paint also served to camouflage the warriors and strike fear in the enemy.

⁜

Ramtouses called for Baduga and Taharga to thank them.

"You two have been a great help to me. I think highly of you both for your success in bringing us here. I will not ask you to fight with us tonight. You both may leave and rejoin your people. Take your men with you."

Baduga said, "Nonsense! We are here to the end and will fight with you tonight."

Ramtouses looked at the two men. "Speak for yourself, Baduga. What about you, Taharga? This is your chance to go home."

"My men and I came for the fight, not just to be your guides and advisors." Taharga spoke with pride and commitment. "We are also with you to the end. You must remember it was our people they attacked first."

Their words filled Ramtouses with pride. He smiled.

"If we survive, you two will become wealthy men. Back home in our country I will award you with treasures from Tungul and Juba."

⁜

Taharga thanked Ramtouses and embraced him before leaving. His heart was heavy with the knowledge of his role in the ruse that brought these men to this place and time. Baduga also embraced Ramtouses and turned to follow Taharga.

When the two had moved a good distance away, Taharga stopped. He told Baduga he wanted to go back and tell Ramtouses the whole truth about their deception.

"I cannot hold this any longer. He is the best man I have ever known and to mislead him like this, I cannot live with it." He turned to go back. Baduga, still bent over in the grasses, grabbed him by the arm while drawing his dagger.

279

"No!" he whispered. "Are you mad? He will put us both to death. He may not even believe you. After all this hard work, he will not stop the attack even if you told him. So what good would it do?"

"But he must know Princess Carnabrara is still alive."

"Quiet, you fool." Baduga hissed. "He will be crushed. Do you believe he will run off and leave his men after all the hardships of this journey? He can do nothing about this terrible situation we have put him in even if he knows the truth." Baduga's anger was rampant. "If you say one more word about this I will kill you myself before you have the chance to tell anyone!"

Taharga pulled away. "I am not afraid of you. Kill me! I would rather be dead for what we did."

Both men grew still, crouched over and glaring at the other.

Taharga considered Baduga's words. "Would he embark on a wild journey to find Princess Carnabrara? Perhaps. I agree with you. I will not tell him now. It is best he does not know the truth at this time. Ramtouses would be devastated, out of his mind with rage. After all that has been done to him, I will not add more injury."

⁙

Ahikar arrived at his quarters after a meeting with the military leaders. Someone knocked at the entrance and called his name.

The voice surprised him and he nearly tripped while rushing to the doorway. It was Judith. He joyously invited her in. *Had she changed her mind?*

⁙

Judith wanted to thank Ahikar for all his input while preparing her for the dangerous task ahead. She caught the look of relief on his face when he opened the door. He hoped she would delay or even cancel her departure because of their feelings, but the plan had to be implemented.

280

*This could be the last time I see him, but I cannot disclose my plan to leave today. If Ahikar pleads with me not to leave, it would make my judgment of the matter more difficult.*

"Don't come to my quarters at your usual time," she said. "There is no need. My maidens and I will be practicing the dance all day."

Judith began to withdrew from his doorway, then stopped. "Thank you so much. I thank God for putting you in my life and showing me my destiny." She left to return to her own quarters.

※

A changing of the guards patrolling the walls of Jerusalem occurred at midday, so twice as many guards and soldiers were on the walls. Their concentration on changing shifts was momentarily diverted. The soldiers kept glancing up, trying to figure out why the sun's brightness changed. The clear, sunny day grew dim and dull, though no clouds gathered in the sky. They grew alarmed. A black wall rushed toward them, snatching up the daylight. Hundreds fell to the walkway, covering their faces, screaming for Almighty God.

※

Judith sat in her quarters looking at her costume ready and laid out for her. The maidens had finished dressing. *Is this the hour to put my plan into action? Is this the right time? Are we really going to do this?*

While she contemplated the dangers and possibilities, the light from outside drew her attention. Slowly, she walked to the window and looked out. She squinted. The sun, somehow, gave less light. For a moment she did not believe the obvious then suddenly she understood.

"Oh, God," she cried, "This is it! It is a sign in the heavens from the Almighty."

Her maids rushed around in circles, obviously frightened by the strange dimming of the sun.

She screamed at them. "Hurry! Help me into my dress, now."

They went to the corner and huddled, shaking. Judith ran over to them and pulled them into action. "This is a sign from our LORD!" she shouted. "Please hurry with the dress. Put it on me quickly. We must go now."

While they attempted to dress her, she pushed another of her maidens toward the door. "Go to the king. Tell him I want to leave now. I request a chariot to carry us. The guards will need to be informed to let me out. Hurry! Run!"

⁜

King Hezekiah stood watching the sky in utter bewilderment when the maid ran in with the message. The guards before his chambers were hypnotized by the sun and did not see her run past.

"My God," Hezekiah's voice was a whisper. "Is this the day you will come?"

Judith's maid pulled urgently on the King's arm. "My mistress must leave now. She requests a chariot, saying the darkened skies are a sign from our God telling her to leave and do his bidding."

Hezekiah looked down at the woman, rushed out and grabbed one of the stunned guards by his uniform.

"Come to your senses, man," he shouted. "Take this pass and obtain a chariot. Wait outside the palace steps for Judith, and then take her to the main gates. Hurry! Our LORD demands it. This is His sign and we will obey."

⁜

The guard shook himself and ran out. Hundreds of people on the streets ran about hysterically. Some even fell to the ground and lay praying for the God of Israel to save them.

He pulled the chariot in front of the palace steps and waited for Judith, as directed. Tiny points of light shone through the leaves of a nearby tree and reflected on the ground as hundreds of crescent shaped images of the slowly returning sun. He looked at the palace and the surrounding buildings. A peculiar pattern, thin wavy lines alternating light and shadow, moved and undulated on the building walls, like the soft lines of sand he once saw left by many waves on an open beach. He marveled at the sight and through his fear of all the strange happenings around him, he thought the scene before him so beautiful that it would never leave his mind.

Judith and her maids rushed anxiously down the steps. Judith wore a black cape. She lifted the hem of her gown so she could move quickly. Each of her two maids carried two large bags. All three stepped into the chariot, and the driver sped off in the direction of the gate.

By the time they reached the walls, the skies had returned to normal. The guards were still praying and asking Yahweh for forgiveness as they continued to watch the sky. The driver showed them the king's emblem pass and they nervously opened the gates.

Judith hurried through with her two maids.

As she dropped the hem of her dress to the ground and threw aside her cape, she said, "Remember everything we practiced. Do not follow me too closely. I must be fully visible to the Assyrians' eyes."

The gown sparkled brilliantly in the brightness of the sun, the many jewels creating a dramatic display of color as she moved. Speckles of shimmering colors danced on the ground and flickered across the faces of the two maidens as she walked. The vivid light could be seen over a great distance. Judith's hair was spectacularly coifed in a great vertical circle across the top of her head and she truly presented an image of wonder.

⁌

**Eclipse shadow bands observed on walls**

Ahikar sat back with his midday cup of tea when he noticed a change in the light coming through his window. Hearing a commotion outside, he stood and walked over to his window to investigate. His eyes widened in sheer amazement as he watched the sky grow dark. He stood motionless. His mouth fell open, but he made no sound. In the street below people cried out in fear. Their screams came from all corners of the city.

Through the darkened scene before him, he saw a chariot racing for the gates and thought he glimpsed Judith. Panic seized him. He felt his face begin to quiver. His heart pounded with alarm as he turned and dashed out of his quarters.

Ahikar leapt down the stairs shouting for Judith.

"Judith! Judith! Oh, LORD, God of Israel, do not let her go."

He rushed into the street, pushing aside the frightened people blocking his path. He ran as fast as he could in the

284

direction of the racing chariot. When he reached the gates, they had already closed behind her. He found a narrow slot in the heavy, metal gate and could see her nearly a rock's throw away.

He screamed again, "Judith. Come back. Come back!"

He knew she would not turn to acknowledge him even if she heard him. Her mission held her absolute focus.

He turned away. "What have I done? Oh, what have I done?"

The sky appeared as if nothing unusual had happened on this bright and sunny day. He cried out, "Oh my LORD, what have I done? Please bring her back to me."

He looked around frantically and saw King Hezekiah with a band of his guards around him ride up on chariots. *Has he come to see the beautiful Judith go off into the Assyrian camps?*

Covering his face in sorrow and regret, Ahikar fell to his knees crying.

"I just helped send the woman who means everything to me to her demise—a sweet and innocent young woman, sent into the den of tormenting heathens, blood-thirsty Assyrians, to her certain death. Oh my LORD, what was I thinking?"

As Hezekiah reached the top of the walls, he called down to Ahikar, "Pray to the almighty LORD."

The people of Jerusalem crowded along the walls, watching their beloved child move closer and closer to the Assyrian camps.

The king spoke to the people. "The sign of the LORD has departed. He works His miracle to save His holy city through our beloved Judith. Let us all pray to the true God."

# 18

# HOLOFERNES MEETS JUDITH

## 701 B.C.E.

J udith stood with her back to the gates of Jerusalem, her two maidens four or five steps behind her. The sleeping potion was tucked inside one of the bags carried by her maids, wrapped and sewn into a handkerchief in such a way that only a slight stretch would tear the cloth and let the powder pour out.

Judith's stunning, glittering gown fit loosely below the waist and barely kissed the ground. She took a deep breath before starting down the main road from the city. The gown moved gently with the rhythmic sway of her body. Even though the potential violence facing her made her fearful, she felt a soothing peculiar serenity. She radiated confidence and the fear that first gripped her two maidens began to ease a bit as they sensed Judith's assurance. The three Hebrew women approached the enemy encampment.

An Assyrian soldier yelled, "Look!"

⁘

Holofernes had not moved since the whole ordeal in the sky began. Now, he turned and saw her.

*What on earth is this? Why are these strange things happening? What do they mean?* The questions flooded through his mind like water rushing over the rocks.

Coupling his hands around his mouth, he shouted to his men. "Stay where you are. Let no one approach them!"

⁛

Judith performed as if her life hung in the balance. It did.

She calculated every move to express grace and elegance. She imagined herself walking on clouds. She let her arms hang loosely and swing back and forth.

⁛

When she got close to the soldiers, Holofernes shouted. "Make a path for her leading up to the mound of my dwelling."

The Assyrian ranks fell back and made way for the three women.

As each step brought her closer, Holofernes could see her more clearly. The woman's eyes seemed fixed upon him. Mesmerized by her astonishing beauty, he imagined how she looked in her natural form. He compared her to all the noble Assyrian women he had known and judged her beauty as equal to any of them, if not beyond.

Her face was sweet and innocent. Her hair was braided and twisted above her head in a design that reminded him of a silky red spider web.

Ahikar's story came to him.

She stopped at the foot of the mound leading to his quarters and looked up, her eyes locked on his. Neither said anything for a few moments, as if they were sizing up one another before a match.

Then Holofernes said, "When I first saw you, it was as if seeing a glittering star from the heavens. Who are you? Are you a goddess of Baal or an angel from the Hebrew God?"

He was astonished when she responded in his language. "I am neither of those. I am the seer of whom Ahikar spoke."

Holofernes stood in silence. His left hand supported his right elbow and leaned his chin on his right hand. He appeared

287

to be thinking. "When Ahikar first told me about you I took him to be mad."

He thought for a few more moments before continuing. "There is the possibility Ahikar and your people are trying to snare me and my Assyrian countrymen. But how could you come from any snare? You are real, just as stunning as he described, and no one, not even the Hebrews, can create such an incredible likeness, red hair and all."

In a clear and haughty voice, the woman said to him. "Do not patronize me. I am here as a seer to prophesy the outcome of this war to you."

Holofernes returned his hands to his hips. "Why do you prophesy to me, not to your own people? Should they not know the outcome of this war?"

She answered with the same, firm tone. "I did prophesy to them. They would not listen. Our LORD demands a faithful people, but they are not steady in their worship. Only in the time of trouble do they turn to the God of Israel. That is why, when the sign came from the heavens, I was thrown out of the city."

*Was this event in the sky a sign from their god? It was no doubt an evil omen.* "Come up here, close to me. Perhaps there is some validity in what you say."

She came close to within an arm's length of him and stopped.

Holofernes snarled and gritted his teeth. It was a ploy he often used to intimidate people. Most people withdrew under his glare, but not this woman. Her eyes remained fixed on him. Her expression remained unchanged. He motioned the maidens to stand back as he walked a circle around the lovely creature, examining her entire figure.

"Looking at my form will not tell you the secrets of the prophecy I hold inside." There was no change in her expression and no inflection or hesitation in her voice.

For the first time since seeing her, Holofernes turned his eyes away. He ordered some of his men to erect a tent fit for an Assyrian noblewoman next to his own. He demanded it be completed as soon as possible. Turning again toward the woman, he bade her reveal her name.

Slowly, softly, she said, "Judith."

Holofernes enjoyed the timbre of her voice. He invited her with her maidens into his large tent until the work on their tent would be completed. He led the way, and once inside, he directed them where to sit.

⁘

King Sennacherib came out of his tent after his prayer and worship time hoping to feel peace after the strange occurrences. A new commotion was about. What could it be?

One of his officers said, "My king, a Hebrew woman was thrown out of the city with two maidens. General Holofernes has contained them and is questioning her."

The king thought this to be no threat. *After all we just went through with the unusual events in the heavens, this is minor.*

He said to the officer. "Is that all? Have General Holofernes give me a full report after he questions her. I will expect him at the evening meal tonight."

The officer and a group of soldiers set out toward Holofernes's tent.

⁘

Inside Holofernes's tent, Judith remained standing but allowed her maids to sit where he had instructed. Holofernes stood several steps away from her when he asked, "Who is this seer who comes to me with prophecy? What is your narrative, Judith?"

Judith answered. "I am of the tribe of Ruben, the oldest son of Jacob. My ancestor Jacob had dreams foretelling the future. I believe that is where I inherited the gift of prophecy. My nobility and wealth come from my ancestry, and my status among the Jerusalem nobles is influenced by my divinations."

"Well spoken," Holofernes said. "Still, there is one other thing that must be addressed. What god do you serve? Feel free to speak the truth of what is in your heart for I respect an honest answer. Though I must say, I have never hurt a man or woman who serves King Sennacherib and our god Baal. If your people had not disrespected them, I would never have lifted up my spear against them."

Judith folded her hands behind her and walked close to him.

"King Sennacherib lives to express the will of his god, Baal, to all the earth. You, General Holofernes, are the power for chastising all straying souls. The industry of your mind is spoken of among all nations of the world. Your excellence and mightiness in the kingdom of Assyria shines above all. It is known what you did to Ahikar for insolence toward your god.

"Your god, Baal, is known throughout the world. Our God is not. He does not have a force to command His glory. Only the tribes here in these small communities know of Him. Let there be no doubt. I am a believer in the God of Abraham, Isaac, and Jacob, the God of all Israel."

Judith's words convinced Holofernes of her sincerity. He studied her for a few more moments before one of his guards interrupted and announced an officer of the king wanted an audience with him.

"Let him enter," Holofernes said. "What is it?"

"The King wants a full report regarding the Hebrew woman when you join him in his tent tonight. Also, he inquires of your war plans after the event in the sky."

General Holofernes said, "Tell him I believe there is a connection between the woman and the strange event in the sky today. I will have information later tonight, but it is unlikely it will be in time for our evening meal. The war effort is temporarily on hold until we regroup." The officer turned to leave, but before he left Holofernes continued, "If he needs me sooner, come back and let me know immediately."

"Yes, General," the officer departed.

Holofernes ordered a guard to stay with Judith and her maids while he went outside to see the progress of their tent erection. The tent was up and being filled with candles, mats, bedding, bathing cloths, incense and oils, water and fruit, all worthy of an Assyrian noblewoman. They even provided covered personal waste bowls. He oversaw the work to the end to make certain everything was done right.

He returned to his tent. "My men have completed your living space. You and your maidens should become comfortable. I will summon your return later."

As Judith left his tent, Holofernes said "I look forward to hearing your prophecy tonight and the story behind the signs in the skies."

Judith thanked General Holofernes for his hospitality.

He watched the women enter their newly prepared tent.

He left strict orders the women were not to leave the tent without his prior approval.

⁘

Judith and her maidens slowly adjusted to the tent Holofernes's men had setup. She looked at her two young companions. They looked tense. She remembered that day when she evaluated all the young women from the city and selected these two over the many others.

*They need words of encouragement,* she thought. *I need encouragement myself. Oh my God, give me the right words to bolster these two young women who are willing to do your will.*

She spoke in a quiet, loving voice. "How can I expect you not to be afraid when I myself feel the danger we are in. I selected you two for reasons other than your beauty. I know you love our people and the one true God. So far you have done even more than I expected. My fear is wrestling with my faith in our Lord? Inside of me the battle rages on with each breath I take, just as it does within you."

She walked directly up to them and said, "Look at me, look into my eyes. We will fight through our fears with the strength of our Lord to support us and subdue our fears.

"You must sing and dance better than ever before, and you must do so in complete tranquility."

She requested extra water from the Assyrians so she and her maids could bathe, perfume themselves and change their clothing. They wore both outer and inner garments.

Believing she had won Holofernes's interest, Judith retrieved the handkerchief from the bag and concealed it in her dress pocket. They sat down and reviewed their task for the evening one last time, then awaited Holofernes's summons.

⁜

General Holofernes summoned Judith and her maids to join him in his tent for an evening meal. He seated the women at a table prepared for him and his guests. His finest silverware and plates adorned the table. He asked Judith to eat with him, but she politely declined and pointed to the bag one of her maids had brought.

"I am pious, and I am obedient to my God. We eat ritually cleaned food. My maiden has our food in this bag." Holofernes did not object to her choice of food.

Her maidens set the food on the table, and the four of them had a quiet meal. When they had eaten, Holofernes asked her to explain the sign in the sky and tell him the prophecy.

Judith stood and walked to the center of the tent. She spoke eloquently with flawless articulation and fluent phrasing.

"This is the prophecy. The Assyrians are colossal in military might. Jerusalem is strongly fortified. The battle shall be frantically fought, extremely bloody, with no treasures for your efforts. The wealth of the city has already been delivered to you."

She pointed to Holofernes whenever she referred to him or his people.

"Truly I say to you, the Assyrians will lose thousands of their men but will find victory. The LORD's anger with Judah is great for they consumed items that ought not to touch their hands. They killed their cattle and drank the blood. They handled unclean grain, wine and oils. Therefore, because they did these things, it is certain they will be given up to destruction.

"As for you, Holofernes," she pointed directly at him again, "because of your tremendous loss of personnel, you will not be able to campaign against Egypt and Ethiopia, where there remain fabulous riches.

"However, by diverting your attention to these nations and bypassing Jerusalem, you will return to Nineveh with slaves, countless booty, and a formidable remaining army."

She walked directly before General Holofernes, her finger pointed at his chest. "Hear my words. Your glory in Nineveh will be surpassed by no man, your legacy will live in history forever."

She turned and moved a few steps away from him, then swung around and continued.

"The event in the sky that was seen by everyone was a sign from our God that he will have a blind eye to the fall of Jerusalem for their little faith and continuous sinning." She lowered her head and with tears flowing from her eyes she finished, saying, "And that is my prophecy to you."

Her credible speech and convincing mannerisms while presenting the prophecy impressed General Holofernes extremely. She amazed him. He asked, "How is it you come to know your prophecy? Does it come to you in a dream? Have you had other predictions and have you ever been wrong?"

Judith responded. "Dreams come to me once in a great while. I have never been totally wrong. Repeated dreams, such as this one, reinforce the facts of their truth."

Holofernes paced the tented space, shaking his head, before he finally spoke. "Judith, I believe you mean well, but I am the general of a very powerful army. I just cannot operate upon premonitions and superstitious beliefs. I have to use my training and experience to guide me in warfare. Perhaps you are correct. Perhaps no wealth remains in this city, but King

Sennacherib desires vengeance. Neither he nor I can see any military reason we cannot overrun this city and still have a strong body of men to go up against Egypt and Ethiopia whose main armies we have already defeated.

"However," he came up close behind Judith, "we will talk about this in the morning." He took his middle finger and rubbed it along the back of her neck, from the base to the hairline. "I will not make a decision on this until after we talk tomorrow."

He bent over and kissed her neck. Judith did not flinch or draw away. She did not want him to feel rejected. From what he had said, she did not believe anything would convince him to not attack the city tomorrow. She now considered her alternate scheme.

He faced her and placed his hands on her shoulders.

*I must stall him, somehow!* She smiled. "Let us have some wine."

When Holofernes reached for the wine carafe, she said, "I cannot drink your wine. We have brought our own."

Holofernes filled his goblet and gave them permission to drink their own wine.

Judith told him of their singing and dancing talents and suggested they perform for his pleasure.

She smiled coyly, trying to please this man who planned to destroy her people. And at the same time, she tried to think of how she could access the sleeping potion hidden away in her outer garment.

❖

Across the open fields, Ramtouses's words reassured and rejuvenated the tribesmen. Their trust in one another grew. Their courage was revitalized.

No patrols guarded the camp perimeters as if the enemy defied an attack. He asked Taharga about what appeared to be a giant wall further away from the camp.

"That is a city wall built by people who fear the Ell."

"Does this city have roads and buildings made of stone and men riding horses like Egypt?"

"Yes."

"When the fighting is over, I want to see this city."

Taharga told him, "You will be a hero to these people."

"Really?" Ramtouses was surprised. "When the world is at peace again, I want to be an adventurer as my great-grandfather and explore the many lands. I am ignorant of so much of the world."

⁙

As the evening drew late, the leaders of the dart men instructed them to move to their predetermined locations, which would bring them within attacking distance of their targets. Once in position, set and ready to engage the enemy, they had only to wait for the signal to attack.

⁙

Ramtouses had taught himself to imitate the many sounds of nature during his boyhood years and had learned the high-pitched bark of the local red fox. During the night, the people of Ell heard this sound periodically and most likely thought nothing of it. Ramtouses used a pre-determined pattern of the barking call for a signal to attack.

He thought back to the night he and Carnabrara sat on a hilltop. He remembered showing her his favorite star. Now, he looked and found it in the low sky to the west when the clouds moved and opened a small window to the sky. He spoke softly to it.

"Carnabrara, my love, I carry you in my heart. You flow with the blood in my arms and hands. You give me strength to deliver the punishing blows with my sword in answer to the excruciating death they inflicted upon you."

His eyes moved from the sky when the clouds thickened and he looked toward the coming battle site. His voice grew hard, and no one who heard his words could doubt their truth. "To the people of Ell, your mental torment and physical anguish shall now begin. And let the vengeance of all mankind fall upon you this night!"

Ramtouses cupped his hands to his mouth and gave three quick barks. He repeated it twice and stood listening as the barks were passed on into the distance.

---

Holofernes took a second drink from his goblet, set it down and walked over to Judith. He stopped so close to her, he could feel the heat radiating off her body.

Holofernes reached out and slowly pulled her to him. He took her into his big arms and held her tightly, lifting her to her tiptoes. He felt the rhythm of her breathing and the soft exhale of each breath. She did not move or say a word. He lowered his head and began to kiss her passionately. He wanted to devour her, moving from her lips to her face and neck then back to her lips.

He kissed her like she had never been kissed before. Then he slipped his hand inside her garment and took hold of one tender breast with his large rough hand while the other hand continued to press her against him. He rotated his finger around the areola and then rubbed the nipple of her breast until it hardened. He pinched it softly then harder, but not hard enough to hurt her. He pulled her garments open so her breasts were bared and focused his attention on the second one. He lifted her up, high enough for one of her nipples to slip into his mouth.

Holofernes believed Judith to be a prophetess and a priestess of the Hebrew people. He did not want to treat her as a slave or servant under his power so he showed more patience and was less demanding.

---

To win his trust, Judith believed she had to give in to his sexual advances and allow herself to feel the strong desires he elicited from her. She wondered if, at this point, she could convince Holofernes to allow them to put on the dance show for his pleasure without upsetting him.

Again, she said, "Let us dance and sing for you."

He pulled her outer garment open further and slipped his hand between her legs, rubbing her gently.

"We dance beautifully, let us perform for you. As we dance you will see our voluptuous figures in motion through our thin gowns."

She looked briefly into his eyes and then moved her glance downward with an alluring smile and a slow nod of her head. "It will add to the pleasures of being with us."

Holofernes finally agreed and released her, then turned to refill his goblet before settling back on the cushioned bench to watch their dance. "If it is so good, let me see if I agree," he commented.

Before they began to dance, Judith and her maidens disrobed down to their very soft, transparent gowns. They placed their outer garments next to Holofernes's table of food and wine. Judith retrieved the handkerchief containing the powdered sleeping potion and gently dabbed her brow, then dropped the soft cloth next to the wine carafe.

※

The silken, gauze-like material covered their bodies but General Holofernes saw every curve through the delicate cloth. Their dance movements caused the gowns to flow and swirl in beautiful patterns, creating a mesmerizing display for his enjoyment. They sang and the sweet notes of a familiar song floated through the air. It pleased him immensely. He smiled and leaned back to enjoy the show.

Holofernes could not take his eyes off the dancers as they moved faster and faster and then slowed to a more deliberate and provocative rhythm.

Judith took the now empty goblet from his hand and swung her hips from side to side while holding it. The dancers turned and bent forward slightly. Their hips continued to rock from side to side. Focused on the sway of their backsides, he relaxed even further.

⁜

She sang and danced her way to the wine carafe with her back to Holofernes. Her hand moved swiftly when she set down his goblet and picked up the handkerchief. In one fluid movement she broke the flimsy stitch, released the powder over his goblet, and brought the cloth to her face in a pretense of gently wiping her nose and mouth. She dropped the handkerchief and refilled the empty goblet.

Judith moved back to where Holofernes sat, never stopping her dance and song. Holding his cup of wine, she brought it to her lips as if to bid an honorary toast. The tainted wine touched her lips but she did not take it into her mouth. Instead, leaning forward, she brushed her lips against his face and offered the cup to him. He smiled victoriously, tipped the cup and drank.

Judith joined her maidens as the three women executed well-timed leaps, kicking their legs up high, one after another, in time to the song they sang.

⁜

Their dancing and singing caressed his stern heart.

They spun around in circles, enticing him with seductive arm and hand movements. Judith came up close to the general and twirled before him. He could see every inch of her spectacular body. Then they moved into a very sensual belly dance, including a tantalizing belly roll, over and over, smooth and in rhythm. Their undulating bodies, wrapped only in the beautiful saris, created a lovely, beguiling dance and Holofernes couldn't take his eyes from them.

Judith spun to a sudden stop directly in front of Holofernes. He looked up and handed the empty cup to her. Taking the goblet in both hands, Judith raised it to her cheek and then to her forehead, she held it out at arm's length and began to sing a new song. The melody sounded soft and faraway, a haunting Assyrian love song Holofernes loved. She brought it near her forehead and moved her head from one side of the drinking cup to the other, repeatedly. Her body swayed with the gentle flow of the music.

⁂

She enchanted Holofernes with her charm. His shoulders swayed to and fro in rhythm with the sweet song and at the end of it, he reached out and took her onto his lap.

He told the two maidens to remove his footwear and he once again started kissing Judith. The maidens removed his big boots. He stood, reached his long arms around the three women and guided them toward the bed. He gently nudged them onto the bed. Stepping back, the great General Holofernes grinned down at Judith and her maidens and started to remove his uniform.

⁂

Judith wondered why the potion had not yet affected him. She thought maybe it required more time and she needed to stall a bit longer. "I have my special bedding with me. It is made from sheepskin. Will you allow us to spread it upon your bed?

In slightly slurred words, Holofernes said, "I would like that very much."

The three women rose from his bed and one of the maids went to fetch the spread. When she returned they covered the bed with the sheepskin.

⁂

Holofernes had to shake his head, to stay awake. *Am I drunk from just a few goblets of wine? Or, am I just very tired?*

He called Judith to him and put his arms around her. Together they stretched out on the bed. He tucked Judith in his arms.

⁂

299

Judith dared not make a hasty move and lay there for quite a while before she slowly slid out of his embrace. As she stood, her body quivered. Plotting this scheme to deceive proved much easier than implementing it.

But the he-man lay fast asleep for the night. Judith instructed one of her maidens to stand at the entrance and give warning if anyone came up to enter. She told the other maiden to lie on the bed beside General Holofernes while she gathered her thoughts.

She walked in circles, thinking. *He is not only a hero to his army, he is their inspiration. To lose him in battle would be devastating to them and a psychological victory for my people.*

Judith thought of her LORD and the people of Judah who depended upon her to complete this mission. She cleared her mind and began to pray.

"Oh my LORD, give me the strength for what I must do. God of Israel, look on the works of my hands this hour. Raise up Jerusalem, Your city, and may I bring to pass that which I have proposed, having a belief that it might be done by You, through me."

She went to the entrance and said to her maid, "Make certain you are not seen watching. And, if someone does come, run over, strip off your garment and jump in bed with us. We want to give the illusion that we have lain with Holofernes." Returning to the bed, she reminded her second maid of what to do if anyone came into the tent.

Her mind on the task at hand, Judith grew nervous and upset again. She kept telling herself to hold fast to her faith. *It will be God guiding me.*

⁘

Outside, the soldiers guarding Holofernes's tent were relaxed. Their general appeared to enjoy his time with the Hebrew women. The song and laughter that came from within confirmed it as much as the quiet that followed. All seemed quite unobtrusive.

# 19

# THE ETERNAL NIGHT

## 701 B.C.E.

The daytime sky slowly slipped into the blackness of night. Ramtouses watched the darkness approach. He remembered the words of Baduga and Taharga in describing the formidable army his men would soon violently awaken, but Ramtouses believed some advantage lay with them. The clandestine attack, warring at night and use of the grating sounds were designed to remove the Ell soldier from his usual fighting element.

The echoes from the fox barks had stopped, but laughter and carousing could be heard from the Assyrian campsites. The tribesmen's plan called for the selection of random targets among the Ell. First would be the men who strayed from the main groups alone or in small groups of three or less. The venom had to work immediately to prevent alerting the whole camp. If a victim yelled or called out, the surprise element of the attack would be nullified.

⁘

The first to fall victim to a poisoned blow dart left his campsite in search of dried grass to build a fire. His arms full of the grasses, he bent over to pick up a bit more. A dart man watched and took aim. The Ell straightened. The tribesman let fly his poison dart. It struck behind the neck. The Ell's hand jerked up and slapped his neck as if a mosquito had bitten him then he dropped onto the grass without uttering a sound. Many more Ell targets became victims.

The tribesmen rose, blew the darts and dropped back down into the tall grass, a continuous up and down motion. They were like a school of fish jumping out of the water to consume the dragonflies hovering near the water's surface and then falling back beneath. The poison proved its extreme effectiveness. Not one Ell soldier had time to cry out for help, but neither would the dragonfly have time to be alarmed.

Ramtouses watched from his distant vantage point listening for any sign of alarm from the camps. In his mind he could picture hundreds of the Ell dying silently. But the oblivion would not last forever. At some point soon the enemy would be alerted.

The time came to give the signal for the archers to move into position to support the dart men as they pulled back. He gave three quick barks, repeating them once. The signal was relayed. Still no disruption in the camps of the Ell.

The tribesmen constituted a bold force, the best archers in all of Africa. They weaved through the tall grass like stealthy hunters of game.

⁂

It seemed to take forever for the Ell to become aware of the attack until the cavalry soldier who sought his companion stumbled upon the body.

He turned, "Come quickly! Come quickly! My partner is dead!" and ran as a dart struck him in the back. He collapsed but too late. The alarm had sounded. More and more men came.

They were easy targets for the dart men hiding in the bush.

The task to cripple and diminish the effectiveness of the cavalry as much as possible continued. The enemy soldiers ran straight into the hidden death waiting for them in the darkness. Hundreds more died.

The cavalry officers ordered the remaining cavalry and shield bearers away from the perimeter. As they withdrew, the dart men rose from the tall grasses and advanced, finding a wealth of targets.

Even though they could not clearly see what was happening in the camp, Ramtouses and the men who remained with him heard the commotion and knew the Ell were alerted. It was a sound like the roar of a lion when rising with an empty stomach after a long sleep.

⁘

It was time, three quick barks with no repetition. It was the final signal. The army moved in. The chanting began.

A shrill, sibilant sound suddenly erupted from all directions, constant and very loud. Thousands of warriors made this piercing, high-pitched hissing noise. It echoed off the hills, resulting in a weird pulsating tone. Deafening. Disturbing.

⁘

King Hezekiah and Queen Hephzibah retired to their chambers for the evening when they heard a strange sound from beyond the city walls.

"What on earth are the Assyrians up to now?" the queen asked.

They looked at each other, puzzled, and after a few moments he said, "Let us go to the gates to investigate this."

They exited the palace under escort of guards, joining hundreds of other bewildered people in the streets. By the time they reached the main gates, the walls were crowded with those hoping to discover the source of the mysterious noise.

Ahikar ran up to the king and asked if he could join them.

"Yes," said Hezekiah. "Do you have knowledge of this atrocious sound? Why do the Assyrians make it?"

Ahikar seemed just as baffled. "King Hezekiah," he said, "I do not believe it comes from the Assyrians."

Hezekiah looked at him. *If not from the Assyrians, then from where, from whom?*

The men and women of Jerusalem stood in wonder be-hind the battlement walls. They looked into the dark night, and listened. They saw nothing. The moon was hidden by heavy clouds.

⁘

Confusion reigned as the Assyrian officers mobilized their cavalry. The hissing sound sorely aggravated the Assyrian soldiers and interfered with their focus and ability to function.

One officer sent a group of soldiers to Field Marshall Holofernes to inform him of the situation and request his immediate presence.

Another group went to King Sennacherib to assure him the problem would be resolved quickly.

King Sennacherib appeared visibly upset by the strange noise and plugged his ears, attempting to block out the sound. "Cease this confounded noise!"

They backed away from his ire, nodding assent as they withdrew.

⁘

In Holofernes's tent, Judith gathered her courage. She flinched at the unexpected interruption, fearful of the noise. For a moment she stood frozen wondering what it could possibly mean.

"What is going on out there?" she asked her maiden standing at the tent entrance.

"Soldiers, many of them, running everywhere," the young woman said.

To her other maiden, Judith said, "Help me undress him."

Once he was naked, they spilled wine on him and the bed and rolled him over.

Just then, the maid watching at the tent entrance turned and began waving her hands around in panic.

"Soldiers are coming here. Now!"

Judith answered in a loud whisper. "Come. Remove your gown."

Dashing to the bed, the three nude women wrapped themselves around Holofernes as if drunk and exhausted.

Several men entered. One rushed to the bed and pulled the women out of the way. He tried for several minutes to revive General Holofernes.

He turned to another man. "Bring water. Hurry."

He splashed it onto Holofernes's face. Holofernes raised his arm and mumbled.

The officer sounded disgusted. "This man is totally drunk. He is of no use to us." He gave General Holofernes one more shake then turned to the others and hurried them all out of the tent.

⁙

By the time the group returned to report on Field Commander Holofernes's condition, the officer second in command, General Rabsaris, had arrived and was directing the course of action.

His assessment of the situation was that some feeble army wandered out of the bush and attacked the cavalry and the pavis shield bearers. The attack seemed to be coming from the close perimeter of the war camp. He ordered the cavalry to mount up at all costs and weed out whatever enemy was hiding in the grass.

The other Assyrian commanders milled about, temporarily confused and uncertain what to do. They did not know who or possibly what could be out there, nor did they understand what part that distressing noise played, if any. To make matters especially difficult, it was all taking place in the dark of night.

⁙

The dart men of the tribes switched their focus to the horses and the grooms who dressed the animals. Hundreds of dart men moved to where the cavalry horses stood corralled and began to kill the animals as well as anyone trying to prepare them for battle.

The Ell broke off a sizable portion of the horse herd from the main body and stampeded them with fire torches, forcing them to race out into the grassy area.

The terrified horses overran some of the dart blowers who were unable to escape their path and were trampled to death under the horses' hooves. Hundreds of others scattered out of harm's way, stalling the attack momentarily.

As the dart attack resumed, the first wave of cavalrymen, a unit of nearly a thousand horsemen, came charging out of the corral. They galloped around the mouth of the camp where the other horses had raced into the fields, hoping to engage whoever or whatever enemy they came upon. The first unit found themselves under heavy attack, but their purpose was distraction to allow the grooms time to get more horses and riders ready for subsequent waves.

The cavalrymen of this first unit put up an outstanding fight but, unable to see their opponents as they would in the light of day, they were ultimately slaughtered. Their sacrifice allowed three more units enough time to mount a charge into the grassy fields.

The horsemen, though highly trained and normally confident, were indecisive and uncertain under these strange conditions. Poor night vision slowed the usually swift pace of battle. Locating their attackers in the tall grass under an almost moonless sky proved to be their biggest problem.

Mobility gave the Assyrian cavalry an advantage, and they fanned out over a large area, hunting the tribesmen, running them down like the cheetah runs down the gazelle. The fighting cleared the way for units five through nine and half of ten to join the battle.

Commanding General Rabsaris received a status report. The report stated nine full units of a thousand riders each rode out to combat and a third of them left without horses wearing their fabric armor protection. The numbers stunned him. The general winced visibly. A tight knot grew in his throat making it difficult to swallow. *What in the name of Baal is happening?* He suddenly thought of the king and Holofernes. *What will they think or do when they hear this report?*

Rabsaris shook his head. *There must be some mistake. Twenty-seven thousand cavalry soldiers down to less than ten thousand!*

⁜

When the stampede of horses came out the tribesmen closest to the camp could not flee in time. Scores of them died, trampled to death by the horses' hooves. The dart men directed their flurry of poisoned darts to the cavalrymen who followed the stampede.

The horsemen carried long lances designed to inflict deadly wounds. With a quick twist and jerk, the rider could free the spear from the victim and have it ready to run down another.

Hitting a quick moving target with a blow dart required a high level of accuracy and the protection provided the horsemen by their shields and armor made it exponentially more difficult. To compensate, the dart men began to target the horses. A third of the horses had been deployed to the attack without the fabric armor to protect them. Those were the easiest prey for the dart men. Once the horse went down and the rider fell to the ground, he could then be killed by the sword or blow dart.

Still, after a time, the battle swayed toward the cavalry. The supply of darts ran low, and the speed and mobility of the horsemen overcame the men on foot. The horsemen routed out the tribesmen and slew them by the hundreds. The tribesmen who had delivered a devastating blow to the elite cavalry now fled for their lives.

Such a withdrawal was part of Ramtouses's battle plan.

The dart men raced to where the bowmen crouched in the grass. As hundreds of dart men retreated into their ranks, the bowmen stepped forward, ready for their attack.

⁜

The Assyrian cavalry now numbered far less than a quarter of their original strength. Even so, their arrogance had them believing they had prevailed, that the enemy was on the run. They followed after the dart blowers to finish them off and rid themselves of this terrible menace.

⁘

The bowmen stopped chanting the sibilant sound and focused their attention on the cavalry coming at them head-on.

The Ell cavalry had taken the bait and ridden straight into the trap.

Forty thousand bowmen whistled their poison arrows across the night sky.

The men of Ell never knew what hit them as men and horses fell victim to the hailstorm of poisoned arrows that rained down from the dark skies. The attack was thorough and devastating. When no more horsemen came riding up before them, the bowmen rejoined their fellow tribesmen and returned to making the loud sibilant chant.

⁘

Less than a handful of riders returned to tell of the horrifying experience. It took some time for the bewildered soldiers to internalize the reality of their loss. They were the mighty Assyrians but that did not make them immune to sorrow. The cavalry, the pride of their military power, no longer existed. It would not be easy to recover from such a loss.

The Assyrian officers and generals did not know what to say, no utterance seemed appropriate. What had been impossible to them had happened.

No one wished to be the one to inform King Sennacherib of the terrible loss, but he had to know. The generals reported the loss of the cavalry at the same time he was told of Field General Holofernes's disabled condition. The furious king ran from his tent screaming at everyone in general, yet at no one in particular.

"What are you fools doing out here?" His ranting continued. The officers who brought the bad news slowly drifted away, out of reach from his rage.

He muttered to himself. "The entire cavalry lost? How can this be? Could the people of Jerusalem be so clever as to sneak out of the city at night and destroy my whole cavalry? No. There must be some other explanation."

The eerie noise came at him from all sides. "These are not the sounds of the Hebrews. Why doesn't it stop? It is maddening. Stop it!"

The king turned back to his officers. "Forget Holofernes for now. Return to the battle. Destroy this new enemy. And stop whatever entity creates this terrible noise."

The officers hurried back to report to the Commanding General Rabsaris.

⁝

The Assyrian culture bred a warlike population, and after moments of grief, sorrow rapidly switched to hatred. A deep need for revenge rose to the surface of each hardened soldier. These aggressive and militaristic men knew nothing but fighting from childhood. They rushed into their assignments and prepared for the coming fight, even as the insane droning penetrated their every thought and action.

General Rabsaris ordered the siege ramps moved into positions within the interior of the army close to the pavis wall. Officers waved and pointed fingers as the massive army took to their positions. About three-quarters of the pavis wall-of-shields forces had survived the earlier attacks and formed a wall to the foremost of the camp facing the grassy fields at their front. Thousands of shields interlocked in a line stretching the length of the camp. With the army now in place behind them and with vengeance in their eyes, they stood primed and ready.

⁝

The people of Jerusalem were assaulted by the sound, unlike any heard before, and fear crept into their hearts like the cold of night chills ones bones. It slid down the neck and across the shoulders, shuddering through the body. Many refused to return to their homes and tried to stake out an area on or near the wall. Others meekly returned to their rooms where four walls blocked out some of the sound.

"I see no movement. We hear only this strange and awful noise. I do not believe it comes from the Assyrians, so what or who is making it? Something is going on," Ahikar said to King Hezekiah. "If it is an indication of conflict or attack, it is not Assyrian. They would not fight at night by choice."

He emphasized the not, his eyes brimming with tears. *What had happened to Judith? Could she be a part of these strange things going on?*

⁘

After the guards left the tent, Judith and her maidens slowly rose naked from the floor. Judith pointed to the tent entrance and the maid closest peered outside. She told Judith no one could be seen around the tent area.

"It is only this deafening noise we hear. No one is nearby."

"Stay there and continue to watch. If anyone approaches we will repeat what we did earlier and join this Assyrian leader in bed once more."

⁘

Ramtouses had divided his army in two. The second group stayed to the rear while the first marched toward the camps of the people of Ell.

⁘

Five siege ramps now stood in the midst of the interior fighting machine. The Assyrian generals perched atop one of the ramps to see if they could distinguish anything of the attacking forces in the dark of night.

310

It was fruitless. If anyone hid in the nearby fields, one way to validate their presence would be to shoot flaming arrows at random into the fields at their immediate front.

The archers quickly received orders to let fly their flaming arrows into the tall grass. If the fire burned, no one was there to put them out. If the fire extinguished quickly, they knew someone was there to smother it. The fires vanished within seconds. The enemy was out there, less than the flight of an arrow away. An attack was imminent, and the soldiers of the interior readied themselves to throw the heavy spears.

⁙

Ramtouses raised his arm high and lowered it quickly, a silent signal which was passed on. Arms raised and lowered all along the massive lines of tribesmen. *Attack!*

The African warriors charged the Ell lines at once. Thousands fanned their way through the grass.

Their approach was visible to the enemy by the light of the flaming arrows flying through the night like torches. The arrows were followed by waves of heavy spears sailing through the air. They crashed down on the tribesmen's wood and skin hide shields. Many abandoned their shields with the heavy spears lodged firmly in them.

⁙

The Assyrian archers on the siege ramps as well as those on the ground found many random targets without protective shields among the attacking enemy. The bowmen weren't certain of their targets in the tall grasses and the darkness. They shot randomly in the general direction of the attacking forces, and not all their arrows met an enemy target. Many of the attackers reached the wall-of-shields and faced another phase of the Assyrian arsenal.

The fighting soldiers standing directly behind the pavis wall-of-shields utilized the narrow slots between the shields. Sharpened spears became their offense in conjunction with the defense of their shields. Anyone running up to the pavis wall to knock it down could be stabbed through the slots. The bowmen could also utilize the slots to shoot their arrows.

A barrage of fierce men rushed the wall-of-shields and buckled it in many places, knocking it down in others. The foot soldiers repositioned themselves to bridge the gaps. Archers joined the spearmen to fight off intrusions and reestablish stability in the wall. Catastrophe was avoided. Infantry came forward to take the places of those killed or wounded shield bearers and realign the pavis wall.

⁘

The tribesmen fired their poisoned arrows. Hundreds of the Ell met death through the slightest wounds from the poison. This kind of fighting continued well into the night with both sides suffering heavy casualties.

⁘

General Rabsaris began to feel anxious and disturbed. How much longer could this enemy support this level of assault? They suffered alarming losses, yet kept coming. The Assyrians faced an attrition rate much higher than in previous wars.

⁘

Ramtouses realized his army suffered heavy losses from this first wave of frontal assault. The time had come for the final phase of battle strategy. His warriors manipulated a strategic retreat. They did not turn and run but fought less intensely and allowed themselves to be pushed back. This required very strict discipline from the tribal warriors, but the Ell had to believe they had killed most of them, they had control and that the battle would soon belong to them.

⁘

The Assyrians saw the enemy attack weakening. General Rabsaris shouted. "Die, you filthy desert rats!"

The sibilant sound had dropped off greatly.

He sent word to King Sennacherib the fighting had come under their control. The king sent them away and stayed in his tent professing he could not bear the discordant cacophony of the enemy.

This behavior surprised his men. Their king never stayed away from any battle. His chariot was always seen at the forefront of battle.

As fewer and fewer men charged the pavis wall-of-shields, General Rabsaris would not accept the enemy's retreat. The army belonged to him now. It was his opportunity to demonstrate his prowess of leadership, to conduct and orchestrate this massive war machine.

"I will allow not one of these insignificant nomads to escape after what they have done this night."

He moved the front wall-of-shields forward and ordered the men to march after the last of the enemy. "I will slaughter every last one of these barbarian animals, cut them into pieces and hang them on poles for all to see."

The shield bearers raised the shields from the ground and led the way forward. The foot soldiers moved in behind them. Mules and men pulled the siege ramps forward using many large logged wheels.

None of the other Assyrian generals agreed with this maneuver.

Some said, "Do not move forward in the night. We can hunt them down in the morning, in the light of day."

"General Holofernes would never do something so foolish."

But General Rabsaris paid no heed to their admonitions. This was his night, his battle, his only chance to excel. The streets would be lined with crowds cheering his brilliance when they returned to Nineveh. He would not wait until morning to destroy the enemy. General Holofernes would recover by then, take back his command and bask in the triumph for the final victory.

"Be silent!" he demanded. "I am in charge of this campaign, and you will all do as I say."

❖

If Ramtouses's men were to have any chance of winning the battle, it was imperative to penetrate the Ell's defensive wall. The maneuver had to be flawlessly timed and executed.

When Baduga and Taharga spoke of this defense method employed by the Ell, Ramtouses had decided to add the red ant versus black ant strategy into his war plan. It required high levels of discipline and control, but Ramtouses had full confidence and trust in his bushmen.

❖

The Assyrians advanced their wall of shields. Here and there gaps appeared, exposing their ranks. The shield bearers continued their forward movement after the remaining tribesmen who still fought before them.

The chanting started to rise again, strident hissing that grated on their ears and worried their minds. To add to their distraction, wounded men began to grab at the legs of the shield bearers causing them to stumble, some even to fall.

Out of nowhere a second wave of the enemy came weaving their way through the grass. A tall, fierce man led them. It happened very fast, with no time to reform their wall of shields, no time to shake off the wounded warriors pulling on their legs.

The second wave of the enemy swiftly swarmed upon them. The wall came down and the onslaught could not be stopped.

❖

The army of Ramtouses pushed forward, overwhelming the pavis shield bearers and brutally slaughtering many of them. Ramtouses now fought the war he wanted, man to man. He fought with his brothers, the men of Juba and Tungul, Baduga, Taharga and their men all around him.

Together they moved as one unit cutting their way through the Ell ranks.

⁂

Judith and her maiden sat on one side of Holofernes's bed when the chanting stopped. She asked the girl who stood watch at the tent entrance what she saw outside.

"I see nothing," the girl answered.

Judith was clear and resolute. "It has been going on a long time now, and I finally know what the chanting means. It is a sign from the LORD instructing me to complete my mission."

Her two maidens seemed alarmed, standing immobile, hands clasped against their breasts, lips pressed tightly together.

Judith walked to the middle of the tent and fell to her knees in prayer. "My God, grant me the courage to do your bidding."

The two maidens began to shake all over when the chanting returned, nearly as loud as before.

"I hear you, my LORD," Judith responded.

She slowly rose to her feet and moved as in a trance, similar to the time when she cut the ropes around the graven idol image of Yahweh in the Temple. Holofernes's weapon hung on the post of his bed. Unhurried, she moved toward it. She grasped it with both hands, lifting his sword from its sheath. The blade shone brilliant as a mirror. When the tip slid free, she turned it upward and held it high, pointed it to the heavens then she lowered the handle along her body with the flat side of the blade close to her eyes.

Her face reflected in the smooth shinny surface. The sword tip reached higher than the top of her head with her arms lowered full length and her hands clasped around the handle. As she positioned herself before Holofernes, she did not look away from the sword.

Outside the haunting, pulsing noise continued.

The maids ran to each other and covered their faces in horror.

With a single purpose, Judith shifted her gaze to Holofernes's nude body face down on the bed, his head hanging off and his neck at the edge.

⁘

Ramtouses and his comrades fought their way deep within the Ell ranks. In a short time they reached the siege ramps where several dozen Ell bowmen nested, shooting arrows from the top of each ramp. The excellent vantage point had allowed the bowmen to kill hundreds of tribesmen from atop these terrible weapons.

The five towering ramps had to be destroyed. Ramtouses directed his men to set fire to them, using the very same fire pots the Ell used earlier to light their arrowheads and reveal the tribesmen's positions.

The fighting was intense. Ell soldiers swarmed and battled, trying to save the ramps. They fought fiercely in defense of the monstrous siege ramps, but after a long bloody battle the Ell fighters gave way. Tribesmen set the towers aflame, and within minutes Ell bowmen leapt from the ramps to escape the flames. Ramtouses and his comrades hacked and chopped at the supporting beams and pulled on the structures until they toppled to the ground, killing or maiming the archers still clinging to their positions on the ramps.

⁘

A soldier on the wall of Jerusalem cried out, "Look!"

The people stared into the black night at the flames.

King Hezekiah said to Ahikar, "Is this some war ritual performed by the Assyrians?"

Ahikar gave a slow shake of his head. "I lived in Nineveh many years and studied the Assyrian culture and history. I have never seen nor heard of behavior such as this. I do not know what is happening."

The people of Judah continued their vigil from the wall.

⁘

"There go the leaders of these Ell people!" Taharga shouted to Ramtouses. "They hope to fight from the higher ground."

A large convoy of Ell fought their way to a mounded area where several large tents had been pitched. Soldiers fought off the tribesmen, protecting the high-ranking officers enroute to the knoll.

The intensity of the battle moved from the siege ramps to the mounds where the officers were headed.

Ramtouses and those he fought with set the higher ground as their objective. The Ells' desire to protect their leaders meant the development of a major confrontation. Ramtouses expected the conflict to escalate to its most fierce level thus far.

The battle began to rage.

Men from both sides fell on that mound of ground, struck down by sword, spear or dagger.

Ramtouses saw friends drop but could do nothing to help or comfort them.

Taharga pointed Ramtouses to a man with a very tall horsehair dressing on his helmet with a long plume.

"Their leader," he screamed.

Ramtouses fought his way over to the man. If this was the commander of the Ell army, Ramtouses intended to destroy him as he had destroyed Carnabrara.

Warriors and soldiers from both sides surrounded Ramtouses and the man with the horsehair on his helmet to keep others from interfering with the fight of leaders.

⁜

Commanding General Rabsaris was an excellent swordsman. He charged Ramtouses and swung at him several times, his long iron sword cutting wedges on the rim of Ramtouses's shield.

⁜

Ramtouses returned the charge but the Ell's shield remained undamaged. The Ell commander was aggressive and charged again, hacking at Ramtouses with a finely honed double-edged sword. Ramtouses's blade was single edged. The Ell dealt offensive blows from the right and left, and Ramtouses was continually on the defensive.

The fighting around them reached a wild frenzy. Scores of bodies lay close around. Ramtouses fought on, but received two blows for every one he gave. His skills proved inferior to that of the enemy.

The Ell leader swung hard, a blow that broke Ramtouses's blade. Ramtouses never hesitated, but charged straight into his enemy before he could recover from such a mighty swing of his sword. The leader fell back and tripped over a fallen body.

Ramtouses was on him, striking his helmet and neck. The Ell leader climbed to his feet, without his helmet and bleeding. Ramtouses moved quickly, pounding the enemy's shield with his broken sword, spurred on as he felt the enemy's resistance weaken. Ramtouses struck again, and yet again, smelling victory, tasting it. His sword smashed down onto the head of the Ell army's leader. He fell. Ramtouses moved over him, knelt and cut his throat.

⁙

At that very moment, Judith raised Holofernes's sword high over her head and took a deep breath. In silence, her mouth formed the words, "Almighty God, I do your bidding."

She brought the sword down with all her might against Holofernes's neck. A loud guttural grunt escaped Judith's throat as the sword swished through the air.

The mighty General Holofernes's body twitched once then lay limp. Blood splashed against the tent walls and on to the floor. Droplets of his blood spotted her belly, breasts, and face. She lifted the huge sword high above her head once more and cried out again with the same loud and forceful grunt as she struck a second time. It was identical to the sound she made in the Temple when she destroyed the graven image.

More blood splashed up and landed on her body and face. The head of Assyria's military monarch fell to the floor. His body no longer moved. The man who terrorized so many no longer existed. No sign of his tyrant soul survived in the corpse of blood, bone and tissue that lay on the bed, with its head fallen to the floor.

Then, there was the silence of an ending.

Tears filled her eyes and flowed onto her cheeks. She dropped the sword to the carpeted ground and stood paralyzed from the shock of what she had just done. She began to tremble. She looked down at her naked body smeared with his blood. Blood and tears streaked her face.

Slowly, life moved back into her limbs. She shuffled a few small steps willing her legs to support her. She barely managed to make her way toward the tent entrance. Exhausted and empty, she felt like an apparition, ephemeral and unreal.

The two maidens clung to each other, on their knees shaking all over. Judith looked out. No one was near the tent, but the sibilant chanting had changed to the cries of war.

She turned to the maidens. "Get dressed and bring me the basket."

They all dressed in silence, their movements slow and precise. The two maidens shuddered as though shaking off some unseen bindings and brought Judith the basket.

"Help me roll him over so that I can remove my blanket from his bed."

They would not go near the dead man's body.

"Help me! Now!" Judith's voice came from somewhere beyond her, resolute and adamant.

Only then did the two women move to help her roll over the body.

She removed her blanket and placed it in the basket. She closed her eyes as she lifted his head by its long, brown hair, set it in the basket and covered it with the blanket. She closed the basket lid. One of her maidens brought a wet cloth and wiped the blood splatters from Judith's face.

They crouched at the tent entrance, waiting for the right opportunity to dash for Jerusalem. The loud cries of battle seemed to be coming from everywhere. Judith's vision was limited in the dark and she grew anxious, afraid that if they ran out they would be seen and killed.

⁂

The lifeless body of the Ell's commander lay on the ground. Ramtouses dropped his broken sword, picked up the general's sword then rejoined his comrades in the fighting.

He soon spotted another Ell with a high horsehair ornament atop his helmet and a long plume dancing with his every move. There was a regiment of soldiers fighting around him. Ramtouses fought his way to the Ell leader and the two men clashed.

Ramtouses fought with the same technique as he did with the other Ell leader. His excellent night vision enabled him to maneuver the general around into a position where he, too, would stumble over the bodies of his fallen comrades. Ramtouses slit his throat when he fell to the ground. This time he discarded his own shield and replaced it with the second dead general's shield.

The tribal fighting force eventually overcame their opposition but not without a tremendous loss of friends and countrymen. Ramtouses looked over to another mound and thought more leaders might be there. He and his men fought off the few soldiers between them and the higher ground. Ramtouses led the way toward a tent on the apex of the mound. There appeared to be no activity near the big tent.

⁂

Judith could see some figures coming toward them. She gritted her teeth at the sight of them. Was this the end? Her heart beat faster, but only for a moment. She thought of Yahweh, lifted her head high and rose to her feet.

320

*Let me die as a noblewoman of Judah, not as a cowardly dog, before my God and my people.*

The man leading the group stood as big as Holofernes, but something registered very different about him. He was not dressed as an Assyrian. His skin color melded with the black of the night, and his eyes glowed white. He seemed to illuminate the space around him with a radiance equal to the stars.

He looked straight at Judith, and when their eyes met, a moment of tranquility flooded her.

That's when she knew the truth. "This is the angel our LORD has sent."

Judith stepped forward from the tent entrance. "Are you here to save us?"

From their faces, she realized they did not understand her speech. She held her hand up high.

⁘

When Ramtouses saw the women, he realized they did not mean to fight; neither did they appear to be women of the Ell. What were three such women doing in the middle of a field of war? Ramtouses remembered Taharga spoke of people nearby who also feared the Ell. Perhaps these women had been captured and taken as slaves.

He held his hand out to his men as a signal to be at ease.

One of the women made gestures to Ramtouses, pointing to the basket she carried. They did not know what she meant to convey to them. He and a few of his men stepped forward and looked at the basket. She opened it, reached in and slowly raised the head of an Ell man by his long hair.

⁘

The black angel and his men stepped back and looked with disbelief on the severed head.

She quickly lowered the head. It made her retch, but she fought back the urge to throw up. She pointed in the direction of the city wall.

⁘

It was the wall Ramtouses had discussed with Taharga who said it surrounded a city of people who also feared the evil Ell. Her gesture meant she wanted to go there.

Ramtouses gathered his fighters around the three women and stepped toward Judith. She looked up at him calmly, handed the basket to her maiden and nodded to him.

He turned his back to her, took both of her hands and placed them on the leather band around his waist that held his sword and dagger. "Hold on tightly and do not let go."

⁘

She did not understand his words but it was clear what he wanted her to do. She put her fingers inside the band. It felt rough, wrapped with coarse animal hair. She gripped it tightly.

One of the angel's soldiers took the basket from Judith's maiden and repeated the angel's maneuver to indicate she should grab hold of his waistband. A third soldier repeated this pantomime to the other maiden.

They began to walk, surrounded on three sides by a larger group of warriors who guided them toward the walls of Jerusalem.

⁘

Judith couldn't identify the shapes of all she saw in the dark, but she knew the sounds meant violence. Awe filled her soul and she felt the power of the LORD walking with them as hundreds of warriors and soldiers fought and died all around them.

A large party of Assyrians confronted them. Heavy fighting escalated and became very intense. Assyrian soldiers charged right into the forces of the black angel only to be cut down. Judith wrapped her arms around her savior's waist. He held his big shield high over them.

The fighting lessened as they drew closer to the tall walls blocking off the top of the hill. There was no further aggression as the men of war stopped before the wall. Judith pointed them toward the gates and the troupe walked horizontally along the wall in the direction she indicated.

⁙

People on the walls saw their approach from between the battlements but did not shout or shoot arrows at them. The surreal noises faded into the night some time earlier and word of the figures moving toward the city walls passed from person to person along the walkways atop the walls.

"Some people are out there near the wall. They seem to be coming to the main gates."

Ahikar and the King and Queen strained their eyes, searching the dark night to catch a glimpse of these people who were said to be approaching.

⁙

Judith, her maidens, the black angel and his men all stopped at the gates.

The warrior who carried the basket handed it back to a maiden who reluctantly took it.

The angel turned toward Judith. He tore off a piece of fur from the band around his waist and handed it to her. She clutched it in her fist.

She began to weep suddenly with immense gratification. So many of her people were saved from slaughter because of him. She reached out and hugged him tightly, holding onto him as if this would be the last time she would ever hug anyone. Moments passed and Judith still would not release the man who was surely an angel of God. How could she thank him for such a brave and courageous deed?

Impulsively, she kissed him passionately on the lips then turned and ran off into the night. Her two maidens followed. About halfway to the gate she stopped and turned to look back.

*Maybe he will come inside.*

"Wait!" she called and started to run down the incline after him, but she saw no one.

Judith retreated to her waiting maidens. She retrieved the basket and clutched it tightly as the three of them started to move steadily toward the gates of Jerusalem.

She called out, "It is I, Judith. Please open the gates. Hurry."

⁘

Ramtouses and his men hurried to join their fellow tribesmen at war.

The tribesmen charged down the incline but found no resistance. The warriors of Juba and Tungul, along with their allies, began to suspect the fighting might be over until they realized the echo of war still sounded. Ramtouses slowed his pace to a near standstill.

"Be quiet."

Everyone stopped and listened to the echo from the nearby hills.

"Follow the sound."

The tribesmen trotted in the direction of the sound that grew louder and louder. After several minutes at this fast pace, the screams and sounds of war became much clearer. Ramtouses and his people could see in the distance a merger of Ell forces combined around another area of raised ground. Warrior tribesmen had also gathered and regrouped around the same area.

From where Ramtouses and his party stood, it looked like an extremely strong force attracted the remainder of the war effort to it. Much like a queen bee draws the other bees to her.

They joined in the battle and it escalated like none other. The killing was furious, the intent savage. Hundreds of brave men butchered each other around the perimeter of this one mound. The occupant of the tent atop the crest became the focus of the entire struggle.

The Assyrians were motivated to protect King Sennacherib, their living god among men, at all costs. The tribesmen warriors were equally resolute to bring the reign of the people of Ell to an end.

⁘

Sennacherib could be seen outside the tent, wandering about, not like himself at all. He carried no weapons and had not dressed for battle. He held a goblet in one hand but did not seem to be intoxicated.

He talked aloud to himself. "Kill those uncivilized rats of the desert! Who are these animals who think they can stand up to the Assyrian army, the creation of Baal?"

⁘

Ramtouses tried desperately to penetrate the Ell ranks after realizing they fought so valiantly to protect the man at the top of the mound. With a massive push he and his comrades generated a minor intrusion but lost many warriors in the move. The Ell refused to yield any ground and sacrificed many of their own to stop the advance of the tribesmen.

Ramtouses's men fought on three sides with him in the center. His arms seemed not to grow weary as he cut down men with the trophy sword and blocked anything thrown his way with the shield.

Lozato who fought near him went down suddenly. Ramtouses backed off his aggression and made his way to him. He tried to lift Lozato as he fought off Ells. Taharga saw this and came to their aid. The two warriors moved Lozato away from the front line to an area free of combat.

They found a pile of hay and eased Lozato down upon it. Taharga covered the brothers as the fury of battle continued behind them.

Ramtouses felt Lozato's pain as he looked into his brother's eyes.

"Please do not die," he said.

Lozato had two wounds above his stomach. Ramtouses removed his upper garment and bound the wounds.

"Hold on, Lozato. We are always together."

Lozato raised his hand to his brother's chin. "Giraffe legs, I love you." He laughed, a little. "The boy who had a dream...I always wanted to know what it meant."

His hand dropped and he lay still. Ramtouses saw the soft rise and fall of breath and knew his brother was alive. He shook him gently.

"Do not go to sleep. I will be back for you soon. I promise!" He stood back and gathered himself.

"I wish I had the time to take him to that city where a healer could attend him." Ramtouses spoke to Taharga as they both turned and began to jog back to the fighting. "But I cannot turn my back on the bushmen who continue to fight so desperately to overcome the Ell. It would not be fair for them to sacrifice their lives without my help."

Taharga moved just ahead of Ramtouses. Abruptly he stopped and fell backward. Ramtouses broke his fall. An arrow lodged just below the throat of his Ethiopian friend.

"Taharga!" He grabbed the arrow to dislodge it.

Taharga stayed his hand and gestured for Ramtouses to come close. Ramtouses bent over to better hear him.

In less than a whisper wet with the rattle of blood, Taharga chocked, "She..." but Ramtouses could not be certain of his words.

Before he could say anything more, Taharga's body went limp, and he died.

Ramtouses let his comrade's body slide to the ground. He raised his head and looked around. Bodies lay everywhere, so many people dying or dead. The fields, now covered with his friends and tribesmen who so bravely rushed into battle, stretched out into the night with no apparent end.

Warriors and Ell all around him were still locked in mortal conflict, each side affording one final push for triumph and, with it, glory. The circle around the Ell's precious leader had dwindled to maybe a hundred still fighting, far less than the thousands of thousands who engaged in battle not so long ago.

The voice of this Ell leader still urged them to war as he stood in the middle of this circle. Ramtouses ran to where the heaviest fighting persisted. A desperate wish to kill this Ell and bring an end to all this hostility burned inside him.

⁙

At the walls of Jerusalem Ahikar shouted, "That sounds like Judith! Tell me my ears do not deceive me."

"I see them! Three women are coming this way." The King shouted with elation. "Hurry! Open the gates."

Ahikar scrambled down from the tower. King Hezekiah and the Queen followed after him. The gates swung open and Ahikar ran to greet the three women, shouting, "It's a miracle! It's a miracle! I can't believe it."

Judith did not run to meet the overly excited crowd but continued a measured walk through the city gates, followed by her two maidens. The gates closed behind them once they passed through.

Ahikar raced up to her and embraced her. Queen Hephzibah and King Hezekiah came next to greet Judith. They seemed to want to touch her as if to assure themselves of the reality of her presence. Their joy at seeing her safe was overwhelming. Soon a crowd formed around them and the families of the two maidens found them.

"Are you well? Did they harm you?" Queen Hephzibah wept and laughed at the same time. "Tell me everything. Leave out nothing, not a single detail."

The King shouted. "Clear the way! These women have had a trying ordeal. Judith will tell us everything later in the new day. Clear the way."

He spoke to his guards. "Bring the two maidens also. Let them all rest. They will speak with no one before the council meets with them."

❖

Judith's mother was feeble and unable to walk far. She stood by the door of their quarters when the guards accompanied Judith to her rooms. She saw the stains on her daughter's clothing but she also saw a strong presence of calm assurance in the manner of her walk. It told Peninnah that whatever her daughter experienced beyond the city's walls she had conquered and survived well.

The Queen joined Judith's mother in the living space but neither woman went into Judith's rooms for the rest of the night. Only Judith's two maidens stayed in her company.

❖

King Hezekiah sent everyone else away and ordered her rooms to be kept under guard.

"Provide for them all that they request."

With his orders given and the guards posted, Hezekiah retired to his chambers, exhausted but relieved. In his mind he was already compiling a list of questions for Judith.

❖

In the streets hundreds of people chanted Judith's name. They did not know why such elation filled them. The Assyrian army still camped in siege beyond the city walls. But somehow, they sensed a good and marvelous thing had happened. Otherwise, why would she be back?

❖

Dawn arrived and found twelve soldiers standing, all bore minor wounds, some with more grievous injuries. Two of them held low officer rankings.

King Sennacherib stopped pacing. There was no activity around him. He ceased his ranting. Silence surrounded him.

Calm, he stood very still and focused on the bodies from as near as an arm's length to as far as his eyes could see in the early morning haze. He gazed along the plane of the field before him, turning in a full circle, while absorbing what had taken place.

"Almighty god, Baal, what has happened to my magnificent army? Am I to believe they all are dead?"

He approached one of the young officers who stood scanning the area as if somehow his eyes deceived him. He laid his hand upon the young officer's shoulder. "How much evil can there be in one place? Prepare my chariot. Hasten."

The battle weary men seemed to take forever, but somehow they found enough stray horses to pull the king's chariot and one for each of them. One officer served as his driver.

King Sennacherib climbed aboard the chariot awash in defeat. There was no victory to celebrate. Death and destruction clouded his mind. The immense trauma of his loss clung to him like a suit of lead, weighing heavy on him, pulling his body down. His world had abandoned him.

He wept, then screamed at the top of his voice, "Holofernes, where are you," then he whispered, "when I need you most?"

As the chariot moved away, he uttered, "I forgave you for everything." He looked around in every direction as another thought came to mind. "Ahikar, you traitor! You will not get away with what you have done to me. In the name of Baal, I will get you, you rat."

They made their way through the field of bodies.

Suddenly, the king yelled, "Stop!" In a very sad voice he said, "We cannot leave Holofernes here. We must find him."

If his friend Holofernes was yet in a drunken stupor, he might yet live. He sent the soldiers to see if they could find him near his tent or in it.

King Sennacherib waited in the chariot beside a pile of hay. His eye caught a sudden movement and when he turned to look, a man rose up and stared at him. Their gazes met and the king screamed in horror, "Get me out of here!"

In a panic, he took the horses reins from the driver and whipped them. The horses jolted in alarm stampeding over bodies and anything else in the way. His screams continued. "Those black fiends are after me!"

The horses increased their speed.

Over the field of trampled grass and fallen men, the soldiers ended their search for the great General Holofernes when they heard the cries of their king. They chased after his chariot to join him. King Sennacherib could be heard screaming repeatedly as they went, "They are after me. I must get away!"

⁂

Lozato had raised his head to see if his brother had returned. After the Ell screamed and sped away, he collapsed back down into the hay.

# DAYLIGHT

### 701 B.C.E.

*A* ray of sunlight pierced the horizon and raced across the surface of the earth. It created shadows behind the mountains and high hills and danced through tree leaves and bushes. It both penetrated and reflected from open waters. In an instant, billions of rays reacted with the molecules in the atmosphere, bringing light and warmth to life upon the earth, revealing a dichotomy in nature.

Just as the birth of life is so beautiful, there also must be the agony of its death. On this morning, the sunlight exposed the secret the night hid.

Earth's finest product, magnificent man, had managed to annihilate close to one-half million of its population in a single night.

The bodies were visible for miles. Some wore boots. Others' feet were bare. Eyes were open but not seeing. Fists clenched weapons no longer in use. There they lay, side-by-side, across one another, in some places three or four deep—onstage before the entire universe.

⁙

Late that morning Judith awoke and lay still, remembering the horrifying events of the night. She aroused her companions, and they freshened themselves and dressed for the council hall appearance. Their guards were ready to escort them. The Queen, Ahikar and Judith's mother joined them.

Many people walked aimlessly around the streets of Jerusalem, some near delirium, praying to Yahweh for a favorable message from Judith. The small entourage walked past them and entered the council hall. Judith carried the basket.

King Hezekiah rose to his feet and called the meeting to session. People stood shoulder-to-shoulder, filling the meeting hall and even crowding out into the corridors. They sat on every available ledge and windowsill leaving no empty spot. They crowded around the building outside and down the streets as well waiting for word of what transpired inside the hall.

The king said, "We all know why we have come to this meeting. Judith, stand and give us your account of the events that took place overnight."

She wore a simple gray gown belted with a black sash. Judith stood and looked around at the crowd of people, her people, and began to speak.

"I thank the LORD for making this day possible. Without his love for Jerusalem I would not be standing here. The LORD fought for our city last night, not I.

"I wanted to convince the Assyrian leader, General Holofernes, to give up the siege of Jerusalem with the telling of a prophecy. He would not listen. He left me no choice but to rob the Assyrians of their prized commander-in-chief. Yes, hoping to destroy their morale, I stole Holofernes, the one most necessary to guide them in war."

She stopped speaking. Every eye in the hall was upon her and every ear waiting for her to continue. Stress began to steal her calm as she remembered the events of the past day and night, but they had to hear the horrific story she and her maidens had lived. Judith breathed deeply to counter the tension. When even an inkling of the memory invaded her mind, it lassoed her whole being, and there seemed to be no escape from the fear. It left a bitter taste in her mouth and filled her with a lassitude so deep that even her breath seemed to fade. At that moment, Judith turned to the one whose promise of covenant care never failed, and she prayed that her LORD stay by her during this time.

With a powerful voice, she shouted, "This mission has deprived me of my innocence. I have taken a man's life, in the name of my God. I answered the calling of the LORD. I felt His will moving in me, giving me the strength and courage to do His bidding. When you believe in the true God, as I do, anything is possible. I demonstrated that when I raised the sword. I am but an unpretentious woman yet was able to strike down the champion of the entire world in war. I fulfilled that deed and here you see the proof."

She opened the basket and raised the head of the great General Holofernes as high as she could by his long, thick hair.

"See the face of the man who led so many into battle."

She turned a full circle, holding high the despicable, decapitated head of Holofernes. Women stifled screams, children covered their eyes, and men took sudden, deep breaths. For a few brief moments the entire room was absolutely still, shocked beyond belief as they viewed this repulsive trophy.

"See his head and know this monster no longer exists to terrify the world. Let this wretched head be a sign to all that Jerusalem's God, almighty that He is, can overcome anyone, no matter how boastful in war that person may be."

She lowered the head back into the basket and felt peace when she spoke again.

"After the deed was done, God allowed us to see His angel and I feel his warmth even now—a large and mighty being, his eyes pierced my eyes and he looked straight into my soul." Judith brought both her hands together in front of her breasts, as if in prayer.

"I knew he came to rescue us from our dilemma. He shielded me and my two maidens as we made our way back to the city. Without his presence we would have died at the hands of the

Assyrians. When I put my arms around him, my soul flooded with a full assurance that he would always be there for me.

"I know his hand smote the Assyrians because the God of Israel so willed it. I did not want this man to leave when we arrived at the city gates. I did not know what to do so I reached up and kissed him and in that second I felt an unconditional love, an everlasting love."

She lifted her arms up toward the ceiling, stretching her body and reaching with both hands, fingers wide open, she shouted.

"If anyone asks, let it be known the Black Angel of the Lord saved Judah's place in history."

Judith stood still for a few moments and said nothing more. She finally sat down. Now it was over. She glanced to the side where the two young maidens sat. Relief was sketched in the set of their faces.

No one moved in the crowded room. Silence filled the air. A hushed paralysis settled upon everyone.

Her words were repeated in the corridors and down the streets. An awesome wave of stillness flowed over the people until most of Jerusalem felt its power.

King Hezekiah finally stood "That is an amazing story, much more than I expected. You are our heroine, Judith. You deserve more than we have to offer."

Before the meeting ended, a messenger reported to the king that the chief of guards on the walls requested his presence.

King Hezekiah immediately adjourned the meeting and hurried to the main gates.

Upon arriving, the chief guard said, "We have observed no sign of life in the Assyrian camps. We watched closely all morning and detected no movement, only images that looked to be prostrate bodies."

"Go out there," the king said. "Investigate and report to me immediately."

Ahikar was granted permission to accompany the scouting party.

⁛

More birds than usual flew high in the blue skies around Jerusalem. As the scouting party walked through the encampment they found the bodies of men who died violently, Assyrians as well as the dead of a dark-skinned people whom they knew as Kushites from Africa or Egypt. The men of the patrol were dumbfounded. They knew nothing of any Kushite presence in the area until that day.

In some areas they saw large numbers of men, both Assyrian and Nubian, laying tangled in death. Wounds and bloody weapons told the story of the battle.

They found no one alive. It was a field of death.

The captain of the company sent word to inform King Hezekiah there was no sign of life except the birds.

After dispatching the report to the king the captain said, "This is the most peculiar day of my life, yet, rewarding."

⁛

In the streets, people came from every corner, shouting. "It is a miracle."

Some chanted Judith's name. Others praised Yahweh.

King Hezekiah got down on his knees. "Thank you, my God." He uttered the words over and over again.

⁛

The military tried to piece together what had happened. It was obvious a battle had ensued between the Assyrians and a Kush or Nubian army. The fact that no survivors were found from either side utterly amazed them. The commander of King Hezekiah's army said, "Someone always lives to tell the story. Where is he?"

They searched for the body of King Sennacherib but did not find it. Judith requested the body of the man who saved them be brought to the city. She described the man as wearing a large waistband with coarse animal hair woven into it, but he also was never found.

The Assyrian dead were hauled off to the mountains and burned with no care or honor. The African dead were carried respectfully into the hills and buried with honor. All of Jerusalem said prayers for them.

⁘

The people honored Judith and her two handmaidens with a two-day celebration.

⁘

Judith retired from the elders' council. She said, "We all have a destiny in life. Most do not know what that fate will be, not even at death. I have been blessed. I strived to accomplish that which Almighty God expected of me.

"You all know how difficult and frustrating it is to be a part of the council. But it is a joy to learn that your decision turns out to be right for everyone involved."

⁘

The Assyrians temporarily held their Hebrew prisoners at a site in Northern Israel. After an extended search, King Hezekiah's scouts found the camp, and the king mobilized his army to liberate his people. The freed prisoners returned to their homelands, some to the North and others to Judah.

⁘

The decapitated head of Holofernes hung high on the newly built extension to the gate tower, a victory trophy that served as a reminder to never forget the sorrow this tyrant brought upon the world. Anyone who came through the gates of Jerusalem could see it.

⁘

King Sennacherib returned to Nineveh. He was not of sound mind. Nightly the sounds of dreadful nightmares emanated from his quarters. He thrashed around, screamed and demanded to see his friend. "Where are you Holofernes, when I need you the most? Holofernes? Come to me. I am your king!"

Then he would quiet, as if waiting for Holofernes, and when no one came, he would shout again with intense anger.

"Ahikar, you traitor, you will not get away with this! I will see your face in torment. I will have no mercy."

Each night, his chambers echoed with the same screams for Holofernes and the loud threats made to Ahikar.

"Stop it! In the name of Baal, stop that eerie clamor! Ahg, I cannot bear that noise."

His words were filled with fearful pleading. "That sound, I cannot bare that chilling sound!"

King Sennacherib could find no peace.

※

For the next four years, Prince Esarhaddon governed the nation. His two envious half-brothers assassinated their father while he prayed in the temple. Their crime was discovered, and instead of gaining power, the princes fled for their lives into northern Babylon. Prince Esarhaddon became the successor to the throne of Assyria.

※

Pharaoh Shabaka died during the deception that brought Princess Carnabrara to Egypt. The hundred virgin maidens became wives to numerous upper-class Egyptians.

※

Carnabrara's wish finally came to fruition, but without the happiness she envisioned. She gave birth to Ramtouses II and, after living in Thebes for three years, married Pharaoh Shebitku's oldest son.

Carnabrara never stopped going out in the evening or early morning to watch for the star of her true love, Ramtouses.

# EPILOGUE

The arrowhead has told its story. Have you heard it before?

⁘

*"Therefore, thus saith the LORD concerning the king of Assyria, He shall not come into this city, nor shoot an arrow there, nor come before it with shield, nor cast a bank against it. By the way that he came, by the same shall he return, and shall not come into this city, saith the LORD. For I will defend this city, to save it, for mine own sake, and for my servant David's sake. And it came to pass that night, that the angel of the LORD went out, and smote in the camp of the Assyrians an hundred fourscore and five thousand: and when they arose early in the morning, behold, they were all dead corpses. So Sennacherib king of Assyria departed, and went and returned, and dwelt at Nineveh. And it came to pass, as he was worshipping in the house of Nisroch his god, that Adrammelech and Sharezer his sons smote him with the sword: and they escaped into the land of Armenia. And Esarhaddon his son reigned in his stead."*
*2 Kings 19:32-37*

## THE END

# Map, Illustration and Photo Credits

*Middle East map circa 750 B.C.E.* digital imaging by Sherry Baribeau

*Ancient beehive tombs in Old Dongola*   Page 122
www.pbase.com/6mcmorrow/image/120774663

*Nubian steep-sided pyramids*   Page 125
http://bristoltocapetown.wordpress.com/photo-gallery/egypt-sudan/
sudan/#jp-carousel-535

*Example of Assyrian battering ram.*   Page 157
www.bible-lands.net/cities/lachish/96-the-seige-of-lachish
www.twcenter.net/forums/showthread.php?348945-traits-and-
Ancillaries

*Hezekiah's tunnel*   Page 169
www.generationword.com/jerusalem101-photos/hezekiahs-tunnel/
toni-wiemers-hezekiahs-tunnel.JPG

*Remains of broad wall at Jerusalem, constructed prior to the 701
B.C.E. siege*   Page 174
www.generationword.com/jerusalem101-photos/broad-wall/
IMG_3617.JPG

*Giant golden reeds*   Page 201
dnr.state.il.us/Stewardship/cd/srs/GR.html

*Statue of Assyrian god, Baal*   Page 232
www.boundless.com/image/man-headed-lions

*Diamond Ring Eclipse*   Page 277
www.dreamview.net/dv/new/photos.asp?ID=101917

*Eclipse shadow bands observed on walls*   Page 284
www.earthview.com/tutorial/effects.htm